BLOCKBUSTER PRAISE FOR DAVID POYER AND CHINA SEA

W9-BLD-770

CHINA SEA

DAVID POYER

St. Martin's Paperbacks

This is a work of fiction. Characters, companies, and organizations in this novel are either the product of the author's imagination or, if real, are used fictitiously, without intent to describe their actual conduct.

CHINA SEA

Copyright © 2000 by David Poyer.
Excerpt from *Black Storm* copyright © 2001 by David Poyer.

All rights reserved. No part of this book may be used or reproduced in any manner whatsoever without written permission except in the case of brief quotations embodied in critical articles or reviews. For information address St. Martin's Press, 175 Fifth Avenue, New York, NY 10010.

Library of Congress Catalog Card Number: 99-055067

ISBN: 0-312-97450-7

Printed in the United States of America

St. Martin's Press hardcover edition / March 2000
St. Martin's Paperbacks edition / May 2001

St. Martin's Paperbacks are published by St. Martin's Press, 175 Fifth Avenue, New York, NY 10010.

10 9 8 7 6 5 4 3 2 1

To all those who have vanished without a trace,
Without a word,
Without a sign
Into the eternal mystery of the sea.
But especially to the officers and men
Of USS Shark, USS Edsall, USS Pillsbury,
USS Asheville, and HMAS Yarra.
The gods forgot you.
But we never will.

ACKNOWLEDGMENTS

Ex nihilo nihil fit. For this book I owe thanks to James Allen, Harry Applegate, John J. Becker, Eric and Bobbie Berryman, Walter G. Clarke, Tom Cooney, Howard Denson, Joe Donohue, Sharon Doxey, Clark Driscoll, Heather Freidel, Noel Galen, Herb Gilliland, Vince Goodrich, Guy Grannum, Frank Green, Pegram Harrison, Cheryl King, Steven Klepczynski, Keith Larson, Carol Lewis, Lee Livermore, Luís Manuel Machado Menezes, Paula Mills, Gail Nicula, Doug Palmer, Kevin J. Philpott, Lenore Hart Poyer, Jarvis Rathbone, Sally Richardson, Mark Roberts, Beverly and Don Rock, Arthur Sanford, Jerry Sapp, Jack Schmock, H. Peter Schorr and the USS The Sullivans Foundation, Sandra Scovill, Maurice Shaw, Rob Taishoff, Jerry Todd, James Tomczak, Doug Undesser, Steve Wilks, George Witte, Elizabeth Wolf, Bob Wright, Andrew Young, J. Michael Zias, and others who preferred anonymity. As always, all errors and deficiencies are my own.

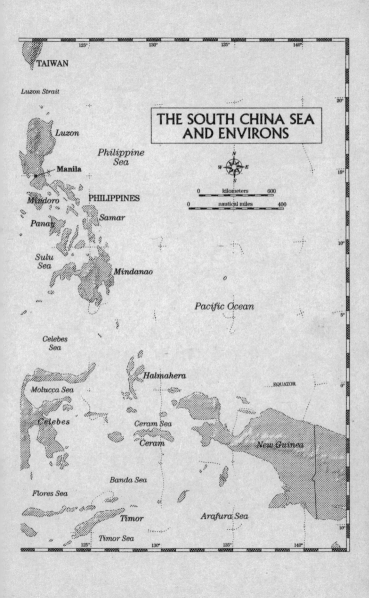

TAIWAN

Luzon Strait

Luzon

Philippine
Sea

**THE SOUTH CHINA SEA
AND ENVIRONS**

Manila

PHILIPPINES

Mindoro

0   kilometers   600

0   nautical miles   400

Panay

Samar

Sulu
Sea

Mindanao

Pacific Ocean

Celebes
Sea

Halmahera

Molucca Sea

EQUATOR

Celebes

Ceram Sea

Ceram

New Guinea

Banda Sea

Flores Sea

Timor

Arafura Sea

Timor Sea

Capt.n Kidd Commission to Seize Pyrates.

William the Third etc. to Capt:n William Kidd Commander of the Ship Adventure Galley or to the Commander of the said Ship for the time being. Greeting. Whereas Wee are informed that . . . Our Subjects, Natives or Inhabitants of New England, New Yorke, and elsewhere in Our Plantations in America, have associated themselves with divers other wicked and ill disposed persons and do against the Laws of Nations daily commit many and great Pyracies, Robberies, & Depredations, upon the Seas in the parts of America, and in other parts, to the Great hinderance, & discouragement of Trade and Navigation and to the Danger and hurt of Our loving Subjects, Our Allies and all others navigating the Seas upon their lawful Occasions. Now Know Yee, that Wee being desirous to prevent the aforesaid mischiefs and as farr as in Us lyes to bring the said Pyrates, Freebooters, and Sea Rovers to Justice, have thought fitt and do hereby give and Grant unto You the said Capt:n William Kidd full Power and Authority to apprehend, seize, and take into Your Custody as well . . . all such Pyrates, Freebooters and Sea Rovers being either Our Own Subjects or of other Nations associated with them, which you shall meet with . . . with their Ships and Vessells, and also such Merchandizes, Money, Goods, and Wares as shall be found on board or with them in case they shall willingly yeild themselves; But if they will not Submitt without fighting; Then You are by force to Compell them to yeild . . . And Wee do hereby enjoine You to keep an Exact Journall of Your Proceedings in the Execution of the premises. In Witness etc. 26ᵗʰ January 1695/6.

Warrant to my Lord Keeper of the same Date to affix the Great Seale.

William R.

20° 05' N, 118° 36' E:
WEST OF THE LUZON STRAIT

THE full moon soared over a hazy sea. Beneath it, like a fallen galaxy, rode a scattering of lights so vast no eye could encompass them all.

But a goldenglowing tactical display did. The maritime patrol plane had been aloft for eight hours. Now it churned through the summer night, back to its base in Japan. The petty officer at the console only occasionally glanced at the picture that reached out three hundred miles. Yellow on black sketched the downward-pointing dagger of Taiwan. To the east, a speckle of islands, then the blunt rump of Luzon. To the west, the coast of China. And scattered across the center of the screen, the ships and aircraft that had maneuvered here over the last week.

That exercise had just ended, terminated early in order to respond to aggression and violence in the Persian Gulf. He was starting to shut down his equipment when he noticed a spike on one of the screens.

It showed the output of a sonobuoy he'd dropped an hour earlier. A dangling microphone, deep in the sea. He debated not reporting it, but finally depressed the switch on his headset mike as he pulled a keyboard toward him. "Charlie Charlie, Delta Lima. We have a surface contact out here. Two four-bladed props, steam propulsion tonals. I call it as a large combatant, nationality unknown."

Forty-five miles astern, on the carrier, a petty officer clicked a transmit button. "Roger, Delta Lima. Have you been advised, we're hauling ass to rescue Kuwait. You're gonna have to keep tabs on the China Sea by your own-selves now."

The aircraft, droning through the dark: "Roger, understand that, but I don't think this is an exercise contact."

On the carrier, the petty officer hesitated. Then he heard the chief's voice, behind him. "You gonna pass that on up or am I?"

TWO minutes later the phone buzzed in the battle group commander's cabin. The admiral blinked himself awake with difficulty. Sleep had been all too short for the last few days. You were supposed to need less as you got older, but he wasn't sure he bought that theory. When you missed it, you didn't feel as sharp as you had at thirty, eager to jump into the cockpit after a long night partying.

"Yeah," he grunted.

The flag watch officer gave him the essentials. An unidentified surface combatant had been detected west of the force. Did he want them to identify it, considering the exercise had ended? "Sure, why not," the admiral said. "Detach a screen unit; let him check it out. No, make it two; include the Japanese if they haven't detached yet."

"Do we need to adjust formation course and speed, sir?"

"I don't think so. What's the Luda group doing?"

Three Chinese warships and a submarine out of the big South Sea Fleet base at Zhanjaing had shadowed the battle group since the exercise began. The staff watch officer reported they were clear to the northwest. The admiral told him to maintain formation course for the Strait of Malacca. He hung up, rolled over, and went back to sleep almost instantly.

USS *John Young* and JMSDF *Takatsuki* reached the ship's estimated location at 0050. So far this was standard procedure. Any surface, subsurface, or air contact in the battle group's vicinity was tracked and identified. If the craft belonged to another navy, it would often try to maneuver into an attack position. Each side would hold contact as long as possible, gathering data and training sensor operators. It was a pickup game at sea, officially denied by all parties, but nonetheless engaged in.

The battle group commander was jerked awake again at 0115. "What is it?" he snapped.

"It's the unidentified contact they reported on the last watch, sir. Message from the surface action unit commander. It's evading."

"Evading?" The admiral came fully awake. "Any identification yet? Anything on ESM?"

ESM was electronic surveillance measures, classifying ships and other threats from the signatures of their radio and radar. "No, sir. He turned west and went to high speed as soon as he realized they were attempting to intercept. *John Young* tried flashing light, but he didn't respond."

"Call *John Young*. Talk to the commander personally. Tell him to maintain the pursuit. Try to identify. But stay outside four thousand yards. Don't crowd him."

The watch officer rogered and hung up. The admiral turned over but couldn't sleep.

At 0120 he let himself into the Command Decision Center. CDC was built of small interconnected rooms lit by dim blue overhead lights. Narrow walkways labyrinthed gray consoles. He pulled himself into a chair, staring at the large-screen display as the tactical action officer began briefing him on increased air activity in the Gouangzhou Military Region.

At 0136 the Tactical Officer's Plot, which tracked the surface picture out to thirty-five miles, called down to advise that the Luda group had altered course toward the task force. The admiral rogered, watching plane after plane rise into the air over southeastern China. A few minutes later he ordered all units to Condition Three.

At 0155 the mass of aircraft stacked over the Chinese coast began moving out to sea. As they moved out of the land clutter, they organized into two groups.

The admiral ordered Condition One, full manning and readiness for immediate action, throughout the force. He passed Air Warning Yellow, sent a Red Rocket message to Commander in Chief Pacific, info Pacific Air Forces, Thirteenth Air Force Clark Field, and the Joint Chiefs, and scrambled his fighter wings. The carrier began launching the standby combat air patrol to deal with the second strike group, now turning southward after the first. She launched a radar surveillance bird and electronic jamming aircraft. The antisubmarine warfare commander pulled his screen in tight around the carrier.

"Sir, the Luda group's still closing the formation."

"I can't act against them at the moment."

"Understand that, sir, but one of them's tracking right down toward us."

"Can't the screen keep him clear?"

"Roger, sir, I'll pass that suggestion along."

THE running lights of the ship ahead were startlingly bright, magnified by the haze above the warm sea. The destroyer skipper listened to his orders, face set, then turned to the officer of the deck. "OK, you heard the man. Get your rudder over now. Figure a course when you see the relative motion. Get between him and the carrier."

"Sir, if he doesn't change course we'll hit him—"

"You heard me. Head him off!"

The OOD had never been ordered to put the ship into a position of danger before, and it took a moment to penetrate. The commanding officer was on the verge of relieving him when he said, "Aye, sir. Engines ahead full. Right standard rudder. Steady on one three zero . . . continue right to one five zero. Steady as she goes. Stand by for collision! Clear the starboard wing!"

The destroyer dug her stern in, heeling as the rudder levered at the sea. Turbines whined, and a white wave grew at her bow as the collision alarm needled into the eardrums of every man aboard.

A radioman coming out for a smoke break gaped up at a superstructure suddenly looming over him from the dark. Cooks clapped lids on boiling grease. Engineers went to their knees, grabbing for stanchions, the route topside through trunks and escape scuttles suddenly vivid in their minds.

The two ships came together with a crunch and lurch, the shock and energy absorbed by bending steel and crumpling strakes. A lifeline caught and peeled back, then snapped with a deadly *zing* across the deck. From the helo deck a knot of aviation mechanics looked across into another bridge, staring at the faces of the men inside, eerily lighted from below.

IN CDC, a television monitor showed a shrinking speck, steam whipping over the deck, the next fighter trundling toward the launch shuttle. At the same moment, a buzzer sounded from the compartment that housed electronic warfare.

"Pass missile warning, red. Air warning, red."

The admiral stared at the gathering storm north of his force. The inverted triangles a hundred and eighty miles out were hostile aircraft. The inverted semicircles closer in were his air patrol. His sensors reported aircraft after aircraft switching on their missile-control radars.

So this was the kickoff. He just hoped they came through without losing too many guys. Leaning back, he tried to stay calm as the data updates made the hostile symbols jump inward every two seconds.

Then he recalled something. He leaned over and pressed a send key. "This is the admiral. Pass to *John Young* to break off prosecution on the surface unidentified, and rejoin as soon as possible."

Three minutes passed, during which the incoming aircraft bored twenty miles closer.

"Antiair warfare coordinator reports verbal warning, no response received. Request missiles released, contingent on detecting weapons separation."

"Granted at crossover zone."

"CAP One leader reports missile lock-on, request clearance to engage tracks A0028 through A0035 with Phoenix."

"Stand by."

An endless silence as the hostile tracks jumped inward again. Checking the surface picture, the admiral noted that the two destroyers he'd sent west had dropped their pursuit of the unidentified ship and were headed back toward the battle group.

The tracks leapfrogged again. The tactical action officer was staring at him, waiting for the order to fire. They'd ignored his warning. It was time.

Then the lead bogey sidestepped, clicking a small but noticeable increment to the southwest.

"Sir? Recommend weapons release—"

"Just stand by one. Just stand by," he breathed.

"CDC, ESM: Fan head illumination ceases."

"Western strike group breaking off. New vector 290. Looks like they're going home."

Just short of the weapons release point, the strike broke off and turned back to the west. The Chinese ships clung to the formation for a few more minutes, then peeled off as the carrier and her escort moved on ahead into the open sea, headed west on the long transit to the Gulf.

The admiral tilted his chair back, watching it recede. At 0255 the chief of staff placed a draft message in front of him. He made two changes and initialed it, then leaned back again. "That was exciting."

"Too damn close for my taste. But what did it mean?"

"They consider this their backyard. Something we did set the dogs off big-time."

"But what? We were peacefully transiting through international waters. If we let them shut us out of the China Sea—"

"Yeah, I agree. But we've got other fish to fry and there's only so many pans. Saddam's invaded Kuwait. They want us in the Arabian Sea as fast as we can get there."

"How do we react here?"

"Not our problem. We've passed it up the line. Now if you don't mind, I'm going to get my head down for a few hours."

PROLOGUE II

THE FORBIDDEN CITY, BEIJING

FOR some obscure reason, the powers that be had decided to hold the reception for the new Danish ambassador in a locale usually reserved for the most portentous of state occasions: the Hall of Supreme Harmony, deep in the imperial compound once known as the Violet City. It was walled by red-lacquered pillars and richly carved screens, decorated with bronze lions with strange uptilted snouts; from its ceiling shone dimly one solid blaze of reddish gold.

Beneath it a captain in trop whites stood in the middle of the vast expanse of floor, looking at the fierce entwining of sharp-clawed dragons high above. Swarthy and barrel-chested, the naval attaché wore dark glasses even though the hall was only poorly lighted. He was admiring a single dragon, which was dipping to suspend an immense golden pearl over the throne, glorious but empty, on a stepped dais near where he stood.

Jack Byrne sipped his drink, thinking about the days when "barbarian" emissaries to the Middle Kingdom had been forced to kowtow on these polished floors.

A middle-aged Chinese approached from the direction of the buffet, accompanied by an aide. Byrne recognized the round-faced, aloof-looking officer as Admiral Mi Guozhong and came to a higher level of alertness. Not only was Mi commander of the South Sea Fleet and, as such, of interest to any naval intelligence officer operating in-country. Not only had his father been on the Long March with Mao and Teng H'saio-ping, but Mi himself was extremely well connected within the oligarchy that administered and profited from the swiftly accelerating industries of South China, the Yangzi valley, and the Guangzhou Delta.

The admiral spoke briefly, and the aide translated in a

high monotone: "Did you know that you are standing at the exact center of the Earth?"

"I hadn't realized that," said Byrne.

"An ancient text states: 'Here earth and sky meet, where the four seasons merge, where wind and rain are gathered in, and where yin and yang exist in harmony.' " The admiral turned slowly, eyeing the long north–south axis. "Here the emperor, as Mencius said, 'stood in the center of the earth, and stabilized the people within the four seas.' "

Byrne knew Mi had more English than he cared to display, just as he himself had more Chinese, but he appreciated the use of the translator. It gave one a few seconds to think and a graceful excuse if something went awry.

"An impressive venue."

"It is Emperor Yung Lo we have to thank for the complex of the Forbidden City," said the aide, without Mi actually having said anything.

"A notable name in China's long history."

"Yung Lo was the first Ming despot, a ruthless usurper and murderer," said Mi, speaking for himself now in a serviceable though accented English. "Capable, ambitious, and cruel. But effective."

"If one must be cruel, one should at least be effective."

"It was Yung Lo who sent out the fleets to the south. Though I understand it is not a well-known event in the West."

Byrne began to pay attention to what had seemed up to now a fairly innocuous conversation. He took a sip of his drink, knowing his role at this moment was less to understand or respond than to recall and transmit, word for word, if possible, whatever message would shortly be conveyed. "I've heard of it. But perhaps the admiral would like to enlighten me further?"

"Gladly," said Mi, tapping a cigarette out and bending his head as the aide snapped open an engraved Zippo. The smoke rose toward the hovering dragons like an offering. "In 1405, the emperor sent out a great expedition under the eunuch Cheng Ho. The first fleet consisted of sixty-two vessels, with twenty-eight thousand men on board. In his seven cruises, Cheng Ho brought under the tutelage of the Middle Kingdom countries from Java all the way to East Africa. Including every state bordering what even you still call the China Sea."

"I seem to recall, however, that his visits, grand though they must have been, were never repeated."

"Unfortunately, that is true. The Mongols were growing in power outside the Wall. The Mings had to shift their attention back to the northern steppe. Save for that, Asia might have been spared the interlude of European exploitation and hegemony."

"And been subject instead to the benevolent attentions of the—how did you put it?—'ruthless' Mings."

The admiral smiled faintly. "Let me ask you a question. Please, answer not in your diplomatic capacity, but as an officer with some influence in the U.S. Navy. As I ask not in an official capacity, but as part of the brotherhood of the sea."

"I understand. Though my influence, as you call it, is very small."

"The recent encounter between your aircraft carrier battle group and our forces, west of the Luzon Strait. What is your navy's view of that incident?"

"We regarded it as an unfortunate misunderstanding," Byrne said carefully. "That's why we didn't make a public statement."

"I don't see it in that light," said Mi. "As a matter of fact, the next time a provocation like that occurs so close to our coast, within waters that are historically Chinese, I believe we should send up our latest aircraft, shoot down your carrier planes, and sweep your very small number of overrated ships from the sea."

Byrne felt disbelief, then rage at the nakedness of the threat but disguised both reactions with a bland smile. "You mean we are a *zhi laohu*," he said, using the old Maoist phrase. "A paper tiger."

The admiral gave a short, harsh laugh, one that the intel-

ligence officer, who had visited many countries and heard
many different kinds of laughter, had never encountered before. "We no longer use that expression, Captain," Mi said.
"But there seem to be elements in American military circles
who still do not understand the changes that have taken
place in China. They seem to think this is still the era when
your Asiatic Fleet was permitted even to violate the Long
River. It is time they understand those days are past."

The attaché thanked the admiral for his interest. After a
few more remarks, mainly about the Danish ambassador's
stately wife, the Chinese excused themselves and strolled
away.

Jack Byrne stood alone again, swirling his drink as he
contemplated what was obviously a back-channel message
from some faction within the Chinese armed services. What
precisely did it mean? And to whom should it go? Mi had
made it clear he wasn't speaking as a government represen-
tative. If Byrne forwarded it through embassy channels,
State would simply file it. And the next time the Navy exer-
cised in those waters, the Chinese might very well carry out
their threat.

It wasn't the first incident like this. It was part of a pattern; one that spelled danger, and that if continued could
end in confrontation and catastrophe for both sides. Someone had to lay down a marker. Draw a line. Make it clear
that there was a limit.

Standing beneath the golden dragons, Byrne said to himself, *We're going to have to come to some understanding
with these bastards.*

PROLOGUE III

MANHATTAN

HE had a name, but not the one he used in daylight. He had a face, but he revealed it to no one. Save to those who looked on it as their last sight on earth.

Through this crowd of beings driven by unthinking desire he moved with the purpose and fixity of the eternal stars.

Etched with light like the gate of heaven, the square at night was a foretaste of hell. Cadaverous men offered drugs, their terrorfilled eyes the best argument against their wares. A man in a crusted vest thrust a flyer into his hand, a come-on for an "adult club." Shabby video stores, topless bars, grimy peepshows where furtive women muttered promises with their lying, diseased lips. As he paused beneath the marquee that advertised live boys, the wind rose between the reefs of buildings, rattling grit and paper cups across the street. Music came from somewhere, distant, distant. Beneath it lay the unending rumble of the subway, a lead foundation under the violet wheels of arriving night.

Tonight the sacrifice selected herself.

"Get outta here!" shouted the cop at the corner of 42nd. "Move on, or I run you in!"

Her face was wide, thin-lipped below wedged cheekbones. Eyes dark as the coming night. She held her raincoat closed with one hand, turning to the silent man who'd stopped to watch. She shouted, "What *I* do? Told you, I got a gig tonight. You get off hasslin' me—"

"What's she done, Officer?" he said.

The cop whipped around. "Back off, mac! This ain't your problem."

"Maybe it is," he wanted to say but did not. When the officer swaggered off, he followed her swinging stride down the pavement.

Just after sunset, but the square was swollen with light and noise. Taxis idled by, horns blaring. Lost youngsters drifted past, bleached hair long, rubber thongs binding wrists. Transvestites paraded in halters and heels. Canadians in shorts towed gaping pale children.

At Seventh the sidewalks suddenly clotted. Beneath the gaudy light, shoes grated on crowd-worn concrete; faces grimaced; lips mouthed shattered words of need and intoxication. Her heels clicked over crucified light. Above the buildings the sky glowed, a shield of phosphorescence damming back the dark.

She disappeared through a gated door. Faint, regular thuds seeped through the walls. He shouldered through after her, folding money into a red-lit hand.

Into a reek of smoke, alcohol, sweat, and electricity. Backlit faces above shadowed bodies. A storm surge of shouting. Shoving his way in, he craned around. Without success, she'd vanished like a stone dropped into the sea. He stood searching, then squeezed his way toward the runway. A blank-eyed hostess asked for his order. When he set the can down, the chilled metal rang hollow.

"Go through those fast!" shouted an old man. "You see how she went for me? I's your age, 'd show her thing or two."

The hostess was back, leaning over him, asking if he wanted more. He shook his head. He was getting up, resigning himself to another wasted night, when orange-and-red spots ignited and he froze, staring up.

She seemed to materialize from the black curtain. The bar went quiet, and in the silence she glided down the scuffed runway and kicked off gold platforms.

Music began, a heavy, rhythmic beat, and her eyes passed over the crowd, darkness on either side of those doors of night. Shinbones like reinforcing steel set in copper. Long thighs, bow-curved to slowly switching hips still hidden by the tail of the blouse.

The lights changed, from hectic red-orange to the hazy tubed purple of ultraviolet. The music changed, too. It became bare feet stamping dirt, the throb of hot blood, the slash of a lion's claw. Ultraviolet played like fire over triangled undershirts, false teeth, creased collars. Cigarettes gleamed from the dark like feral eyes. Smoke streamed like violet fog.

The blouse fluttered to the curtain, hung for an instant, glowing pearl against black, and fell.

The music accelerated. Now it was the lion's leap, the jaws at the throat, the triumph of lust and death. She danced it with teeth bared and cords standing out in her neck, faster and faster, till the final chords crashed to a halt and her breasts heaved, her naked body a sweaty mirror as the lights rose again.

Their hands touched as he handed the money up. Her eyes locked with his, and he saw that she knew, that the bargain was accepted. Straightening, she did a slow grind, lips curled, and trotted away as cheers and whistles erupted.

"Damn," whispered the old man. He raised his glass, grinning as if he'd discovered the back door to heaven. "Ain't a man till you split a black oak."

Outside, the clouds, lit from below as if by furnaces, streamed westward above the topless towers. Above them were stars and for minutes at a time a swollen moon.

He waited for hours in an alley behind the club, far from the light. When she emerged alone, he followed her down the ways of the city.

His left hand, thrust deep into his pocket, clutched the bundle of nylon cable ties. The knife was cold against his right. His heart was pounding so hard sparks drifted at the edges of his sight. He had dreamed, yearned, imagined his way toward this night for so long. But he saw as he passed a dusty window that his face showed no eagerness, no passion, no emotion at all.

Till at Seventh and 41st cars lifted like offerings on metal jacks behind torn chain-link and darkness submerged them like the rising sea.

She struggled at first. Tried to scream, until he chopped her in the throat. At the last she pleaded with him for death.

There is an Angel of Death. There is a Sword of God.

Toward the approaching darkness I move without a face. His tool, His puppet, obedient to His will.

Fingers still sticky with the fragrance of a crushed and scattered rose.

I

THE SHIP

1

U.S. NAVAL SHIPYARD, PHILADELPHIA, PENNSYLVANIA

THE 727 shuddered, bucking turbulent air as it passed over the rain-lashed Delaware. Lt. Comdr. Daniel V. Lenson looked down at the moored shoals of heavy cruisers, auxiliaries, destroyers. The mothball fleet, ships the Navy didn't need now but thought it might someday. He was in civvies, slacks and a windbreaker; with sandy hair and gray eyes that were starting to gather sun wrinkles at the corners.

"There's the old *Des Moines*," said Comdr. Greg Munro, leaning to peer past him. "Started my career on her, when I was a seaman deuce."

"Can we see *Gaddis* from here?" Lenson said.

"Should be over to the right—no, forget it; we're coming in for the approach."

Munro was the chief staff officer of Destroyer Squadron Twelve. It was Munro who'd called him at his stash billet in Norfolk the week before and asked if he was Dan Lenson, surface line officer, executive officer experience in frigates, coming in the zone for commander?

Dan had said, "Yeah, that's me. Why?"

"Just out of curiosity, ever serve on a 1052?"

"I was on *Bowen* my second tour. Why?"

"Got any objection to taking one over on short notice?"

"You putting me on? Who is this, anyway?"

Munro had identified himself then and assured Dan it wasn't a joke; they needed a short-fuze relief for the skipper of *Oliver C. Gaddis*. He advised Dan to say yes fast, before someone else heard about it. *Gaddis* was home-ported in Staten Island but had had a boiler explosion at sea and was limping into Philly for repairs. "I'll be sketchy on this, but the commodore's been thinking of slotting another player in there for a while now. It didn't seem urgent, because of the circumstances of the command. But this latest . . . we called over to see who SURFLANT had in pocket. They said your board was coming up; if you had command time it'd help you out."

"Well, I'm sure it would," Dan had said. "Uh, sir, what do you mean, 'the circumstances of the command'?"

"You're what, a senior 0–4? With this in your jacket you'll be a shoo-in."

"I wouldn't be too sure about that." Dan had a Silver Star and a Bronze Star. He also had a Navy–Marine Corps Lifesaving Medal for keeping his men together and alive through two days in the water after his ship had hit a mine in the Gulf. But along with them, his jacket held a letter of reprimand, a midtour relief, and more than one equivocal fitness report.

So at last he'd told the voice on the phone sure, he'd give it a shot. And now they were descending into Philadelphia International, past blasted-looking marsh and refinery towers bleeding a sulfurous pus into the sky, and the FASTEN SEAT BELTS light came on and the announcing system warned them to stay in their seats, to be prepared for rough air on the approach to their final destination.

MUNRO had been quiet on the plane, but in the taxi he cleared his throat. "OK, time for the details. Why you're here, what we expect you to do."

"Shoot." Dan concentrated, determined not to miss a word.

"The commodore has lost confidence, as the saying goes, in Dick Ottero's ability to command. I'm not going to cite you chapter and verse. It's enough to say he's been counseled before."

An unpleasant thought occurred to Dan. "He knows he's being relieved today, right?"

"I called him last night. Enough about him; let's talk about the ship. You know we're ramping down the frigate force, right?"

"Yeah, now we don't have to worry about convoying the Army to Europe against submarine attack."

"Exactly. So *Gaddis* is being disposed of as excess, transferred overseas under the Foreign Military Assistance Program."

Dan's dreams suddenly froze, like buggy software. As the screen faded, he muttered, "Oh. Uh . . . when? Who's it going to?"

"Here's how it works. Once the Navy decides we don't need a ship, the CNO decides if he wants to offer it as a foreign military sale asset. That's handled out of something called NAVOTTSA—Navy Office of Technology Transfer and Security Assistance. I won't bore you with the process, but it ends up with the gaining country signing what's called a Letter of Offer and Acceptance." Munro pulled a fat envelope out of his briefcase. "Your copy, plus the Security Assistance Manual, the Joint Security Assistance Training Regulation, and the Hot Ship Turnover Training briefing. She'll be first of five frigates we're turning over to the Pakistanis."

The taxi's tires droned. Looking out, Dan saw they were lifting on a long bridge. Past a cage of green girders the Schuylkill twisted like a strangling snake beneath a rainy sky. The pointed towers of downtown Philly pricked the clouds. Then across a brown waste of marsh he caught the gray island of a carrier, stacks and masts and the slab hulls of oilers and tenders.

"When's it happen? The transfer?"

"I'm getting to that. This is what they call a 'hot turnover'—where the original crew ramps down simultaneous as the foreign crew ramps up. There's a total twelve-week turnover period. *Gaddis* was in week twelve when they blew one-alfa boiler—"

"How'd they blow a boiler?"

"One of the snipes, showing off. They were under way doing their engineering casualty control exercises, and in the course of that they go to put fire back in one of the boilers. They'd pulled fires in it, so it's still warm, and one of the chiefs says, 'Hey, we don't use those goddamn books. Here's how we do it in the real Navy.' So he lit it off the back wall. Know what I'm talking about?"

"Usually it works. Unless you don't purge before you relight."

"Exactly what happened, and he hits it with a shot of fuel and *kaboom*."

Dan said cautiously, "Not necessarily the skipper's fault."

"Wait'll you get there; you'll see why we decided to clean house starting at the top. Now, normally the way this would work is the commodore would fly down, relieve Ottero, and leave the exec in charge till the Pakis get under way. But the commodore's in Rosey Roads doing an exercise, and Lieutenant Commander Juskoviac's really not command-qualified. So I'll get you pointed in the right direction. The ship transfer officer'll help if any roaches jump out of the process."

Dan sat back. The closer he got, the less attractive it looked. A careless fireroom gang, a relieved skipper, an exec who'd have been acting CO—commanding officer—if not for him. Still, it was better than pushing paper in Norfolk.

A lofty ironwork gate. "Here's the yard," said the driver.

"Pier six. Straight down toward the river." As Munro flashed his ID for the gate cop, Dan caught sight of a straggling line of what he at first took for strikers. Then he saw the signs. U.S. HANDS OFF IRAQ. PRAY FOR PEACE. He lifted his hand in a wave, searching their faces, drawing a quizzical glance from Munro. Then the cab was moving again, past the marchers into the bustle and grime of the yard.

THEY passed 1870s-era brick barracks, a parade ground, then slowed, bumping over patched asphalt along barbed-wire-lined alleys into the steamwreathed heart of the shipyard. A line of destroyers lay derelict and listing, rusting in the rain. Stone dry docks cratered the wet-glistening earth.

Out of one loomed a mountainous hull, clifflike sponsons. USS *Constellation*, CV-64.

"Pier Six," said Munro at last. The concrete shelf extended a quarter-mile out into the Delaware, into mist and river fog. "We better walk from here."

She took shape slowly from the inchoate gray, as if she were steaming toward them over the gray-green river. He'd always considered the Knox-class frigates graceful-looking ships. About the same displacement as the Gearings he'd started his career on, but roomier and more modern, with aluminum superstructures and low-maintenance design. Strange to think they were already passing out of the Fleet, outmoded less by time than by the changing realities of world politics.

He shook off the depression that thought gave him. The high Atlantic bow faced him as he stepped carefully across the grease-caked rails the pier cranes rode on. It was topped by the rounded housing of a five-inch gun. Behind the ASROC (antisubmarine rocket) launcher rose the sheer front of the bridge. Above towered a gray cone topped with a drumlike structure, a combined mast and stack unmistakable from miles away at sea. Then he saw something he didn't expect.

"What's that on the fantail? And the boat deck?"

"The Pak Navy wanted more firepower. So we went rooting around and came up with some old forty-millimeters. We put twins on the boat decks and a quad mount on the stern. They're getting twenties, too, but they're not installed yet."

A chunky blond in steel-toes and wash khakis loped down the brow. Munro introduced Lt. Comdr. Evilia Beard, the ship transfer officer. Dan followed her and Munro aboard, aware as he faced the flag and then the OOD that every man on the quarterdeck was watching them with outright hostility.

THE outgoing CO's lips were crimped like the edges of a metal can. His eyes were reddened and glossy behind plastic-framed lenses. As they shook hands outside the captain's cabin, Dan understood the squadron commander's decision to relieve him. 0900, and Richard Ottero's breath was bourbon-ripe. Dan had noticed other symptoms of a carelessly run ship on the climb up from the quarterdeck: a holstered pistol hanging unattended, paint on gaskets and knife edges, out-of-date inspection labels, trash in the passageways.

"Sorry we had to meet this way," Dan told him.

"Don't take it personally if I don't say welcome aboard," Ottero said. He turned to Munro. "Let's make it short and sweet."

"OK by me. Dan?"

"Sure."

Ottero's hand trembled as he made sure his uniform pockets were buttoned. He faced the ship's exec, a thin lieutenant commander with a long head like a greyhound's, fine light brown hair receding in front. "Greg, how do I look?"

"Good, Skipper. For a guy about to get the shaft."

Ottero told Dan, "You can have the damn job and to hell with you. But take care of her. I know she doesn't look so hot right now, but I've been undermanned since day one. She's a good ship. Too good to be giving away."

Dan felt like he was watching something he didn't want to see. Alcohol and humiliation. He remembered. He said, "I'll keep that in mind. Captain."

"By the way, where's Khashar?" interrupted Munro. The exec said the Pakistani CO and the incoming crew were on the berthing barge. He hadn't seen any reason for them to—

Ottero interrupted, "Right. OK, get 'em mustered on the flight deck, Greg. Give me a ring when they're ready." To Dan he said, with what seemed a touch of irony, "Care for a drink?"

"No thanks. I had to quit, myself."

They stood silently for a few minutes. Then the phone squealed, and Dan and Munro followed Ottero aft.

2

WHEN the short and all-too-tense ceremony was over, Dan went back to the captain's cabin, started to knock, then stopped and let himself in. Someone had been busy during the change of command. The floor was vacuumed, the closets cleaned out, his laptop set up on the desk. But he could still smell cigarettes and the unsettling reek of whiskey.

He hadn't had a drink for three years, but that didn't mean he didn't still want one sometimes.

No, he wasn't going back to that. It solved nothing . . . and he'd made a promise. The woman he'd given his word to was dead, but if anything, that bound him all the more tightly.

On some obscure prompting he went into the little attached head, the most private place on the ship, and washed his hands. An assured-looking officer in creased khakis with three rows of ribbons looked back from the mirror. He took a deep breath, trying to convince himself he was the Skipper now.

The turnover ceremony had been brief. When he and Ottero arrived on the helo deck, Juskoviac had called the crew to attention. Chiefs to the right, officers to the left, the crew facing him, shoulders hunched under working jackets and peacoats. The flag crackled in the misty wind. Ottero had read his orders first, a bland paragraph transferring him to the squadron staff. Dan had followed with his, just as terse: "Report to USS *Gaddis* and relieve as commanding officer." Traditionally, the outgoing captain then gave a closing speech. Ottero had simply saluted Dan and Munro and said, "I stand relieved." Then said to the silent ranks, "Good-bye, men, and good luck."

Twenty steps back into the hangar, the sound of his voice

on the quarterdeck, and he was gone. A sigh rustled the crew like a breeze over a calm sea. Dan gave it a moment. Till their eyes turned to him, curious and apprehensive. But he'd said only, "I'll speak to you all in the course of the day. Mr. Juskoviac, ship's work, please."

Now he ran a comb through his hair, wondering what he was going to say. What would Jimmy John Packer do? How would Tom Leighty or Ben Shaker or Barry Niles approach this? Every leader had his own style, but there were a few things the good ones shared. Make your expectations clear up front. Make sure everyone knew what his job was. Start everybody with a clean slate.

The most important thing was to make it perfectly plain to every man aboard that a new day had dawned.

For gnawing at him now was the last thing Munro had said, pausing by the brow for a farewell handshake. "Good luck, Captain. Get her ready for sea as soon as you can."

"We'll try not to let the turnover slip too far."

"I didn't mean that." Munro hesitated, then added words that had brought Dan suddenly to alertness. "We may need her."

He figured he knew what the chief staff officer meant. War was imminent in the Gulf. *Gaddis* and her sisters might be called on again.

Thinking that, he went out into the cabin and soon found what he was looking for: a small cabinet with sliding doors and a brass lock.

"Buzzed me, sir?" A kid in his teens with bushy red eyebrows and freckles like a high-water line across his nose stood in the passageway.

"Carry on. What's your name, sailor?"

"Foley, sir. Seaman Foley. Welcome to the 'Ollie Maru,' sir."

"Thanks. What's in this locker, Foley?"

"That's Captain Ottero's liquor locker, sir."

"That's what I thought. Got a key to it?"

"Me? No, sir, Cap'n kept that himself."

"OK, here's what I want you to do. Who's the chief master-at-arms?"

"That'd be Chief Mellows, sir. 'Marsh' Mellows, they call him. Can't miss him; he's the guy looks like Mr. Clean in the commercials."

"OK." Dan remembered him from the helo deck, a large, patient-looking senior enlisted with a shaven head. "Have him cut this padlock. Put everything in an open box. Take it all down to the Dumpster on the pier and pitch it in. Hard, so all the bottles break. Make sure everybody sees you do it."

Foley squinted, then grinned. "Got you, sir."

Dan picked up his cap, checked his alignment, and headed aft.

HE ran into the exec on the ladder. "Hi, uh, Greg. Wardroom assembled?"

"They're standing by," Juskoviac said. Sullenly, not meeting Dan's eyes.

"I want to see the chiefs and first class, after that. Then the rest of the crew, on the mess decks."

"When do you want to meet Captain Khashar?"

"How about him and Commander Beard for lunch? If they're free."

The XO spoke into a handheld radio as Dan headed down the ladder. Lenson said over his shoulder, "Greg, anything you and I ought to discuss now? What's our muster look like?"

"They started the personnel drawdown three months ago. We had a hundred and forty-two white-hats, ten officers, at quarters this morning."

"That's below even a reduced combat readiness manning."

Juskoviac nodded.

"Equipment casualties?"

"Minor stuff on the combat systems. Major problem's the boiler."

Dan headed down the 02-level passageway. "Give me the short squirt."

"Uh, I know the explosion warped the casing, split some brick."

"Have we got a repair estimate yet?"

"Jim Armey might. He's the CHENG."

That was shipboard slang for "chief engineer." Dan was a little puzzled the exec didn't seem to have all the details on the damage at his fingertips but let it pass. They were outside the wardroom door when Juskoviac added, "Can I ask you something?"

"Sure."

"I figured, this close to turnover, they'd fleet me up to acting CO. Either that or send somebody down from the staff. How'd they come up with you?"

Dan had to admit the guy was up-front. "I'm out of a staff billet. What they told me, they couldn't fleet you up because you weren't command-qualified."

"I *am* command-qualified."

"Well, I guess that word didn't get to wherever it had to get. Announce me."

Juskoviac slammed the door open. "Attention on deck!" he yelled, and the officers surged to their feet.

"Seats, please," Dan said, taking the head of the table. He scanned their faces, taking a sip from the coffee that had appeared at his elbow, and looked to make sure the galley slide was closed. "Who's missing?"

"This is everybody, sir. We're dual-hatted on several billets."

"OK, let's get down to business. Commander Juskoviac's given me a rundown on our readiness for sea and personnel status, but I'd like to hear it in more detail. Let's start with Supply. Please introduce yourself, I need to start getting faces with names."

A sallow, slim, dark-haired lieutenant. "Dave Zabounian. We did a complete inventory to get ready for our turnover. Aside from what we used coming down from Staten Island, we're at a hundred percent."

"Is everyone getting paid?"

"Yessir. I got a first-class who's pretty hot on the disbursing end."

"What exactly is the status of the ship itself, Dave? In terms of this turnover? Can you talk to that?"

"Sure. The Pakistanis are signed up for a five-year lease. With that, they get what's on board for parts and consumables and so forth. Ammo's a separate account; they bought that outright."

"How hard would it be to jerk her back to full-op status, say if this Kuwait thing escalates to war?"

Heads lifted around the table. Zabounian said cautiously, "I don't believe there'd be any major problem with that, sir. We'd need a personnel augment from somewhere, though."

"OK, good. Let's continue."

Chet "Chick" Doolan, the weapons officer, looked like a young Hemingway, with a broad chest and black hair curling aggressively over a white triangle of undershirt. He briefed on the guns, the ASROC, and the torpedo tubes. The operations officer had no outstanding problems, though the news that most of the crypto and radio equipment had been stripped off was a downer.

Finally only a lean, uneasy-looking black officer in coveralls remained. "Jim Armey, right?" Dan said. "Tell me about our plant."

"The inspector's aboard; I can ask him to come in—"

"I'd rather hear it from my chief engineer."

"We're in Condition A except for our boiler and some sea suction valves. The bottom paint's reasonable considering we haven't been out of the water for four years. This isn't a new ship, but it's in good condition."

"Tell me about the boilers."

"We've got Babcock and Wilcoxes, type D. CRMO headers, mag-moly drums, carbon steel in the waterwalls. Thirty-nine thousand steaming hours on them."

"I meant, how bad's the damage."

"The explosion warped the casing. First off that's gotta

be replaced. Once the yard checks the burner fronts and does the hydros, they'll replace the damaged tubing; fix the refractory brick, with the grout and the mud and so forth; then do the light-off exam. Now, normally they'd put us in dry dock for tube and brick work, but I think I've got them argued out of that. That saves us three weeks just to set the graving blocks up."

"That's the direction we want to go in. How are the drums?" Dan asked him.

"Far as we know now, all we've got to do is replace a couple of downcomers."

"How long's it going to take?"

"My seat-of-the-pants estimate would be there's three to four weeks' work there, once the yard turns to."

"I'll get with you around eleven, take a look." Dan glanced at his watch and stood. They scrambled to their feet, taken by surprise.

He said, "Gentlemen, you tell me *Gaddis* is in good shape. But I see a dirty ship, a slovenly ship, one that can't steam safely because of her crew's carelessness.

"Here's how I do business. There's only one test of a warship: her ability to steam and to fight; to take punishment and inflict it. I don't believe that simply because we are due to turn this ship over so many weeks from now we have an excuse for letting it be less than a fully capable fighting unit.

"The standards we set in this room are the ones our men will judge themselves by. I have high standards. I expect you to bust your tails till this ship meets them. Until the moment we haul down the flag, *Gaddis* is a U.S. Navy warship and I will run her as such."

No one spoke, but he could read their thoughts in their eyes. He nodded coldly and went out.

To pause in the passageway, wondering. The words had come almost without him, fruit of the years he'd spent at sea and the men he'd served under, good and bad. If you watched them all, learned from them all, maybe it wasn't really that much of a stretch to step up and take your place after them.

Anyway, he'd do his best.

HE was on the bridge later that morning, leaning thoughtfully over the splinter shield, when he noticed several seamen sauntering down the pier. He said to the quartermaster, a Cajun named Robidoux who looked like he had a basketball under his dungaree shirt, "Who's that down there, Louis?"

"That's the Pakis, sir. They only do half-days. Fridays off, too."

"And Saturday and Sunday?"

The QM nodded.

"*And* half-days?"

"That's their routine, sir."

"You know Captain Khashar?"

"Yessir, sure do." The petty officer glanced around, as if making sure they weren't being overheard. "Ever hear the phrase 'a menace to navigation'?"

"All right," Dan told him. "I'd better form my own opinion of him. Get a chance to start over, if you know what I mean."

"Sure, sir. It might help; him and Cap'n O. sure didn't get along."

Three of the Pakistanis, in USN-style dungarees but different ball caps, came rattling up the inboard ladder. Two immediately lit cigarettes. Dan glanced at his watch again and saw it was nearly time to meet Armey.

HE stood in front of the wrecked boiler in steel-toes and borrowed coveralls as the chief engineer introduced the fire-room team. "And this is Chief Albert Sansone," Armey finished.

Dan studied Sansone. He looked young for a chief, stocky and young. He also gave the impression of being both pissed off and startled, maybe because he didn't have any eyebrows. His skin looked as if it had been microwaved. "You the one blew this boiler up, disregarding the operating standards?" Dan asked him.

Sansone met his eye. "Is that what they told you, sir? All due respect, that's bullshit."

"What's your side of it?"

"Sure, I lit it off the back wall. Just like everybody does, when the boiler's warm. It works great, long as you got draft. I get ready to light her off; I turn my head and yell over to Abdul Number Two, 'Check and make sure the forced draft blower's on high speed.' He ambles over to look, then gives me the high sign. Next thing I know I'm laying in sick bay with half my face burned off. And fucking one-alfa looks like a tank ran over it."

"Let's take a look," Dan said. He jackknifed himself and slid in through the manhole.

An odor of oil and metal and smoke stuffed his nose. Brick grated against his back. He rolled over and got to his knees and then to his feet, crouched over, so he wouldn't whang his head into the slanted ranks of water screen tubes above him.

Steel-cold now, but when it was lit off this bathroom-sized cave was the blazing heart of the ship. Burners sprayed hundreds of gallons an hour of Distillate Fuel, Marine, into a tornado of fire that cooked the water in the tubes into an invisible gas so charged with energy by heat and pressure it could cut rubber or cloth or flesh like a shearing blade. Knox-class plants ran at over 1200 psi, double that of previous destroyers. A crack or break in the piping would fill a compartment in seconds, cooking or smothering anyone who didn't get out in time.

The blackened brick swallowed the light so that you had to bend close to actually see the surface. He shuffled forward, noting where it had blown out of the fire wall. The fractures were paler than the flame-blackened surface around it.

A scrape, a cough, and Sansone joined him, twin fetuses in a hellish womb. The chief pointed above their heads. "All that side of the casing's bent. That brick's all got to be chipped out. There's the tubing we gotta replace. Then it's all got to be hydroed and certified, then rebricked and go through light-off. It's a good six weeks of work."

"Mr. Armey said three or four weeks."

"Ain't impossible, but the forty-one shop'd really have to get their butts in gear. Which I don't see happening yet. This yard's way overbooked. We're like parked in the front lot; they'll get to us when they ain't got nothing better to do."

"OK, I got a question for you. What would it take for us to fix this ourselves?"

Sansone touched one of the tubes. "Sir, I'd like to tell you we could. I mudded brick before, on the *Harry Yarnell*. But we couldn't do the tubes, or the headers. I'll tell it to you straight. It'd be a goddamn bomb waiting to blow." The chief spat into a dark corner.

"Has anybody showed up yet from the shipyard?"

"There's an estimator or something up in the log room."

"Let me have a minute with Mr. Armey; then we'll go talk to him." Dan ran his hand over the damaged section. The firebrick came apart under his hands, gritty and frangible. It could take a thousand degrees of flame, but it was delicate as porcelain. It left a black stain on his hands that didn't rub off even when he was back in his cabin, washing his hands as he changed for lunch.

HUSSAIN Khashar was in British-style whites. Dan stared at the four broad stripes on Khashar's wing-curved shoulder boards. A shock, and not a pleasant one. He'd assumed everyone called the Pakistani "Captain" because he was taking over as skipper. Khashar was nearly six feet tall, but his legs were short, making him seem top-heavy as he grasped Dan's hand and revealed strong yellow teeth. "*Assalam o-aleikum*. The blessings of God upon you."

"Uh, upon you, too," said Dan. "You know Commander Beard and Commander Juskoviac." Khashar nodded to the exec but didn't seem to see the ship transfer officer.

They sat down to fish sandwiches and fries. Foley

served, not with any flair, but he got the plates from the tray to the table.

Khashar took out a pack of Camels when the meal was over, and Dan noted a jewel-encrusted Rolex on his wrist. He lit a cigarette and opened with, "I wondered whether to show up for your change of command. Finally I decided it should be an all-American function. Commander Ottero and I had differences."

Dan said, keeping his voice bland, "Differences?"

"My government has put twelve million dollars into this account. As far as I'm concerned, this is my ship. We won't be working together long, you and I, but I hope you'll be more helpful, more flexible, than he was."

Dan turned to Beard, asking if they might take a look at the turnover schedule. She spread a file before them. In a flat voice, she pointed out where they should have been by this time. Dan frowned. "You mean we were three weeks behind even before the explosion?"

"Purely administrative," Khashar put in. "The only essential element is the training. And that's on schedule."

"It's *not* on schedule," Beard told him. "Withdrawal of personnel from schools without meeting test standards does not constitute acceptable training."

"It does if I'm satisfied with their progress."

"I'm talking about operating the automatic combustion controls. Weapons system maintenance. Sonar acoustic analysis. How can you judge their progress?"

"But you insist that all training, and all tests, must be conducted in English." Khashar spread his hands. "How much can we realistically expect? If they can demonstrate basic knowledge of the systems, we can figure the rest out in service."

Beard said, "On the job, you mean? You could train on the auxiliary systems that way. But engineering, ordnance, that's a stupid approach." She stopped herself. "Not *stupid*—I didn't mean that—just risky."

But her apology came too late. Khashar had withdrawn

to some higher plane, where he neither heard nor could be bothered with those below. He sipped his coffee, lit another cigarette, and stared out the porthole at the upperworks of a passing freighter in the channel.

A double rap on the door, an inthrust shaggy head. The ponytailed man in an old-fashioned foul-weather jacket introduced himself as their ship supervisor. "Can't stay long, Captain. We're working everybody overtime on the *Connie.* May be longer than you like before we can get to you."

"I meant to ask you about that. If it's a question of triage, getting hulls into service fast, we're a better investment than a ship with a big backlog of work."

The ship supe looked puzzled. "Right, but I understood you were slated for overseas sale. Isn't that right? Transfer to, uh, Egypt?"

Dan hesitated, caught between Munro's warning and Khashar's questioning look. Finally he said, "No, Pakistan. But the end result's the same, another combat-capable ship in the Middle East."

"I'd cut you a break if I could. But we're at capacity right now."

"That's not what I hear."

The supe looked surprised; then his face hardened. "What do *you* hear? Captain?"

"I'm told if this gets tagged as a hot job, management can ask for volunteers from the planners and supervisors, to go back to the tools and help out. I've got a committed wardroom and two committed crews. Put them together with some experienced craftsmen and we'll get this job done."

"And why should we tag this as a hot job?"

"Because the United States of America made an agreement with a foreign government. I'm willing to go to twelve-hour shifts, seven days a week, to keep that commitment." Dan got up, picking up his cap. "I'm headed over to the shipyard commander's office. Captain Khashar, Commander Beard, would you do me the favor of accompanying me?"

"You're not going to make yourself popular over there, pulling that card out," Beard said.

"Sometimes you have to accept that as a cost of doing business," Dan told her.

3

NINE days later, he held tight to a jagged hot sheet of steel as a volcano of sparks flamed past his squinted eyes. After long seconds the howling torch waned. Blinking, he sucked smoky air through his dust mask. Then the man holding the air arc shifted his boots and jammed the nozzle against the casing again, and the roar built anew.

He was in the boiler room, surrounded by ship's force in green coveralls and yard workers in disposable outfits and red and gray hard hats. Since they'd started, Dan had been going down several times a day to observe. He didn't think of himself as a back slapper, but he knew every man worked harder if he saw the CO was personally into getting the job done.

Jim Armey, who seemed to spend twenty-four hours a day on the job, had explained that ripout was the first order of business. The boiler was surrounded by fuel lines, fuel oil control valves, air flow transmitters, and sensing piping. It all had to be torn out or moved so they could gain access to the work area. That had taken four days. Next, they had to remove the damaged casing panels. There were actually two casings on the boiler, inner and outer, separated by stainless-steel stiffeners that allowed movement from thermal expansion. A few of the least damaged panels could be repaired in place, but most had to be cut out. The air arc, from which his ears were still ringing, combined a high-temperature welding arc to melt the metal with an air jet that blew it away. It made a deafening roar and filled the boiler room with dense black smoke, but it was fast.

The next job, which they'd start at midnight, was to begin air-chipping out the firebrick and mortarlike cast refractory that covered the firetubes. Only then would the boilermakers be able to reach the tubes themselves.

As the deafening whine built again, he headed for the ladder, pulling himself out of the engine spaces into the only slightly less grimy passageway outside the mess decks. His coveralls, like those of the men he left behind, were coated with a gritty powder.

They were making progress. But it had taken a personal call on COMNAVBASE Philadelphia, two meetings with the shipyard commander, and an appearance before the Metal Trades Council, the shipyard's equivalent to a union council.

Of course there'd been a price. Admiral Girault had been faultlessly correct, but icy, and Dan knew word traveled. He had a reputation already as a loose cannon. Add to that a name as a troublemaker, and he could kiss his career farewell.

The second price had been with the crew. He'd called BuPers and told them he was holding personnel they'd slated for transfer. Juskoviac had been in his cabin within the hour, protesting that Lenson was lousing up arrangements he and Ottero had made to get career-enhancing billets for the men being transferred off.

Dan had studied his exec's sulky pout for a moment. His initially neutral impression of the man was changing rapidly to dislike. Juskoviac's moods altered unpredictably, almost manically. At times he was all energy and enthusiasm, like a puppy who wants to be picked up. At other times he was sullen and hostile. Dan could live with emotional lability, but he'd also noticed Juskoviac had to be reminded, warned, and bird-dogged in order to get anything done, a fatal drawback in a ship's XO. Now he said, "Sorry, Greg. I already made the call."

Juskoviac had closed the door. "We're going to be facing a real morale crash when this gets out."

"Then they'd better hear it from us first."

"You'd better announce it yourself. Sir. Because I don't think it's necessary."

Dan overlooked his tone, for the moment. He remembered how difficult it had been when he was an XO to speak bluntly to Captain Shaker. "You know what we've got to do, Greg. We've got to have the bodies to do it with."

"But have we really *got* to do it? Screw the guys on their next assignments and work them like dogs, just to turn it all over to the Pakis two weeks early? You're letting this acting CO thing go to your head."

Dan had risen then, letting his anger show. "I can't force you to agree with me, Greg, but I damn sure expect you to support me in public. Or, if you can't do that, keep your mouth shut. Yeah, I'll go on the 1MC and explain why we're holding people."

And Juskoviac had been right, at least in part. Chief Mellows had filled Dan in on what was circulating on the mess decks. He was aware of a coolness when he made his daily rounds. But there hadn't been any actual protest, no notes in the suggestion box or calls from congressmen. The enlisted were holding off, giving him the benefit of the doubt. Dan knew why, or hoped he did. The Allies were building up their forces in the Gulf, flying in air wings and troops. Everyone still hoped Saddam would back out, retreat from the occupied territory, but there was no sign yet of anything but a determination to hold.

"We may need her." That was how Munro had put it.

Back in his cabin, Dan stripped off the coveralls. There was enough shore steam for hot water, and he tried his best to relax in the sheer animal pleasure of floods of it.

The phone, right outside. No matter if you were squatting on the can, there was always a phone near the CO. He shut off the water reluctantly. Naked, shivering, he said, "USS *Gaddis,* commanding officer, this is a nonsecure line."

"Dan? Is that you?"

"Blair," he said, smiling.

He'd met Blair Titus in Bahrain, during what was for him an all-too-brief port visit during Operation Earnest Will and for her a tour as defense staffer for Sen. Bankey Talmadge. At the time Dan had thought that was it: one snatched night; knowing only that he'd always remember her; that in years to come he'd see her likeness in others who passed him on the street, in malls, on beaches. She would be part of what made him himself; he would take the smell of her hair and the feel of her lips with him into the darkness. But then he'd found her again on the heat-baked tarmac at Manama when he arrived with the other *Van Zandt* survivors.

Since then they'd spent weekends together and gone hiking and camping in the Blue Ridge. He'd been out to Charles County to meet her family. No promises, no commitments, just a strange sort of camaraderie, respect, and (he had to admit) great sex.

Neither had much time for the other. Or for much of anything but work. That was the price you paid, he figured, for being dedicated to what you did.

But sometimes he wondered if what you got was worth what you were charged. He came back to being naked, dripping, holding the phone and her saying, "I was calling because the base closing commission's going to be in Philly and I can make it an overnight. If you want."

"Sure. We're pretty busy here, but—sure! When?"

"Thursday. I'll have my assistant set something up. I don't think I want to be down near the shipyard area. That's in South Philly, right?"

"Yeah—why not?"

"Haven't you heard? About the Philly Ripper?"

"Sorry, I haven't been following the news."

"They found one woman dead, and pretty badly mutilated. Another was attacked and escaped but couldn't give much of a description."

"No, I haven't heard about that. I've had my head inside these repairs. Thursday, fine, it'll be nice to see you. What time'll you be in?"

She said she wasn't sure but would have her assistant call. She made a kissing noise and said good-bye.

A tap at the door: Foley. The seaman stared, then

coughed into a fist. "Excuse me, sir. Quarterdeck wants to know where you wanna hold the progress conference."

Dan grabbed for the towel. "Uh, make it in the wardroom. Call damage control central, see if they can get the word to Mr. Armey to meet me there."

HE was on his way when shouting came from a ladderway, a clang of metal on metal. He wheeled, dropped a deck, and came off the ladder into a pushing, shouting melee.

"Marsh" Mellows, the big chief master-at-arms, held two people apart at its heart. One was a livid Pakistani; the other, a snarling woman in coveralls and a yellow hard hat. "What's going on?" Dan said as all eyes swung to him.

"Got a situation, is all," said Mellows, still holding them both, the Pakistani and the woman, well separated. He *did* look like Mr. Clean, just as burly but sort of friendly at the same time, with knotted curly eyebrows like Leonid Brezhnev. "You don't need to get involved in this, sir."

He liked Mellows—had come to depend on the chief master-at-arms's calm efficiency, the way he seemed to know everything the crew said or even thought. Still, he didn't like the mix of angry sailors. "Maybe I'd better."

The chief said reluctantly, "Seaman Usmani here. Sounds like the son of a bitch couldn't keep his hands to himself."

"How about it?" Dan asked the woman. Before she could answer, someone else said, "She's one of the yardbirds. She says he came on to her, started humping her ass like a dog."

"Is you the captain? I'm filing a complaint on this filthy animal." Powell was young, stocky, a grimy canvas toolbag over her shoulder. "This little prick been hassling me all day. Make sucking noises when I go by. Then I goes to get a drink of water and he come up behind me. That's when he says it."

"What did you say to her, Usmani?"

"All I say, I bump into her, I say, 'Excuse me, please'."

"Like shit. He said, 'Screw me, please.' Then he start

pushing his crotch into me. I'm putting in a paper. This ain't right, that all—"

"Great, great." Dan looked at the guy, already sorry he'd gotten involved. Mellows had tried to warn him. More people were arriving, coming down from the mess decks, hanging on the ladder. He couldn't let it go by. On the other hand, he wasn't certain how far his authority over the foreign crew extended.

"Is there a problem here?" said a British-accented voice.

Dan half-turned, but Khashar was already pushing past him.

The sailor's eyes had time only to widen before the captain slapped him, followed by a torrent of abuse. Khashar turned to Powell. "These men see American television, movies. They watch the women naked in bars, offering themselves. They think this means all American women. This man will be broken in rank and restricted to the ship until we return to Pakistan. I hope this will be satisfactory?"

"You didn't need to hit him," said the worker. "I figured chew his ass a little, that kind of thing. . . . You didn't have to hit him."

Dan said, "So you're satisfied?"

"Long's it don't happen again, and none of those others starts grabbing me. I'm here to do a job. Leave me alone, it'll get done."

Usmani stood against the bulkhead, face blank, cheek reddening where he'd been struck.

Mellows shouted, "You guys all got work to do, don't you? Or do I need to think up something?"

The knot broke, drifted apart. The situation seemed to be defusing itself. But when Dan looked after the dispersing sailors, he noted the way the Americans stayed an arm's length from the Pakistanis, how they didn't intermingle at all.

4

THE lobby of the Four Seasons smelled of perfume and flowers. Low sofas and armchairs and an antique sideboard holding an immense Chinese vase of fresh gladiolas were scattered over the silver-veined marble floor. The concierge asked, "Can I help you, sir? You look as if you're lost."

"No, no, just waiting for someone."

He was turning from an eighteenth-century engraving when he saw her through heavy glass, a doorman dressed like a Ukrainian general ushering her in. He lifted a hand and her face lit up and she swung toward him, tall and cool and looking so damn good, feeling so damn good in his arms.

"How fares the BRAC? Are we losing the navy yard?"

"I'm not actually on the committee. But base closing and consolidation's obviously one of Armed Services' prime concerns." Blair Titus checked out the lobby, then him. "You look tired. How about tea? Or would you rather just do room service?"

"I've never been a big fan of tea."

THEY lay together, when they were both exhausted, close as the twists of a cruller, and the touch of her legs against his, scratchy here and petal soft within, was sweeter than powdered sugar. He felt himself relaxing for the first time in weeks. He opened his eyes to examine her closed lids, the lashes lowered to shade the penetrating intelligence of her gaze. He cupped a white breast and let his drift closed, too.

The first time, in Manama, he'd been wary of her, wary of love. Disappointed twice, once by divorce and once by death, he'd tried to fight clear. But it hadn't worked, and though he hadn't told her yet and they had never discussed it seriously, he knew now he was one cooked gosling.

Some time later she stirred, and he jerked awake. She yawned, lifting a bare arm shining with fine golden hair to check her watch. "You awake?"

"Sorry. Didn't mean to drift off."

"Don't apologize. You did great for somebody who looked as bushed as you did. Are we going to lie around here all evening?"

"Sounds like a plan."

"Are you really that sleepy?"

"No." He rubbed his eyes. "What do you want to do?"

"It's almost dinnertime. Then I have to make this reception, at least for a little while." She half-rolled, then stopped at his choked protest. "Have I got something caught?"

"Let's just say I'm not in a position to object."

"I sense signs of returning life. Let's investigate."

Looking down at her shining hair, he lifted his body in a half-protesting arch, then resigned himself to her friction-less caress. A moment later she mounted him, taking him with a sudden ferocity that matched the mouthwatering impulsion he'd brought to his first ingress, and rode him to her own eye-clenched climax and then, changing rhythm and grip, with a mischievous grin and quick vertical strokes brought him to a second exquisitely near-painful discharge that left him sagged back sweating into the damp, wrinkled sheets as she swung a leg off and went briskly into the bathroom.

THE restaurant was dim and the chandeliers glittered above white linen. After some encouragement he ordered braised Norwegian salmon and black truffles. Blair decided on lamb *en crèpinette*.

"So how's the overhaul going?"

"We should be done in two more weeks. Maybe sooner, if the hydros go well."

"You were having trouble with the foreign commanding officer, weren't you?"

"Actually, that's smoothed out. Khashar doesn't do things the way I would, that's for sure. But he's not actually around all that much. I wind up dealing with Commander Irshad; he's the operations officer and general whipping boy."

The wine steward. She ordered a pinot noir. He asked for orange juice and tonic.

"The trouble is, you get attached. I have to keep reminding myself she's only mine for a little while. Unless the transfer's preempted by operational considerations—"

"Meaning Desert Shield."

He nodded, wanting to ask her if the Allies were going to attack but knowing he had no right to. He had no doubt she knew, though maybe not the exact hour. He couldn't ask her about *Gaddis*, either, whether Munro's charge to him was based on a concrete plan for canceling her transfer. So instead he asked about the base closing commission, and she sketched diagrams on the tablecloth with her fingernail to show how reduced infrastructure translated into force modernization.

"That's why all our ships are going away?"

"There's no reason to keep them. Iraq, Iran, North Korea—none of our remaining potential adversaries is a sea power."

"What about five years down the road? Ten years?"

"I don't want to get into an argument with you. But there's a real question how much insurance an obsolete ship actually represents."

"It's a lot quicker to install up-to-date equipment and put an old hull to sea than it is to design and build a whole new one. We proved that with the battleships. *Missouri*'s on her way to the Gulf right now, loaded with Tomahawks."

"I take your point, but we have to look at political realities. The shipbuilders don't want those old hulls around. The Navy would rather build something glamorous like Arleigh Burkes and Seawolf. Weighing it all, we've approved leasing or selling them. We get a political advantage out of it; the smaller allies are happy; on paper there's even a cash flow." She waved a hand. "Anyway. Have you been back home?"

"Yeah. I went to see my mom."

"How is she?"

"OK."

"I haven't met any of your family yet."

"Yeah, sometime I'll have to take you up there."

She was silent for a time, then said, "What is it? You look uncomfortable. You don't want to talk about your family. And now I think about it, you never have. Have I said something wrong?"

He looked at her, shining in a simple black evening dress, and admired that poise, that coolness she could turn on and off like flipping a switch. "It's nothing you did. I'm just not used to all this."

"You mean this hotel? The restaurant? What?"

"All of it. I was pretty poor growing up."

"But it's all show. No one here sees you as a poor kid, with holes in your shoes."

"I know. It still makes me nervous, though."

"Like you don't belong here? You're some kind of impostor?"

"Right. I know; it's silly." He was also, though he didn't mention it, remembering another woman, one who'd thought whatever you had beyond your needs was not far short of theft from others. To her this sumptuous display, these rare foods, would have been an obscene theft from the poor and the homeless.

"Well, you worked your ass off to get here," Blair told him. "You graduated from Annapolis. You're commanding a ship. You've done damn well, and you have every right to enjoy it." She signaled to their server. Dan reached for the check, but she was too fast. "Courtesy of the Senate Armed Services Committee," she told him, scribbling their room number on it. "All right, let's go do our duty."

* * *

A SIGN at the entrance of the Museum of Art read: CLOSED TO THE PUBLIC. PRIVATE RECEPTION, but the men in dark suits smiled at Titus and swung the doors wide. She told Dan to keep his cap, not check it, and he tucked it under his arm.

He felt uncomfortable, like a stuffed dummy in service dress, following her into a reception area set up with a drink table and canapés. Titus circulated fast, into each small circle of tanned older men, perfectly groomed women, shaking hands and exchanging chitchat. She knew everyone. She introduced him as "Captain Lenson." After half an hour she turned to him suddenly and said, "That's enough of that. Let's go someplace more interesting."

She led him into the museum, through dimly lighted display areas, then out a back door and down a flight of stone steps toward the sound of rushing water and the scents of flowers. They strolled through a small wood of azaleas and oakleaf hydrangeas and emerged at the bank of a river. Looking back, Dan saw the classical roofline of the museum and below it the chaste and beautiful pillars of a small Greek temple.

"I remember this," she said. "I visited the University of Pennsylvania when I was in high school. Thinking I might want to go here. I thought this was incredibly romantic. I remember hoping someday I'd stand here with someone I cared for."

"You're right. It's nice." He looked across calm water that reflected colored lanterns hung above distant boathouses. In the evening light he could see the line where the calm water broke into falls, the Schuylkill pouring over the race with a dull roar and whirling downstream in pools of faintly glowing foam.

"You really think you don't deserve anything nice?" she said to him. "Because what that means to me is maybe you think you don't deserve me."

"I never said that."

"I can read it in your expression sometimes. Something not too far from contempt."

"It isn't contempt. If it's anything, it's intimidation."

"Dan, these people are no different from you. Surely you realized that when you were in D.C., working for Barry Niles. They may have more money. But they're not a bit smarter, or harder-working, or more honest."

He grinned in the dark. For some reason it struck him as funny, her trying to prove to him he didn't feel the way he felt. "OK, Doctor," he said. "But you see, it started in my childhood—"

She pinched his arm, hard. "Because sometimes, when you act like you don't like me very much . . . I start wondering."

"About us?"

"About us, yes." She hugged herself, looking not at him but out over the water. "I mean, it could be perfect. Together when we want to be. Apart often enough we can do what we need to do. Then every once in a while, something wonderful—like tonight. There are lots of navy jobs in Washington. You wouldn't have to go to sea. I mean, if you didn't want to."

He cleared his throat, knowing what he said now counted, the very words he chose mattered. "Sometimes I wonder, too. I mean, you're there; I'm wherever the Navy sends me. You're on your way to being somebody. I'm sort of—well, if I make commander, that's going to be it. All the ups and downs on my record."

"You have friends, too. People you've impressed. If you do a standout job on this assignment—"

"Sure, but you don't get promoted by being different. That's the kiss of death." He pondered. "But the rest of it— I get jealous sometimes. I don't see you often enough."

"That's up to you. It's always been up to you."

"I thought it was up to you."

"Then we were both delegating?" She laughed, but it wasn't amused; it was almost sardonic. And he couldn't think of anything else to say or do but back her against the low railing till there was nothing behind her but a twenty-foot fall to the cold-smelling river. Nothing to do but kiss her, amid the scent of the azaleas, and the cool taste of her lips mingled with the dead smell of the dark water rushing past below endlessly out of the hills, out of long-abandoned coal mines where, he could not help thinking, the bones of his ancestors lay.

5

HIS alarm went off at 0500 on that final day. An hour earlier than usual, but he was determined the last event under his command would go off flawlessly, professionally, and on time. Today USS *Oliver C. Gaddis* would officially become PNS *Tughril*, the newest commissioned warship of the Islamic Republic of Pakistan.

They'd taken her to sea for two days after the yard was done with her. The boiler tests had gone well, though the at-sea drills, with the Pakistanis in charge, had been less than inspiring. At one point Khashar had nearly gotten them run down by a supertanker.

Dan pushed that scary memory away, reviewing the schedule of events as he dressed. The ceremony would begin at 1000. The official guests included the base commander, the Pakistani attaché, the deputy chief of NAVOTTSA, and three of *Gaddis*'s former commanding officers. It promised to be a clear day, thank God, fall-cool but tenable for a ceremony he hoped to hold to an hour.

He found Greg Juskoviac in the wardroom with Commander Irshad. Helping himself to coffee so fresh the brew light hadn't gone on yet, Dan said, "You two are up early."

Juskoviac gave him the eager-to-please grin he dreaded. All too often, he'd learned, it masked a lack of follow-through. Dan sat them down and went over the preparations: cleaning, rigging the quarterdeck and flight deck, vans to meet dignitaries at Philadelphia International, escorts, hotel reservations. "And test the PA system again; we got too much feedback at the rehearsal. Talk to the men on the jacks and halliards. Those flags should come down slow, not *snap, snap, snap*." The XO noted busily away. Finally Dan said, "Well, that's all I've got; I'll let you get to it."

Juskoviac jumped up, upsetting his coffee cup, and ran off. Dan wondered what he should be doing himself, then knew. Paperwork. The final draft of the turnover letter, official thank-yous to the guests, et cetera, et cetera. Then he had to pack; he'd planned a leisurely drive back to Norfolk, a weekend in Georgetown with Blair en route. He called the ship's office and told them to bring up the morning's grist.

HE'D designated *Gaddis's* wardroom as a VIP reception area, with his own cabin reserved for the Pakistani attaché and the two-star from Washington, Admiral Sapp. At 0800 he changed into service dress blue with sword, medals, and white gloves and went down to the ship's office to get out of their way.

When he went back up at 0915 the wardroom was filled with men in business suits and uniforms, women in long dresses. Jim Armey stood against the bulkhead, looking uncomfortable in blues instead of coveralls. Dan squeezed his arm, wondering how he could make the man loosen up. He wasn't married, hardly ever went ashore, and had no outside interests Dan had been able to elicit. "We enjoying ourselves yet?"

"Not yet." The chief engineer forced a bleak smile.

"You did a great job getting her ready for sea, Jim. But you can't stay in the hole forever. Pick somebody out and start a conversation." Dan drew a breath and plunged into the social maelstrom, forcing a smile to his face and a heartiness into his handshake that he didn't feel. At 0950 he headed back to the fantail.

The day was bright and thank God the wind off the river not as sharp as it could have been. It set the bunting flapping where it was cable-tied to the helo deck netting. He looked down and across to the pier. The tent for the guests looked crowded. A murmur of conversation swelled across the strip of water. To his surprise, applause broke out as he appeared. He smiled, uncertain how to respond, then threw them a salute and went back behind the superstructure, out of sight. He checked the flat gray Delaware, his mind formulating a

vision of an out-of-command merchantman crashing into
them as they lay by the pier. As long as she sank *after* the
turnover. . . . He checked his watch again, startled to see it
was ten already. Where the hell was Juskoviac? Dan was on
the point of sending a runner after him when the exec
bounded out of the quarterdeck shack and took his place on
the dais. When Dan nodded, he bent to the microphone.

"Ship's company: atten-*tion*. Will the guests please rise
for the arrival of the official party and remain standing
through the invocation."

The band swung into ruffles and flourishes as a U.S. admiral arrived. A pause, then more music and piping as a
short man in a peaked military cap and British-style uniform overcoat bustled up the brow.

Juskoviac bent to the mike. "Parade the Colors."

The U.S. color guard stepped high as they proceeded
from the head of the pier. The Pakistani guard's marching
was crisper; they swung their arms British-style and
stepped out like toy soldiers. The green-and-white moon-
and-star met the Stars and Stripes in front of the platform.
Marching in step, they did a slow wheel and halted, left,
right, *halt*, facing the guests.

"The national anthems of the United States and of Pakistan," Juskoviac announced.

Dan stood with the rest of the official party, holding his
salute till the last brassy note died away on the wind.

"Post the colors," said Juskoviac.

Dan bent his head for the invocation, then relaxed into
his chair as the crew, lining the rails, snapped to parade
rest. He felt inside his blouse for the square of paper. His
remarks.

"I now introduce Rear Admiral Jerry Sapp, Deputy
Commander, Naval Office of Technology Transfer and Security Assistance."

Sapp acknowledged the general, the former skippers, the
family and friends present, "shipmates, and guests." He focused his opening remarks on *Gaddis*'s service career. "Designed and has performed as a mainstay and a workhorse.

. . . Carried our nation's flag during the closing phase of the cold war . . . a total of fifteen deployments literally spanning the globe, most recently during Operation Checkmate, interdicting drug traffic in the Aruba Gap and Colombia Basin." He gave numbers and specs, horsepower, speed, weapons. He went on to congratulate the crews who had manned her and the captains who had led her, naming each, nodding to those present on the platform. Dan noticed he wasn't included, but kept his expression relaxed and benign.

"We gather today to celebrate a job well done. We say good-bye to a ship that has given much, that has been well maintained by the literally thousands of sailors who have passed over her decks.

"At the same time I sense exultation among our friends from Pakistan, a nation with which the United States has long enjoyed a special relationship." Dan's attention wandered as Sapp praised the alliance as a force for peace in the Mideast, then returned as the admiral closed with a tribute to the crew that had worked so hard to prepare for turnover. "For you, the journey continues," he said at last. "To new ships, new places, new challenges. Take the spirit you learned aboard *Gaddis* with you. Godspeed; fair winds and following seas. I will now call the commanding officer forward."

Dan cleared his throat and rose, but Juskoviac was there before him.

"Ship's company: atten-hut. General Saqlain will present a letter of appreciation to Lieutenant Commander Daniel V. Lenson, United States Navy."

Dan stood at attention as the little man handed over the scroll and shook his hand. He saluted him, then glanced at the exec.

"Captain Daniel Lenson, Commanding Officer, USS *Oliver C. Gaddis*. Ship's company: Parade *rest*."

His turn at last. Snapping open the paper, Dan looked out over the pier, the green cold-looking water beyond, the bright sky. A freighter was coming around Windy Point, windows flashing golden in the sun.

"General, Admiral, sponsors, honored guests, plank-owners and former skippers, relatives and friends. Welcome to the official transformation of USS *Gaddis* into PNS *Tughril*.

"Any decommissioning is a bittersweet occasion. I myself have only had a few weeks to know her as a ship. But even in that short time I have come to understood what she means to her former crew members. It is hard to say farewell. But in this case we all know the ship we loved will sail on, under a new name and a new flag, but still in the defense of freedom and the maintenance of peace.

"As you see her now, poised to make the transition from U.S. to Pakistani man-of-war, I will say for all the crew: the best of luck to her new owners. What has made these last few weeks special has been the close bonds of friendship that have grown up between the two crews as they worked together, side by side, to pass the skills of one seafaring nation to the seamen of another. And between myself and Captain Khashar. It is a tribute to him, his officers, chiefs, and men, that the process has gone so smoothly and that I can hand *Gaddis* over knowing she will be well taken care of."

Hoping he would be forgiven for that, he lowered his eyes to the second page. "I will now read my orders. 'From: The Chief of Naval Operations. To: Commander in Chief, U.S. Atlantic Fleet. Subject: Decommissioning of USS *Oliver C. Gaddis*.

" 'You are hereby directed to decommission USS *Gaddis* no later than 30 September 1990. The ship will be transferred to the Islamic Republic of Pakistan. Upon completion, report same to Chief of Naval Operations. Signed, Frank B. Kelso the Second, Admiral, United States Navy.' "

The guests were silent. He gave it a second or two, for the old salts, the plankowners, those who'd put their youth and dreams into a piece of metal. Then said, "Executive officer: Haul down the colors."

The guests came to their feet, too, as Juskoviac read from a card concealed in his glove: " 'The commissioning pennant, when hoisted to the mast, symbolizes the moment when the service of a ship begins. Therefore, when the pennant is finally lowered from the mast and handed to the commanding officer, the ship is officially retired.' "

The guests looked upward, shading their eyes as the whiptail crept down, cracking and writhing as if fighting to stay aloft. The jack and the ensign sank with it. Chief Mellows came back aft and handed Dan the pennant.

"Debark the crew," Dan said.

The passed-on command echoed away into the depths of the ship as the division officers called their men to attention, faced them right or left, and marched them down ladders and over the brow to the pier. They fell into ranks again there, guiding onto duct-tape markers on the concrete, and snapped to parade rest opposite the patient Pakistanis.

"Sir, the watch has been secured."

"Very well." Dan turned to Sapp. "Sir, the watch aboard USS *Gaddis* has been secured."

"The transfer of ex–USS *Oliver C. Gaddis* to the custody of the Islamic Republic of Pakistan will now take place. Ladies and gentlemen, Commander Lenson."

Dan took his place at the mike again. "The document transferring ex–USS *Oliver C. Gaddis* to the government of the Islamic Republic of Pakistan has already been signed by representatives of both nations in Washington. Admiral Jerry Sapp, USN, will now officially transfer the ship to General Saqlain, for subsequent turnover to her new commanding officer. Ladies and gentlemen, Admiral Sapp, General Saqlain, and Captain Khashar."

Sapp took Dan's place. Without a cheat sheet, he bent his height toward the mike and said, "Sir, I present to you the ex–USS *Gaddis*, the best warship in the United States and Pakistani Navies. I will now introduce the Honorable General Muhammad Saqlain, defense attaché of the Islamic Republic of Pakistan to the United States of America."

Saqlain dilated on the history of the Pakistani Navy, the long partnership of the United States and Pakistan, and its role in preserving peace in the Middle East. He praised

Khashar as an officer of the highest professional accomplishments and a bright future, then, switching to Urdu, spoke for several minutes while the Americans tried to look interested. After he paused, it took some time for everyone to get the idea and clap. "I will now introduce Captain Hussain Khashar, the new commanding officer of PNS *Tughril*."

Khashar delivered a few remarks, then switched to English to thank Sapp and the turnover crew for their efforts. He spoke smoothly and with a little smile. Then he asked the guests to rise.

"Commander Irshad: Hoist the colors."

Both crews came to attention as the Pakistani colors ascended the mast. The band played the anthem. Irshad spoke a few words; then the incoming crew sprinted up the brow. They fell in along the starboard side, facing the pier. Khashar ordered the first watch set, then asked the guests to rise again. Turning toward the frigate, he said, "Blessings be upon thee in the name of Allah, most merciful, most compassionate. May this ship and all who sail in her strike the enemy, with your aid."

A puzzled silence succeeded when he stepped away. Finally Dan took the mike again, since no one else seemed about to. "This concludes the ceremony. You are invited for light refreshments in the helicopter hangar. Ship's company"—he looked around one last time at the bright morning, the expectant faces, at the closing of a short and not, after all, a very significant incident in his career—"dismissed."

THE windup of the ship's Morale, Welfare, and Recreation Fund left almost a thousand dollars. When he put the question to the Welfare and Rec Committee, the crew opted for a Farewell Ball. They reserved a hall in town and invited the Pakistanis as well. When Dan had passed this invitation to Khashar, the captain had seemed more doubtful than pleased, especially about enlisted and officer ranks mixing. Dan had pointed out that the fund came from the ship's store, thus from the pockets of both khaki and bluejackets, U.S. and Pakistani; he couldn't bar anyone, and having separate events would double the cost. Khashar had said nothing, and Dan assumed that meant he agreed. But now, adjusting his cummerbund in the cloakroom, he noticed there weren't any Pakistani enlisted here, though all the officers were, gathered around the attaché and his wife, a sylphlike woman in a very smart cocktail dress.

Evilia Beard looked professional in women's mess dress, a dark blue skirt and jacket. Dan joined her in the receiving line to welcome the guests. The first one through was a frail lady who told him she was Oliver Gaddis's half sister; she'd been there with the ship's sponsor, his daughter, during the christening at Avondale. Since then the daughter had died, such a lovely girl, but here she was still. He said, "Ma'am, you need to be in this receiving line."

"Oh, no, I'd rather just sit and look at the young men."

Dan smiled and pressed her hand again, feeling the fragile bones beneath the satin skin.

The guests passed and the crew. Chick Doolan pushed a tiny woman huddled in a wheelchair. She was child-small and one shoulder angled forward. Her face, ovoid and pale beneath short strawlike hair, was that of a suffering angel. The husky weapons officer bent to take her hand. "Honey, this is Captain Lenson," Doolan said. "Sir, this is my wife, Jill."

"Chick's told me a lot about you, Captain. He's pretty impressed."

"Call me Dan, please. He's done most of the impressing around here, Jill. Getting those twenty-millimeters installed practically singlehanded. You can be pretty proud of him."

When the receiving line drifted apart Dan joined the other dignitaries in front of an immense sheet cake. FAIR WINDS PNS TUGHRIL, it said in pink icing on a green sugar sea. Strobes flashed as Khashar cut it. Dan blinked, chasing afterimages.

He moved aside and stood watching the room for a time, now and again digging a fork into cake he didn't really

want. Maybe it was knowing the ship wasn't really his. Or
maybe this was the isolation of command he'd heard so
much about. But looking at his officers, his chiefs, and his
crew, watching them enjoy this respite, he realized how
solitary and isolated he felt from them.

It was a puzzling feeling, depressing, too, and he dug
into it as Yeoman First Ribiero, who was DJ tonight, kicked
the first tape into the sound system. A jangle and purr of
electric guitars, then Bonnie Raitt's whiskey voice filled the
room.

When he'd been just another guy, it seemed like he'd
known the men around him a lot better than he knew *Gaddis*'s crew. As if being a CO, even an acting one, meant you
saw them from a higher angle, an elevated distance from
which you saw only the glinting surface of their personali-
ties. It was a hard concept to articulate, and he stood struggling with it for a few seconds. It seemed important,
something he needed to understand to understand himself.

Juskoviac sauntered by. When their glances crossed the
XO's went elsewhere, like a refused épée. He and the exec
had had an unpleasant encounter yesterday, when Dan had
called him in to read his detachment fitness report.
Juskoviac had quivered in injured innocence. He'd said they
were both in exactly the same position, waiting for boards.
He'd helped push the ship through the yards in record time.
He would most definitely be submitting a statement in response to this unfair fitrep. The implication was clear:
Dan's adverse grading of him was nothing more than knif-
ing his temporary subordinate in order to make his own
chances better.

Robidoux, carrying punch for a platinum blonde in a
pale sheath dress who reminded Dan of a Q-Tip. Sansone,
alone, shifting from foot to foot as he listened to an older
gentleman in a Pearl Harbor Survivors Association ball cap.
Dave Zabounian, with his wife, Sarah. Zabounian, Dan had
noticed, wore the maroon good conduct ribbon that identified ex-enlisted, what the Navy called Mustangs. He had

four small children, whose photos he kept in the card pocket inside his cap. His wife had a stunned look, like an axed steer. Zabounian, Dan remembered, was on the list for the MTT: the Mobile Training Team, the remnant of the U.S. crew that would ride the ship from the commissioning port to the receiving country.

"Marsh" Mellows, beside him. Dan lifted a glass to the towering chief master-at-arms. "Marsh, how you doing. Ceremony went real well."

"Thanks, sir. Nice speech."

"You didn't invite your wife? Correct me if I'm wrong— you're married, right?"

The broad smiling face didn't alter. "Was, sir. You know how it is when you deploy. Haven't seen the ex for five years. The kids have got a new dad now."

"I know just exactly what you mean," said Dan, thinking of Susan and Nan and the dermatologist, what was his name, Feynman. The showcase house in Utah. But he didn't want to think about that; the taste was too bitter. "Your name's on the MTT list, too, isn't it?"

"Yessir. Been a while since I've seen that part of the world."

"Just stay out of Captain K.'s way." They both chuckled, and Dan added, "Seriously, Marsh, you've been a big help, keeping the two crews working together, backstopping the exec as chief master-at-arms. I really appreciate it."

"It's not that tough keeping the guys in line, sir. Just make it your business to know everything that's going on. Know what makes 'em tick. A little reminder here, a little favor there. Long as they figure you're gonna find out what-ever's going on, they're not gonna give you much trouble."

"Well, I appreciate your fine work. I signed your evalua-tion out yesterday. Should help you on the E-8 board."

Mellows's smile dimmed a few watts. "I'm not gonna be going up, sir. This here's my last tour."

"You're getting out? You don't have thirty yet, do you?"

"No, sir. It's a physical problem." Mellows didn't elaborate, and Dan didn't get the impression a probe would be welcome. He lifted his beer bottle and Dan nodded farewell and the broad back drifted off toward the chief's table.

Someone took Dan's arm. When he turned, there was Captain Munro. "Commander. Sorry I haven't been much use to you the last few weeks."

Actually, he'd seen the chief staff officer exactly once, after the at-sea tests, when he came aboard for a hurried lunch. Khashar had been there, too, so Dan had been hobbled in discussing both his doubts about the incoming crew's readiness for sea and the question that had nagged him ever since he got this assignment. So that now, free in the hum of chat and music to speak, he said, "Nice to see you, too, sir, but . . . I sort of expected to hear from you before this. Before the turnover, I mean."

"You expected to hear what from me?"

"About what you mentioned when I relieved."

The CSO smiled politely. "Sorry, I'm not certain what we're talking about."

Dan struggled to keep his tone level. "I was under the impression—what you said to me, just before you left that first day. At the brow, on your way over the side. You said to get her in shape; we might need her. Or words to that effect. I took that to mean that in view of what was happening in Kuwait, there was some consideration going on of retaining her on the active list."

Munro looked over his shoulder, obviously not riveted by the conversation. "Retaining her? No, I never heard anything along those lines. I may have said something encouraging, but I don't think I said *that*. Excuse me a minute, OK? Talk to you later."

Dan stood still, seething with disappointment and anger. Cursing himself for being credulous and overbearing, for having sacrificed his own work and his crew's arrangements on the basis of a misunderstood phrase.

But, goddamn it, that was what Munro had said. It wasn't possible he'd misunderstood or misheard.

Foley walked by, beer in hand, giving him a respectful

nod. Dan forced a smile, fighting for calm. He knew why he'd done it, of course. For *Gaddis*, for a ship that for one bright moment he'd thought of as his, hoping against hope he could save her, almost singlehanded.

Instead his destiny was a pookah in Norfolk, checking the message traffic every day to see whether he'd been promoted. If he wasn't, he'd have to retire.

All he'd ever wanted was to be allowed to do what they'd trained him for. Could it really be that acting CO of *Gaddis* would be the closest he'd ever get to having his own ship?

He stared at the wall with unseeing eyes, then gathered the saliva in his mouth and spat the cloying taste of too-sweet cake into his paper napkin.

HE was heading for the exit, making his bird, when he saw Beard and Admiral Sapp vectoring to intercept. He forced another smile. "How you doing, sir? Good to have you with us."

"A well-run ceremony," said Sapp. "A good-looking ship. I had seen her before, when Dan Ottero had her. You've done a job, turning her around."

Dan wondered about the slip, calling Ottero "Dan" instead of "Dick." But instead of correcting the admiral he just said, "Thank you, sir."

"Did you get to speak to the general?"

"Yessir, had a few words with him. Nice of him to come down."

"Sometimes the ambassador makes it. Busy now, I expect, because of their government shakeup. . . . I was impressed with how quickly you got *Gaddis* out of the yard. Evilia didn't think she'd be ready before spring. How'd you get them turned to so fast?"

"Some size-ten leadership, I'm afraid. The shipyard commander's not happy with me."

"Don't worry about him. The staff corps's there to support the fleet." Sapp cleared his throat and looked around. "I've been getting your turnover status reports. Apparently you have doubts as to their conning and navigation readiness."

"Yessir. They don't strike me as fully trained in those areas yet."

"How about fireroom and engineroom manning? Are they safe to sail?"

This was a complex issue wrapped in a code phrase. "Safe to sail" had several meanings, from material condition, to crew size, to the potential legal issue of whether someone could be held liable for ordering an unready ship to sea. Dan took a deep breath. "Sir, if you want it laid on the line here, the short answer's no. The CO was on deck for the sea trials. I went below for a few minutes, and he damn near got us run down. The boiler team's still acting like they've never been to A school."

"They've already paid us for this material, Lenson."

"Yes, sir, understand that, but—"

"Let me make a further point: that the replacement crew's state of training is not in the end your responsibility. The final responsibility is Khashar's, as the incoming commanding officer."

"Well, sir, I understood from Commander Beard here that it was the U.S. skipper who certified them safe to sail or not—"

Sapp smiled grimly. "I strongly doubt CNO would appreciate us having a lieutenant commander vetoing a foreign four-striper. No, the political reality is, they're going." He cleared his throat again. "However, I got a call today from Security Assistance Office, Islamabad. The Pakistani government's asking us to beef up the MTT."

Dan knew there were normally thirty-some guys who rode the ship over; the officer in charge, usually the chief engineer, and the rest boiler techs, machinist's mates, and various other senior ratings. "Beef it up, sir?"

"Especially the steaming watches and nav personnel. To ensure a safe delivery."

"I'd say that's a good decision, sir. After watching these guys operate."

"I hope you're more diplomatic with our foreign friends," Sapp said.

"I try to be, sir. But I'm down to fifty-five bodies right now, and they've all got orders cut, travel requests in—"

"How many engineers?" said Beard, cutting as usual to the chase.

"Excuse me. Evilia, let me see what the two of you finally come up with," said Sapp, and headed off toward the general and his wife.

Dan and Beard went around on bodies and numbers. Finally she said, "So you'll need roughly fifteen more snipes, three more quartermasters. I'll hand that to the squadron, see if they can find volunteers." She hesitated. "I'm sorry if this impacts your personal plans."

"Wait a minute. *My* plans? Jim Armey's heading the training team."

"We read your reports. About Khashar and that near miss. A collision en route wouldn't look very good for our training pipeline, would it? We'll extend your orders and fly you back from Islamabad. Admiral Sapp will be your reporting senior, which will give you a two-star flag endorsement on your last fitrep before the board meets." She gave it a beat. "Is that all right?"

"Actually, I'm not sure I've caught up to you yet. What would be my status?"

"Officially, head of the MTT. Unofficially, you'd be sort of co-skipper with Captain K."

He thought about it, swirling his drink. It meant steaming *Gaddis*—no, dammit, that wasn't her name anymore—halfway around the world. Every destroyerman dreamed of independent steaming. On your own at sea, no tactical commander running you ragged, no carrier to hawkeye around the clock. The divided command didn't sound so hot. But whoever had dreamed it up was right about one thing: *Tughril*'s chances of arriving in one piece were a lot better if somebody was backing this bozo up.

Dan had never really been her skipper. But maybe he owed her that, her and the guys who'd take her to sea; yeah, the Pakistani crew, too. It wasn't their fault their boss was who he was.

He lifted his glass to Beard. "To a swift and uneventful passage."

"Fair winds and following seas."

Just then, he noticed Khashar watching them from across the room.

II

EASTING

6

THE NORTH ATLANTIC

SEVEN hundred miles from land, ten-foot seas followed *Tughril* like wolves loping after a solitary elk. The wind was at force five, air temperature high thirties. The sun was a fluorescent tube behind white plastic. Color shifted around it in the overcast sky like fragments of frozen rainbows. Dan stood shivering forward of the ground tackle, fists jammed into his foul-weather jacket.

Poring over the October and November pilot charts, he and Commander Irshad had roughed out the crossing in two great-circle legs, Nantucket Shoals to the Azores, then on to Gibraltar and thence into the Med. The deep tanks aft of Frame 120 held 212,000 gallons of Distillate Fuel, Marine. Steaming one boiler, with two burners pulled, the ship's most economical operating speed was 14.5 knots. At that speed her range was 2,700 miles. Pub. 151, *Distances between Ports*, gave 2,098 nautical miles from New York to Fayal, Azores, and another 1,096 past that to Rota.

That struck him as a little close for comfort. If they got orders halfway across to divert for a best-speed transit to the Gulf, he'd have to request replenishment at sea. But since there still wasn't anything on the street about their heading for Iraq he left it at that, reasoning they had the current with them and a generally following wind till midocean.

The days before departure had passed in a blur. He'd met Blair for an all-too-brief weekend in northern Virginia, then snapped back to backstop Armey on the final preps for getting under way.

Meanwhile the augmentees had been reporting aboard, already bitching about being restricted to the forward berthing. They kept to themselves. They didn't, some of them, even look like sailors, and Chief Mellows had to order several ashore for haircuts. Dan understood. When you asked for volunteers, you got the guys nobody wanted.

Anyway, it wouldn't be for long. He figured total transit time to Karachi at twenty-eight steaming days. Add port calls and the Suez Canal, a month and a half. He figured he could hold things together that long.

Today they were three days out, and he sucked the cold air with a sudden lift of his heart. Some cruises had been milk runs; some had been hell. Two had ended in disaster. But despite the bad memories and sometimes dreams, he'd never forget the clear sunsets of mid-ocean, the smoky red dawns of the Persian Gulf, the howl of an Arctic storm. He'd left his youth somewhere in the wake, but on a day like this he remembered it imminent and tangible as the first time he'd ever seen salt water, coming from State Circle down to the Academy on a bright morning in June.

Behind him the ship rolled, a barely perceptible haze whipping off the uptakes. Someone was looking down at him from the bridge. He lifted his hand, but the distant figure didn't respond. He turned back, knowing he ought to get to work but unwilling to break away just yet.

From the outthrust bow, cantilevered to protect the sonar dome, his gaze plumbed straight as a lead line. The heaving deep was blue as boot-camp dungarees at the surface, but beneath that a transparent blue-black sucked his gaze into lightless depths. The forefoot scalpeled it open with a roaring hiss. It spackled the undulant skin, smooth as melted glass, with spatters of spray before peeling it up and apart in a transparent curve that shattered into a crash of foam. The steady roar sounded like a gigantic sheet of Velcro being ripped apart. Beneath it millions of tiny bubbles boiled aft along her belly, then tore apart in the enormous whirling of the thrusting screw.

A bell caught his ear, followed by a hornet hum. He turned to witness the tapered barrel of the five-inch quiver, then rise swiftly till it pointed to the zenith. It paused there, then swept down, rotating till it aimed off to starboard.

The hollow clank of the transfer tray, and the barrel

jerked. It whipped toward him, then halted again, quivering. The dark rifled lumen of the bore pointed straight at him as he stood at the bullnose. His grip tightened on the lifeline. Then the internal motors died, their pitch descending the scale, and the weapon reverted from uncanny life to inanimate metal.

Out of nowhere, he remembered the day before they got under way. The crew had been loading stores, U.S. and Pakis tossing the moon-marked boxes aboard side by side, when Evilia Beard had come down the pier. Swinging along, she mounted the aft gangway and saluted the Pakistani ensign, then faced the OOD, who had come out of his slouch to confront her where the brow debouched onto a wooden pallet. There was a short exchange, during which she suddenly blanched, at which point Dan strolled over.

"Something wrong?"

"Khashar," Beard snapped. "Is this *his* idea?"

The OOD: "It is Pakistani Navy regulation. No women are allowed on board Pakistani ship."

"*What?* Horse shit! You get him on that J-phone and—"

"I'll have a word with him, Evilia—"

"You stay out of this. This is me and him." She turned back to the Pakistani. "*Did you hear me, mister?* Get your commanding officer on that phone. Tell him I'm waiting out here."

They waited for several minutes. Finally he came back. "You are not permitted aboard," he said. Beard stood motionless, fingers working. But at last she'd spun, clattered back down to the pier, disappeared.

Dan really couldn't say why he'd thought of that just now.

Shortly thereafter, he went aft.

HE put in an hour in the Weapons Department office, now the Mobile Training Team admin area, going over the training schedule with Chief Warrant Officer Engelhart. Engelhart was one of the augments, a somber, hollow-chested Uriah Heep who looked older than anyone had a right to be and still go to sea. Still he was fit enough; Dan had seen him clambering around the SLQ-32 arrays at the top of the mack. Another fanugie was the sonar chief, Bernardo Tosito. A native of Guatemala, "Tostito" was stony-silent as a graven image. He'd been recalled to sea duty from a shore billet in Tampa to run ping ops scheduled with a Turkish diesel sub when they got inside the Med.

From *Gaddis*'s old crew he had Dave Zabounian, the supply officer, who Dan had discovered was a steady conning officer, too; Chick Doolan, still in charge of the Weapons Department; and Jim Armey. Greg Juskoviac had been left behind in the States, to Dan's undisguised relief.

He had about twenty senior enlisted, including Marsh Mellows, Yeoman First Ribiero, and Quartermaster Second Robidoux. Foley had gone ashore, bound for USS *Thomas S. Gates*, a new Tico-class cruiser. Not without envy, Dan had shaken his hand and said so long. He still had Sansone, who'd taken a bust to first class. Dan had noted at his mast how hard Sansone had worked during the yard period, how the explosion itself most likely had not been his fault. But the saying that even ill winds blew good to somebody did not apply in the surface Navy. Ottero had paid. Armey had gotten a letter in his jacket. Sansone had been lucky to make it out of admiral's mast with a bust to E-6 and a $500 fine. He worked now with a closed self-absorption that discouraged conversation.

Armey came in, and Dan tossed him the schedule. The engineer suggested deleting a two-hour drill on manual operation of the Hagen automatic combustion control console. Dan said, "They need to work on the Hagen, don't they?"

"Right, but first they got to be comfortable with running it automatically."

"They've been to school on it."

"They sat in the seats, you mean." The chief engineer sat, passing a long hand slowly over his face like a blind man recognizing someone he had once known.

"You doing all right, Jim? You look beat."

"I'm OK, sir. Just pulling too many hours in the hole."

"Just call me Dan; I'm not the skipper anymore."

"OK—Dan. As soon as you turn your back they're cutting corners. Al says even when he points out they're not lining things up right, they're not listening anymore. Two fellas started throwing punches down in Aux Two last night—"

"Throwing punches? You mean our guys and—"

"One of the augmentees. Guy named Pistolesi. They call him 'Pistolero.' He's been trouble from the second he came aboard."

"Get him up here." Dan slammed his chair down. "The son of a bitch can't keep his hands off people, I'll restrict him to his bunk and off-load him in Rota."

Armey tried the phone, but whoever answered it hung up when he began to speak. "They hear English, they hang up," he said. "I'll go down. When you want him?"

"Make it ten hundred. OK, so the rest of the schedule looks good to you?"

"SIR. Commander Armey said you wanted to see me."

Dan measured him in silence. He'd expected a hulking brute, but Pistolesi in person was slender and fine-boned, with a sharp, nervous face. A scar or wound had healed irregularly across his left temple. A blue dotted line of old tattoo showed at the collar of his coveralls. His name was Magic Markered over his pocket, not stenciled or in block letters, but in fancy Olde Englishe script.

"Where you from, Fireman Pistolesi?"

"Hack's Neck. Sir."

"I mean, you joined us from where? Stapleton, right? Staten Island?"

"That's right, sir. Off the *Iowa*."

"Were you with her when she had that turret explosion?"

"Month I came aboard. Was down in number three fire room when it went."

"I understand you were involved in a fight in the spaces yesterday. I also see from your record that you went to mast for fighting on the *Iowa*."

"Sir, you didn't stand up for yourself on *Iowa*, the fuck-ing nig—the fucking blacks'd cut you to pieces."

"I see. What about this time?"

"I cuffed one of the fucking ragheads to get his fucking attention. Yeah."

"One of the *ragheads*? Look, Pistolesi—"

"Sir, due respect, but you sit up here and drink tea with the officers. K-man and them. We got to straighten these fuckers out before they blow this fucking ship up. You whale 'em one upside the head, they pay attention. That's the way their own people treat 'em."

Dan relaxed. Pistolero could be dealt with. "OK, you got a point. Now listen to mine. Number one: *you* are not in the Pakistani Navy. You are in the U.S. Navy. Number two: We are now on their ship. We're eating their food—"

"Their fucking food sucks—"

Dan came out of his chair and roared face-to-face, "You got a bad habit of interrupting me when I'm talking. Don't interrupt me again, Pistolesi!"

"Uh—yessir!"

"I agree, they do things differently. But this is their ship now and you'll treat them with respect. You don't like their food, try bread and water in one of the fan rooms till we hit Spain. You receiving me?"

"Yes, sir." The fireman was breathing heavily, eyes still on the deck. But he said nothing more.

Dan watched him for a couple of seconds, then added, "I need your help getting us safe to Karachi. We don't have enough people and we need you. So work on your self-con-trol. Dismissed."

Pistolesi wheeled and left without another word.

AT 1100 a short fellow in a stained jacket appeared at his door. Between his gestures and the time of day, Dan gath-ered Khashar wanted him in his cabin for lunch. He nodded and said all right, he'd be there in a few minutes.

His former stateroom had undergone a subtle change. Khashar was nowhere in sight, but the prayer rug on the floor, the bulkhead photo of an ex-British Battle-class destroyer—one of his previous commands, no doubt—lent the room what little personality a shipboard space could assume. Dan nodded to the waiting officers. They were all smoking except for Irshad, who looked green. Dan felt ill himself from the closed-in haze but was able to ignore it. He found *Tughril*'s gait pleasant, a rolling pitch that put him in mind of a trotting horse.

The cuisine reminded him of Bahrain. Lamb and rice in a baked *biryani*. Hot nan bread. A tray of sweet hand-molded items and fruits. The officers ate with tableware, though he'd seen the enlisted men, on the mess decks, dipping in with their right hands. There wasn't much talking at first, till Khashar, wiping his mustache with a napkin, said, "*Alhamdulilah*." The others murmured and sat back as the steward served out sweet tea white with milk.

Khashar turned to Dan. "I was watching you up on the bow this morning. Communing with nature?"

"Something like that." They discussed the buildup, Desert Shield, the increase in U.S. forces Bush had announced just before they sailed. Dan was cautious about his opinions, but they seemed unanimous in their protests that Saddam had to be put down, that he was as much a menace to the Arab world as he was to the West.

AT 1300 he pressed the buzzer outside Radio. A face appeared at the grating; the door clicked and unlocked.

The little room was walled by gear racks, but most were empty. Power cables and antenna feeds dangled like tied-off arteries. The main transmitters had been left aboard, but all the cryptographic gear had been stripped out and jumpers plugged in to make the system work without them. Radioman Chief Compline was one of the new gains. He was short and rotund, and something was wrong with one of his legs, making him lurch when he walked. Dan sat and began going over the daily situation report. Paragraph 1 gave their noon position and whether they were ahead or behind planned progress. It gave percentages for potable water, feed water, fuel, and the rate of consumption. Para. 2 was a training update. Para. 3 was materiel status and casualty reports, including parts or circuit cards they'd need en route. Para. 4 was personnel issues, and Para 5 was any comments or concerns he had as the officer in charge.

"Look all right, sir?" said Compline.

"Send it out." He handed it to the chief, who swiveled around and pulled a key toward him. Dan watched fascinated as he dot-dashed it out. High-frequency CW, same as the *Titanic* had sent as she went down, in an age of computers talking to each other in thirty-two-bit code.

THE deck was rolling too hard to go for a run, so he drifted through the spaces. The very air smelled different. She was turning into a Pakistani ship already.

At 1500 General Quarters sounded. He knew the schedule, so he was on the bridge wing when the alarm went. The high-pitched electronic bonging was unchanged, but the excited Urdu that followed it over the 1MC struck his ear strangely. The thunder of boots and the slamming of watertight doors, the clang of dogging wrenches, were reassuringly the same. He was tucking his pants cuffs into his socks when Khashar and one of the junior officers undogged the door and came out to join him.

Khashar ignored him, speaking rapidly to the OOD. Dan slid away to give them room, steadying himself against the signal-light stanchion as *Tughril* rolled. The seas were growing. Toward midocean a tongue poked down from the stationary low that parked itself south of Iceland. He wouldn't be surprised if they hit some heavy weather.

Behind him a rushing roar spooled upward. Brown smoke shot out, unscrolling across the pearly sky. *Tughril* accelerated smoothly, roll diminishing as her speed increased. Peering into the pilothouse, he saw the handles of the lee helm at flank. Dan noted the time. Khashar was the boss, but with five tons of fuel an hour going up the stack, he might benefit from a reminder if he left the pedal down too long.

Below and aft of him Dan could look down now directly onto the boat deck, where the crew was pulling the rubberized gun covers off the forty-millimeter.

He'd never seen one in active service, but he recalled these long barrels with their wraparound springs and cone-shaped flash hiders from World War II movies. They'd been manufactured for the big push on Japan and then greased and laid away in some cavernous government warehouse to sleep the decades away. Now oiled steel gleamed in the dull sea light as the trainer spun furiously at a handwheel. A crewman in flash gear and heavy gloves hoisted a curved clip of the fixed shells, looking for all the world like over-size rifle cartridges. From above him came a yell and a clatter, and looking up, he saw the twenty-millimeter swing to the same bearing.

Hammered together from fruit crates, shoring lumber, and empty drums, a spindly shape bobbed in the smoothed road of *Tughril*'s wake. Then it began to sway, picking up the rhythm of the waves. The ship plowed on, at full speed now, throwing out a hissing arc of spray each time the bow guillotined down into a sea.

Khashar swung himself up into his seat on the starboard wing, crossing his short legs jauntily. Dan leaned over the splinter shield, shading his eyes as the frigate leaned into a snap turn. A paint can darted from some hidden nook and launched itself over the side like an old-fashioned depth charge. It hit the sea and was immediately overwhelmed and obliterated in the tearing surf *Tughril* now dragged behind her.

He took Khashar's intent. Drop the target; run straight for a mile or two; then execute two ninety-degree turns, till you were headed back parallel to your original course but offset a thousand yards from it. The target was out of sight now, behind the superstructure as *Tughril* began to roll beam on. He leaned in to check the radar for any passing traffic.

Another hard right at flank speed. Khashar liked to maneuver fast and with a lot of resultant motion. The wind thrummed in the signal halliards, pressing itself against his face.

Dan got his ear protectors out of the little vial on his belt. The clamor of wind and sea retreated, replaced by the thump of his heart. He focused on the target, rolling violently half a mile away.

The sound made him flinch, the whip crack of the twenties above, the rivet hammer of the fifties. The five-inch unleashed a blast that rattled the gratings under his boots, and a choking cloud of brown powder smoke swept back on the wind. Below him the forty fired with alternate balls of instantaneous flame, succeeded by puffs of burnt propellant sucked instantly aft as the ship bulled forward. Wave spray broke in a cold glowing spatter across his face. Brass clink-tinkled across nonskid.

A thousand yards away, ivory spray hearted with black high-explosive smoke suddenly sutured the water, some well short of the target, others far over. He opened his mouth to the captain, then closed it. If they'd been firing at a real ship, some of those overshots would be superstructure hits. Some of the short rounds would ricochet up off the water.

And it really, really wasn't his concern anymore.

LATE that night he was carrying a towel under his arm, headed aft in his worn gray sweats for the weight room, when the counterbalanced door to the escape trunk at Frame 100 slammed open in front of him and sailors rushed out yelling into the narrow passageway. He caught "*Chaloy jaldi jaldi,*" or words to that effect. Flattened against the bulkhead, he grabbed at one of them. "What is it? What happened?" but was thrown off. "*Jaldi Jahaz say bahar niklo!*"

As soon as the trunk was clear he jerked the door open and stared down.

The stink of burning oil hit his face, and with it shouts muffled by steel. At the same moment the GQ alarm went. He stuck his head into the passageway, but all he saw were rapidly retreating backs. He grabbed the ladder and swung himself out.

The emergency escape trunk was a square steel well, closed off from the spaces through which it passed by watertight access doors. Its vertical walls were set with welded-on handholds. Some anonymous artisan had put in innumerable hours wrapping each rung with marline work, not just for decoration but also to improve the grip for desperate greasy hands. As he climbed rapidly downward, another wave of shouting sailors surged up. He swung into the corner, catching a boot in the neck as they clambered over him, then kicked himself free and dropped. His running shoes rang on the inner bottom. He jerked the door open that led into the lower level of the engine room.

Scorching hot air hit his face. He was looking aft and thwartships, at the space-filling bulk of the low-pressure turbines and the main reduction gear. To his left were an electrical panel and a vacant log desk. The telephone pendulumed at the end of its cord. His ear tuned through the tremendous hum of the gears, the multitudinous vibrations of pumps and turbines. He didn't hear anything out of the ordinary. The only hints of danger were the haze that filled the slanting brightly lit air and the unmistakable smell of burning petrochemicals.

More excited voices on the 1MC. Someone slammed the door open at the top of the trunk. Letting go the bottom door, Dan grabbed an emergency escape breathing kit off a rack. If the smoke thickened, it would give him a few minutes. Then he moved cautiously out into the space, slipping across the slick gratings beneath which oil-sheened water eddied. His eye snagged on a CO_2 extinguisher. He flipped the clamps free and dragged it after him, staying low to avoid the smoke. He couldn't stay long. He had no safety line, no backup man to get him out if he lost consciousness. Maybe the best thing to do was retreat, get out, and trip the Halon flood. But if anybody was still down here, unconscious or hurt, he'd be smothered by the inert gas.

The smoke rippled up on a current of heated air above

the huge gray bulk of the reduction gear casing, disappearing through the gratings into the upper level. He couldn't see where it was coming from till he crouched between the lube oil service pumps. He dropped to his knees and peered beneath the gray sheer sides of the casing, down through perforated metal into the shadowy recesses of the bilge. Only it wasn't shadowy now. It glowed with smoky orange flame. The flame danced quickly over a darkly gleaming surface, turning an ebony pool to a lake of fire.

He glanced behind him, to see Al Sansone and Jim Armey stepping out of the trunk. Dan pointed, voice useless in the clamor of the turbines.

The first-class took off running, plunging past Dan into the smoke down the aisle between the main gear and main condenser. Armey took a more direct route up, leaping onto the condenser intake and hammering a grating loose from below with the heel of his hand. Suddenly alone again, Dan jumped back as a meter-long tongue of smoky red flame licked up between his Nikes. He jerked the cylinder around, gripped the release lever, then hesitated. In this closed space, if he started pumping out carbon dioxide, what were they going to breathe? Pushing that thought aside, he jerked the pin out and aimed the nozzle, vision dissolving from the rapidly growing heat.

THEY had the fire out in less than ten minutes, working together just the way they'd all drilled over and over for a Class Bravo fire in a main space: Sansone coming down the ladder from the fire-hose rack, Armey feeding slack off the reel. Dan had circled the sump tank, driving the flames back with roaring jets of cold white gas, till Sansone reached him. Then he'd dropped the extinguisher and fallen in as number two man, helping the boilerman control the suddenly rigid hose as Armey spun the valve open. Sansone braced his boots on the grating and pulled the bail back to Mist. Suddenly the smoke vanished, the water bloom cutting through the haze. The flames retreated as the mist advanced, the blast of seawater fog not so much quenching the flames as sucking heat from them till they could no longer sustain ignition. They circled the casing, Sansone bending to send the mist probing and swirling into the bilge, chasing and exterminating a final lunge of the flames.

Then it was out. The boiler tech laid the hose carefully out in the aisle, and they took a break, wheezing, clutching their knees.

Armey came down the ladder with a flashlight. He pulled up a grating and disappeared beneath it. He emerged from under the lube oil purifier, forearms and chest smeared with oil and soot. "It's out!" he bawled, over a clamor Dan realized was lessening, winding down.

He recalled himself then, remembering the haste and terror with which the engine-room watch had shoved past him, and sprinted to the log desk and grabbed the handset. No one answered. He tried the 21MC next and finally raised a voice that switched only reluctantly to English. "We abandon the ship," it said. "Get on deck. Help us put boats in water."

"You're *what*? Listen. I'm in the engine room. The fire's out. Get the steaming watch back down here. We need the repair party, need a blower rigged for desmoking." He had to argue for some time before he was sure the message had gotten across.

"What's going on up there?" Armey said, coming up, wiping at his eyes with a bright blue bandanna.

"Apparently they were trying to launch the boats."

The engineer gaped. "For a li'l lube oil fire like that?"

Sansone said, "That's the way it's been down here since day one, sir. Anything goes wrong, it's the will of Allah. No point doing anything about it. I figure we watch over 'em every second, it's even money we get to Karachi before it all goes to shit in a real serious way."

Dan nodded slowly. He looked around the space, then looked at his hands. Armey offered his bandanna. Silently Dan took it.

7

THE AZORES

THE land was a black barrier, mountaintops erased by the low overcast. They'd been volcanoes in the dim past, the spiny outcroppings of the Mid-Atlantic Ridge. The sea heaved uneasily, deep blue as an old watch cap, still dimpled by rain from the low steel clouds. When Dan lifted his binoculars he could make out the humpy peninsula that screened the old city and, past it, straggling up the mountain, the glowing whitewashed buildings of Horta, capital of the Azores and the largest city on the island of Fayal.

For a week after the fire they'd steamed east by southeast, angling toward an imaginary point well south of Fayal. In all that time the seas had grown, harried and maddened hour after hour by a roaring wind that had backed around, opposing itself to all progress eastward. Fleet Weather reversed its original recommendation after forty-eight hours, advising ships in the central Atlantic to stay north of forty degrees north latitude. Too late for them, of course; they'd doglegged south following the meteorologists' earlier advice and had to pay for it in two days of thirty-foot seas and seventy-knot winds.

They actually could have made port last night, but Khashar had decided not to run in close under the island during the night; they'd passed the darkest hours steaming slowly on an east–west course, then turned north at 0500. The sky was still overcast, but the wind had dropped during their final leg in and the anemometer wavered now between ten and fifteen knots.

Ever since the fire, a standoff had existed between the halves of the crew. Like a creature with two brains, two wills, *Tughril* had staggered eastward with a divided heart. Dan had pulled all his men off training and reorganized them into a shadow watch team. He stood watch on the bridge, trying to keep an eye on things and at the same time stay out of Khashar's way. Every time Dan was around the captain, he had an uneasy sense that the guy was waiting for an excuse to blow. He had a job to do, so he did it, but he kept out of the captain's way except at mealtime. Khashar kept inviting him to lunch. It was tense, but he figured he was in a sense being the lightning rod. The downside was that he was getting really sick of boiled lamb and greasy rice.

Khashar had never mentioned the night his men tried to abandon ship. Not once.

"Three thousand yards to turn point," murmured Robidoux. Dan told him he didn't need continuous reports, just to let him know if anything didn't look kosher. This wasn't a demanding evolution. Just proceed in toward Horta Light, hang a right on a radar range, pick up the pilot, then let him conn them in. Warships usually took the last berth on the mole, and it was always a port-side moor. He raised the glasses again and examined the cottony wisps of squall that clung to Pico Alto, miles off to starboard but still perfectly clear in the rain-washed air.

A rattle on the outboard ladder, and Jim Armey hauled himself up. The engineer's face was gray and his coveralls stiff with dirt and dried sweat.

Dan returned his salute. "Jim. How's it looking down below?"

"Got the bus transfer problem nailed down. They're flying the circuit board in to the air base." Armey rubbed his eyes, squinting forward. "That a C-5?"

They watched the huge aircraft in the distance, so huge and slow it seemed to float. Dan said after a moment, "Stopping to refuel. On its way to Saudi."

"Gosh, we're almost in."

"It's a short sea detail." Swinging the Big Eyes—the huge pedestal-mounted binoculars—around, Dan took him on a tour of the island.

"You been here before?"

"Twice, but you never stay long; it's just a stop on the way someplace else. Like for Columbus. There's a park at the top of that volcano, a mile across and about a thousand feet deep. Kind of a *Lost World* thing. You going ashore?"

"Like to, but we've got the fuel barge coming along-side—"

"Take a damn break, Jim. We can get a decent dinner, at least."

Armey said he'd think about it and went below again. Dan turned back to the nearing land. He could make out individual buildings now, church spires rising on the hillsides amid masses of trees, the long black line of the mole. He lowered the glasses and looked down.

Into a sea clear and blue as sapphire. It appeared harmless and welcoming, ruffled by faint cat's paws of wind. Sometimes, when it looked this lovely, it was hard to remember the placid surface hid a thousand fathoms of darkness, an unquenchable craving for the bones of ships and the lives of men.

Beside him the port bearing taker spoke urgently. A moment later yelling came from inside the pilothouse. The deck leaned as the bow came right, swung too far, and corrected back to within a point of the peninsula that screened the town.

The engine-order telegraph pinged, and the ripple and rush of the hull slackened. Glancing down at bits of weed rocking past on the paling sea, he estimated they were making ten knots. The dark knobs screening the town slid away. Masts and white-shining hulls came into view past the breakwater. The gleaming upperworks of what looked like a cruise liner were slowly being revealed, just forward of where the frigate would moor.

He went below for a head call and refreshed his coffee from the pot in the Combat Information Center. When he came back up, Horta spanned the horizon. He checked the chart with Robidoux. The QM said the Omega fixes were plotting three hundred yards east of the visuals, but the error was consistent. He went back out on the bridge and lost himself in reverie as *Tughril* slowed further, pivoted. The mole stretched out like a black barring arm of volcanic stone, then opened, welcoming them in. Old men in ragged shirts and straw hats swung nets into the water. A windmill stood on the mountain, arms clicking rapidly around in the steady wind. The water was even paler now, the tint of female turquoise.

He looked down at an excited man in a tossing small boat. He was yelling up, whipping his cap back and forth. He pointed at the bridge, at him, and after a perplexed moment Dan raised his hand to return the greeting. The gesture seemed to drive the fellow into a rage; he threw his hat down into the boat.

It was bobbing in the wake when Dan suddenly realized who it must have been. He did a double take, focusing the glasses. Yep, a black-painted *P* on the boat's side.

"Sir." A crisp salute never hurt with this captain. "We've missed the pilot. Small boat just passed down the port side."

Khashar turned a lazy gaze on him from out of a cloud of smoke. "This doesn't look like a very challenging harbor."

"He's required by Portuguese regulations, sir."

"If necessary I will apologize to the harbormaster." The Pakistani stared ahead, making it obvious that the exchange was over.

Dan wavered, then shrugged inwardly. It looked straightforward enough. The mole lay ahead to port. Their berth was closest to the entrance, just aft of the moored cruise ship. Ahead were a small military pier and a patrol boat, to starboard a shoal of pleasure craft cupped by another, smaller seawall and beyond that the town. Khashar had brought the ship's speed down, though they were still surging ahead faster than Dan liked. The stern of the cruise liner walked steadily closer, a red-and-yellow Spanish ensign flapping briskly. Dan liked the wind. All Khashar had to do was park himself fifty or sixty meters off the pier and the sail effect would sideslip him into the berth. The captain spoke to the helmsman sharply. The bow came left, then left a little more. Dan tensed, but it stopped there.

"Sir, I'd take this a little slower if I were you. She doesn't back very efficiently."

Khashar didn't answer. He stared rigidly forward at the rapidly approaching mole. Dan hesitated, looking at the others on the bridge. Not one of them met his eyes. He looked at the liner again.

There is a moment, dreaded by every ship handler, when the momentum of thousands of tons of steel means collision can no longer be avoided, but it has not yet actually happened. These are the longest minutes ever made, and Dan stood gripping the rail and staring as the high rounded stern of the liner drew closer. He saw the line handlers staring up at it from the forecastle. "Get back!" he yelled, accompanying the order with a violent pushing-away motion. They glanced up, seemed to grasp their danger all at once, and ran. The strip of milky green water narrowed steadily. Gray-haired passengers stared down from the stern gallery of the liner. He waved them back, too, and they retreated hastily. The lee helm pinged then, but far too late. He couldn't help baring his teeth and tensing his forearms as if to push off as the bow coasted into the liner's quarter.

The sound was tearing and gritty, like a dozen Dumpsters being dragged over concrete by a bulldozer. The spray coaming along the gunwale bent inward, then the lifeline, stanchions wrenching inward one after the other as they popped and twisted off their bases. Bolts cracked and bonged across the deck. Each stanchion left its own separate black gouge across the white-painted hull of the liner. The jolt came back along the hull, rocking him gently as the greater mass of the bigger ship shouldered *Tughril* off. As the bow rebounded to port, the frigate continued to move forward. The result was that the point of impact moved steadily aft along the starboard side. The grinding and screaming continued, marching steadily closer, scuppers popping up and writhing like live things as they were crushed, stanchions snapping inboard, held now only by the vibrating lifelines. Steel grated and screamed. The liner's high hull was still swelling outward at the level of the frigate's main deck, and as the point of impact moved aft it gradually rose.

As it reached the bridge, Dan grabbed the bearing taker and hauled him into the pilothouse and dogged the door. The white hull, so close Dan could read a palimpsest of previous chippings and paintings, bit into the splinter shield where he'd stood a moment before, snapping up the wooden handrail and gnashing it into varnished kindling. A white-uniformed steward stared at them through a porthole. Then the curved wall receded, and the squealing and groaning moved on aft, accompanied by reverberating bangs.

Khashar was yelling, berating someone, Dan couldn't tell who. A knot of men in work clothes gaped up from the pier.

He was opening his mouth to suggest a hard backing bell, to be followed by a nudge ahead, when Khashar shouted what was obviously an order. The helmsman and lee helmsman yelled back, and the engine order telegraph pinged. It looked like hard rudder and a full ahead bell. Son of a bitch . . . he was about to speak again when Khashar yelled again, and the ahead bell came off and the handles went back, and the rudder angle indicator swung back to amidships. The vertical line of the jackstaff hesitated, then swung slowly to the right. The mole loomed closer and closer, the black rock and concrete looking extremely hard and jagged. Then the back bell took effect, and from the forecastle lines uncoiled in the air.

Chick Doolan, beside him: "What the hell was that? I was down in the breaker, all of a sudden it sounded like a train wreck."

"We had a close encounter with the liner, there." Dan looked up, saw people gathered along her rail, examining the gouges. There wasn't anything more he could do, but he still didn't leave his post until *Tughril* lay moored at last, snugged to solid rock while above her, rank after rank, the white houses gazed serenely down.

HE avoided the wardroom for the next half hour and sent Doolan down to muster the guys in the port breaker. When they were assembled he laid a few groups on them about conduct ashore. The Azores were pretty pro-American, but a sailor could get into trouble anywhere if he didn't use his head. The moment he dismissed them, they stampeded for the brow. There, that was done; at least they were off the ship for a few hours.

Back in his room, he hauled himself up into his bunk. For a few minutes he lay staring at the overhead. The ship seemed to reel inside his head, then suddenly reorient, as if he were drunk and staggering. He felt something cocked and tense inside him slowly release. Then it was black.

WHEN he came out on deck again late that afternoon the sun had burned off the overcast and the sky was clear and brilliant. He stood on the quarterdeck in slacks and a short-sleeved shirt, looking out across the mole and the strait at Pico. The volcano towered like Fuji, black and ominous. Scattered clouds lingered about its upper slopes. He'd called Jim Armey, asking about dinner, but the engineer begged off. Dan decided to go in alone, get off the ship for a couple of hours, maybe find someplace he could make an international call, see if he could get Blair. He owed his daughter a call, too.

A sun-swarthed Azorean with long hair pulled a taxi to the curb as Dan came down the mole. "To hell with Saddam."

"Yeah, to hell with him."

"You American, right? But that's not an American ship."

"We just sold it to the Pakistanis." Dan declined the ride politely. What he wanted more than anything was just to walk along a street, look at human beings he didn't know, reassure himself a world existed outside *Tughril*'s steel shell. He turned back to look at her halfway down the mole. She looked so incredibly small.

THAT evening he ended up halfway up the mountain, at a half-house, half-restaurant whose outdoor patio looked down over a spectacular view of the strait, looked up to hawks skating the updrafts. From here the ship was a scale model. Most of the other diners were German. He refused the *angelica* with some difficulty, declined beer as well, and had sparkling local water and a fish soup and tried a stewed octopus dish that turned out to be quite palatable.

He was sitting back, waiting for the main course and enjoying the twinkling of lights below as night came to the sea, when he saw Chick Doolan at the bar.

The weapons officer wasn't alone. His broad shoulders were hunched attentively toward a twenty-something woman in a lavender pants suit, with long dark hair and a melancholy look that was focused alternately on Doolan and on the wine at her elbow. Dan watched them for a moment, then turned his mind away.

Then he looked up and there Doolan was, coming toward him. Blue cotton slacks, a Polo shirt. Rugged heavy-jawed face flushed, whether from the drink he carried in his hand or at being discovered, it made him look more like Ernest Hemingway than ever. Behind him, the girl, following close as a tow through a crowded strait. Doolan said aggressively, "Commander. Didn't know you were headed up here."

"Hi, Chick. Bring anybody else with you?"

"No, most of 'em are down at the Estalagem." Doolan waved the glass at the horizon. "You can see all the way to Philly."

"Just about."

"This is Lorenza; she's from Lisbon—"

"Not 'Lorenza.' Lavina."

Dan got up, waited for her hand; she didn't extend it. He noticed Doolan had taken his ring off. Dan didn't say anything, just stood there smiling, and after a moment Doolan took the hint, either that or figured he'd discharged his obligation to acknowledge his presence. He said, "Well, enjoy your dinner," and added something in an undertone to the girl that made her smile. On the way back to the bar he put his hand on her back. Dan looked after them, watching her turn her head and half-smile as Doolan shifted his hand to her waist. Then Dan switched his attention to the deep-sea crab.

HE found a telephone post by the marina and called Blair and Nan on his card. After punching in many many numbers, he got to talk to two answering machines. The ship was quiet, though the bars were still going on the main drag, and he turned in at 2200 to catch up a little more.

The next day their parts were still not in. The air force said they'd arrive by light plane at 1000. Khashar took the news silently, but it was not a resigned silence. When they finally arrived, at 1130, he canceled lunch and ordered them to cast off. The pilot was on the bridge this time, a small man with several days' stubble and no compunction about taking cigarettes out of the pack in front of the captain's chair.

Dan stood in his by-now accustomed place on the wing as Horta's hills gave way to the open sea again. Getting under way went without incident, except for the cigarette-filching pilot drawing a glower from Khashar. He debarked outside the breakwater, into the same speedboat they'd passed by coming in. When it was clear the captain spoke sharply, and the OOD flinched and shouted orders. The whoosh of the intakes rose to a whine, and they rolled to a moderate sea.

An hour out the GQ alarm sounded. He was in the combat systems office, going through his mail. A letter from Blair, putting him in a better mood. He took it along as he ran up to the bridge, figuring to read it over again there.

He got there to find the train warning bell clanging and the five-inch slewing out to port. He blinked, staring past the muzzle at the island of Terceira. Almost immediately the long tapered tube depressed, scooted all the way around the deck, and rose again on the starboard side. He breathed out and sprinted up the ladder to the flying bridge.

Here no overhead protected him from the glaring sun. He flipped the binocular strap around his neck and rastered the horizon, wondering for a moment if they were outside

Portuguese waters. Then shrugged inwardly, a response that was becoming habitual.

He was tucking in his earplugs when he saw Doolan duck under the gun barrel and disappear around the mount. Dan frowned. Not a good idea. In fact, against the NAVORD safety precautions. He watched till Chick reappeared, loping bent over across the deck. The weps officer glanced up and saw him, raised a thumb. Dan lifted a hand in acknowledgment.

Khashar emerged onto the wing. He glanced at his Rolex, looking down at the mount. His impatience and anger were clear as if they had been lettered in a comic-book balloon above his head. The barrel rose and fell with the roll of the ship, intent on some distant target. An imaginary one, apparently, because when Dan scrutinized the sea horizon through the Big Eyes he saw nothing but far-off clouds, the sparkle of afternoon sun off the waves, and *Tughril*'s own shadow, lengthening across the inkblue sea. Then without warning the gun let go a blast and flash that, despite his having held himself ready for it, made him flinch so hard he skinned his knuckles against the coaming.

He'd figured it was just a quick-reaction drill, but the gun kept firing, round after round, sometimes in full auto, sometimes a round every thirty seconds. Empty powder canisters clanged on the deck. Smoke and paper fragments blew aft. Either Khashar was running some sort of reliability test or else he was just taking out his frustrations by firing seventy-pound projectiles into the empty sea.

The mount fell silent, still pointing south. Khashar stood drumming his fingers on the splinter shield. It had been hastily hammered back into shape and primer slapped over it. The captain snatched his hand back and examined sticky red-orange on his fingers. He turned and yelled into the pilothouse.

Doolan came out and said something to Khashar. Dan looked on from above, only mildly interested. The captain made a hurried dismissive gesture and turned his back.

Doolan stayed. Dan leaned down, cupping his ear to catch Chick's next remark.

"Sir, you've got to get them out of there."

"They'd have to do it in battle."

"We're not in battle. You'll lose four guys if it goes off."

"Perhaps that will motivate them to find out what's wrong."

"That's not a smart way to operate, sir. In fact, it's damn dumb."

Khashar, colder than liquid helium: "You will go to your stateroom, Mr. Doolan. At once."

Dan came down the ladder, joining them on the wing. The gun was still trained out. The mount door was open, and he glimpsed a fear-drawn face within. He said to them both, "Hot gun, Chick?"

"Right. We've got to get those guys out of there, get a stinger down the barrel, and commence cooling."

Five-inch ammo came in two sections, the shell and a separate propelling charge. The loading mechanism lined them up and rammed them. But if a primer misfired or the firing circuits failed, it was possible to end up with a shell in the breech and no way to either fire or extract. If the gun was relatively cold, no problem, but if a number of rounds had already been fired, the residual heat quickly began cooking the shell—and the live explosive within it.

"Chick's right, Captain—we've got to get them out of there."

"I told you to go to your stateroom," said Khashar, face immobile as iron.

Doolan stood rooted.

"Go on, Chick," Dan said.

The weapons officer wheeled and disappeared into the pilothouse.

Dan said, "Can we commence cooling now, Captain?"

Instead of responding, Khashar spun, making for the ladder leading to the main deck. Dan followed him down, then forward through the breaker.

On the sunlit forecastle the mount still pointed off to

starboard, motors humming an ominous obbligato. Khashar ducked his head into the open hatch, beginning a shouted exchange in Urdu. Dan stood a few steps off, looking down at the stinger, a long metal wand connected to a three-inch fire hose. There was no sign or hint of danger, no smoke or noise other than the ominous hum and the hollow clank of a tool. But inside, hidden by the breech and mechanism, was a live shell steadily approaching cook-off temperature. He bent and picked up the stinger. All he had to do was thrust it into the barrel, twist the valve on, and run like hell. Unfortunately, the 54-caliber barrel was so long he couldn't get to the muzzle with the mount trained outboard. He moved up behind Khashar. "Cap'n? Have 'em go back to ready surface, and I'll get that barrel cooled down."

"They're almost ready to fire."

"That's good, but we need to get some water down there . . . sir?"

A hollow metal clanking came from inside the mount. Simultaneously the men within yelled. Khashar backpedaled hastily, and Dan got through the breaker door and slammed it behind them a split second before *ka WHAM* slammed through the steel and shook the bulkheads around them. *Ka WHAM*, *ka WHAM*, *ka WHAM*, jumping dust and paint chips up from the nonskid to hang in the air like smoke. He stared at Khashar's sweat-glistening face in the dimness.

"You Americans are too easy with your men. You treat them like children. No wonder they act without respect, without self-control. You are so obsessed with perfection. If they have no freedom to fail, how can they succeed?"

Dan stared at the strong sallow teeth.

"Lieutenant Doolan. I do not wish to see him about the ship until he apologizes to me. I cannot permit disrespect."

Suddenly the ship was unfamiliar, the space Dan stood in was strange and separate and other, as if he had boarded for the first time and knew nothing and no one here. He stared at Khashar, then turned, still wordless, and left him standing in the empty passageway.

8

THE MED

THE Rock was a violet wedge splitting lavender clouds. As dying beams of gold and scarlet flashed across the sea, Dan shaded his eyes to a needle of light that stitched the gathering dusk. It paused, and beside him the shutters rattled, the signalman flicking his wrist with cool expertise. Then the rapid flash from the Rock resumed.

The Strait of Gibraltar, a day after leaving the NATO base at Rota, Spain. An overnight there to fuel and have the maintenance activity do a little metal bending and stanchion welding along the side. His sight bridged two continents: the mountainous darkness of Africa to starboard, the purple gloom of an equally precipitous Iberia to port. *Tughril* moved steadily east, surging occasionally to a swell. The air temperature was fourteen degrees Centigrade and the sea sixteen. The wind was from the north at twenty knots, the sky clear save for the luminous and slowly fading clouds that hovered behind them, over the Atlantic. Which, he could not help reflecting, the frigate would never see again. She'd serve out her life in the Far East and end reduced to anonymous metal for Toyotas and Hyundais.

The days since Horta had passed peacefully, but with a sullen undertone he didn't like. Khashar had released Chick from restriction after twenty-four hours, though Doolan had not apologized. Dan had taken Doolan off the bridge watch, moving him to CIC for the rest of the transit. Keep them apart, that was about all he could think to do. Anyway, they'd be in Karachi in another three weeks.

The straits were as busy today as they'd been every other time Dan had transited, to his surprise; he'd expected the loom of war to keep ships in port. It hadn't, at least in the West Med. There were a score of contacts on the vertical plot, containerships and colliers plowing past in the stolid ox plod of commercial shipping.

Now he lifted his glasses to the ships that moved rapidly closer out of the eastern darkness. He studied the lead one as it grew to the unmistakable icebreakerlike silhouette of an Udaloy-class cruiser. Accompanying it, four thousand yards astern, were the cutter bow and complex tophamper of a Kashin-class destroyer. As they passed, he followed them with the circle of enlarged sight, watching the sunset light flash scarlet and brass off paint and glass, catching high on the cruiser's mast top the white, red, and blue flicker of the new Russian flag. He remembered passing their weapon-bristling warships close aboard and wondering when the final challenge would come. Now it appeared it never would, that the long faceoff would end without the Armageddon both sides had anticipated and feared for so long.

Behind them the sun turned redder as it fell, sending rays of luminous violet shooting up into the sky. The clouds were pink continents, edged in luminous gold. The sea glittered copper, then tangerine. The sun's lower limb slowly spread as it touched the sea, as if kissing it with parted lips.

Dan raised his glasses again. The flat russet disk, tint and heat dulled by miles of air, sank steadily, eclipsed moment by moment by the rising horizon. Then, as the distant darkness sheathed the last curved edge, a sudden flash of brilliant emerald darted toward him across the darkening ocean. It was so vivid and so unexpected he jerked the binoculars from his eyes. Then it, too, was gone, leaving only a dwindling hue in the violet sky, an expiring, fatal maroon like venous blood. Till all that remained was a fading glow, a luminous wash of phosphorescent gold, lingering like memory over the windy sea.

HE was sitting in his stateroom that evening, playing a computer game on his Z180, when the GQ alarm went again. Another fire. He got down to the galley fearing the worst, but by the time he arrived it was out, though white smoke seethed and the air smelled like scorched doughnuts. The deep-fat fryer, probably the biggest fire hazard in the ship. Someone had used his head and tripped the Gaylord hood. Others stood around with CO_2 extinguishers. That was good, a better response than showing their heels. A man lay on the deck, the normal batch of gawkers close around him as the Pakistani corpsman squatted. Through the surrounding legs Dan caught a glimpse of skin as the medic stripped off clothing. It was coming off with the cloth. The burned man was completely silent. Then suddenly he began to scream, endless and deafening in the sealed metal room.

THE open Mediterranean, dark and winter-windy. Their next landfall lay another thousand miles ahead, past Algiers, Palma, Sardinia, Tunis, and Sicily. He and Irshad had laid the track down well clear of land, except for a close passage off Cap Bon to cut a few miles off the last leg to Malta. The decision to lay over at Malta had been the Pakistanis'. Malta and the U.S. Navy had not been on good terms for some years now. *Tughril* steamed eastward over the next few days, out of sight of land but never out of sight of shipping. The Med seemed more crowded every time he returned to it. He recalled his first deployment, how vast and empty it had seemed. Now he looked at the chart and felt cramped.

The burned man from the galley died after a day, and they buried him at sea.

Dan spent most of his time on the bridge, standing for hour after hour on the wing or parked in the chair in the nav shack. Khashar was up there a lot of the time, too. Which would have been fine, except he was continually taking over the conn. Whenever a closing contact forced them to maneuver, he gave orders direct to the helmsman. Dan could see it wrecking what little confidence the OODs had gained. Not only that, but Khashar changed course when *Tughril* was bound by the rules of the road to hold course and speed. The first couple of times it happened, Dan pointed out he was courting danger, that sooner or later both ships would put their helm over in the same direction. Misunderstandings at high closing speeds could be fatal. But the wall was up. The third time he brought it up, the captain cut him off with the brusque statement that he'd been commanding ships for years.

THEY lay over in Valletta for two days. The second day in port, Dan was in the wardroom, watching an Italian television report on the Desert Shield buildup. He could follow the diagrams and video clips if not the torrent of speech. Five seconds of jets dropping napalm, then a shot of Saddam looking at a map, surrounded by fawning generals. Then the bulkhead squealer went off.

Dan hadn't been in Khashar's stateroom in a while. The coffee table was covered with papers. The two men on the sofa stood as he came in. They were both stocky, one fair and balding, the other dark, both in lumpy gray suits. The one who spoke first sounded German or maybe Dutch or Flemish. He shook Dan's hand. "Mr. Lenson? I am Mr. Wint. This is Mr. Selmunit. We're with Interpol."

"Pleased," said Dan. He looked from one to the other.

"Well sit down," said Wint. "You are the senior American, correct? I understand that there's something of a divided command aboard this ship?"

"There's only one captain," Dan said. He glanced at Khashar, who sat fingers tented, dark eyes hooded. The smell of tobacco smoke lingered in the room, but none of the men in it were smoking now. There must have been a confab of some length before he had been called. What had Khashar told them during it? Why did cops always come in pairs, anyway? No answers offered, so he went on, "But I report to him, for the U.S. contingent."

"Very well. I will repeat what I've already told the captain, then. We're here because of a death that was reported in the Azores. A young woman was found murdered in a park. She was found not far from the waterfront, the day after your ship left port."

Dan looked at the deck, sobered, getting a quick vision of his own daughter—"a young woman"—Nan, dead in the grass. "I don't think there's anyone aboard *Tughril* who'd—"

"Nor do we, really. We're simply following up on a request. In a case like this, the local police have charge of the investigation. We act on their behalf. If we develop any suspects, there are, I believe, status-of-forces agreements that would govern return of the suspect for identification, and so forth."

Mr. Selmunit said in an accent Dan couldn't place, "I will want to interview every man who go ashore. One alone at a time."

Dan sat thinking as they discussed how to set up the interviews. He was remembering a night high on the hill and the sad eyes of a young woman at the bar. Chick Doolan, coming over to him at his table, aggressive and defensive at the same time. Doolan, drunk. With his wedding ring slipped off.

Dan said to Wint in an undertone, "Do you happen to have a photograph?"

Wint blinked, giving an impression of interest but also of a certain detachment. "Of the victim? Yes, I do." He flipped open a plastic portfolio and slid out what looked like some sort of high-quality fax, centered it in front of Dan, then studied his face as he leaned forward.

He straightened after a moment, relieved. It wasn't Lavina, the melancholy girl with the long dark hair. This woman was dark, too, also long-haired, but her face was quite different. Rounded, heavier, with a different shape to her mouth. Not the same woman at all.

"Yes?" said Wint politely.

"Nothing. I thought I might have seen her when I went ashore."

"In whose company? Or did she approach you? There's some indication she may have been a professional or at least semipro—"

"Neither. I mean, I didn't see this woman, at all." He didn't see any point in aiming Interpol at Doolan over a one-night stand. Even if he *was* married. "I'll be happy to go over my movements for you or give you any other assistance I can. I have a first-rate chief as my master-at-arms. He'll help you organize the interviews, get everybody in you want to see."

The other agent, Selmunit, had been watching as he and Wint examined the image. Now he said, "Let me show him the other picture."

"All right," said Wint, and Dan found himself looking at another. His breath stopped involuntarily.

"This is what the body looked like when it was found," said Wint. "Notice the pattern. Genitalia. Intestines. But above all, the obviously obsessional attention given to the eyes."

Dan pushed the photo away. He'd seen death and wounds before, but never anything like this. The image seemed to have gone right to some primitive horror-center deep in his brain. He tried to speak but for some reason couldn't get a word out.

"All right then," said the agent, getting up. "Thank you both for your assistance. Captain, how do you suggest we begin?"

The agents spoke to everyone who'd gone ashore, which was pretty much everybody aboard, but didn't spend much time with any one man and left that night.

THE next day they got under way again, passed under the ancient walls of Fort St. Angelo, and ran east for the next two days at twenty-five knots. A fast passage, but this was a short leg. The wind veered northerly and the seas ran eight to ten feet, rank on rank of cold dark green seas, marching down from the Adriatic and the coast of Greece. Dan watched them pass with a strange sense of *déjà vu*. It hadn't been far from here that he and Red Flasher and Jack Byrne and the rest of the Task Force Sixty-one staff had tried to

keep their butts from being ground up between Greece and
Turkey, in the clash over Cyprus, then reoriented east for
Operation Urgent Lightning.

He stood immobile, clinging to the pitching ship, and
stared through it into the past. Hearing again the crack of
three-inch fifties, the popping of aircraft cannon, the rising
howl of engines. Seeing again what he'd thought then
would be the last thing he'd ever see. Silver birds above a
green-gray sea. Blossoms of yellow fire, perfect rings of
smoke, whipping past him on an icy wind . . . muzzle
flashes from the leading edge of wings, the cutting brilliance of aluminum. They bored inward still, and always
would, inexorable, invulnerable, eternal nightmares in the
tranced sight of irrevocable memory.

9

THE SUEZ CANAL

THE moonlit desert was made of blackness and straight lines. Forward of *Tughril*'s blade-sharp bow stretched the straightest and strangest of all: a kilometers-long gutter of dun-muddy water long ago rendered lifeless by the churning props and furtive bilge pumpings of half the world's commerce. Nearly sixty miles of ditch, varied only by the occasional pumping station or the scooped-out bays that were called gares. Speed in the canal was limited to seven knots, and the frigate glided through the night almost silently save for the occasional hiss of her safeties lifting.

Dan stood watching from the bridge as a patch of darkness ahead slowly grew into trees, unnatural and somehow ominous-looking in the surrounding waste.

What the chart called Al-Qantara was lined with trees, what kind he didn't know, but surprisingly tall in the silvery light of a desert moon. The flat banks were dotted with an occasional low white building that might be a house, though they looked awfully stark for homes. The bank was littered with broken concrete or stones against which their bow wave washed with a rippling roar that in the immense stillness sounded creepy as hell. He saw no people. The distant barking of a dog was the only sound of life. The tidal buoys showed almost no current, floating quietly at their moorings until the frigate's passage set them nodding like obsequious courtiers at the ends of their chains.

The Suez connected the Mediterranean to the Red Sea. He'd been through it before, on *Turner Van Zandt*, and the unease he'd felt then was unchanged. The constriction of a ship, the freest thing on earth, to a narrow channel; the weirdness of sea amid desert; the uneasy sense that, like their passage, all human presence was transitory, irrelevant, perhaps even illusory.

Their passage had started from Port Said at midnight. Now *Tughril* steamed with a searchlight on her bow, a loran-C position reporting transmitter on the starboard wing, and a skeletal revenant in sere khakis standing centerline with his hands in his pockets. As long as they were in the canal, he and not Khashar controlled the movements of the ship. The canal pilot was at least sixty years old and very soft-spoken, but his tired brown eyes missed nothing. He'd tested the engines, steering console, rudder angle, and RPM indicators and done comm checks with the bridge radios as well as his own. He made sure the boats were ready for instant lowering, in case he needed them to carry a mooring line, and that the engines were tested and the fuel tanks topped off. Dan couldn't help contrasting his attitude with Khashar's. For the first time in weeks, he felt safe.

THEY anchored in the Great Bitter Lake as a desert sunrise ignited the calm waters. What riveted Dan's attention when he came topside, though, wasn't the sun, red and swollen as a blood-filled condom above the shimmering desert. It was the blocky superstructure of a Ticonderoga-class cruiser a quarter-mile away. She swung to her hook in the warm air, the octagonal shields of Aegis radars glowing in the ruddy dawn. Her hull number was 56, USS *San Jacinto*, and after looking across at her for several minutes, listening to the music from the boom boxes out on deck, he went below to ask Irshad if he could borrow a boat.

SWEATING in the airless heat—even this early the gray steel radiated it like an oven—he tossed off a salute as he stepped onto the quarterdeck. "Permission to come aboard."

"Permission granted." A chief returned his salute.

Dan showed his ID, showed the portable radio he carried, too, in case there was any question later. The chief asked him who he wanted to see. He said the operations officer, if possible, and got handed off to a messenger to escort him up to CIC.

Following him down wide, polished tile passageways waxed so brightly they reflected the overhead, he felt the existential anxiety of a sailor aboard a ship not his own. The air, so icy chill his sinuses immediately began to hurt, smelled of fresh paint and familiar chow. He got curious glances as he trailed the messenger up ladders and along more passageways to CIC.

After a couple of seconds of jealous staring around—the Tico-class cruisers were the most modern ships in the fleet, with state-of-the-art phased-array radars and computers that could track hundreds of targets at once—he found the ops officer, studying a red-bound publication that he closed as the messenger brought Dan up. Lenson introduced himself. "Van Miralda," said the other officer, shaking hands. "Yeah, we saw you coming in to anchor and looked you up. Pakistani, right?"

"We were *Oliver C. Gaddis* till last month."

"I didn't know we were giving ships to Pakistan. There was something on Armed Forces Radio; they're doing something we don't like—"

"Well, this is a done deal." Dan looked at the command displays enviously. "You're lucky to be here."

"You sound bitter, man. What're you doing over there? You a tech rat?"

"No. I had her for a while. Just long enough to get attached. We're just making sure they get her home in one piece."

They traded backgrounds, finding they'd both been in Destroyer Squadron Six, in Charleston; Miralda had come in after Commodore Niles had left. The lieutenant glanced at the bulkhead clock. "You want to come on down, catch second seating for breakfast? Food's nothin' special; we're doing some kind of reduced-galley-manning test."

"You kidding? After four weeks of lamb and rice?"

Miralda started to get up, then said, "Did you have some questions for me? Before we went down?"

"Yeah. We don't have Fleet Broadcast, so we don't get much news. You don't have to tell me classified stuff; just I'd like to know what's going on."

Miralda said that Saddam—he pronounced it "Sad-*damn*"—had probably intended Kuwait as the first stage in a two-stage offensive. The second would have taken a bite out of Saudi Arabia, advancing to a line south of Dhahran that would take in the country's oil production, ports, and desalinization facilities. The president's ultimatum, backed up by the *Independence* and *Eisenhower* strike groups, had made him pause. Now the Army and Air Force were ramping up rapidly. The Navy was concentrating its main forces in the Persian Gulf, to support an air offensive and prep for an amphibious assault.

"That's why we're headed over. You've heard of Tomahawk."

"I helped develop it."

"Is that right? You're familiar with the capabilities of the weapon then. We have the vertical launch version. And something new." The ops officer told Dan about a new kind of warhead, loaded with hundreds of spools of superfine carbon fiber. On detonation over transformer stations and other electrical infrastructure, the spools would unwind, shorting out power but causing little permanent damage. The lieutenant explained the awesome forces that were building up to retake Kuwait, push Saddam back into Iraq, and decimate his military force to the point where his government would fall, brought down by the anger of long-oppressed minorities.

A white uniform passed the sonar curtain. Miralda said, "Want to meet the commodore?"

"Sure, who is he?"

"Fella named Leighty."

Dan sat rigid. "Not *Thomas* Leighty."

"That's him. Sir? Commodore?"

Commodore Thomas Leighty, USN, still carried himself with the air of conscious drama Dan had noticed when they'd served together aboard USS *Barrett*, DDG-998.

Leighty's hair was a more distinguished silver now; that was all. They stared at each other, and Dan remembered very suddenly running through the passageways with this man, riot gun in hand; kneeling over him, thinking he was dead. Leighty must have remembered it, too; he nodded slowly, and a shadow crossed his gaze. He extended a small manicured hand. "Why, Dan. Where did you pop up from, out in the middle of the Great Bitter Lake?"

Confronted with Leighty's crisp whites, Dan was suddenly conscious of his own unstarched, wilted khakis. "The Pak frigate, sir. I'm OIC of the MTT."

"It's been a while. Since we went after Jay Harper."

"I still think about the King Snake. In my nightmares."

"This was the spy, right?" said Miralda. "You knew him, sir?"

"I was his CO. Dan here was his department head."

"And you never had any idea what he was doing?"

Dan took that one. "No, the King was smooth. We knew there was a leak, that equipment was missing. But he'd have been the last guy I suspected. The superpatriot and all."

"Were you there when Naval Intelligence took him out? I heard something about Cuba, a rumor you were actually inside territorial waters—"

"You know how scuttlebutt gets exaggerated," said Leighty. "Anyway, I have to say, you're the last person I expected to see out here. You say that's a Pakistani ship you're on?" He listened intently as Dan explained the transfer program. "And how are things going over there?"

"There's strain. Occasionally."

"Between the crews?"

Dan said reluctantly, "No, not so much among the men. There was at first. The cultures are so different. But the biggest problem's between me and the Pak CO."

"I find that hard to believe. You were always perfectly loyal to me. Personality conflict?"

"More like different leadership styles. Won't be much longer, though; another week to Karachi and we'll be done."

A smooth-faced young aide appeared beside Leighty. "Sir, we've got the covered round robin coming up," he said, giving Dan a dismissive glance.

Leighty looked around for his cap; Dan saw that if he was going to bring this up, this was the time.

"Anyway, sir, I did have something to ask you. It's about Desert Shield."

"Go ahead, Dan."

"Sir, I just wanted to say, once we hit Karachi, my orders are to fly back to Norfolk. But if there was a spot for me on a battle staff, or an extra fill on a combatant, I bet I could get temporary orders. If it comes to that, I've got leave coming—"

"Whoa there. Whoa!" Leighty chuckled, holding up his hand. "I should have known, if there's anything going on, you'd want in. I'll bear you in mind. All right?"

"I'd appreciate that, sir."

"Good, then." Leighty held out his hand. After a moment Dan took it, conscious of the skin touching his, the faint smile on the commodore's lips.

"It would be nice to serve with you again, Dan," Leighty said softly, at which Dan got a level scalpel flick of a glance from the aide, who seemed to really see him, then, for the first time.

He stayed for breakfast, then excused himself. He called up to the bridge, asking the anchor watch to give *Tughril* a call on Channel 13, let them know he was ready to be picked up.

He stopped just before stepping out on the main deck, enjoying a last moment of air-conditioning before he returned to the growing heat outside. Giving himself a once-over in the reflective Plexiglas of a bulletin board, he couldn't decide if he looked salty and self-assured or like a passed-over loser.

10

THE RED SEA

THE incident with the ferry happened the second day out from El Suweis. All that morning they'd steamed south, hugging the west coast, a low, pale, sandy plain rising toward distant mountains, passing only an occasional island scrubbed with low brush. The Sudan, land of war and famine. The temperature hovered at eighty. Dan hated to think what it would be like here in August. A gusty north wind pushed them along. He was in the nav shack late that afternoon, reading a velvet-paged copy of *Watership Down*, when the 21MC broke out in urgent Urdu. Simultaneously he got a call on the sound-powered phone, which had by now evolved into a U.S.-only comm channel. When he picked it up, Chief Compline said, "Commander? Radio. Call coming in on 8364."

Eight-three-six-four kilohertz was the international maritime distress frequency, one of the four emergency frequencies the ship monitored around-the-clock. Dan said, "Got a posit yet?"

"Call you back when. Just wanted to make sure you were up there."

"Surface ship? Or aircraft?"

"Commercial vessel of some sort. Sounds like it might be close."

Dan told him to send somebody up with the message when they had a hard copy. Not four minutes later Compline himself was at the folding door. Dan glanced over the handwritten carbon and turned to the chart he had taped down and already marked with *Tughril*'s most recent fix and a running dead reckoning line from there.

The message was from something called the MV *Al Qiaq*. It reported taking on water and requiring assistance at

L 20° 34' N, λ 38° 17' E. She was making 030 at between two to three knots, destination Jedda, on the eastern coast. He walked the dividers out. "About sixty nautical miles," he said, running a DR line toward her advance position and marking it hour by hour. The other ship was headed north-east, generally across *Tughril*'s bow. He calculated two courses to intercept, one at twenty-five knots and the other at flank speed. He wrote them in ballpoint on his left palm, along with the estimated time to intercept, and took the message out into the pilothouse.

Khashar was standing at the chart table with Irshad and the Pakistani OOD. Past them a lapis sea surged and bil-lowed, the wind whipping spray off a breaker to rattle like spent shotgun pellets against the windows. None of the three looked up till Dan cleared his throat. He laid his copy of the message against their original, which was already lying on the chart, and said, "I thought we could check our intercept courses against each other."

"Do you feel we need to respond?" said the captain after a moment.

"Sir, we've already responded. Chief Compline rogered for their distress call. It's only about twenty miles off our intended PIM anyway."

Khashar looked doubtful as Irshad laid out his recom-mendation: a thirty-knot course to intercept. Dan said, "Sir, I concur with that."

"Come left, one-three-zero," the CO said at last, turning away as he said it.

Dan and Irshad looked at each other; was that a helm order or what? The OOD checked with Khashar, who was back in his chair now, lighting a cigarette, and got an angry response. He suffered it in silence, passed an order to the helm. The gyro swung around to steady at 130. The speed was unaltered, though, and presently Dan pointed this out. The lieutenant said, "If the captain had wanted the speed in-creased, he would have said so."

"You know as well as I do that if we maintain this speed, we'll pass astern of the contact. He forgot it, that's all."

The lieutenant wouldn't meet Dan's eyes; he obviously didn't want to fall afoul of the silent officer in the chair. Dan sighed and tried Irshad next. He didn't even answer, just stared ahead through his binoculars. For a moment Dan considered reaching over, seizing the shining polished brass handle, and yanking it over to "ahead flank" himself. To hell with it. He crossed the bridge and said, maybe too loudly, but he was getting sick of tiptoeing and scraping, "Captain, we need to increase speed."

Khashar breathed smoke out and watched it curl off the inside of the window. "We're already at twenty knots. There's no indication we need to go any faster."

"They sent a distress signal. Sir, our obligation under international agreements governing distress at sea is to respond as quickly as possible."

Khashar spoke angrily. The engine order telegraph pinged.

Dan, sweating for some reason, turned away. Then he forced himself back. "Sir, we've got two hours plus till we intercept. I'd recommend using that time to get organized. Get the boats ready and the gear loaded, flake out a towline, get a damage control party ready to—"

"That will do," said Khashar coldly. "You really do not have to instruct me in any of these matters, Commander. I know my duty, I know my men, and I know international law and my own regulations. You do not need to instruct me, and I do not believe I require your presence on my bridge. I would recommend that you return to your book and your coffee in the wardroom." He turned his head.

Dan debated a response, debated against what frustration, anger, and growing hate pressed him to say, finally decided none was called for. He said, "Aye aye, sir," and went back to the charthouse, feeling the gazes of the enlisted men following him. Hard to tell, impossible to guess, what was going on behind those expressionless black eyes.

He was really looking forward to Karachi.

THE next message came in fifteen minutes later, saying the water was rising and assistance was needed fast. This time

Compline said that an Italian merchie had answered, too, but its position plotted well to the south, at least six hours away at the best speed she indicated she could make. Jedda had promised a tug but had been unable to provide a sailing time yet.

The distressed ship came up on radar at sixty thousand yards. Dan felt the bridge team's eyes on him every time he came out to dip his face into the repeater or to scan the sea ahead with his binoculars. Taken at face value, what the captain had just said barred Dan from the bridge. And he was tempted to take Khashar at his word, to go below and play passenger for the rest of the voyage. But he'd decided he wasn't taking any hints. He'd stay here doing his job till they threw him off by force. One good thing about the sideswiping in Horta: it would lend him credibility if Khashar entered a complaint against him. Once you'd established that you were acting in the interest of safety, a court-martial found it hard to hold your actions against you. Rain rattled at the windows, then slacked, leaving a sky the color of wet concrete.

At 1700 the lookout must have reported sighting the other ship, because everyone rushed to the starboard side and focused their glasses on the same point. Dan stood at the chartroom door, not bothering to look. According to her reports, *Al Qiaq* wasn't making as much headway as she'd hoped. For a moment he wondered why they were headed upwind; then the chart gave him the answer. Downwind lay shoal water, swash islets, and the black symbols of wrecked ships. The Sawakin reefs. *Tughril* came farther right, to 145, heading for what in a few more minutes he could make out with his naked eye: a distant white speck against blue-black. Even at this distance there was something irregular and disquieting about its motion.

Robidoux had been poring over a pub and now nudged him with an elbow. "MV *Al Qiaq*," he said. "Saudi registry. Twin diesels. A passenger ferry."

"Thanks, Robby." The photo showed a modern vessel with a short forecastle, high superstructure carried up from the main deck, a single funnel midships, and a mast on the afterdeck. He couldn't make out from the picture if there was ro-ro access forward, but there was clearly a ramp aft. "Take it out to the OOD," he said.

He went out to the wing and looked down at the RHIB. The dark gray inflatables—*RHIB* stood for "rigid-hull inflatable boat"—were nearly as big as the old-style motor whaleboats, but much lighter and far easier to launch and get back aboard. Instead of diesels they had fifty-horse outboard Johnsons. A couple of familiar faces down there. Pistolesi, shrugging a black coil of cable into the boat. Usmani, the fellow who'd fondled the shipyard worker in Philly, looking glum as he manhandled a pump along the deck. For a moment Dan wished he were going with them, fighting something honest like a separated seam or a cracked intake casting. But his place was on the bridge, trying to flatter and kick-start Khashar into the right decisions. Lips set, Dan went back in, checked the radar, made sure the bright dot that was *Al Qiaq* was tracking down the grease-penciled line to intercept.

Irshad muttered, "What's your thought on this?"

"Me? I'd run up alongside and send the repair party over. See if we can help 'em out."

"They look very low in the water. What if they sink?"

Dan frowned, swung up his glasses. In the half-light he saw what the Pakistani meant. The ferry was down by the stern. Some sort of dark liquid eddied about her afterdeck, but he couldn't make out what it was. Her stern rose, wallowed about, then dropped into a trough with the grace of a sack of sand. For a fraction of a second he'd seen a hollow interior, caught a glimpse of a ramp.

"What if they sink?" Irshad muttered again.

Dan glanced at him, surprised to see he was licking his lips. "We'll have to take everybody off."

"I don't know if we are ready for that."

"Well, we'd better get ready. There's a section in the rescue and assistance bill on what we've got to do to embark refugees and stuff. That'll cover where we put them and so forth."

He headed toward Khashar, but before he got there the captain swung down from his chair and walked past him. Lenson spun nearly in a circle, watching Khashar go on past the helm console, open the door that led to the ladder down, and vanish without a word or a look back.

The OOD removed his eyes from the glasses long enough to glance at the empty chair, then said to Dan, "Sir, we're going alongside?"

"Too soon to tell, Lieutenant. We need to establish comms, find out how bad off they are. See if you can raise the bridge on UHF."

After several calls, while the ship ahead drew steadily nearer, an excited voice answered. Unfortunately, Dan didn't grok Arabic, and it seemed to puzzle the Pakistanis, too. Or maybe the man on the tossing ship was trying to speak English, but it wasn't coming across. The signal light clattered. After a long pause, a burst of light came back, but modulated by no intelligible communication. OK, Dan thought, so this wasn't going to be easy.

"Is the boat ready to go? Repair party, pumps, lines aboard?"

"I will check. I believe so."

"Take a look at the wind direction. You want to give the RHIB a lee to lower into. I'd cross the wake, then pull up and match speed off her port side. As close as you can without banging into her."

The OOD muttered something, touched the speaking tube, then decided against it. He brought the head around by eye, lining the tossing ferry up on the pelorus. In the failing light Dan went out on the wing. The wind ironed his khakis against his chest as he searched the bridge opposite. A heavyset fellow in a black fisherman's cap looked back. Hard to tell at this distance, but he seemed to be wearing a beard. The others must be below, working on the leak.

Letting his binoculars drop to their strap, Dan swept his arms up and down several times. The man opposite stared at him. Dan then climbed onto the little platform that ran along the outer edge of the wing. From there he hauled himself up another couple of feet, till he was straddling the corner of the splinter shield.

The man opposite raised his glasses. Excellent. Dan bent over and thrust his rump out. He pointed to it several times, then with a flattened hand mimed something hinging or folding down from it. He noticed the Pakistanis watching him from inside the pilothouse. Their faces were carefully noncommittal. He faced the other ship again and was rewarded by a vigorous nod and wave. The man in the cap disappeared.

Dan jumped down to the gratings as a curtain of spray hurtled over the port side and rattled over his head, then craned out, trying to see into the fast-falling darkness. They'd have to do this right the first time. Would it be easier if they were steaming into the wind? No, it'd give them better helm control, but it wouldn't give the RHIB the shelter they needed to launch safely. This course was as good as it was going to get. *Al Qiaq*, of course, was still hoping for Jedda; that was why she was on it. He slammed the door open, wrestled the wind for it, and dogged it closed. "How far to Jedda?" he yelled to Robidoux. "And what's the tide doing here?"

"Wait one . . . about sixty nautical miles, with a dogleg around the Mismari Reef. Tide . . . that's a tough one, sir. There's no tables for Sector Six, and the sailing directions mention frequent crosscurrents."

Irshad: "At least a day yet, at the speed he's making good."

"If we can keep her afloat that long. You want to make sure the RHIB's loaded, all personnel have life jackets on and secured, that they have lights, and that their radios work. Tell the boat officer the easiest approach will be to make for that ramp on her stern. Do you see the ramp?" Irshad nodded.

"They'll be dropping it in a couple of minutes. That'll be a lot easier than trying to get up those sheer sides. Once it's down, we lag back to give them a lee, smooth that pitch out, and they can head on over. You sure you don't have anybody who speaks Arabic?"

"Not the kind of Arabic they're speaking."

Dan picked up the portable radio. It was on Channel 16, a line-of-sight distress frequency. *Tughril* was angling in, approaching the ferry's wake. The big seas were rolling through it, but the wide, flat stern of what Dan saw now was a rather larger vessel than he had at first thought had ironed them down to five to seven feet. Events were accelerating now, taking on that vicious smooth velocity that could at any time career out of control into utter disaster. He lifted the radio again, figuring to try French on them, then thought, *Wait a minute; Compline got their distress message.* He thumbed the 21MC. "Radio, Bridge: Chief Compline there?"

"Speaking."

"Chief, when the distress call came in, how did you copy that? We can't seem to get through to the other fella's bridge team."

"There's at least one guy speaks English over there. 'Cause I was talking to him."

"Call him back. Keep it short, but ask him to lower their stern gate. Think I got that message across nonverbally, but make sure. Number two: I want them to maintain present course and speed, their best man on the wheel, and hold the swings to two degrees max. Number three: See if your English speaker can come up on Channel 16 and translate; we're gonna have to coordinate our movements pretty closely while we're running alongside."

Compline rogered. Dan double-clicked the lever and checked the relative positions of the two hulls again. Maybe five hundred meters back, *Tughril* was coming left now to parallel course, ratcheting up steadily on the heaving ferry. Looking across to her, Dan saw a party of seamen at the stern gate. As he watched, it came slowly down, and they scrambled back as a sea licked at their boots. He saw also that what he'd taken for oil or loose water, a mobile darkness on the ferry's decks, wasn't oil at all.

"Good God," he breathed.

They were human beings, hundreds of them, lining the gunwale as the frigate moved in, shedding speed to fall in on her port quarter. The ferry's crew seemed to be fighting to move them away from the rail. But the passengers weren't obeying. It would be difficult to get the assistance party aboard if they couldn't keep the stern gate area clear. And what if those panicky hundreds suddenly decided they'd feel safer in the RHIB? It was a disaster in the making.

But if the other ship foundered, they'd be trying to pick people out of the water in a heavy sea, at night. They'd die then, a hell of a lot of them. And he had only a few more minutes of light to do anything.

He was still staring across, making sure there wasn't something he'd forgotten or overlooked, when someone cleared his throat behind him. He moved aside as Khashar emerged onto the wing, cigarette in his jaw. The captain surveyed the approaching ferry, the seamen waiting on the boat deck. The stolid dark face with the heavy Stalin mustache looked icy calm. For a moment Dan felt relieved.

Then Khashar swung and shouted an order through the open pilothouse door. The helmsmen's faces flew around. Their hands tightened on the wheel. Irshad gaped from the chart table. Dan didn't know what the order was. All he saw was the astonished expressions, the glances they exchanged.

Khashar spoke again, angrily and threateningly, but the faces did not alter and no hand moved to obey. Instead they did a strange thing. Their glances flicked to Dan, then returned to their work, their charts and instruments, or else they simply stared ahead, as unresponsively as if the bridge were peopled with wooden images.

Khashar blinked as if disbelieving what he saw.

Trying to head off what was going suddenly and horribly wrong, Dan took his arm, realizing as he did so that save for the obligatory handshakes, he'd never touched the man before. He said, "Sir, we have a clear duty to render assistance here. We need to get in there before this light fails, get the assistance party over there."

Khashar shook him off, not even favoring him with a look. Instead he spoke again to the silent listeners. This time the Urdu sounded incantatory in the pilothouse, mingled with the rush of wind.

Irshad slowly etched a line on his chart. The lee helmsman stood immobile at parade rest, only the nervous flickering of his clasped fingers betraying life. The helmsman stared with oblivious intensity at his gyrocompass.

Khashar shouted, his rage filling the enclosed space. The men paled, but yet again not one moved. Dan saw that the helmsman was holding them in position, glancing over at the ferry from time to time, then back at his repeater.

The captain bit savagely at the ends of his mustache, then turned to Dan, his face suffused with blood. He said, as if each word cost him an effort, "What were you suggesting, Commander?"

Dan explained his plan. When he was done, Khashar nodded. "I have reported this situation to Islamabad. We will wait for orders."

"We can't wait for them to get back to us, sir. Look; it's getting dark."

The captain chewed his mustache for a moment more, then grunted, "Carry out the assistance," and moved a step forward, out of the way.

"Aye aye, sir." Dan forced his horrified attention away from the crew's silent disobedience, Khashar's rage-flushed cheeks, what would happen to them and to him as soon as this revolution was over. He leaned through the wing door. "Right ten degrees rudder! Steady course zero-four-zero. Engine ahead two-thirds, indicate RPM for ten knots."

The helmsman shouted his reply; the lee helm answered up. Dan motioned Irshad over. He came unwillingly, glancing at Khashar, but the captain ignored them now. He was staring off toward the ferry, which was rapidly growing larger as they came up astern.

Both ships were rolling, but out of sync, the seas coming in on their port bows, lifting first *Tughril*, then *Al Qiaq*. The gunwales were black with people. By now Dan could make out individual heads. He told Irshad to pass to the boat coxswain to trail on the sea painter till he gave them the cast-off signal from the bridge. Once in the water, they'd proceed directly to the stern gate, put over a bow line, then debark everybody but the coxswain. The crew of the ferry would have to help with the pumps and eductors; a davit near the stern gate might help. "And tell them to keep their hard hats on and buckle those life jackets tight," he finished.

He watched the ferry's stern draw nearer. The closer they got, the safer the RHIB's passage would be. On the other hand, too close and the hulls would suck together; plus the ferry's yaw and wallow didn't give him a hell of a lot of confidence in their helm control. He wanted to drop into a slot about fifty yards off her port quarter. He called Irshad out onto the wing again to explain. "Just like an underway replenishment, only you're going to have to keep a sharp eye on her stern," Dan told him, conscious at each word of Khashar's back, still turned to them. "That's where you'll see the first motion if she's going to yaw significantly or come around into you. Maybe you should have your OOD watch the stern, yell if he sees her kicking out. OK, got it? Now goose her in the ass and get in there."

Tughril surged ahead and Dan tensed, but Irshad chopped power just as the stem passed the stern gate. The frigate rolled hard as she slowed, and he wondered if they could hold this position without slamming into the ferry. All it took was an unexpected sea, a second's inattention at the helm. But the helmsman was concentrating. Dan saw him sweating. "Tell him he's doing good," Dan said to the OOD.

"What?"

"Your helmsman, Lieutenant. Tell him he's doing good."

The man smiled briefly, not looking up. Dan watched as they crept up, then seemed to stop, relatively at least, hammering along seventy yards off *Al Qiaq*'s port side. The men on the ferry's bridge were yelling something. He couldn't make it out above the mingled wind and blowers and diesels. He glanced again at Khashar's back, then leaned in and yelled, "Captain! Permission to put the boat in the water?"

He'd meant it to help the man save face, but the momentarily turned eyes held a depth of hatred he'd seldom read in a human visage. OK, so be it. He leaned over the shield and gave the boat crew the signal.

Pistolesi waved, and the inflatable dropped. The crew scrambled down a jacob's ladder as it surged and bumped against the hull. "Cast off!" Dan howled down through cupped hands.

The outboards whined, and the boat curved off into the patch of slightly smoothed sea between the heaving, rolling hulls. The OOD, without coaching, dropped four RPMs and drifted back fifty feet, then nudged the bow in with one-degree course changes till they were riding so close to the other ship Dan could have underhanded a softball down to the afterdeck. He saw the bright-colored curved roofs of cars, the wet shine of lacquered metal. The passengers were women, in black veils, *chadors*. Children, too. He rubbed his face anxiously, watching the RHIB try a tentative first approach to the gate. It came in too fast and sheered off, and the wind caught the bow and lifted it and blew it scudding backward like a paper boat on a pond. The coxswain caught it deftly, though, spun it through a full turn in the wake, and surged back again in a full-throttle roar that was audible all the way up here on *Tughril*'s bridge. They disappeared for a moment, screened by an immense green-hearted swell, and Dan's hands tightened on the rail. Then they reappeared, and he saw a spider thread of nylon stretching from the bow over the stern gate.

Suddenly a jet of black diesel smoke shot from the ferry's stack. Dan cursed, hammering the freshly repainted splinter shield as Irshad yelled into the pilothouse. Increasing speed, but *Tughril*'s steam plant couldn't accelerate as fast as the ferry's diesels. What the *hell* was the ferry's captain doing? Then he saw the stern squat down into the water, sucked down by the increased thrust of the screws, and at that same moment a line of men squatted back along a white thread and the black wedge of the inflatable boat surged up and out of the sea like a beaching seal, sliding to a stop on the wave-washed afterdeck.

THEY dropped back a thousand yards and plodded along after the ferry as the sun dropped out of sight in a final brief blaze followed by the stars that had accompanied Sinbad. Khashar went below without a word to anyone. Dan wasn't looking forward to the explosion. He'd never seen a captain defied on his own bridge like that. He would have simply left declining even to witness, except for the obligation to provide assistance. For the moment, that took precedence over everything else. If it tore poor damn *Tughril* apart, that would have to be accepted.

He retreated inside the pilothouse to warm up, propping a shoe on the radiator as he checked the ferry out through his glasses. Her lights burned bright half a mile ahead, their reflections on the heaving sea now and then silhouetting the RHIB, swimming astern. He wanted to call Pistolesi, see how it was going, but didn't want to interrupt them. They would be pretty busy. It was hard to tell, it was surging up and down so fast and so far, but he had the bad feeling that the ferry's stern was riding lower than when he'd first seen it. The maneuver to dip her stern and get the boat aboard had been nicely done, but he hoped it hadn't made them take on more water.

The PRC crackled about half an hour later, in Urdu, and he listened as Irshad went back and forth for a couple of minutes, then called down to Main Control. Dan waited till he was done, then sidled up. "How's it going over there?"

"They're dewatering two compartments on the starboard side. That's why everyone was over to port; they were trying to even out the list. Not sure where the leak's coming from. Maybe a split seam. Our eductors don't fit the hoses on the ferry. So they're trying the P-250s."

"How about fixing her pumps?"

"They're working on it." He didn't have anything more, and Dan took a turn or two around the bridge, then checked the chart. The navigator had laid out their DR straight to Jedda. Fifty-some more miles.

Several hours passed with no change and only occasional reports from the damage control party. They reported gaining on the leaks and an estimated repair time of 0600 on one of the ferry's pumps. Around midnight the Italian merchant reported in. Dan asked them to stand by just in case, then signed off and stood looking ahead at the steadily rolling lights.

HE came awake in the red-lit dark of the chartroom, tilted back in a chair, with somebody shaking him. It was Irshad. He said, "The ferry is sinking, Dan."

He followed Irshad out of the chart room onto a silent dark bridge. The sea had not moderated. If anything, it was heavier, and *Tughril* labored around them. He rubbed his eyes and stared at an unlighted shadow ahead. "When did they lose power?"

"About five minutes ago. They ran out of gas for the pumps. The water's gaining fast now."

Useless to ask why they hadn't awakened him sooner. He checked the radar scope, trying to flog his tired brain into something resembling attentiveness. At least the ferry was still under way, had even increased speed a bit. Straining every sinew to reach port, no doubt. A bright contact off to the south was labeled as the Italian ship. Nobody else close enough to assist. The chart showed a little over thirty miles to Jedda. He wished like hell for an island, even a shoal, but the chart showed nothing but coral reefs. The dark sea beneath their rolling keels now was seven hundred meters deep. They could alter course right, try to anchor when they got closer in, but what the chart showed as the Abu Shawk Reef didn't look inviting; if the anchor dragged, in this wind, they'd be on it.

"Any word on the tug?"

"It got under way from Jedda. We don't have it on the scope yet."

On the radio, Pistolesi said he'd tried his best, but the rising water had shorted out the generators. Now it covered the pumps, too. Dan looked around the bridge. He should call Khashar. But Irshad hadn't, and he didn't feel like going through the charade. Finally he told Irshad to close up to two hundred yards astern of the ferry and to get the crew to rescue and assistance stations. As the GQ alarm went off, he called Compline, who was still in Radio, and told him to patch voice UHF to the Italian freighter, to a remote on the bridge. The chief said he had it up and tested; he would be speaking direct to the *Sant' Oreste*'s master. He spent ten minutes making arrangements with the Italian, then signed off and switched his attention back to the ferry, which was coming up fast. He was opening his mouth to caution the ops officer when Irshad snapped an order and the lee helm kicked back to one-third.

Out on the wing, Dan snapped the switch over on the signal light. He flipped the shutter handle down and swept the beam along the length of the ferry. In the sudden brilliance hundreds of faces looked back at him. Women raised their arms as if to a deliverer. Some held out black wrapped bundles. He tore his eyes from them, focusing on the bridge team. This would take iron nerve. They didn't have the boats to transfer that many people, there wasn't time to rig transfer lines, and if the passengers went over the side in this weather he'd lose them downwind in the dark and they would go spinning down before the seas and in a couple of days there'd be bodies on the beaches of Eritrea.

This was the only way it was going to work.

"Need a hand?" Chick Doolan, at his elbow. "Since *he* isn't up here?"

Dan said thanks, he could take over on the circuit to the *Sant' Oreste*. He outlined his plan, then jogged aft to make sure the deck-edge nets outboard of the helo pad were going down as ordered.

The Italian loomed out of the dark, red and green side-lights burning, then showing green alone as she passed through their wake. Dan sent the new course, 010, to *Al Qiaq* over Pistolesi's walkie-talkie. Irshad spoke tersely, and *Tughril* gradually dropped back, clinging to her flank as the ferry lumbered around. Dan tensed, watching her begin to pitch. Please God, it wouldn't open any more seams. He had to have both ships steaming upwind for this, with *Sant' Oreste* close aboard, crossing their bows in a diagonal zigzag, thirty degrees to either side of their base course.

The ferry was slowing. He didn't know if they were doing it for him or because they were losing power. He cupped his ear and didn't hear any engines at all.

The little PRC-10 crackled: "*Tughril*, this is the assistance party. Our engines just crapped out."

God damn it. At the worst possible time. "All stop," he snapped to Irshad. Into the walkie-talkie, "This is *Tughril*. Abandon the engine spaces and stand by the boat." He clicked off and yelled to Doolan, "To *Sant' Oreste*: 'Disregard previous plan. Request you heave to in your current position and begin pumping now.' "

He couldn't see it, but in a few minutes he smelled it. The petroleum reek of lubricating oil, coming down the wind. As it reached them, he felt the seas smoothing, gentling, as if a sheet of plastic had been glued down on the swells. It was almost miraculous, but he didn't stop to contemplate it, just snapped, "OK, move in. Keep everybody clear of the nets when we hit. And for Christ's sake, put the smoking lamp out."

The heaving black sea between them narrowed as Irshad took her in. They drifted together so slowly it looked almost tender, a gradual embracing one ship of the other, but then metal clanged and snapped from aft as the outfolded deck-edge nets hit the side of the ferry.

Lenson took a deep breath and swung the loud hailer up. "Passengers first! No baggage! Passengers first! Take your time. We have plenty of time." Which wasn't true at all. It was going to be a close race between the other ship slipping away stern-first and capsizing, but he didn't want to trigger panic. He passed the megaphone to Irshad, who repeated the message in songlike Arabic. Watching the upturned faces, mouths open as if drinking the words. A keen wavered into the wind, followed by a babble of voices.

Then it began. A slow, wriggling stampede, only marginally channeled by the united efforts of the ferry's crew and *Tughril*'s. Pistolesi lifted an old woman, black cloth flapping around her frail body, and half threw her across the gap between the rolling hulls. Doolan and the fantail party were tossing cargo nets over the moving metal junk into which the seesaw crashing and rolling of the mismatched hulls were rapidly grinding the nets and lifelines. Dan stood on the wing, staring down as the black tide of pilgrims advanced like ants transferring from rocking leaf to leaf in a storm. Some drew back from the passage, clutching bundles or luggage as they glanced terrified between the ferry, whose stern was now nearly submerged, and *Tughril*'s afterdeck. Others shoved their way forward, clambering hand over hand out over the tossing bridge, hesitating at the brink, then hurling themselves forward. An obese fellow in a long white shift tripped as he stepped across, stumbled, flung his arms out with a hoarse despairing cry. He was plummeting for the gap between the rolling hulls when Chief Mellows leaned out, swept down a muscular arm, and hoisted him straight up as effortlessly as a power winch.

Dan took another deep breath of the choking oil smell, watching helplessly from above as the weird uluation broke out again among the huddled pilgrims. He didn't understand the words they were crying below him, but he could guess. They were praying, and they were right. He'd done all he could. They'd all done all they could, on this dark night.

Their lives were in the hands of Allah now.

11

KARACHI, PAKISTAN

THE hot wind smelled of petroleum and swamp, mud and smoke and shit and dust. On the way in they'd passed a refinery, then a railroad yard; to port stretched low black mangroves and, closer in, miles of exposed and drying mud. Dan wasn't sure why they were going in at low tide, but then, he hadn't spoken to any of the Pakis for days. The pier walked slowly closer, grimy worn concrete left over from British times. Forward of it a steam dredge was puffing and pumping, not far from where *Tughril* was expected to go alongside, if one judged by the men leaning against the bollards.

Dan stared down from the main deck, the only place outside the skin of the ship he was allowed to go. His stateroom, the wardroom, and the main deck. Since the ferry incident, Khashar had restricted all the U.S. officers to their quarters, forbidding them to set foot on the bridge or CIC. An enforced leisure cruise, without the shuffleboard and dance extravaganza.

They'd debarked the passengers at Jedda, robed in black and chattering to one another, carrying the bundles and cheap suitcases that despite all Irshad's and Dan's shouted warnings they'd insisted on pushing or carrying across with them when they abandoned the *Al Qiaq*. Which had apparently gone down, because the salvage tug that had reached her position a couple of hours after the frigate had cast off, having embarked all her passengers and crew, had found no sign of her. He tried to console himself with that: not a single life had been lost and only three injured, one fractured pelvis and two twisted ankles. That helped, to think they'd rescued nearly three hundred people from certain death.

But here they were at last. The passage was at an end.

His seabag and B-4 were already packed and a set of civvies laid out for the taxi or bus or however the local security assistance guys had set up for them to get to the airport. A few hours and they'd be on their way.

The pier drifted nearer and beyond it the flat mass of city. The mysterious East. Only from here it looked pretty workaday, the industrial face every port city presented to the arriving seaman: railyards, water towers, oil tanks. Only needled minarets and an occasional dome gave any clue to what lay beyond.

The first hint something unexpected was going on was when a silver Mercedes turned onto the pier, accompanied by two covered army trucks. The trucks stopped and troops began jumping down. Chief Mellows, who had come up to watch beside him, said, "You know what's going on over there, sir?"

"Damned if I know, Marsh," he told the master-at-arms, then shaded his eyes, staring in disbelief across to the pier. "Hey. You see who I see? There in the civilian clothes and the big hat?"

"I can't really say, sir; eyesight ain't what it used to be. Where you looking?"

Dan shaded his eyes. "I thought I saw Commander Juskoviac." It had certainly looked like him, in a blue windbreaker and the flamboyant straw Panama Greg liked to wear on liberty. But that made no sense. Dan had left the former XO behind and never missed him—in fact, quite the reverse.

When the brow went over, the soldiers presented arms. A white-uniformed dignitary emerged from the Mercedes, followed by another character in a business suit. They marched up the brow, looking grim.

"Your presence is requested in the captain's cabin," the messenger told Dan a few minutes later.

When he knocked at Khashar's door they were all there. All wore war faces, and the smoky atmosphere was hostile. As he entered, a bulky form in whites and broad-barred shoulder boards, a familiar enraged face, swung to him.

Khashar said, "Here he is. I was explaining to your attaché here, Lenson, your role in the near-rebellion of my crew."

Dan said carefully, still at attention, "I'm not aware of any rebellion, Captain. Nor have I ever intended you any disrespect."

The man in the suit cleared his throat and introduced himself as Capt. Marion Sasko, the assistant U.S. naval attaché to Pakistan. The man in uniform was Capt. Ahmed I. Uddin, Chief of Staff, Pakistani Fleet.

Uddin said heavily, "Sit down, Commander. Captain Khashar: Is this rebellion or mutiny the subject of an official report? Or is it a figure of speech, meant to illustrate the depth of your disappointment with this officer, while he was under your command?"

Khashar hesitated, and in that moment Dan knew he had never reported any such thing, nor would he. To do so would be to admit he'd so estranged his crew and even his officers that they preferred the direction of a foreigner to his. Finally he chain-lit another cigarette without answering. Uddin said, "Now, how long will you require to offload your crew, officers, official publications, cryptographic materials, personal gear, and all ammunition?"

"I have not yet been ordered to do so," said Khashar.

Uddin resumed speaking, but now in Urdu. Dan didn't follow it, but Sasko leaned forward to slip him a photocopied message. When he lifted his eyes he had the picture.

The transfer was on hold. Because of Benazir Bhutto's avowal of a previously secret nuclear weapon development program, all transfers of U.S. weapons, ships, and aircraft to Pakistan had been frozen under the terms of the Pressler Amendment.

Uddin turned to him. "Commander, are you up to speed on all this?"

"Uh, this is the first I've heard. You mean we're taking the ship back? But we already transferred it."

Sasko: "It was a lease, not a permanent transfer. The contract always contained provisions for early termination."

Uddin said, "That is not quite correct. The provisions for

termination, I do not recall the exact terminology, but they state that the material involved may revert only for certain reasons, such as the U.S. needing the ship in case of war or the receiving country not meeting the lease payment. Which case is it, Captain Sasko? War or nonperformance? And why *now*? I am sure you have known about our nuclear programs for years, with your wonderful satellites."

"I would say noncompliance with the nonproliferation pact."

"Which no nation bordered by China and India could dare take seriously. We have invested several million dollars in acquiring this ship and the others scheduled to follow her. This is extremely offensive to my government. However, in the interests of continuing a defense relationship that has been of value to both sides for many years, I have been directed by my service to acquiesce in *Tughril*'s temporary relinquishment. Contrary to my own instincts in the matter. We insist, however, that we retain title, and if this matter is not resolved in a reasonable period of time, we will pursue restitution in the appropriate diplomatic venues and in U.S. and international courts."

Dan waited as heavy silence larded the too-warm air. Finally he cleared his throat. "Uh, maybe I misunderstood, but you mentioned something about off-loading ammunition."

Uddin barely turned his head. "The ship herself may have been leased, but the ordnance aboard was clearly purchased outright. We own it, and our personnel are setting up to off-load it now."

"You're not taking my ammunition!"

Three four-stripers glared at him simultaneously. Khashar succeeded in getting the first word out. "You see. This is the sort of 'cooperation' I have had to put up with."

"Relax, Lieutenant Commander," Sasko said warningly, extending a hand as if to hold the others back from physically attacking Dan. "This will all be settled at a higher level than ours."

Dan set his teeth, forcing himself back into his chair. They were retaliating for losing the ship by taking every round of ammo aboard. "Well—I understand that, but look; you've got to leave me something for self-defense. Fifty-cal, at the very least. Some of the twenty-mil."

No one answered him. The attaché said, looking away, "It's unpleasant for all concerned. But the bottom line: As the senior officer on scene, I have verbal direction for Commander Lenson to assume duties as OIC, receive an additional draft of augmentees, and get under way at once. You will not permit your men to go into town, Lenson. Anti-American sentiment is very high at the moment."

"Meaning, they would be torn apart," Uddin said, as if he felt a certain satisfaction at the prospect.

GRAY GMC trucks showed up half an hour later, and the Pakistanis began shifting ammunition to them. Dan made sure Doolan was on deck enforcing safety precautions, then went down to his stateroom and started punching the pubs to put together the reports he had to make. He kept glancing at the phone, expecting a call from Khashar. Despite their differences, he expected some sort of turnover, even if frosty. But it never came. When he gave up at last and phoned the CO's cabin, no one picked up.

He got his cap and went out on the main deck. Tosito and Zabounian were watching the last of the forty-mil going over in cases, two sailors to a case. Troops watched stone-faced from the pier, automatic rifles slung ready to hand. "You seen the captain?" Dan asked them.

"Aren't you him?" said Zabounian.

"I mean Khashar."

"Special K left with the chief of staff. Took the log with him, too. I started a fresh one. One question: What's our name now? *Gaddis* or *Tughril*?"

"Make it *Gaddis* again," said Dan.

"They leaving us any ammo at all, Skipper?" Tosito asked him.

"We might have a couple of clips left for the quarterdeck pistols."

"You serious, sir?"

"Well, not quite. The small-arms ammunition and the pyrotechnics are still ours, but that's it. I tried to talk them out of a self-defense allotment of the heavier stuff, but there wasn't any give. Dave, I put together a draft logistics request message. Check it out and add what else we need; give it to Captain Sasko in the wardroom." He took a breath, tried to shake himself into something resembling an in-charge mode. "We better get hot. They mentioned augmentees, but we can't wait. They want us out of here ASAP. I'll call Jim and make sure he has a steaming watch. If you can take the bridge and Chick the deck gang—"

"There's somebody coming," said Tosito.

A bus was trundling down the pier, weaving through the departing ordnance trucks. The troops flagged it down, climbed aboard, then waved it through. Men in civvies, white and black but unmistakably American from their size and clothes and the way they carried themselves. They filed up the brow, lugging seabags and suitcases.

A familiar voice from behind him. Juskoviac, in khakis now, rendering a reluctant salute. Dan returned it with the same lack of enthusiasm.

"I didn't volunteer for this," were the first words out of his ex-exec's mouth.

"I didn't either, Greg. But here we are. Are you listening?"

Sullenly: "I'm listening."

"You know these men? Where they came from?"

"Whoever didn't want 'em, far as I know."

"I see. Well, get them into their berthing areas. Get 'em into uniform. Pass the word: under way in three hours. Tell Jim to fuel as quickly as possible. Have Chick inventory every round we have left. Dave, see what consumables you can scare up and get that logistics request off. Muster everybody on the fantail at eleven hundred for word."

At 1100 the crew, or what he had for one, fell in for muster, instruction, and inspection. Dan looked them over, noting the paucity of officers and chiefs. He had Chick Doolan, Jim Armey, Dave Zabounian. Engelhart, with his

melancholy visage. And now Juskoviac, already looking
cheerful and aggressive again, which meant absolutely zip.
He had Compline, Tosito, and Mellows. Sansone, too. It
was time to fleet him up to chief and damn the paperwork.
Not a heavy command structure and a damn light crew to
go to sea with.

He took five minutes to welcome the new men. He made
sure they had bunks and were assigned to divisions. Once
they got to sea he'd promulgate a watch, quarter, and station
bill, set up watch sections, and shake things down into
steaming order. He went on to the tasking that Sasko had
passed verbally, with the promise of official orders from
CINCPAC—Commander in Chief, Pacific—to follow
shortly.

He said dryly, pitching his voice to carry over the creak
of seagulls and the talking that would not stop in the ranks,
"Since the withdrawal of deployed forces for Desert Shield
started, piracy has flared up in the Singapore area. Cargo
ships, tankers, and yachts have been boarded, crews killed,
cargoes and even ships stolen. In the most recent incident, a
Dutch captain and Filipino first officer were shot on the
bridge by pirates who emptied a tanker's safe.

"Local nations thought they had a handle on the situation by leaning on Jakarta, resulting in twenty Indonesians
being shot. And it did stop, for a while. But now that most
of the Seventh Fleet has deployed to the Gulf, it's broken
out again, and now the gangs are more ruthless and better-
organized.

"Right now State and UN authorities are trying to coordinate combined action against the pirates. But what's left
of the Pac Fleet has to stick close to Korea, in case things
heat up there.

"That leaves us as the only readily available force for
antipirate work. So we are getting under way in one hour,
first stop: Singapore. Detailed directions will follow, but it
is most likely we will take our place in an ad hoc task force
made up from those states that border the China Sea and
Malacca Straits area.

"Are there any questions?"

The men stared back at him, the new drafts wearing the tough, unimpressed faces sailors shipped when they joined a new command. He nodded to Juskoviac. "Take charge and dismiss the men. Sea detail at noon sharp."

Sixty minutes later, he stood on the bridge and looked around slowly, still unable to believe it. Then he pressed the switch on the 21MC. "Main control, bridge."

"Main control aye."

"Ready up, Jim?"

"Ready to answer all bells, Skipper." Armey sounded relieved, too. "But you know, they wouldn't furnish fuel. We're down to fifty-two percent."

"We've still got diesel we can burn, right? For the motor generators?"

"Yeah, we still got that."

"And you know, I can't blame them. It really was their ship."

"Well, it's ours again now." For the first time since Dan had known him, the engineer sounded almost relaxed.

Dan clicked the button twice and went out on the wing. The line handlers on the pier were gone. The tug was gone, too. The Pakis weren't making anything easy. Well, he could understand that, too.

"Take in all lines!" he yelled down, and Topmark began shouting orders. The last dripping line snaked up through the fairleads, and yellow water burbled as the screw began to revolve. The pier fell away, and the ship that was now his again slowly wheeled, pointing her bow toward the flat blue edge beyond Manora Point as from the mast, once more, the Stars and Stripes blazed out like white smoke and red fire in a steady wind from the sea.

TNTF

12

01° 09' N, 103° 51' E: THE STRAITS OF SINGAPORE

THE humid air was in the high eighties. Rain that smelled of petroleum smoke and decaying vegetation was pouring out of a gray sky, drumming and whooshing on *Gaddis*'s forecastle and windshields as if she were cycling through a Robo Wash. Dan stood irresolute at the chart table, having penciled in a course curling in around Sentosa Island to the pilot pickup point.

He felt wrung out and groggy, not just from the tropic heat some seventy miles from the equator but also from having been awake for two days and nights. The trek south along the coast of India, then east past Sri Lanka and across to the Nicobars had been routine till then. But a cracked bilge pump casing followed by a night passage of the Strait of Malacca didn't make for calm nerves.

A cracked casing could ruin a skipper's sleep all by itself, since if it gave way it could flood the engine room in a matter of minutes; but the nighttime run through the strait had been the capper. The traffic separation scheme required westbound traffic to hug the Malaysian side of the deepwater channel and eastbound ships the coast of Sumatra, to the south. He could deal with weirdly lighted local fishing craft, crossing traffic, strong tidal currents, and numerous shoals and sandbanks. But around 0200, a huge contact had detached itself from the glowworm-green parade across the scope and cut due south, into the eastbound lane. The effect was like a tractor-trailer plowing across a median into oncoming rush-hour traffic, except that heavily laden tankers and containerships have no brakes. Ships had backed and veered in all directions, and from a frictionless flow shipping had splintered into chaos for hours, rammed even tighter by the still-incoming pressure at either end of the strait. At one point a huge supertanker had come barreling down on *Gaddis* as she hugged the ten-fathom curve against Bengkalis Island. Somehow they'd missed each other, the frigate crowded into water so shallow Armey had called up telling him they were sucking mud into the intakes and they'd have silted exchanger tubes if he didn't get into deeper water. And Dan shouting back to get everybody topside fast if he heard the collision alarm. But somehow they'd squeezed past each other, the tanker towering over them in the dark, then gradually fading to a shrinking stern light. And after some hours of the Vessel Traffic Information Service manager shouting himself hoarse over Channel 73, the scattering of shiplights, like confused and wandering stars, had finally resumed their steady plod east and west, welding Asia and Europe and the Americas with a bridge of floating steel.

And now dawn and heat and the monsoon wind pushing black clouds trailing rain like the stinging tentacles of Portuguese men-of-war across the blue-green hills of Sumatra. The prickly scatter of island returns on the radar and ahead the tip of Malaysia and the city-state where he hoped for fuel and parts and ammo. Without them, he wasn't going anywhere. And orders; he needed orders and a chat with the local authorities.

Ah, the joys of command. This was what he'd wanted, wasn't it?

The funny thing: despite it all, it was.

Scrubbing his face hard with his palms, he forced himself to concentrate once again.

BY noon they were clipped into a back pocket of the world's second busiest port, moored outboard of a worn-out breakbulk whose rusty indented sides looked down on *Gaddis*'s pilothouse. When he was satisfied the lines were right, he passed "secure the engines" down to Main Control. The rain had let up temporarily, trailing its skirts inland, and he looked across the south basin at a shining mass of glass and steel rising from a jumble of particolored roofs. To seaward spread a second city of anchored ships, scores of them riding the dark green surface. Beyond Singapore low hills rolled into the distance, the deep light-sucking hue of rain forest and jungle. Dan remembered how the Japanese had bicycled down out of them in 1941 to take the "impregnable" fortress from the rear. Not Western imperialism's finest moment.

The squealer, while he was musing on history. He snatched it off the bulkhead. "Captain."

"Sir, Chick here, on the quarterdeck. Fella down here in a boat says he's the consul."

"Great, great! Just the boy I was going to try to find. Take him to my stateroom. Tell Usmani coffee and cake, if we have any."

THE consul was extremely meager and almost seven feet tall, an astonishing apparition whose head brushed the acoustic-tiled overhead of Dan's cabin. He wore a gray silk pin-striped suit and carried a calfskin briefcase and a furled umbrella. They shook hands. "Dan Lenson, commanding."

"Pleased to meet you, Captain. Derek Kingon, U.S. consul to the Republic of Singapore. Our younger visitors call me 'Klingon.' I really have no idea why." Kingon had a Boston accent so pronounced and nasal that for a moment Dan's brain hesitated, trying to decode what he had just said. But at last it computed, and he waved Usmani in as the messman appeared at the door. The Pakistani set down coffee and a dish of crackers—supplies were getting short—and left, easing the door to. Dan drained his cup and poured another from the carafe, fighting to regain some alertness. Kingon eyed the crackers doubtfully, took a perfunctory sip at the coffee.

"Well, and how may I be of service? I can recommend some tour companies. Your crew will want to see Pasir Panjang and the Tiger Balm Gardens. All guides Tourist Promotion Board–certified. If you can give me some idea of how many—"

The squealer. Dan said, "Excuse me," and grabbed it. "CO."

"Fuel barge alongside, Skipper. They want to know how we're going to pay."

"Tell him he can start pumping, I'm with the consul now and we're going to discuss that." Dan hung up. "Sorry, Mr. Klingon, I mean, damn it, *Kingon*, you were saying . . ."

"Tours, about how many men you would be needing tickets for—"

"I'm sorry." Dan suddenly felt apprehensive. "We can talk about tours later, but I'd hoped you'd have instructions for me. I've been making reports daily, asking for orders, but I haven't gotten any response. I left Karachi for here on verbal instructions. It would make me feel a lot better to get confirmation. We need to talk about how to charge our fuel and water and port fees, too."

"How are your communications?"

"Not good. I'd like to send a cable or something back to Pensacola, if you could help me do that. For the last few days there didn't seem to be anyone on the circuit when we were ready to transmit. I've been sending my sitreps anyway, in case the problem's in my receiver, but I want to send some kind of land-line wake-up call."

"I can take care of telegrams or telex, if you would like me to. As for your fuel and so forth, well, all I can say is that Navy ships often call here. The Regional Contracting Center arranges supplies, I believe. I'd contact them with any problems in that arena." The consul waited, cup poised. "Anything else?"

"You really don't have anything for me? Have you checked at your office?"

Kingon smiled. "I'm sorry, Captain. I wish I did. All I can suggest is the regional Navy center, as I said—"

"You wouldn't have a number, would you?"

"Oh. Certainly!" Kingon brightened, taking out a notebook. He gave Dan two numbers, for admin and officer in charge, and a home number for the OIC as well.

Kingon moved on into what was apparently a set speech.

Singapore was clean, efficient, and relatively free of corruption, but at the same time, it was not far from a police state in some respects. There was one party, the People's Action Party. Criticism of it or of the prime minister was not tolerated. Drugs, long hair on men, and any sort of public rowdiness would attract instant police attention. One could be fined up to five hundred dollars Singaporean for jaywalking outside the double yellow crossing lines, for failing to flush a public toilet, for smoking in a public place. "You might have heard about an American teenager, his parents are residents here, who was publicly caned for possession of marijuana. Mr. Lee Kuan Yew is very concerned about narcotics. Warn your crew that both possession and attempted purchase are illegal here. The punishments are quite draconian."

Dan started to say he didn't have any drug activities aboard, but then he remembered how when he'd been an XO one of the hospitalmen on *Van Zandt* had not only been buying hash ashore and selling it to the crew, but had also been looting morphine from sick bay. The point being just now he had a lot of men aboard he didn't know very well.

That made him think of Usmani, and he said, "I'll make sure they know that, about the liberty environment. Another question. I discovered a stowaway on board after I left Karachi. Hiding under one of the RHIBs. The man who served us a moment ago, actually. He's a Pakistani national. If I might turn him over to you—"

Kingon grimaced and was shaking his head before Dan had gotten past the word *stowaway*. The consul absolutely could not take custody, had neither police powers to confine a man nor funds to send him home. "Nor will the Singaporean authorities accept him. Stowaways are a real headache. No one wants them, and yet the shipowner—I'm thinking merchant captains now, but you're under the same obligation—is required to afford them humanitarian treatment. I'm very much afraid he's going to be your problem for a while. There are two solutions. The legal one is to retain him aboard until you encounter a ship under the Pakistani flag, a warship, I guess—you said he was navy?—and turn him over to its commanding officer."

"What's the illegal one?"

"Give him an opportunity to escape and look the other way. Only I'd wait till I was somewhere else than here; the island's so small and the authorities are so efficient, you'd have him back in hours."

Dan said, "Well, he seems happy enough to be aboard, at least for the moment. Thanks for the warning, about the drug laws and so forth. I'll have my XO put it out to the men. And thanks for the offer to send the cable. I'll write that down right now and you can take it ashore with you."

HE let the starboard watch go ashore at 1300, after warning them along the lines Kingon had laid out. As they trooped up the brow to cross the merchie, boisterous at the prospect of a few hours off the ship, Chief Compline reported that the phone connection was complete. Dan hunched over the little linoleum-surfaced desk in the port-side vestibule and listened to the phone burr at both numbers for the USN contact team. When he tried the home number, a Chinese-sounding female answered. She told him everyone was out. Dan left a brief message saying USS *Oliver Gaddis* was in port, asking someone to call back as soon as possible, but he wasn't totally certain the woman understood.

After which he went out on the fantail and stood irresolutely next to the 40mm tub, wondering if it was going to rain again, wondering what the hell he should do next. He was desperately sleepy but too wound up to turn in now. If he tried, he'd only stare at the overhead for hours. The only answer that suggested itself was to go ashore and get some things done and perhaps take a look around while he was at it. He called down and asked Jim Armey if he had any plans. The engineer said he wanted to visit a marine supply company that might have spare parts for the pump.

"BAN Leong Marine Supply," Armey told the cabbie, who seemed to be Chinese, as, indeed, most of the people they had seen so far, walking down the pier and then checking in at the port captain's office, had been. He folded his bony length wearily back into the seat. "It's in Tuas Tech Park, if that helps."

"Tuas Tech Park, Ban Leong, sure, we go there chop-chop," said the driver. Dan wasn't sure if he was making fun of them or just speaking pidgin.

"She's sure as hell got built up," Armey said, staring out at the enormous buildings at the city center. They were modern and featureless, geometric and inhuman as electronic components. But closer to ground level, as the cab navigated along painfully clean roads, was the surging life of millions of people crowded onto a tiny island. Their alert black eyes met Dan's as they edged through the street. He caught the glances of attractive Asian women, their features reminding him of Susan's. Then the battered but clean old Honda pulled out onto a modern expressway and headed west. And without any urging or anything on his part Armey suddenly started telling him about coming here in the early eighties, when he'd deployed to the Indian Ocean and West-pac aboard USS *Sterett*, CG-31. "I pulled my first liberties in Singapore and Hong Kong. I was just a kid. I did some stupid things."

"Who doesn't?"

"I mean really stupid. Things that hurt people."

Dan sat astonished. It was the first statement of a personal nature he'd heard out of his chief snipe. Finally he ventured, "I pulled mine in the Med. You're young, you screw up sometimes. What the hell, Jim—you learned from it, right?"

Armey didn't answer, and when he looked at the engineer's reflection where he had pressed his face against the glass Dan saw, to his amazement, that he was close to weeping.

When they were done at the chandler's the taxi dropped them back near the waterfront. Armey had clammed up again by then. He was headed to Arab Street to do some shopping. He'd most likely be there a while. Dan took the

hint and said he'd check out Change Alley, have an early
dinner, then head back to catch up on sleep. When he
glanced back a moment later, Armey was lost in the crowd,
gone, which seemed odd; he stood a head above nearly all
the Singaporeans. He'd ducked down some side street or
into some shopfront.

Suddenly Dan realized he was alone.

It was always a shock, after weeks or months at sea. The
seaman, the officer, even the commander, who had more
privacy than any other aboard, still lived surrounded by others, directed, informed, hemmed in both physically and by
the manifold forms of duty. Maybe it was a spiritual discipline. Certainly it chastised the will, for good or ill, because
from waking to sleep there need never be any question as to
what you "wanted" to do. "You," as an individual with individual desires, barely existed. Sailors even tended to go "on
liberty"—revealing terminology—in conspecific groups,
not as individuals, taking the ship with them in microcosm
even when ashore. So that now, standing sweating in civilian slacks and light shirt on a street corner on Raffels Quay
Road, he felt the same existential dread a marrow cell
might, removed from the body and placed in a rich nutrient
solution.

A shrine he entered increased his unease. It was
thronged with Chinese in bright yellow T-shirts banging
gongs and setting off firecrackers. Through the noise and
heat and smoke, the smells of gunpowder and incense, joss
sticks and sweat, a pudgy man was slicing his flesh with a
pair of swords before a statue of a scarlet-faced, grinning
god surrounded by a forest of flickering red candles. No one
objected to Dan's presence, but he left hastily and headed
back toward the waterfront, through twisting streets that became steadily narrower and more thronged. Till he reached
the oldest section of town.

Change Alley was an irregular roadway lined on either
side with shop houses, two or three merchants selling
watches, cameras, boom boxes, small cabinetries, porcelain, carpets from the same open storefront. The streets

were nearly impassable with human beings, spilling off the sidewalks into the roadway despite the rules. He priced some toys, thinking of Nan, then remembered: She was in junior high now. A diminutive saleswoman chattered to him in Dutch, tying brightly colored silk scarves around his wrists. After prolonged bargaining, he settled on a teak jewelry cabinet inlaid with mother-of-pearl.

Then he stood with the wrapped gift under his arm, staring about at the black-haired river. The Singaporeans had obviously overcome any need for personal space between human bodies. Evening was arriving across the sea. Beyond expressways and the spindly inverted Ls of gantry cranes, standing like watchful herons above building sites, the sky was gradually darkening, the night stealing toward them out of the East like a black falcon spreading its wings over the earth.

HE was having dinner in a storefront restaurant in Little India, eating a flame-hearted curry off banana leaf, when a white-bearded man in a rumpled lightweight suit dropped at an adjoining table with a grunt. Pale blue eyes surrounded by sun wrinkles surveyed Dan and the package at his feet. Then the man muttered gruffly, almost unwillingly, as Dan wiped his fingers, "A brass bird cage is my guess. Arab Street."

"Actually, it's a jewelry chest. For my daughter."

"Sorry to interrupt. Shouldn't. Bad habit."

"Not at all."

"You're the skipper of that Yank tin can, are ye not?"

On his assent the other leaned forward, crimping his fingers in a hard salutation. "Eric Wedlake, master of MV *Marker Eagle*. I'm the white ro-ro just forward of you. Was inspecting my deck stowage as you slipped in this morning. Saw ye on your bridge. Have not seen your ship before, though, and I've spent a good deal of time out here. And where are you in from?"

Dan invited Wedlake to join him, and they fell into conversation. Wedlake advised him on the *murtaba*, and they ate companionably for a time, the Britisher alternating between asking him about *Gaddis* and telling him about himself. He'd been born in a small port in Somerset called Watchet-on-the-Mud, on the Bristol Channel, taking in esparto grass and pulp for a paper mill and exporting iron ore to South Wales. The very town, he said, on which Samuel Coleridge based "The Rime of the Ancient Mariner."

"You probably know how the antihero shot the albatross, et cetera, et cetera, and how he lived to retell the tale at a wedding at the 'church on the kirk,' or something like that. When I was young, I used to sing in the choir of that same church. Then when I was a bit older Mum moved to the Pembroke Dock–Milford Haven area for a while. Had a stint in the Royal Navy, on submarines east of Suez. And then Mr. Eden decided we had no business here and left it to you. Which perhaps you haven't done all that badly, though Vietnam was unfortunate." He stopped himself. "Perhaps I shouldn't say that, considering, no doubt, that you served there."

Dan pulled out his wallet and tried to convert Singapore dollars to U.S. "I was on the east coast then, at the tail end of it. The Atlantic coast."

"I do recall running ammunition in to Saigon, under a Captain Surtees. Captain Surtees surely loved his whiskey. Sailed with a barricade of crates of it, around his desk. Will never forget old Surtees. So you're here to protect us against the godless communists?"

"Actually, we're supposed to be linking up with an antipirate task force."

Wedlake beamed, mopping his shining brow with a napkin. "The U.S. Navy, fighting pirates in the China Sea. And about bloody time someone did! I'm headed back to the cow, myself. Care to stop up for a scotch? Maybe I can pass on some information you'd not mind knowing. Since you're new to these waters."

Dan considered. He was sleepy, but not so far gone he couldn't put it off for another hour. That would still get him in the sack by eight. At last he said, "I'll pass on the whiskey, but I wouldn't mind seeing your ship. I did just want to stop by *Gaddis* for a moment, see if any orders have come through."

DOOLAN, who had the command duty, said there was no news, no orders, and no one had returned any calls. The duty section was at work, painting over the Pakistani numbers at the bow with haze gray, but they'd discovered they were out of white paint to put their former hull number back on. Dan told Doolan to add it to Zabounian's shopping list ashore, then recrossed the breakbulk and joined Wedlake on the pier.

The rain resumed as they headed up the broad concrete pier toward the *Marker Eagle*. Seen from astern, the roll-on, roll-off looked huge. She was fairly new but less meticulously kept than a warship. Rust streaked bloody tears down from the stern chocks, and her hull paint was pocked with black half-moons where tugs had lipsticked her. Her stern ramp was angled in to serve as a wide gangway. As they reached the shelter of her hull, Wedlake nodded to a black-bearded Sikh in a turban, who sat tilted back in a chair, barely glancing up from a portable TV that was showing a soccer match. His hairy legs bulged from Bermuda shorts; basketball socks sagged above greasy high-tops. An aluminum baseball bat leaned against a sheave. Dan followed the master's vigorous bulk up ladders and through deserted hot passageways painted off-white, then down an access corridor.

A portrait of the Queen hung in a lobby area, above a cap table with a silver dish. Dan eyed the dish with regret. A chance at last to leave his calling card, and he hadn't brought one. A welcome chill met them past a steel door with patches of fresh paint along the hinge area.

Inside the roomy sea cabin an air conditioner hummed its self-absorbed *om*, dispelling the smell of cooked metal. Dan noted carved teak furniture, a large modern-style oil of a harbor by night screwed to the bulkhead, and a side door, no doubt leading to a sleeping area. Wedlake's suede bucks whispered on carpet. He pulled back a curtain to reveal rain trickling down what was very nearly a picture window, protected, outside the glass, by vertical steel bars. Beyond it spread the strait, islands dark on the horizon, passing ships gray shadows in the rain. "Wife will be back shortly," he said, noticing Dan eyeing a woman's sweater hanging on the back of a chair. "Wanted to get her hair done properly. One thing we can't do aboard, though we had a chap from Thailand who did a decent job. Lost him in Hong Kong, unfortunately. You married, Lenson?" His voice became hollow, and Dan, turning, saw his head ducked into a dry bar, the gleam of glass and chrome.

"Was once. I'm seeing a woman in Washington now."

"Now, that will be with ice if I'm not mistaken. Don't tell anyone, but I favor Suntory." He held up a bottle labeled with a bright red flower. "Japanese, but somehow when they make this they give the impression they wear kilts."

"A Coke would work. Or ginger ale. I've had to taper off on the drinking." As he always did around Britishers, Dan heard his own diction changing.

A refrigerator door sucked closed; ice shattered. "Takes a wise man to know that. Haven't had that problem myself, but seen it in far too many. At sea and not. Happen to have Schweppes; will that do? . . . Well then." Wedlake handed Dan the glass and plumped down on one end of a sofa. "To pirates. You'll have to excuse me; as well as being an old China hand I'm something of a history buff. Have you ever heard of Rear Admiral J. R. Hill? Met him in London. Wonderful man, did a fine book about privateers and pirates. Had an encounter with them myself."

"You have?" Dan said, but Wedlake was off.

"Course, there've been pirates in the China Sea for centuries. Most any fisherman will turn pirate, if the opportunity offers. In my view. Plenty of inlets and channels to hide in along the coast. So strong now and again they could dictate terms to the imperial government. We battled them all through the eighteenth and nineteenth centuries. One of my forebears was at the Battle of Tylo Bay. Which no doubt you recall."

"Sorry, can't say I do."

"Eighteen-fifty-five, and odd you never heard of it; the U.S. Navy was there along with us, USS *Powhatan*."

Obviously enjoying himself, Wedlake replenished his glass, then launched into a long tale about a punitive expedition in the Zhu Jiang in which the U.S. and Royal Navies had cooperated. One Sir Castlemayne Hellowell had been part of the expedition, which had recaptured several merchant ships, killed one Lee Afye, the pirate chieftain, and dispersed those pirates who had not been shot, blown apart, or drowned in the action. Dan caught himself starting to yawn, disguised it just in time as a cough.

"But now the White Ensign's gone from these seas. More's the pity. I should have been glad to have them about when we were boarded last February."

"You were boarded? Where?"

But just then heels tapped outside. Wedlake rose as a wan-looking woman in a light cotton dress burst in. She was no longer young but was still striking, with spindly arms and ankles, a pointed chin, a quick sparrow's way of moving, and an expressive, mobile mouth. "I'm back, and they said there wasn't any such thing as a—" Then she saw Dan. "I didn't know you had a guest. A handsome one, too."

"Darling, this is Captain Lenson, from the destroyer just aft of us. Let me introduce my wife, Bobbie."

Her hand was cool and firm. "Great haircut," Dan said. "What do you call that?"

"Why, thanks. This is my street-urchin look, I'm afraid."

"Midwest?"

"Abilene, Kansas. My grandpa grew up with Ike Eisenhower. You?"

"Pennsylvania, but I've spent life since hopping around from one navy base to another."

"Bobbie and I met in New York some years ago and kept up our acquaintance. At last I persuaded her to join me."

"When my former husband decided he preferred the company of men," Bobbie said. "Though Eric would never reveal anything that personal. He's the quintessential stuffed-shirt Brit. As you already noticed, I bet."

"Actually, he was holding my interest. Said you'd had a run-in with boarders."

"You told him about the boarding?"

"Just getting to it, my sweet. Shall I fetch you a gin-and, and let you start?"

"Just a short one—actually, just ice water would be better; it's dreadfully hot out there. The boarding. Eric can tell you exactly where; I just know it was somewhere east of here. The first thing we knew was when they appeared on the bridge. Ugly, jabbering little men with guns. They wanted the safe. Once Eric opened it, they duct-taped him. He was rolling around on the floor. Then they wanted the crew's valuables. Once they had those, off they went."

"I was under way at about ten knots, slowed for the changeover in the traffic scheme. Obviously they knew that. I remember passing through a group of lights. I thought they were fishermen."

"They weren't?"

"Rather clever, actually," said Wedlake. "The way they got aboard. Two small boats, a few hundred yards apart. A floating line from one to the other. I steam between, picking up the line on my stem. The small craft are pulled into my shadow, just below my quarter. From there they reach up with long hooked poles and skinny up them, onto my aft deck."

Dan said, "In the Strait of Malacca? A ship was out of control there last night. Came across the dividing line and plowed straight through the eastbound traffic."

"May well have been pirates on the bridge. There are a lot more incidents than get reported. The Russians have it the worst. Their navy has evaporated, and they typically carry plenty of cash. Since no one will take their cheques anymore. . . . Smaller craft, yachts and fishermen, of course, if they are taken over, one might never know, if the crew's killed and thrown overboard. But to cargo shippers, time is money. We can't linger over to make reports, give evidence, and so forth. The demurrage charges alone would kill us.

"But there's sort of a conspiracy of silence about it. So it's only a matter of time before we have some enormous disaster. A liquid natural gas carrier goes astray and rams a passenger liner and explodes. Then we'll see some frantic finger pointing. Till then, the shipowner buys the drinks, and the crew takes the risks." Wedlake sucked his cheek for a moment, then picked up Dan's glass. "Refill?"

"Thanks."

"Since then we've taken a few precautions. When *Marker Eagle* was laid down, no one thought about security. But I've welded steel bars over all the windows and put in extra-heavy doors to the bridge. When we're under way I have cables rigged over cargo hatches and I secure the hinge pins on the weather deck doors. At night a motion sensor turns halogen lights on over the ladders. When we're at anchor, I keep my pumps running to the fire hoses and drill my crew in blasting intruders off the ship with the high-pressure jets. Those will only help if they're unarmed, though."

"Do you carry arms?"

"The IMO recommends we don't arm our crews."

"That's not quite a direct answer, Captain."

"Do you carry nuclear weapons aboard your ship, Captain?"

Dan grinned and said the rote words: "I can neither confirm nor deny the presence of nuclear weapons aboard any U.S. warship."

"So there you have it. What precautions we can take and, as a last resort, a hidey-hole Bobbie can duck into and pull in after herself. I must say it helps me sleep, but it's not a permanent answer."

"What's the permanent answer?"

"Wiping out the hornets in their nests. As my ancestor did, at Tylo Bay."

"No, Eric. Not Bishop Hell-o-well again—"

"He only became a bishop much later, pet—"

"He's already told me that story," Dan assured her. Mrs. Wedlake passed a hand over her hair in mock relief. She had a few years on him, but he still found it hard to take his gaze away from her. With her street-gamine face, erect carriage, and tight-lipped smile, she would have looked perfectly at home on the Champs-Elysées.

"But the Chinese are still the worst threat," Wedlake continued, boring toward what, apparently, he had been waiting all evening to say. "I can cope with these fellows in the straits, now that I know. Keep my speed up and have the lads ready with fire hoses. What I'm not looking forward to is going into Hong Kong again."

"Eric is worried about what happened to a friend of his," Bobbie explained.

"He had the *Hiei Blanco*. Cars, appliances, and manufactured goods, Vietnam to Hong Kong. He was hijacked by men in fatigue uniforms, speaking Chinese. They took her to Kwungtung. Held them for nearly three weeks, without letting them send a letter or make a phone call—like prisoners of war, they were. When they finally let them go, they refused access to the ship. That was six months ago. He still hasn't gotten his ship back, his cargo, even his personal effects."

Dan said, "You said in *uniform*? Are you saying the Chinese government was behind them?"

Wedlake stroked his beard as if it were a small pet. "I shouldn't want to say exactly that. But I've been sailing these waters for twenty-five years now, and I don't believe these boyos are operating freelance. It will be good to have you out there. May restore some sense there's a bobby on the block. . . . Have you admired my wife's painting?" Wedlake hoisted himself laboriously, crossing to the oil. "It's Hong Kong, if you're not familiar with the backdrop."

"Actually, I was looking at it when I came in. You did that?"

"I don't usually do landscapes. I thought it would be fun to try something different."

"Portraits?"

"No," she said.

He took the hint. Glanced at the night outside the window, the twinkle of distant running lights out in the strait, and heaved himself up. "Well . . . thanks for the drink and the talk. It was a nice break. I'd better get back to the ship now, try to catch up on my sleep."

"Understand perfectly; thought you looked a bit peaked," said Wedlake at once. "Let me make a call, have the gangway lowered for you. We take it up when the sun goes down. I'll take you down to the debarkation door."

"An attractive woman. Very bright," he told the captain on the way down. "You're a lucky man."

"Don't I know it. Hoping she'll come along from now on. Wouldn't be a problem for her; she paints in one of the spare crew staterooms." Wedlake blinked, looking puzzled and wary, as if glimpsing something on the horizon he wasn't quite sure of. "There's not so much happiness in life I shouldn't try to grasp what I can. Way I look at it. Well, perhaps we'll see each other again at sea."

"Perhaps so, sir." Dan gave him a salute and headed down the gangway.

GETTING back to *Gaddis*, blinking with suddenly insistent fatigue, he found Doolan speaking with a man on the quarterdeck. The weapons officer saluted as Dan stepped aboard. In civvies, Lenson nodded to them both.

"Sir, this might interest you. Gentleman here says he has orders to report aboard. This is our CO, Dan Lenson."

"Lieutenant Commander Dominick Colosimo, sir."

Dan shook hands, looking Colosimo up and down. He was clean-cut, earnest-looking, fit-looking. "You say you have orders to *Gaddis*, uh, Dominick?"

"Go by Dom, sir. No, sir. Not exactly."

"What exactly do you have?"

Colosimo produced a folded mass of paper and flashed a pink ID card. Dan took it beneath a deck light as Colosimo explained. "I'm a reservist, out of Cincinnati. My orders are to Exercise Oceanic Prospect II. They don't specify the ship I'm to report aboard, but the ord mod says I meet it in Singapore. This is Singapore, and you're the only U.S. Navy ship here."

Dan rubbed his face, trying to focus. "Sounds tenable, but we haven't heard of anything by that name. What kind of exercise is it supposed to be?"

"Anti-pirate operations in the South China Sea."

"Aha," said Doolan, with great satisfaction. "Tell us more."

"The conference is tomorrow, at the Hyatt on Scotts Road. I have a copy of the schedule, and the op order."

"Funny they didn't send us one," said Chick.

"Yeah, I'm getting the impression we're at the far end of a definite informational bottleneck," Dan told him. "We didn't get any answer yet from that cable the consul sent, did we?"

"Not that I know of."

"No response on the sitreps. No orders waiting here. We've got to tap into Fleet Broadcast somehow. I'll just bet somebody at the communications station dicked up and there's fourteen million messages waiting for us we can't get to because we don't have the crypto capability."

Colosimo bent to his briefcase. "You can copy mine if you want, sir. The operations order, I mean."

"I might do that. And you're what, a liaison of some kind?"

"Yes, sir; I write the op orders, then go out to help run the exercise. I'm supposed to attach to the foreign flag officer, but I suspect I'll be reporting to you as well. I've done one of these before, last year. Oceanic Prospect I was in the Mosquito Bay area, between Jamaica and Nicaragua."

Fighting off the urge to fall asleep, Dan went through the op order quickly, picking up the essentials. *Gaddis* was to be part of a multinational task force. The TNTF would rendezvous at such and such a lat and long in the South China Sea and patrol to suppress piracy and conduct such other activities as COMTNTF may direct. "What's *TNTF* stand for?" he asked Colosimo.

"I made that one up. Somebody else asks me, I'd say 'Territorial Neighbor,' meaning they border on pirate-infested seas. But actually it means 'Tiny Nation Task Force.' "

"Cute. Chick, we need four copies of this as soon as possible. Me, the XO, you, and a CIC-slash-bridge copy. Welcome aboard, Dominick. How long will you be with us?"

"Just two weeks' active duty, sir."

"What do you do when you're not Navy Reserving?"

"Well, sir, in real life I do initial public offerings for new companies, selling stock when they go public."

"Oh, yeah? Mr. Juskoviac will put you in a stateroom. We've got plenty open at the moment. Hope you like standing bridge watches. Chick, what else is going on tonight?"

"Mr. Armey came back and a truck and crew came in from Ban Leong and they're all down there welding the crack and getting the pump back together. Oh, and the local cops called. They picked Pistolesi up down on Pink Street. Said he fit the profile of a drug dealer. I had to make a call to the local hoosegow to spring him. They're bringing him back under guard."

Dan said fine. He took a quick tour of the decks, paying particular attention to moorings and fenders, then suddenly checked his watch. He did a time-zone calculation in his head and sat down at the phone in the quarterdeck shack. He was out on his feet, but this was the right time for the Far West. It took twenty minutes to find the right combination of numbers and an operator who would take his phone card. But at length it worked, and he got to talk to Nan for three or four minutes before she went to school. He told her about Singapore, that he loved her, that he'd be sending her something. She sounded less than interested, but it was still good hearing her voice. Finally she said she really had to go or she'd miss the bus. He sat looking at the phone for a few seconds, then decided to try for a double.

But all he got at Blair's apartment in D.C. was her answering machine. Her office phone didn't answer at all. He called the apartment again and left his number and his schedule, told her where he was, to call him back. Even held on for a few seconds after that, hoping she'd come out of the shower, or whatever, and pick up. But it didn't happen.

He stood and stretched, his mind illuminating momentarily with the remembered glory of her naked body. But then that memory was replaced, intercut, with a shutter-flicker image of Bobbie Wedlake's, half-glimpsed, half-imagined through the clinging dress. He blinked, confused, then yawned again, so hard his jaw damn near locked open, and with that simple bodily act utter exhaustion sucked the last erg of energy out of him. Sleep dragged his eyes closed at last, irresistible, undeniable. They were in port. They were safe.

He barely made it to his cabin, barely got his clothes off when it struck, sudden and dark and overwhelming as the black bar of a squall to a craft that has been at sea too long.

13

THE fuel agent was still smiling, but another expression was becoming visible beneath it. He held out the bill again. "Someone must pay. Who will pay, Captain?"

"Let me speak to my supply officer," Dan told him. "Can I get back to you on this? We won't be getting under way today. Hey, we won't run out on you."

The agent hesitated, obviously unwilling to leave it at that. Finally he said, "I will wait, Captain." He went out on the starboard wing, stood watching a gray-black wall of squall that moved south toward Sumatra, or Sumatera, as the charts called it. Behind it, apparently undeterred by the just-departed downpour, traffic zipped by on a parkway built across the shallow green sea.

Dan reached Zabounian in the supply office, asked him to come to the bridge. When he got there, he pointed out to the waiting back. "He wants paid. Now."

Zabounian looked embarrassed. "Well, we got a problem there, Skipper."

"What's the deal, Dave?"

"The thing is, we're broke. I briefed you on the OPTAR fund status after we got under way from Karachi. I was hoping there'd be something in the mail for us here, but there's zip."

The OPTAR was the fund for spare parts and supplies, what a ship ran on. The cash came from fleet funds. Normally the squadron commander maintained the account, setting allowances for each of his ships. *Gaddis* had had an account in Staten Island and Philly, when she'd been part of DESRON Twelve, but they'd spent it down to zero before the decommissioning. After that, Khashar had paid *Tughril*'s bills from Pakistani accounts.

Now they were back on their own. Dan spread his fingers out on the bulkhead, wishing he'd paid more attention to Zabounian's warnings. The financials were dull, but without them a ship didn't steam. Normally the XO kept his eagle eye on them, but Dan was past expecting much on that score. He grunted, "OK, how are we going to take care of this? The fuel part first; we've got the guy standing here with his hand out."

The supply officer recapped how things usually worked. Logistics requests went up the chain of command to CTF 73, the Seventh Fleet support entity that coordinated port visits and went through the bid process to select chandlers. He said he'd sent their request from Karachi, and Dan recalled signing it. "But we never got a reply, and now nobody seems to know who we are."

"What do you mean, nobody knows who we are? We inchopped to Seventh Fleet—"

"We *tried* to. Did you ever see a response? Look; I've been over all this with the NRCC boys here. They say, '*Gaddis* is an Atlantic Fleet ship; report your problems to your own squadron.' I say, 'No, I'm transiting to a PACFLEET area of responsibility, and I need logistic support.' They say, 'Give us the funding data and we'll provide all the support you want. Otherwise, we can't help you.' End of discussion."

"This is ludicrous. Did you talk to the man in charge? Tell him we're in Exercise Oceanic Prospect?"

"Right, I did, and they say it's not a Seventh Fleet exercise. I'm telling you, I arm-wrestled this squid all afternoon."

"So what's the next step?"

"Well, we could use a Gold Ticket. That's a Form Forty-four, emergency procurement. We make it out and give it to the vendor. He takes it to the Contracting Center here in Singapore."

"So why can't we do that?"

"I don't have a number for the fuel account in this port.

We have to have a number, or anybody could come in here and fuel up and say, 'Charge it to the USN.'

"But Mr. See here comes alongside, says he's our boy, so I told him to go ahead and fill 'er up. But he wants payment now and—" Zabounian's face hardened. "I don't have it, sir, that's all, and we're going to have the same problem with everything else we need. I've been standing steaming watches because you said we needed the bodies. And I'm happy to do it, but we can't neglect proper supply procedure. Or when it comes our turn for an inspection—"

Dan reflected sourly that that was all they needed, an inspection. It would be perfect timing for one. Aloud he said, "I know, and you've done great so far, Dave. But where are we going with this? Can we get under way for this Reluctant Dragon, whatever they call this thing?"

"We're getting critical on parts, tools, and consumables. The low-level alarm's going off on rags and toilet paper. We've got a lot fewer mouths aboard, so our dry stores are still pretty good . . . but if we want fresh food and milk, we're going to have to pay for those, too."

"I can't believe this is the first time a Navy ship's ever been in this position, Dave. What's the supply manual say to do, a case like this?"

"Sir, unless it's wartime, I'd say, just sit tight. Let the contact team send a message to Honolulu. Get a firm account number; get some bucks in our billfolds before we poke our nose out of harbor again."

"You're saying this is a showstopper."

"You asked for the book solution."

"I guess I did. But if we're supposed to play in this exercise, I can't see sitting by the pier and saying we can't go because we don't have the right numbers to put on our chits. That isn't the Navy way. What's the non-book solution?"

Zabounian outlined two. He still had, in effect, "checks" from their old DESRON Twelve account. He could charge fuel and consumables to that account and send a message back to Staten Island explaining what they'd done, so the

N-4 there could pass the buck up the chain of command to be routed laterally to Pacific Fleet.

"This vendor might not want to take anything billed to somebody he doesn't know."

"OK, fallback, I fill in a Form Forty-four with numbers out of the air, give it to him, and have him take it over to the contact office. We'll be out of port by that time."

"You mean like forging a check?"

"Well . . . not exactly. The Navy'll pay him. But I got to warn you, either way it could get you in trouble, Skipper."

The fuel agent chose that moment to come in off the wing. Rain roared on the overhead, splattered against the windows, dissolved the world into running streams of liquid light. "Captain, I must go over to the Australian frigate. If you would effect payment now, please."

Dan rubbed his hand over his forehead. "We've got it straightened out. Lieutenant Zabounian will write you a chit on our squadron account."

The agent looked around the interior of the bridge, as if appraising the brass and brightwork, the binoculars slotted in their holders, just in case. Then, to Dan's relief, he bowed. "Thank you very much. I look forward to serving you again when you return to Singapore."

He and Zabounian left. Dan took a short tour around the pilothouse, fighting a gnawing unease as the downpour rose to a hollow roar. Glancing at his watch. He needed to go over to the center tomorrow, get this situation straightened out. This was ridiculous.

The growler. It was Doolan. "Hey, Chick. What you got?"

"Sir, I'm going over to the *Darwin*, see if they got any small-arms ammo. Want to come?"

"Yeah, but we're going to have to head right to the Hyatt after that. I want you to go with me to the presail conference."

"Trop whites?"

"Whites would probably be best for the conference. Take

your rain gear, though; it's coming down hard up here right now."

Doolan said, "Aye," and hung up. Dan stood motionless for a moment, then spun on his heel and clattered down to his cabin.

Usmani wasn't there. Dan checked his watch. It would be 8:00 P.M. in D.C. Maybe Blair would be at her apartment now. A quick change, and he'd try calling again. He was snapping his shoulder boards onto their loops when Juskoviac tapped at his door. Dan said, "Yeah, Greg, what is it? I'm pressed for time right now."

"A problem with Pistolesi."

"I heard he got sent back aboard under guard."

"Right, but just now he's refusing orders."

"What orders? Whose?"

"Mine. I ordered him to stay aboard."

"You restricted him to the ship?"

"Uh—that was what I told him. But he says he's not going to."

Dan started on his ribbons, replacing one that was starting to look grubby. "Well, Greg, you sort of have to impose your will on these guys. One way or the other. I've heard it called leadership."

"It doesn't make a lot of impression on Pistolesi."

Dan sighed, trying to distinguish between unleashing his frustration and trying to motivate the man who stood perfectly willing to obey, but without force, resource, determination, or impetus of his own. Attempting to get anything done through Juskoviac was like trying to throw feathers over a wall. "What do you want me to do about it, XO? You want me to talk to him? Then why are we paying the chiefs and division officers and you? Why don't we just fire all the in-betweens and let me do everything?" Juskoviac started to pout, and Dan gave up. "OK, let me see him. I don't want a mast situation, though. Just have him come up." He reached for the squealer as the exec left.

As Dan finished snapping his cap cover on a few minutes later Pistolesi came in. Sullenness and resistance were plain in the set of his shoulders, the way he came to a halt on the carpet, hat in his hands.

"Pistolesi. How's it going down in the spaces?"

"Shitty, sir. Nobody likes not getting paid."

"Not getting paid? That's the first I've heard of it. You sure of that?"

"We checked our accounts at an ATM when we went ashore yesterday."

"I'll have Mr. Zabounian look into it. Now, how about last night? I heard you hit a cop."

"These little assholes ain't going to tell me what to do. I threw a cigarette butt in a ash can. Only I missed by a couple feet. And then they started hassling me."

"You were warned what kind of place Singapore was. What I heard was that you fit the profile of a drug trafficker."

"Sir, to them that means I needed a haircut. Anyway, everybody there was chewing gum and smoking and spitting. These little prick cops, they pick on me because I'm white—"

"All I want to know is two things. One: did the exec pull your liberty?"

"Yessir, but if he thinks he can—"

"Two: Are you staying aboard tonight, in compliance with that order?"

"No fucking way. I ain't going to—"

"Then I'm confining you until we get under way again." Dan crossed to the door and jerked it open. Chief Mellows filled the corridor, beefy arms crossed, handcuffs glittering on his belt. His two assistants stood behind him. "Marsh, take him down to the supply office."

"You got it, sir. Let's go, Pistol. You and me got a date with Mr. Zabounian, see if he's got an empty stores cage."

Pistolesi looked surprised. "Wait a minute. You got to give me a hearing—"

"That was it. But I didn't hear what I wanted to hear."

"You oughta think about this, Captain. There's other

people aboard you and Godzilla Boy here need to keep your eye on. Not me."

"What's that mean, Pistolesi?"

The fireman hesitated. Finally he muttered, "Nothing."

"Let's go, man," said Mellows, coming into the room. Dropping his arms, letting the other measure his chances. Dan waited.

Finally Pistolesi shook his head. "All right, you win, Chief. I stay aboard," he said to Mellows. But his look at Dan as he left conveyed his defiance just as clearly as words could have.

THE boat crew was waiting when he got down to the quarterdeck, they were running behind schedule, and he had to skip calling Blair. The RHIB was open, unlike a gig, and that made it much wetter as it bounced across the choppy waters of the anchorage. That, combined with the dirt that had accumulated on it, made him wish for the old days. The crew steered between the rain patches as Dan, Doolan, and Colosimo clung to hand lines, discussing rebelting CIWS rounds for *Gaddis*'s twenty-millimeters and trying not to wipe out their whites as the silhouette of a warship emerged from the anchored merchants.

He'd seen HMAS *Darwin* coming in, thought for a moment he was looking at a U.S. fast frigate. And in fact it had been built in Seattle, a Perry-class, just like the ship he'd lost in the Gulf. It felt creepy climbing a familiar-looking accommodation ladder, stepping aboard a familiar-looking quarterdeck, then saluting the Southern Cross. The Aussies were welcoming, though. He and Doolan constructed a deal with the captain whereby *Gaddis* traded away most of her helicopter support spares for enough 20mm and 50-caliber ammunition that Dan felt comfortable in a small-craft board-and-search situation. The 20mm was uranium-cored, not explosive, but it would go through an engine block without stopping, and he felt much better getting it aboard.

He put his name on the unfamiliar supply documentation

with the same uneasy feeling he'd had endorsing a rubber check to Mr. See. The words *inspector general* and *audit* did not figure well in any fitness report. He wasn't happy with the way things were going with the crew, either. The problems with pay and funding and communications . . . He shook the sense of impending doom off as he said his farewells. He had a presail conference to attend.

THE lofty lobby of the Singapore Hyatt, with Doolan and Colosimo trailing Dan in out of the rain. He stopped to strip off his rain gear, noting a sign announcing that the International Maritime Organization meeting was in the Sir Henry Keppel Room.

Then his ear played back the last sentence that had come over the television, and he wheeled to stare at the screen as a still of a pretty Asian girl came up, apparently a snapshot, because it was blurry and a little off-color.

". . . The latest news from Television Corporation of Singapore.

"Authorities today report the body found last night was that of Ms. Nguyen Minh Dung, a Vietnamese immigrant who had been employed as a waitress in an establishment on Stamford Road. Ms. Dung was last seen in the company of several of her friends. Authorities are disturbed at the condition of the body. The murderer obviously had spent some time with the victim before leaving the scene of the crime. The investigation is proceeding, but pending its resolution females are warned not to proceed alone after dark in the China Town area.

"A major traffic pileup on the Pan Island Expressway this morning. A live report from our traffic correspondent . . ."

He stood watching the program for a moment more. Remembering a murder in Philadelphia, another in Staten Island, recalling the faxed face of an Azorean woman.

Could it be that this horror was following *Gaddis* from port to port, halfway around the world? And if it was, mightn't that mean—

"You OK, sir?"

"Yeah . . . yeah." He shook himself back into the moment. "Come on; let's find this thing."

Two military policemen stood guard in British-style uniforms, revolvers on their hips, just outside the meeting room. One examined Dan's ID, then waved them in. As the doors closed, Colosimo did a quick scan of the group around the continental breakfast, then tapped his shoulder. "Sir, a couple of folks you ought to meet."

A diminutive, leathery-faced character in a civilian suit looked up from a Danish. "U.S. Navy?" he said, examining Dan's uniform.

"That's correct, sir. *Oliver C. Gaddis*." They shook hands.

"Admiral Suriadiredja, Republic of Indonesia Navy. Pleased to meet you, Captain Gaddis. I will be very glad to have you with our force."

Before Dan had time to straighten that one out, Colosimo introduced him to the Singaporean armed forces chief of staff. Then someone tapped on a water glass. The three Americans followed other officers in varied uniforms to seats. At the head of the table a slim, fortyish Chinese woman was dressed very soberly in a suit coat with felted lapels and a matching skirt. In a voice combining Mandarin and Oxbridge, she called the meeting to order.

"Good morning. General Lee, Minister Tong, Admiral Suriadiredja, other distinguished officers, jurists, ministers, businessmen, and guests. I am Dr. S. Mei Guo, from the International Maritime Bureau, London. To open this morning, I would like to share with you several case histories.

"The first concerns a ship called the *Maria Katogiritis*, Cypriot flag, Greek owner, Serbian captain, and a mixed crew. She loaded sugar in Hawaii for transport to India. As she crossed the China Sea headed west, she was boarded by pirates in balaclava helmets. They boarded from a fast boat after shooting up the radio room. They took all jewelry, money, and watches and locked the crew below.

"When the crew was permitted topside once more, three

days later, they found themselves off the coast of Vietnam. The pirates forced them overboard, onto two painter's floats, without food or water. They then fired automatic weapons over their heads, to encourage them to paddle off. One float promptly overturned in the shark-infested water. The captain and first mate were not seen again after that. Those men on the other float were picked up four days later by fishermen from Hong Kong, but only three members of the crew survived.

"The vessel next surfaced in Bei Hei, China, as the *Corral Sea*. Note the misspelling. Her cargo manifest showed 250,000 bags of 'grade A sugar,' although sugar is not graded. A year later, the ship is still at anchor in Bei Hei, the cargo has disappeared, and no action has been taken as far as charging those responsible.

"Another example. On June 11 of last year, MV *Kaituren* sailed from Singapore en route to Osaka with general cargo, including lubricants, bonded goods, and chill stores. She was apparently hijacked east of the Paracels, getting off a fragmentary message before the radio shut down. The owner chartered a small plane to search for it. The aircraft found the *Kaituren* off Hainan Island, alongside a ship resembling a destroyer. The ship has not been heard from since, nor have any of the crew been found. A protest was lodged with the Chinese government, which after three months denied any knowledge of her whereabouts or any involvement in her capture.

"This is a disturbing trend. Ships are disappearing into mainland China with alarming frequency. The cargo vanishes—either confiscated, under a pretext of 'smuggling,' or else simply vanishing. The ships are either sold back to the owner for cash or else used as transports for illegal immigration—we have reports of several either sinking en route or being intercepted. The IMO is now gathering facts in order to make a representation to the UN and to the Chinese government."

Dan noticed concern taking the faces of the men around

him. They were of different nationalities, wore different uniforms, but they were all seamen.

"The previous examples have all been commercial ships. I would also like to point out a continuing pattern of attacks on small craft in the Gulf of Thailand and the western reaches of the South China Sea, where a nearly continuous flow of refugees attempt to escape conditions in Vietnam. These craft set out overloaded and are usually barely seaworthy to begin with. They are nearly always intercepted by members of a swarm of part-time pirates, part-time fishermen. The typical *modus operandi* is to approach them offering assistance, then threaten them with firearms, board, and begin looting. The engine is removed or stripped of useful parts. The looters strip the boat of personal belongings, fuel, water, and food. They then force the younger women and girls into the fishing craft, where they are repeatedly raped, often mutilated, and then thrown overboard. Upon the looters' leaving, hand grenades are thrown into the derelict, to remove all possibility of witnesses.

"A final example, closer to home for our Singaporean hosts. The night before last, the MV *Grand Gedeh*, laden with 150,000 tons of liquid petroleum gas from Algeria bound to Korea, was boarded by unidentified men in the eastern end of the Strait of Malacca. We still do not have a complete report, but apparently four crewmen were killed with machetes during the robbery. The ship made a complete turn in the strait, causing a major disruption in east–west shipping before the pirates departed and the crew succeeded in regaining control."

Dr. Guo turned to a screen and put several slides up showing false manifests, forged registries, and altered documentation; rusty, dinged-up "phantom ships" with hastily painted-over names and home ports; dejected, ragged men sitting glumly in what looked like a zoo cage.

"The problem of piracy is not a new one. Historically, it wanes in periods when one power or combination of powers controls the sea and returns when a power vacuum develops. It is also entwined with other criminal or social manifestations; an increasing tendency for cargo to disappear en route, not always without the knowledge of the shipowner; political and economic refugee movements; and the rise of warlordism and separatism in countries passing through phases of weak central government.

"In opening this conference, let me leave you with this thought. This is not the age of sailing ships, when remote islands could serve as havens. All modern pirates are based ultimately on land. That means someone has jurisdiction over them and, if they continue to operate, that 'someone' must be benefiting in some way from their actions.

"Pirates are rational actors but not moral actors. The core of their activity, as it is of all criminal activity, is to reap benefits themselves while externalizing the costs to others. It's up to us, the maritime community, to ensure piracy is not tolerated. Otherwise, we will continue to pay the price. For example, four years ago the Lykes Lines reported several assaults by pirates off Taiwan. The Taiwanese government sent out fast patrol boats, and the piracy stopped.

"It will never be possible to sweep all pirate operations from the sea forever. Maritime history since Pompey the Great tells us this. The most we can do is apply a deterrent to ensure the continued flow of vital commerce.

"The nations bordering the China Sea pride themselves on emerging from colonialism. More recently, the withdrawal of Russian and, consequently, of most American interest in this area of the world has also reduced the military presence that formerly restrained criminal activity at sea. Unfortunately, the vacuum has not been filled by local law enforcement authorities.

"Exercise Oceanic Prospect is the first step toward providing a more powerful deterrent to criminal activity directed against commercial shipping.

"I will now introduce our principal speaker, Admiral Waluyo Supryo Suriadiredja, Navy of the Republic of Indonesia."

Consulting the op order, Dan saw that Suriadiredja was the commander of the task force.

"First slide, please," said the admiral, and a chart of the South China Sea came up on the screen. A rough comma, with the head curled against North Vietnam and China, the Philippine Archipelago at its back, its tail curling past Borneo and the Malay Peninsula up into the Gulf of Siam. Dotted across it were small red triangles. They formed three clusters of activity. The first was the Strait of Malacca; the second, west of the Philippines; the third, wider in extent but more densely populated, off the south coast of China.

Speaking a slow but understandable English, Suriadiredja began, "The South China Sea stretches three thousand kilometers north to south, twenty-five degrees of latitude from the Tropic of Cancer to the equator. Seven nations border it, and half the commerce of the world transits its seas.

"Our goal in the multilateral exercise titled 'Oceanic Prospect' is to test and extend the integration of surveillance and communications assets, identify pirate strongholds, and demonstrate the unity and determination of coastal states to free the seas of these scourges of commerce. The operation will take place in three phases. Phase One will sweep the island groups from Singapore east to Borneo. Phase Two will proceed northeast along the line Brunei–Palawan–Luzon, with Detachment A entering the Sulu Sea for operations in shallow water off Mindanao. Finally, in Phase Three, the high-seas-capable units of the task force will operate in the northern half of the South China Sea."

Dan, recalling Dr. Guo's remarks, saw that at least on the surface this was an evenhanded sweep through the three main areas of pirate activity.

"Next slide, please." The admiral went on to outline the forces involved and his concept of operations. What he called the core squadron consisted of six oceangoing ships, two Indonesian, one Singaporean, one Malaysian, one Filipino, and one American. Patrol craft from Brunei would participate south of the Spratleys. Maritime surveillance assets included Thai P-3s and USAF reconnaissance out of Clark Field. Intelligence assets included support from Russia, South Korea, and Japan. As the force proceeded counterclockwise around the China Sea, land-based police and coast guards from the littoral states would join it in rooting out criminal elements from their lairs. Suriadiredja emphasized that it was not the primary mission of the task force to give battle or to conduct hot pursuit into the territorial waters of the littoral states. He concluded with a few remarks about command arrangements.

At the break, an Indonesian officer approached Dan and Doolan, who were standing a little apart, hoping for coffee, although there didn't seem to be any. "Sir, I am the admiral's aide. He has asked me to inquire if you have any objection to his breaking his flag aboard *Gaddis* during the first part of the exercise."

"Uh . . . I wasn't prepared for that. You mean he'd be sailing with us?"

"No. He will board at sea day after tomorrow and remain aboard through Phase One. If there is a problem with serving as flagship?"

"No, no problem, but . . . how many staff will be coming with him?"

The aide said between six and eight. Dan said he could provide hotel services, but that there might be communications shortfalls; if they could bring their own comm gear and technicians, the admiral would be better served.

Shortly afterward, Dr. Guo sailed past. He admired her legs, as well as her steely poise. After Susan he was leery of Chinese women, but he couldn't help respecting the way the doctor had dominated the meeting. Her gaze passed over him without stopping, and she disappeared and did not return.

The next presentation was by a meteorologist from New Zealand, who outlined the weather conditions they'd be operating under. The northeast monsoon dominated these waters from November on, bringing heavy cloud cover, rainy afternoons, sudden intense squalls, and heavy periodic downpours. This was also typhoon season in the China Sea, and the forecast this year was for several destructive storms. Dan wondered why they were patrolling in such challenging weather conditions. Not too much later, the conference broke up. Doolan lingered, discussing the arrangements for the admiral's boarding with the aide; and when he was done, they all left.

14

00° 21' N, 106° 49' E:
THE SOUTH CHINA SEA

TWO days later, Dan stood in the hangar, swaying to the rise and fall of the deck and worrying about the fact that he'd traded away to the Aussies the protective suits his crew would need if the incoming Bo-105 helicopter, now a speck against the clouds, burst into flames or crashed. He'd ordered fire hoses laid out, but his fire party looked apprehensive in cotton dungarees. He couldn't help it now, so he just squared his shoulders and sighed, glancing from the approaching aircraft back toward five gray shapes lurching against an uneasy sea.

For the past day and a half, the TNTF had steamed generally east under the tactical direction of the CO of the *Nala*. *Nala* was an Indonesian frigate slightly smaller than *Gaddis* but more modern, armed with Exocets and a 120mm gun. The other ships in the formation were *Monginsidi*, another Indonesian, the former USS *Claud Jones*; a German-built Singaporean missile boat, RSN *Sea Lion*; the second largest ship in the task force, the Malaysian RMN *Hang Tuah*, a British-built all-gun frigate; and RPN *Miguel Malvar*, a Filipino corvette that *Jane's* said had been the *Ngoc Hoi* when there had been a South Vietnamese Navy and before that USS *Brattleboro*, a destroyer escort built by the Pullman Car Company in 1944. It suffered several breakdowns a day and usually trailed far astern of the rest of the group. On the plus side, it carried World War II–issue forty-millimeters. Doolan was already laying plans to get over to her at the first opportunity, to beg, cumshaw, or steal a few rounds of ammo.

Altogether it was a farrago of modern ships and museum pieces, as interesting a force as Dan had ever sailed in, and possibly the most dangerous. Not to any enemy, but to itself. Communications were uneven, with radio frequencies all over the spectrum, language difficulties, and no common signal book. Someone was sure to misunderstand even the simplest course change, leading to several extremely close shaves when they had attempted to maneuver in a circular formation. The Singaporeans and Malaysians had been trained by the British; the Filipinos, by the Americans; and the Indonesians seemed to be in a league by themselves. The weather didn't help, with squalls and a monsoon-driven sea from the northeast that had the smaller craft nearly on their beam ends much of the time. At last, to Dan's relief, *Nala*'s CO had given up the night before and put them in a line ahead at a thousand yards' interval. Now each ship simply followed the one in front of it, like a chain of circus elephants swaying trunk to tail across the island-dotted expanse between Borneo and Sumatra. This worked better, except, of course, when a ship had to sheer out for one reason or another, such as Dan's moving out now in order to get the wind on his bow. *Hang Tuah*—"*Hang Tough*," as the crew had immediately dubbed her—had swung out to follow him, then realized her error and hastily reinserted herself into the column.

The little helicopter's engines became audible, and shortly after it touched down on its skids as lightly as a dragonfly finding a perch. Dan noted the anchor-in-pentagon of the Indonesian Navy. Bundled in a green flight suit, Admiral Suriadiredja jumped out. Lenson glanced over his shoulder, seeing that the signalmen were on the ball; the task force commander's pennant was already snapping out into the steady wind. The flag officer straightened, spied Dan as he stepped forward, and met him, hand extended. Dan saluted, then shook the admiral's hand, noting that the flight suit was stained dark under the armpits and at the neck. No wonder; the heat was intense and the humidity could only be higher if they were actually underwater. Dan led him forward as the chopper began to rev up again preparatory to taking off.

On the bridge rain rattled against the windows. The

doors thumped as the boatswain dogged them down. Usmani clawed his way up the ladder, one hand for himself, the other balancing a tray of iced tea and sandwiches against the plunge and heave as *Gaddis* presented her port bow to rollers the color of dollar bills.

Suriadiredja refused Dan's offer of the skipper's chair with a curt shake of the head. He stood before the chart table instead, eyeing the column as *Gaddis* neared, angling in to resume station. *Hang Tuah* had moved up, not understanding the U.S. frigate was going to return, and only a narrow slot presented itself. Dan had a word with Zabounian, who was conning, warning him to fall in slightly off-bearing to port, then ease the helm over a degree at a time, give the ship behind a graceful interval in which to fall back. Suriadiredja listened, weather-worn face expressionless as graven teak. He did not touch the sandwiches but drank half his iced tea before he said, "You're a cautious ship handler, Lenson."

Dan couldn't help remembering Khashar and wondering what the Pakistani skipper was doing now. "I try to maneuver smoothly, sir. There are enough surprises out here."

"I have to ask you something." The admiral looked around at the bridge team, all staring forward or down into radarscopes or otherwise intent on their work. He thumbed through the ready charts on the chart table, selected one, and tucked it under his arm. "Is there somewhere we can speak privately?"

"My cabin, sir, one deck down. Careful on the ladder."

"Do you recall Dr. Guo? At our conference in Singapore?" were Suriadiredja's first words after Dan's door was closed.

"Certainly do, sir. Impressive woman."

"Did you know that General Lee is Lee Kuan Yew's son?"

"I didn't know that."

"Dr. Guo had an interesting theory, about these phantom ships. Remember what she said? How they were disappearing into China?"

Again Dan said he did, and Suriadiredja nodded as if to himself. He gazed out at the surging gray sea. "It is possible one of our submarines will be able to join the exercise off Palawan."

Dan blinked, not sure he was following the change of subject, whether the Indonesian was just making small talk or aiming at some point. He cleared his throat. "One of the 209s, sir? Having a submarine might be useful. For surveillance, I mean. Pick up any pirates before they know they're being followed."

"We may be acquiring more," Suriadiredja said. "You may know of our plans to greatly increase our surface fleet. We may be purchasing several command destroyers and frigates from the Dutch. We already have a program for twenty-three new frigates, all locally built. We did not have such a good experience with the hydrofoils we had contracted for with Boeing."

Dan gave the task force commander a sidelong glance. Why the mention of Boeing? What did this man know about him? "Not every new program works out," he said tentatively.

"No. But Indonesia is doing well from this crisis in the Persian Gulf. Petroleum sales are very good. Most of it is being refined into jet fuel in Singapore." Dan remembered the smoky pall smothering the harbor. "The question will be how to expend that foreign exchange in the best interests of the country. There seem to be two schools of thought. Submarines, more destroyers, air forces . . . there is also the OPV school." OPVs were offshore patrol vessels, like the *Sea Wolf*.

Dan said, "As far as optimal force mixes, that would be an interesting analytical problem. But I'm sure you have better advice than I could offer you, sir."

"Perhaps. However, I understand that you are close friends with several Washington policy makers."

Dan took his time and thought about that one, realizing that the subject had ratcheted a notch closer to whatever goal the man opposite had in mind; realizing, too, that getting to it might take time, judging by the conversation to date. "Close friends? I don't think so. I know a few—"

"Miss Blair Titus. Senator Bankey Talmadge. Dr. Edward Szerenci. If there is a change of political climate in Washington, they could be very high in the new administration."

Dan would have gaped, but the bridge buzzer gave him a moment to recover himself. He said "Excuse me, sir," and took two quick steps to it. "Captain."

"Sir, OOD. We're back in formation. A little tight fore and aft, but we're shoehorned in."

Dan told him very well, to keep a sharp eye on the weather and the radar and make sure all contact reports were made to *Gaddis* now, as the flagship. He fastened the cover on the speaking tube and said to Suriadiredja, "I don't think there's any possibility President Bush will lose in '92. Unless he totally plows this war with Saddam. Which I don't think's going to happen."

"Nevertheless, you have the contacts."

"I know those people you've mentioned, yes."

"And I understand that you have also had a certain interest for some time now in the Chinese."

Dan was finding this more and more astonishing. When they'd first met, at the Hyatt, Suriadiredja had not even known his name, had confused it with that of his ship, called him Captain Gaddis. Now the man knew his history, his associates, might even know that he'd been suspected of being a Chinese agent when he was working with Joint Cruise Missiles in Crystal City. He said, tightly, "I've acted under orders at all times."

"I don't doubt it, considering that those you acted against caused the death of your wife."

"My fiancée, but yeah, that was one reason. How come you know so much about me? Sir?"

"I was in Washington then," Suriadiredja said. "As a student at your National War College, but I tried to make contacts outside that rather narrow circle. I knew the military attaché from the People's Republic, for example."

Dan went cold inside, recalling the heavy features of the man he even now, years later, would not mind killing. "You knew Colonel Zhang."

"Not intimately, but we met more than once."

Dan nodded slowly, trying to fight off the bad memories. "You said you had a question for me."

"Just your personal opinion. I wanted to ask you: What is going to be the impact of Tienanmen Square on U.S. policy toward Southeast Asia?"

"I don't think it will have much of an impact," said Dan. "Maybe slow down some technology transfer. But I doubt much more will happen."

"That is unfortunate. But only to be expected, I suppose."

Seeming disappointed, though by what aspect of their conversation Dan could not tell, the admiral unfolded the chart he'd taken from the bridge, spreading it out on the table. It was a small-scale chart of the South China Sea. He placed a finger on a group of tiny dots off the coast of Vietnam.

"The Paracels," Dan said.

"The *former* Paracels. Owned and garrisoned by South Vietnam until in 1974 the Chinese saw an opportunity. Saigon was isolated. America had withdrawn her support. The Soviet Union was not interested. North Vietnam was too dependent on Chinese supplies to protest. The Chinese invaded, fought a naval battle, sank several Vietnamese destroyers. Now they are the Xisha Islands, with radar surveillance sites and a naval base."

Dan studied the chart. "We'll be patrolling considerably to the east."

"In Phase Three. That is correct." Suriadiredja cocked his head and sucked air between his teeth. "But I'm not talking about our current operation, Dan. I'm talking about the strategic picture. Jakarta is concerned about the gradual extension of Chinese hegemony southward."

"I don't really see them extending hegemony," Dan said.

"In the same way none of us can see a tree growing," said the admiral. "It is a very gradual expansion, by a regime that plans not in terms of the next quarter but of the next century. But they have already advanced claims to the entire South China Sea, reserving the right not only to develop its resources but also to prevent passage through it."

"By 'resources' you mean fishing rights?"

"Fishing certainly, and transit rights, but most likely the real attraction is twofold: the recovery of past Chinese glory and the exploitation of subsea oil reserves. They intimidate their neighbors with probes and veiled threats while at the same time protesting that they are a peace-loving and trade-loving nation. But each time opportunity beckons, they take another step. They are gradually territorializing what was once open sea, and the overall intent is plain."

Suriadiredja indicated the Xishas again. "As I said, the western boundary of the sea basin is already secured, by their island-grabbing in the Paracels. Truly unfortunate, that the United States permitted that to happen. China could have been stopped at her doorstep. Since then the Russians have withdrawn from Camh Ranh Bay, leaving Vietnam isolated as China builds airfields and bases on Woody Island. We were no admirers of the Soviets, but it is unfortunate their Pacific Fleet is leaving. It is one less obstacle to China's creep south. In 1997, Hong Kong will revert to rule from Beijing. On the east, the Pratas are Taiwanese; whenever China moves to reincorporate Formosa, they will pass into their hands. The Philippines are too weak to resist. Only American support maintains their claims, and the United States is steadily retreating from Asia.

"So far each step has been tiny. An uninhabited reef. A reverting colony. But their next step is a long one." He placed his fingers on several dots north of Borneo. "Two years ago they landed military forces in the Spratley Islands. If they continue to occupy them, the entire bowl of the China Sea will be encompassed. They will have taken de facto possession and, with application of air power or an aircraft carrier, will be able to back up their occupation with force. We are attempting to settle the matter peacefully, but China refuses to discuss her claims."

Dan suddenly realized why he was being treated to this treatise on power politics in Southeast Asia. The naïveté of the admiral's assumption made him smile. He said, "Sir, if this is some kind of diplomatic démarche, if that's the right word, I'm not the guy you want to carry it."

Suriadiredja shrugged. "Perhaps not. But I am looking into the future. And, in a way, into the past. For what I fear is that history will repeat itself. As you know, the Second World War began in Indonesia."

"It did?"

"Yes. Once the British, Dutch, and Americans cut off their petroleum supplies, the Japanese had to decide whether to give up their conquests in China or move south for our oil. They decided to attack. Pearl Harbor, the Battle of the Java Sea, the fall of Singapore and Corregidor and the Philippines was the result.

"What I fear is that what interest America has in the rest of the world will vanish with the end of the cold war. Your leases on Clark and Subic Bay will run out very shortly. If they are not renewed, your withdrawal will accelerate. Meanwhile China advances into your place, intimidating or absorbing the regional powers one by one. In the end, the ASEAN powers could face a resurgent China across a sea she wholly dominates. A resurgent nationalism could unite her populations in Singapore, Thailand, Malaysia, the Philippines . . . and my own country, which has large numbers of overseas Chinese. The only power by then capable of opposing her in South Asia will be Indonesia. Our population is nearly as large as that of the United States and far larger than that of Japan or Vietnam. We will fight, if we must, but we should prefer not to have to fight alone."

"If China attacked you, I'm sure the United States would be by your side."

"As she was at the side of the Philippines when Japan struck?" said Suriadiredja. "And South Vietnam? Your country has a strange blindness. You do not seem to be able to recognize your enemies. As long as your commercial interests profit from the relationship, your leaders will not call China to account in any other way than with words or possibly token restriction of armaments sales. We do not propose to share that strategic procrastination. The time to fence in China is now, not after she has gained powerful positions and built up her fleet."

"Well, sir," Dan said, "basically, I wish you well. If I have a chance to speak to anyone in Washington, I'll be sure and pass on your concerns. I'm not an admirer of the People's Republic, though I like the Chinese as people. But, basically, *Gaddis* is here to help you operate against pirates."

Suriadiredja nodded, face relaxed. "And do you know something? I have the feeling that if we search diligently, we may just find some. Let's pull out that operation order, now, and make sure we understand Phases One and Two."

THE admiral said he'd changed his intent to move to *Gaddis*, that *Nala* would remain his flagship. When he left, the helo rising again into the sky, Dan stood looking after it till it vanished from sight. He caught a distant glimpse of the Indonesian corvette sheered out to the north. "Secure flight quarters; secure the ready boat crew," he told Engelhart. The warrant nodded, and Dan headed forward again. He swung his gaze up and down the column, confirming that Zabounian was headed back to station again, then ducked inside the skin of the ship, slamming the door to as a wave crashed into the side, reaching up a rattling spatter of warm, salty spray.

He stopped briefly in the radio room to discuss Compline's attempts to make contact with Pearl Harbor. The radioman chief said he'd been trying, but no one seemed to be guarding the clear termination. He'd keep at it, and he had other ideas about getting back in touch, but he suggested they duck into Subic as they went north, later in the exercise. They still had the racks and power supplies; all they needed was one old KW-7 to plug in and they could be back up on Fleet Broadcast. Dan said he'd see; maybe they could do that.

His next stop was in the chief's mess, where he'd asked

Mellows to meet him. The big torpedoman was the only one there, sitting at a freshly wiped table over a mug of battery acid. As Dan came in Mellows was looking off into the distance. With his massive arms, deep chest, and bald head he looked like some torpid yet powerful oriental god. Dan motioned him down as Mellows noticed him and came to his feet. "Hi, Chief. Look, put your chief master-at-arms hat on, OK? I want to talk about something that's been bothering me."

He'd had to take somebody into his confidence, and he didn't trust Juskoviac. Not because he suspected him—the exec had been back in the States when the ship was in Fayal—but because the guy was incapable of keeping his mouth shut. And whatever duty Dan assigned him, he'd still have to get somebody else to actually do it.

He'd settled on Marsh Mellows for a couple of reasons. The chief master-at-arms was the closest thing to a police chief there was aboard ship. Aboard larger units, cruisers to carriers, the position was a primary duty, with rated, professional chief masters-at-arms. Aboard *Gaddis*, with her withered, hodgepodge crew, it was an additional duty. Mellows had volunteered for the post, replacing a chief who'd been detached before Dan had reported aboard in Philly. The fact that Mellows had no torpedoes aboard gave him the time, and he'd studied up on the two-volume master-at-arms rate manual. His two assistants were volunteers, too.

Another reason was that Mellows knew the enlisted crew better than anyone else aboard. Most of the chiefs and first-class knew their divisions intimately, their own departments less so, and did not concern themselves overmuch about the rest. As the master-at-arms, it was Marsh's business to know everyone, and it was a business he'd applied himself to. Any hour of the day or night, Dan had seen him circulating, chatting with enginemen, auxiliarymen, supply personnel. The only other person with the same kind of proprietary interest in the whole crew was the exec, and Mellows was far better respected among them than Juskoviac. The last reason was that Dan just liked Mellows's easygoing, cheerful presence. He was reassuring to have around. So Dan had shared his suspicions with him, before they left Singapore, and asked him to think about what they should do about it.

Now Mellows nodded, lowering his usually booming voice. "I did what you said, sir—made the assumption we were talking about, trying to figure what if it was some wacko aboard here, slicing and dicing those hookers, a girl in every port. Now, these boys ain't angels. We had a couple of scuffles I had to break up in forward berthing. But I still don't think it's going to be one of ours."

"You're probably right, Chief. I just got a bad feeling when those cops came aboard in Malta. It made me think. Those prostitutes in South Philly. The girl in Fayal. Now, what sounds like the same thing, only in Singapore."

"Fuckee-suckee girls get in trouble every day, sir. Don't mean we got Ted Bundy aboard."

"Well, I hope you're right. But just in case, who did you come up with?"

Mellows pulled out what Dan recognized as the current muster and said slowly, rubbing his scalp, "Well, sir, first I sort of crossed off all the Pakis. They were here for Staten Island and Philly and Fayal, but they left before we got to Singapore. So I limited this to the U.S. crew. Here's who I got, people who were aboard that whole time."

Dan clicked his teeth together. Over forty names on the list. Including people he'd already thought about: Doolan, Pistolesi, and Armey. "I see you're on here, too," he told Mellows.

"Yessir, go by this, I'd have to be a suspect." The chief looked at the list again. "So would you."

"Well, we've got to narrow it down. How about liberty sections? Can we bounce who was on liberty those nights in the Azores, in Singapore?"

"Sir, I could try, but you know how the guys swap off on duty sections. The chiefs and div-ohs make sure we got enough bodies for the fire party and so forth, but we don't keep any permanent records. We'd have to hale everybody in and start doing cross-examinations, who you went on libs with, were they ever out of your sight, that kind of shit. I'll try if you want, but I don't think those odds are with us even if he is aboard."

"What about checking around with the leading petty officers? Whoever this is, he's got to be giving off signals. Obsessing about women, threats, violent remarks—"

"Gonna be hard to rule out a lot of sailors, you call it like that," said Mellows. "Anyway, I don't know if you're right, sir, that he'd stand out. What I read about them—you're talking Son of Sam, Boston Strangler guys, right?"

"Throw in some Jack the Ripper," said Dan. "This one might have a thing for prostitutes."

"Well, like I say, a lot of these psychos, they look just as normal as you and me. You could be talking to him and he's Mr. Meek—till the moon gets full. But if you want me to start the ball rolling, I'll be happy to do that."

Dan pondered it for a couple more seconds, then got up. "Could you do that without its getting out among the crew? Because if he knows we're after him, he'll pull into his shell. We'll never catch him then."

"Can try, sir. Think up some cover story, somebody's wallet's missing or something. We been having thefts down in forward berthing; they'd probably buy that."

"What about that fire alarm the other night? The false alarm?"

"Can't tell you who phoned that one in, sir. Could have been anybody. I just hope they don't start doing the firebug act for real."

"All right . . . another thing: Till we either find us a suspect or I get satisfied somehow I'm wrong, I'm wondering if I should grant any more liberty."

The thick eyebrows cranked upward. "That wouldn't go down real well, sir. Nosir, that wouldn't make the mess decks happy at all."

"I understand that, and I sympathize, but if we have

someone like that aboard, at least here he's on safe. No prostitutes or women aboard, whatever triggers him off—you see what I'm saying."

"Right, sir, but you got to understand something, too: This ain't your usual ship's company no more. You got some bad actors cooped up down there. Only thing keeping them off each other's throats is the idea they're gonna cut loose in Subic or Yokosuka."

"Well, I'll think about that one. Just keep the lid on as tight and as long as you can," Dan told him, then reached out, giving way to the impulse, and slapping Mellows on the shoulder. "I appreciate your help and advice, Chief. Makes a tough job easier."

"That's what I'm here for, sir, but thanks for the vote of confidence."

Dan glanced at the list again as he got up. If he was right, one of the names on it was that of a murderer. Someone in the grip of a compulsion so sick and savage that it had driven him to kill at least three times as USS *Gaddis* plodded halfway around the world and changed her flag twice.

He hoped like hell he was wrong.

15

OFF BORNEO

THREE days later, morning came brighter than it had for a week. A watery, pale sun penetrated the overcast to shine through the bridge windows, upholstering the green tile deck with yellow pads of light. Dan woke facing into the light, feet propped on an L-beam. He rolled his head in the CO's chair to find Usmani holding coffee and toast. How long had the Pakistani been standing there?

As he spread jelly, he reoriented himself. Engelhart had the deck and the conn, the ancient mariner saturnine on the far side of the bridge. *Gaddis* was in Form One, line ahead, steaming at 045 degrees true at twenty knots. Three surface contacts were on the board, none threatening. No land was visible, but over the curved lens of silver sea to the east lay the coast of North Borneo.

He stretched, reflecting on how little they had to show so far in the operation.

The biggest excitement in the last two days had been *Hang Tuah*'s report shortly after midnight one morning of two unidentified small contacts tracking east out of the Banka Strait. The Banka, Gelasa, and Karimata Straits were choke points between Sumatra and Borneo. Pirate attacks had been reported there. The Malaysian frigate reported a radar track moving toward the shipping lane east of Belitung Island, at speeds varying between eighteen and twenty-five knots. Admiral Suriadiredja had quickly reoriented the formation, which was strung out across twenty miles of sea. *Sea Lion*, the fastest unit in the task force, headed west, to cut off the northern exit of the Banka Strait. *Hang Tuah*, the southernmost ship and the one gaining initial contact, was to close slowly, maneuvering to keep the targets out of radar shadows. *Nala* and *Gaddis* went to flank speed for the Karimata Strait, leaving the two older ships maintaining the patrol in the eastern half of the Phase One op era. *Nala*'s helicopter wasn't cleared for night ops, but Suriadiredja had radioed for Indonesian air surveillance assets.

For four hours the eastbound element held its course, steadily closing on a scatter of islands past which the main Singapore–Surabaya shipping lane, and, not incidentally, the main route to Australia, ran. Dan had set GQ for the bridge and CIC team and told Doolan to be prepared to man up what guns he had ammo for.

For those few hours in the dark *Gaddis* had seemed suddenly to pull herself together. She charged through the night as with a single mind. Men answered with alacrity to orders and busied themselves preparing for action. At one point the radarmen reported they were tracking the suspect go-fasts, range 85,000 yards on the starboard bow. Knowing it was way too far yet to see anything, even if they were showing lights, still Dan had taken his binocs out on the wing. And stood holding them, the utterblack monsoon sky overhead, steel vibrating under his feet, and savored the excitement of the chase. The warm wind smelled of flowers and spices, and ghostgreen phosphorescence flickered as the bow wave crashed endlessly out from the stem. Standing there, he remembered that these were Conrad's seas, bordered by Conrad's lands: Malaya and Sumatra, Java and Borneo. Almayer and Lord Jim and blind old Captain Whalley had threaded these islands and sailed the sea where secrets were shared and old iron held longer than anyone had a right to expect and men crossed the shadow-lines within themselves.

But just before dawn the two contacts had suddenly reversed course south of Belitung Island, then shortly afterward turned north and merged with land return. *Sea Lion* had reported in from the south end of the channel not long after, but after several hours of searching, Suriadiredja had recalled the force. Colosimo guessed their quarry had de-

tected the radar signals from the converging hunters and
ducked into a handy inlet. That had been the only significant event in three days' patrolling, and shortly afterward
the flagship had re-formed them into the now-familiar column and began leading the way northeast, toward a refueling stop in Brunei before proceeding to the Sulu Sea for
Phase Two.

Now he blinked as the growing light gave him back an
eternity of water, high clouds bandaging the sky like old
gauze, the thin tapioca-colored glint of sun. Since then
they'd sighted only the plodding highway traffic of merchant shipping, churning down the straight-line routes that
laced this shallow sea: containerships, tankers, bulk carriers, barge and tug combinations, even the occasional jack-
up drill rig, dragged reluctantly behind straining deep-sea
tugs. No fishermen, though the water was plankton-rich.
Colosimo said they abandoned the area during the monsoon, snuggling the western coasts of Sumatra, Borneo, and
the Malay Peninsula. Dan wondered if that was where the
TNTF ought to be, then dismissed it. That was the admiral's
problem.

He swung down at last and went below. A stop in CIC, to
check the electronic warfare station, then aft and down
through the awakening ship, past the clatter and food smells
of the mess decks, aft and down again till he stepped off the
ladder into the steam-heated stuffiness of the engine spaces.
Armey and Sansone were in the air-conditioned booth of
Main Control. Or *usually* air-conditioned. When he
clamped the door shut behind him this time, it was quieter
but just as hot as in the engine room.

"What the hell, Jim? Don't you guys believe in AC?"

"Sure—when it works."

Armey explained he was having to gradually shut down
the ship's air-conditioning plant, as compressors and pumps
failed without parts or bearings to repair them. "We're at
about seventy-five percent of capacity now," the chief engineer said. "The A gang's been working hard getting them

back up, but . . . when are we going to get some logistic support? Any idea? It'd help me plan how to deploy my spares."

"I hope soon," Dan said. "I left a complete logreq in Singapore, but I never got a response. I'm hoping for parts and ammo in the Philippines. Fuel, we should be OK for a while after this top-off in Brunei."

"But can we can pay for it? Dave told me there was something fucked on the supply end, when we fueled in Singapore."

"This one's courtesy of the Brunei government. They don't have much of a navy, but they're floating on oil. So that's their contribution, a complete fuel load for the whole task force. It's a big contribution, too—crude's gone to forty dollars a barrel since Saddam took over Kuwait."

Sansone had been standing silent as the two officers talked; as Dan paused, he nodded to Armey and left.

"Well, I hope they come through as advertised," said Armey, and worry engraved his face as, Dan had noticed, it did more and more these days. "We're down to thirty percent. Running one boiler and two burners, we're going to just about make it there."

Dan told him he was doing a good job, to keep on stretching it, and Armey said Sansone was doing exactly that. "Matter of fact, sir, I wanted to ask you about fleeting him back up. We're short chiefs and he's doing the damn job; he might as well pin his anchors back on."

"No objection here, Jim. We'll do it tomorrow, muster on the fantail and frock him. Probably take pay a while to catch up, though."

"None of us are getting paid, Skipper. Whatever the foul-up is, it's major and it's shipwide."

Dan said unhappily that he and Zabounian had done all they could; everybody would just have to suck it up until the logjam got unjammed.

He left the engine room disturbed and anxious. If they didn't get parts soon, the breakdowns would cascade, as overworked equipment failed and dropped more load on what remained. So far Armey and Sansone had kept *Gaddis* steaming, but sooner or later they'd lose mobility. He didn't relish having to ask for a tow, but the question that stumped him was where they would be towed and how they would pay for repairs when they got there.

He let himself out on the helo deck at Frame 118. The air was hazy, but across an expanse of ruffled sea he made out a pallid ghost slipping from a cloud-shadow astern. *Monginsidi* and, far behind her, lagging as usual, *Malvar.* The rest of the horizon was empty. He took a turn around the flight deck, trying to shake the tension that seemed to increase every day.

The 1MC, sudden and loud: "Captain to the bridge. Captain to the bridge!"

Thirty seconds later, sucking wind, he slammed the wing door open and yelled, "I'm here! What the hell—"

"Sir, the bo's'n's got a situation down in the sonar dome. Says you better take a Mark Five with you, though."

HE didn't quite need a gas mask, but he understood what they meant when he stood with Chief Mellows and Boatswain's Mate First Topmark at the bottom of the ladder, all the way at the pointed stem of the ship, that led down *Gaddis*'s sonar trunk. They were in a tiny circular space walled by electroacoustic elements and thick black cables. They were actually below the keel, below the ship, submerged, in the bulbous dome deep below the stem that housed the sonar transducers. It was the most remote and obscure space in the ship.

"You got to wonder why he didn't just dump it overboard," Mellows said, squatting to lift the head. It came up easily; Dan remembered dimly that lack of stiffness meant a body had been dead for some time. The blue-green, puffy flesh of the face seconded that estimate. He swallowed, as a second look told him the sockets beneath the blackened swollen lids were . . . eyeless. The smell welled up as the chief master-at-arms let the chin drop. A dark fluid drooled from the open lips. Dan's look traveled downward, and then he had to turn and grope blindly for the ladder.

"It hits you, don't it," said Topmark when Dan came back, wiping his mouth with the back of his hand. "And judging by that rag in his mouth, he wasn't dead when they started cutting."

"Who is it? Anybody recognize him?"

"This here's Clayton Vorenkamp," said Topmark, sounding surprised Dan didn't recognize him; and as he heard the name he did: a slightly built young man with a trusting air who had worked on the mess decks.

"Seaman?"

"Seaman apprentice. Hey!" The boatswain bent and felt around under one of the cables.

The paper square snapped into a curl when he held it up.

"What is it?"

"Polaroid film. The backing, or whatever you call it. The part you rip off and throw away when you take a picture."

"I'll take that," said Mellows. "Where exactly did you pick it up? Right here? Lay it down carefully till I can get an evidence bag."

"I don't recall anyone mustered as missing movement in Singapore," Dan said. The close, musty air in the cramped space, the smell, the dizzying up and down motion here at the very bow, it was all getting to him.

Mellows: "Right, sir. So he got put down here after we got under way."

"Vorenkamp. OK. What do we have to do, Chief?"

"Well, sir, before we start fucking around with him, we better get some pictures. Put that rag and the film backing and any other evidence in Ziplocs. I'll get out the fingerprint kit and see if we get lucky."

"Make sure you check the hatch at the top of the ladder," Dan told him. "Whoever put him down here had to lift that access. And the rungs, climbing down that long trunk. Unless they were wearing gloves, they left prints."

"What you want to do with the body after that, Captain?" said Topmark hesitantly.

None of them was looking at him, and Dan realized suddenly they were afraid. Of him? Of the perpetrator? Or perhaps they thought *he* was the one responsible for this. A bitter laugh rose in his throat till he looked back at the butchered meat. The seaman's hands had been tied behind him. The smells of blood and shit and grease and rubber and decay were suddenly so dense he could barely force the air in and out of his lungs.

"Do like Marsh says. Let him dust for prints and so forth. Check all the corners; look for the knife. Then get the pictures," he told them. "We want the pattern of the . . . injuries." He swallowed, feeling water spring in his mouth, fighting nausea with logical thought and what little distance he could muster. "Then put everything in a body bag and take it down to the reefers."

HIS cabin, an hour later, with Mellows, Juskoviac, Doolan, Topmark, and the only member of *Gaddis*'s Medical Department left aboard, a sallow, indolent-looking third-class named Neilsen. Dan left them all standing and took the settee. He began harshly, "Neilsen, why aren't you in a complete uniform?"

"Sir, I got this here soccer shirt in Singapore—"

"I don't want to see it again aboard ship. Bo's'un. How's it look in the sonar dome?"

"We got all the, uh, the material out of it. Best we could, anyway. I got men washing it down with freshwater and buckets."

Dan reflected that meant the news would be all over the ship five minutes after the cleanup party was secured. Well, so be it. Maybe it would help, to have everyone on guard now.

It was the worst nightmare he could imagine, to have a murderer aboard ship.

"OK, it's pretty obvious we've got about the most seri-

ous situation we could have out here. Number two: This is
the same son of a bitch who's been cutting up women in
the ports we've been hitting. Chief Mellows and I discussed this before. But we had no idea he'd start going
after his shipmates."

The exec said, "I don't know if you can assume this is
the same guy—"

"Look at the mutilations," Dan said harshly, because just
thinking about them made him sick to his stomach again.
"They're the same things Interpol told me about in Malta.
Genitalia, intestines, but above all, the eyes. It's the same
bastard." He restrained himself; the men in front of him
were not to blame. He went on in a lower tone, "All right,
what do we know about Vorenkamp? Who's his daddy rab-
bit? He's not one of our nucleus from Staten Island.
Karachi?"

Topmark cleared his throat. "Right, sir, he came aboard
in Karachi. I don't know too much about him. He didn't
raise the IQ level when he walked into a room. The lights
were on, but there wasn't nobody home. I sent him to mess
duty and forgot about him." He cleared his throat again, fiddled with the marline work sheath on his deck knife, looking into the far corner of the cabin. "I heard he'd suck a dick
if the price was right."

"Mess deck scuttlebutt?"

"I don't know, sir. He didn't act like he had a lot of hair
on his chest."

Dan recalled the intimate darkness of the sonar dome, its
isolation and distance from the work centers and passageways. It was possible. That the body hadn't been dragged
there, dumped. That the young man had accompanied another willingly, all the way forward, down the narrow little
cable-walled trunk, into the tiny intimate space, not understanding till help was out of earshot that there was a point at
which their mutual intentions diverged.

"Chick, you were his department head. Got anything to
add to what the bo's'n said?"

"No, sir. I knew the kid, but he stayed under your radar."

"Greg, you're pretty quiet. Any comments?"

The exec just shrugged. Dan stared at him for a moment, then told them all, "OK, I want whoever did this. It can't be that hard. Vorenkamp went down there, into the dome, with somebody. Someone saw them together. Somebody knows who did this, or can guess. I want names, and I'm not too goddamn particular at this point how you get them."

Juskoviac: "I'm not sure what you mean by that, sir."

"I mean I want this guy in custody now. We've got eight hours till we go to sea detail for Brunei Bay. Before we do, I want a list of the guys who knew this kid and bunked near him, anybody from his hometown, anybody who got it on with him before. This is like state's evidence: they get a free ride on anything else if they come clean on what they know about him. Understood?"

They all nodded, quickly, and Dan told them to get out.

BY the time they reported back, *Gaddis*, last in the line of the now slowly plodding ships of the task force—*Malvar* having limped away northward, detaching from the formation and heading home for repairs—was threading the coral islands, oil-drilling rigs, production platforms, and coastal traffic on their way in. Dan felt his guts loosen at the smell of gas flare-offs and crude oil. It was the same greasy stink that hovered over the Persian Gulf, where *Van Zandt* and thirty-two of her crew had died over two hellish days and nights in the water, drifting in the sullen silent heat, torn at by sharks and sea snakes.

He felt sweat break on his forehead and winched his mind back from that abyss, forcing himself to concentrate on the here and now. The coast ahead was a solid green wedge of rain forest. Low clouds writhed over distant hills. Drops of water stood on the bulkheads, wrung from the air itself by the passage of the ship. But for the moment, it wasn't actually raining, and he listened in silence from his fold-down seat on the bridge wing as Juskoviac and Mellows briefed him on their investigation. They'd talked with the rest of the messmen and swab pushers on the mess decks, plus the guys who shared the cramped space of the supply berthing with Vorenkamp and one who had known him at boot camp at Great Lakes. They'd identified three suspects, guys who'd been friends with the blond seaman or who had been seen with him after the departure from Singapore.

When they were done, Dan asked one question. "Any of those three come aboard in Karachi?"

"One, sir. Seaman Hesey."

"Let him go. The guy we want's been aboard since day one. Who's that leave us?"

Chief Mellows told him, "Two suspects, sir. MMFN Pistolesi and EM3 Machias."

Dan examined the stern of a large ship they were passing, threading among the anchored behemoths as they neared their assigned berth. It read: KEISHUN. PORT KLANG. He had no idea where Port Klang was. Through a half-open side port he made out rows of hoods, Honda or Kia sedans colorful and identical as M&Ms, swathed in protective plastic like sleeping parrot fish. Then he looked at the two men on the wing with him. They were a study in contrasts, the exec bent forward slim and nervous, his fine-boned greyhound head tilted to one side as he waited for orders. Beside him the chief master at arms stood relaxed, big hands hanging at his sides.

Dan asked them, "What did they say when you came down on them?"

Mellows: "Nothing, sir. I read 'em Article Thirty-one and the Tempia warning, and they both clammed right up."

"Have you searched their lockers?"

Juskoviac, sounding injured: "No, you told us to do the interviews and we did those first—"

Dan called on his patience. "Yes, Greg, I did tell you that. And now I'm telling you to search their lockers. Don't forget their work spaces, either. Let me know what turns up."

"What you want done with 'em, sir?" Mellows asked. "We're not gonna be at a U.S. shore facility, anyplace we can turn them in for safekeeping, for a while."

"Lock them both in a fan room for now. No, make that separate fan rooms. Treat 'em fair, I don't want them on bread and water or anything, but I want to make sure they're segregated from the rest of the crew."

Juskoviac looked uncertain, as if he was about to object. Dan snapped, "Cough it up, XO."

"I'm not sure you can confine people without charges and a formal mast. In fact, I know we can't, not under the Uniform Code of Military Justice."

"I don't have time for a formal mast, Greg, and I don't want a serial murderer going over the side and getting away on one of these bumboats. Understand? Call it protective detention if it makes you feel better." Juskoviac hesitated, then nodded reluctantly. Dan went on, "OK, next, I drafted this message to PACFLEET. It reports the circumstances of the discovery of the body and our steps to date. It requests a Naval Investigative Service agent to meet us ASAP. If they hustle, they can maybe get somebody to the airport here before we shove off in the morning. If not, they ought to be able to hop somebody out from Subic to the Phase Two op area. Meanwhile, Greg, I want you to put together the initial investigation report, what we need to hand over to the NIS when they get here. Marsh can show you the forms. Anything else you guys can think of we ought to be doing?"

"Are we going to off-load the body here, sir?" Mellows said.

"I mentioned that in the message, Chief, but if they don't want us to it should be OK in the reefers till we hit Subic."

" 'Scuse me, XO. Coming up on our anchoring bearing, Cap'n."

"Thanks, Chick. Go ahead and drop when she bears." He had a moment's flash-image of clotted blood and tissue, what he'd seen in the sonar dome, took a deep breath, blotted it from his mind.

His eye, roving along the jumble of cranes and godowns and water towers, snagged on something out of place. The sultan of Brunei didn't believe in skyscrapers the way Lee Kuan Yew did. There didn't seem to be a building in Muara

over four stories. But it wasn't the buildings that had caught
his eye. He lifted his binoculars. The ships of the TNTF
were anchoring out, all except the flagship, which was
scheduled to be alongside at the Commercial Port. That fitted him fine, he wasn't letting a man ashore . . . but then
what was the gray silhouette that lay ahead, already alongside the quay wall? Whatever it was, it was signaling; flashing light was stuttering away on her superstructure,
apparently aimed at *Nala*. He tried to copy, but it came too
fast. A rumble shuddered through the ship's bones, the anchor chain running out. Topmark stepped to the 1MC, lifting his pipe; the call echoed through the ship: *"Moored.
Shift colors."*

"Sir, one other question," said Juskoviac, and Dan realized they were still standing there.

He said, irritated, "What, damn it?"

"The port authority people are going to be out pretty
soon. Well, about the kid—"

"What kid?"

"Vorenkamp. About him, what if they ask, like—"

"Let's close hold it for now, till we can get Naval Investigative aboard and maybe some public relations help,"
Dan told him. "From here until further notice, I want the
ship sealed. Nobody ashore except on official business. No
boats alongside. I don't see why the Brunei authorities
need to be told. It didn't happen in their waters, we're a
foreign-flag ship, and I'm sure they'd be just as happy not
to know about it."

"Are you going to mention it to Admiral Suriadiredja?"

"I'm thinking about it, Greg. Along with thirty other
things. OK?"

But Juskoviac still didn't go away. Instead he said
doggedly, "Sir, I realize this might not be the best time to
bring this up, but I've already had a couple of the men ask
me about liberty—"

"Are you listening to me, Greg? I said official business
only. We're anchoring out, fueling; we'll be under way
again tomorrow. There'll be no liberty."

The XO's head was lowering, his features taking on the stubborn, petulant cast Dan knew all too well. "I don't get it. If we got the guys who did it locked up—"

Lenson slammed his hands down on the chair rests, losing it. Heads snapped around inside the pilothouse; even the line handlers waiting on the forecastle looked up, startled, as he shouted, "God damn it, Greg, how many times do I have to say no! *No* liberty for anybody! Now get that message off and lock those two up."

The XO's eyes fell, and he backed away. Dan heard the murmur of voices in the pilothouse for a moment or two afterward, a nervously cleared throat, and then came silence.

THE word arrived flashing light from *Nala* as they secured from sea and anchor detail. COs of the task force were invited aboard the flagship at 1700. They would not return to their ships till 2100. A launch would be sent. Dan grunted as he read it and buzzed for Usmani. After telling the man to get his whites out he stalked the length of the bridge, first regretting his angry outburst at Juskoviac, then admitting the guy had rated having his head ripped off for a long time. The men on anchor watch stood silently as he paced, not looking at him. He felt hot and sticky and desperately tired and abruptly wheeled and plunged down the ladder.

Beneath a thin sprinkle of tepid water he pondered the likelihood *Gaddis* had harbored a serial killer since Philadelphia. This would not be a good story from the Navy's point of view. A U.S. warship voyaging from port to port, bearing with her a ravening monster. It would be raw meat for the media. Raw meat, like in the sonar dome. . . . He snapped his mind from that image, realizing even as he did so that part of his aversion and disgust was the knowledge that he, too, had once fantasized about such things, perhaps everyone had. When he'd looked down at what had been left of Clay Vorenkamp he'd experienced one swift moment of near-recognition, followed by a revulsion as much physical as emotional.

He turned the shower off and soaped down. The violence

of his emotional response told him more: that the murderer was in the grip of an overwhelming compulsion. Pistolesi, no surprise there, but Machias was an unknown quantity. Dan knew the man, of course. A lanky electrician's mate, third who had, to the best of his knowledge, kept his record clean aboard *Gaddis* except for one incident of overstaying liberty. He ought to go down and see them. But not now, not now. . . . The shower felt good after what he'd seen that morning. He turned it back on guiltily, enjoying another quart of the scarce freshwater.

When he stepped out, Usmani was bent over by his bunk, peering at the picture of Nan in her tennis whites. The Pakistani straightened guiltily, then dropped his eyes from Dan's nakedness and hung his freshly pressed trop whites off his locker. "Your uniform, sir. Shall I get the ribbons?"

Dan told him no, he'd do the rest himself. He dressed and sat impatiently until the squealer sounded off, letting him know the admiral's barge was en route. He grabbed his cap and headed down to the boat ladder, careful not to wipe out his white bucks on the knee knockers.

As he waited at the top of the accommodation ladder, he raised his eyes to see dozens of men staring at him. The crew looked down from the top of the helo hangar, the 01 level, the covered gallery beneath the flight deck where the snipes lingered of an evening to smoke a butt and get some air. They watched silently, leaning on the lines, and he noticed suddenly how hardly a man was in a regulation uniform. Colorful shorts, T-shirts, and bare chests were mixed with articles of uniform. The same symptom he'd noticed with Neilsen. As he thought this a sailor stepped out from the weather deck hatch above him, carrying a fishing pole. Dan called up, "Hope you catch something," but the seaman stared as if he'd addressed him in Malaysian.

Swell, if they thought he was going ashore to enjoy himself . . . but their silent regard was not a good sign. An explosive mix was building aboard *Gaddis*, impalpable yet deadly as methane in a coal mine. Her crew had been Frankensteined together from half a dozen sources over the

long trek east. They had no loyalty to the ship and, composed as they were of scrapings and AWOL leftovers, probably not much more to the Navy. Add to that no pay, no
liberty, the heat and boredom, their total lack of contact
with home . . . the fights and thefts were an ominous symptom. He had to defuse it before it got out of hand. Either
crack down or give them something to do. He decided to
think about it later, see what came out of this conference.

The launch came in, throwing spray like a frisky dolphin, the Indonesian flag fluttering at the stern. He judged
the distance and stepped onto the gunwale as it bounded
past the platform. The coxswain sheered off skillfully, and
Dan composed himself into the captain of USS *Gaddis*, settling into the seat cushions, forcing a smile to lips that did
not feel like smiling at all, nodding with friendly dignity to
the other commanders already aboard.

THEY were met with all due ceremony. White-uniformed
sideboys stood at taut attention. Pipes shrilled as they
pulled themselves out of the launch, mounting the boarding
ladder in order of seniority. The flag captain returned their
salutes with crisp slashes of his white-gloved hand. Dan
was junior and last. He marched between the immobile
ranks of sideboys with a strange sensation. He'd rendered
honors for senior officers many times, but this was the first
time he'd been piped aboard himself. When the group was
assembled, he trailed it up ladders and down shining passageways to a curtained space high in the superstructure.
The air-conditioning was blessedly icy. Plaques and awards
were screwed to the bulkheads, mostly from European and
Japanese ships. The flag mess, he guessed, accepting tea
and several small, round cookies or biscuits from a steward.

Suriadiredja came in a few minutes later, weathered
cheeks crinkled in greeting. He didn't waste time, just
shook everyone's hand and invited them to take their seats.

The flag captain spoke first, reviewing the lessons
learned from Phase One. Dan sat flipping his Skilcraft back
and forth, only occasionally pressing it to his wheelbook.

The flag captain had taken the liberty of preparing a formation steaming guide and signal book, which he distributed. The cover showed the five national flags fluttering above a skull and crossbones. They would evaluate it during Phase Two. If successful, it would be expanded in future exercises. The Indonesian reviewed the unsuccessful intercept of two nights before. In view of their targets' possession of what appeared to be sophisticated radar warning devices, it would be necessary to fine-tune the emissions plan. However, the craft they would be operating against during Phase Two would be less advanced, so for the moment no change in tactics was recommended. Meanwhile Lenson disassembled the pen, studied the parts, then put it back together.

When the flag captain was done, Suriadiredja stood. He asked for comments thus far. There weren't any. He nodded to a lieutenant, who put the first of a series of large charts of the Sulu Sea on an easel.

At last the briefing was over. The commanders stirred, gathering their materials and notes. Suriadiredja said then, face expressionless, "We have been invited to make a short visit to the vessel forward of us. If you will follow me to the pier?"

THE ship looming over them had been at sea a long time. A glance told Dan that, details he no longer saw consciously: blood rust seeping beneath fresh paint, the shadow of kicked-up water along the boot, the faded flag at her stern. Her hull number was R327. A weak stream spurted from an overboard discharge, splashing onto the pier. Three or four times the displacement of *Gaddis*, she towered above *Nala* as well. A bulbous-bodied helicopter of a make he didn't recognize, roughly the conformation of a U.S. Sea Stallion, squatted with blades drooping on a platform. Men in olive fatigues regarded them from the rail. The superstructure was capped by antenna-laced masts bracketing a single squared-off stack. He didn't see anything he could positively identify as a weapon. Heat radiated up from the con-

crete, reflected and concentrated by the steel cliff above
them as they paused at the foot of a ladder.

Dan lifted his cap and smoothed back sweat-soaked hair.
It wasn't just the heat that was making him sweat. He didn't
want to board this ship. But there was no graceful way out.
He followed the others, Suriadiredja at their head, up onto
the quarterdeck.

Fans roared steadily in the hangar. A red star with two
golden ideographs on a chain-fouled anchor was mounted
high on one bulkhead. The stream of warm air only seemed
to accentuate the humidity, but he was grateful for the
shade. The receiving line was made up of the commanding
officer, whose name he didn't catch, and several others—
department heads, most likely. Each bowed, shook his
hand, then dropped it instantly and turned to the next guest,
who in this case was Suriadiredja's flag aide. When Dan
emerged from the gauntlet he collected a glass of lemonade.
He glanced at the admiral, hoping this wouldn't be a long
visit. After a moment, he strolled out toward the helicopter.

Before he escaped the hangar, he was intercepted by a
crisp young fellow in a red-tabbed, slightly rumpled uniform. "United States Navy?"

Dan straightened, then reluctantly returned his head bob.

"How do you do. My name is Shan Jihong."

Dan took the limp hand for a moment. "Daniel Lenson."

"Welcome to *Dajaing*. I hope you will not mind if I prac-
tice my English with you. I last saw U.S. Navy officers in
Shanghai. I was translator for the Military Mission in 1989.
Do you know General Ferguson? U.S. Marine general
David Ferguson?"

"I don't think so."

"I see you are admiring our helicopter. That is a French
helicopter. The Super Frelon. We will be building our own
version soon, but with many improvements."

Shan was not as young as he'd seemed at first glance.
Dan leaned out past the edge of the hangar, far enough to
get a glance across the choppy green bay at *Gaddis*. She

looked OK, tending around a bit to the west from where she had originally hung at anchor. A fuel barge lay alongside. He turned back and said to the Chinese, "You have quite a ship here. I was wondering, actually, what type of craft this is."

"*Dajaing* is a research ship."

Dan nodded, trying to disguise his surprise at this piece of news. He took another hit off the lemonade and said, as blandly as he could, "You do a good deal of hydrography, I imagine."

Shan did not answer that one, simply smiled. "I am not involved in that work."

Still thinking about the implications, a submarine support ship this far to the south, Dan pushed the next pawn forward. "What's your position aboard, Mr. Shan?"

"I am the political officer of *Dajiang*. And you are the commander of *Gaddis*? Part of the Indonesian task force?"

The oppressive feeling Dan had fought at the foot of the ladder returned. "Political officer" meant Party member. But to him it meant the people who'd ruined his career at Joint Cruise Missiles, driven an espionage network into the Pentagon and Congress and the Air Force, and hired the gang bangers who'd killed Kerry Donavan on a towpath in D.C. He took a deep breath and eased it out. In a controlled voice he said, "That's right. But it's multinational, not Indonesian."

"You are sailing under Admiral Suriadiredja's flag."

"With ships of many coastal nations, on a mission of commerce protection."

"China would have been pleased to participate. I wonder why we were not invited."

Because you're the assholes behind the worst of it, Dan thought, but aloud he just said, "I wouldn't have anything on that for you, sorry."

He was excusing himself, turning away, when a smooth-faced Chinese-Singaporean he recognized as the *Sea Lion*'s commander joined them, and with him another officer who introduced himself as on the staff of the Royal Brunei

Armed Forces Flotilla. Dan thanked the latter for the com-
plimentary fuel. The discussion then turned to the develop-
ing tropical depression east of the Philippines and the
possibility it would move west into the Phase Two op area.
Dan felt uneasy discussing their intended movements in
front of the Chinese. He tried to relax, tried to look as if he
were enjoying himself swapping shop talk on a hot afternoon. But presently Suriadiredja drifted over, too. The task
force commander stood listening without comment to the
patrol craft's skipper. With the admiral was another Chinese
Dan recalled from the receiving line. The *Dajiang*'s captain
was slight as a boy, but with crow's-feet around penetrating
eyes that flicked from face to face with sour amusement.

When the Singaporean was done, he turned to Dan. "So,
America has returned."

"We never left."

"We thought so for a time. After Vietnam." He smiled
around the group. Dan straightened, a flash of anger pumping his blood pressure so high he felt a sudden pain in the
small of his back. Was the son of a bitch taunting him? He
started to snap back, then caught Suriadiredja's glance.

"There are political differences between China and the
United States." The Bruneian, with an unpleasant smirk.

"Political developments are always of interest," said
Shan, and the little circle's attention came back to the political officer. "But it is unfortunate you halted our technical
and scientific partnership. I personally do not understand
the reason."

"Tienanmen was the reason," Dan said.

"The few students wounded at Tienanmen were an internal matter. Like your Kent State massacre. China needs discipline. The people's rights to material development must
take priority over bourgeois concepts of political liberty.

"But if America prefers to break her commitments, we
have been through the same process with the Soviet Union.
First assistance, professions of friendship, and then abandonment. We managed to continue modernizing. Our new
Luhu-class destroyers will carry French missiles, German

diesels, British radar, and Chinese nuclear-capable antiship missiles. They will be the equal of any ship in the United States fleet. Mr. Gorbachev, too, seems quite willing to discuss sales of advanced systems."

Admiral Suriadiredja coughed into a fist, and the others fell silent. The Indonesian said, "There are questions about your government's intentions in the southern reaches of the South China Sea. We attempted to negotiate the subject of the Spratleys. The response was evasive. Something about Chinese imperial dynasties and national heritage."

Shan listened to a statement from *Dajaing*'s CO. He said something that sounded reassuring and returned to English. "The captain cautions me that these are matters of high diplomatic importance, not for us to venture opinions on without guidance. I will only repeat Chairman Deng's words, said many times over, that China has no desire to threaten other countries or to play the hegemon.

"You must bear in mind, however, that we have been deprived of large areas in the course of our history. Russian imperialists occupied our territory in the north. France, Britain, Germany, even Portugal seized cities and harbors. The Japanese annexed Manchuria and stole Taiwan. China's leaders depend on peaceful evolution for the rectification of these historic injustices. For myself, though, I will point out that all these southern seas were unquestionably Chinese before the piratical incursions of the European powers. The People's Republic will defend our historic rights."

Dan observed, before he could stop himself, "Your historic rights seem to extend farther and farther out to sea as time goes on."

"Along with every other nation in the world," said Shan. "Last year the Japanese extended their naval boundaries one thousand miles, all the way to the Paracels. We are simply moving our defenses outward from the homeland as we take our place in the community of powers. Just as America has. One could say your ship has little business in what even you call the *China* Sea."

"We're acting in concert with other nations to restrain piracy on the high seas."

Dajaing's captain spoke again, in Chinese.

Shan said, "My commanding officer asks me to caution you. He has seen notices to mariners your task force has filed for operations in the Tungsha Tao area. That is within China's coastal sea. It would not be perceived as friendly to the Chinese People's Liberation Army Navy if a task force operated north of fifteen degrees latitude. That is an area which it is our duty to defend."

The group was silent for a moment; then Suriadiredja said something about the UN Law of the Sea Convention boundaries. But Dan had had enough. He couldn't take it any longer, couldn't hold a lemonade glass and listen to courteous threats when what he wanted was to shoot every son of a bitch who wore a red star. He turned his back on all of them, if that was impolite to hell with it, and went out onto the open deck to check on *Gaddis* again. Damn it, he was getting CO-itis. Juskoviac was aboard, in temporary command while he was absent. Yeah, and that was the problem. If that anchor started dragging, Greg would be the last guy to notice. . . . Chick and Dave were there, though. He was getting paranoid. He sucked at the hot wind and tried to push away the anger and the regret, the sense of impending danger and past loss that ached in his bones like the residue of some toxic heavy metal.

Past the sheltered bay a lilac sky glowed like distant fire beyond the black smudge of the low coast, beyond the dark immobile silhouettes of shipping anchored in the roadstead. The wind had fallen as evening came; and an immense and brooding stillness hovered above the waiting sea, which reflected, in its turbulent depths, the flame and color of the dying sun.

16

THE SULU SEA

IT took two days to transit from Brunei to the Phase Two op area. En route, *Hang Tuah*'s commander notified the CTF that he had received a recall from the Malaysian naval headquarters, to operate in the Gulf of Thailand after an incident with the Thai fishing fleet off Kota Bharu. She detached minutes after Admiral Suriadiredja's terse acknowledgment and dropped rapidly astern.

That left *Nala*, *Monginsidi*, *Sea Lion*, and of course *Gaddis*.

The TNTF staff promulgated Suriadiredja's orders for the second phase of the operation by flashing light as the group transited the Balabac Strait. The message sliced the island-hemmed diamond of the Sulu Sea into rectangles of various sizes according to the surveillance capabilities of the ships assigned. It read: "Units will maintain constant and alert radar, radio, electronic, and visual watch, concentrating on the waters, islands, and passages bounding their assigned patrol areas. On detection of possible pirate or smuggling activity, inform CTFOP, other TF ships, and Philippine or Malaysian coast guard commands as indicated below."

Gaddis was assigned patrol area Zamboanga, a fifty-by-hundred-mile rectangle of shallow sea dropped athwart the main shipping channel through the Sulu Archipelago. Colosimo, who had taken over the vacant billet of operations officer, briefed Dan in his cabin about the most effective way to clamp a blockade on the most active area of pirate activity in the Philippines. "They operate out of Basilan Island," he told Dan, unfolding a Defense Mapping Agency chart that had what looked to him like suspiciously widely scattered depth markings.

Lenson sat forward over it, studying their carefully drawn area of responsibility, then perused the labyrinthine scatter of islands that bounded it. "How close in do you think we should patrol?"

"I'd be wary about closing any of these islands. The *China Sea Pilot* says not to trust the charts. They're based on old Spanish surveys. The coral heads aren't marked, and you won't get any warning from the fathometer, no preliminary shoaling, before you hit one. Strong tidal currents. Nothing's marked, no buoys or lights. Worst of all, like you know already, loran's spotty this far south. It's satnav, radar, and putting our balls on the table."

"What else?"

"It's typhoon season. That's probably the most serious threat. If one closes in, Admiral Suriadiredja will probably direct us to maneuver independently. I'd get the hell out of the Sulu, look for sea room west of Palawan."

Dan agreed that trying to ride out a major storm in the reef-fretted Sulu didn't sound like prudent seamanship. But he wasn't sure committing a ship with failing machinery and an already too small and increasingly disgruntled crew to fight it out on the high seas was a stellar idea, either. "What if I wanted to take shelter? Port Isabela?"

"You don't want to go into Isabela," the reservist told him. "That's Basilan, where these local bandits are out of. We're talking hundreds of them, and what amounts to a civil war the Philippine government's waging against Muslim separatists and communist insurgents. You'd have to set up machine guns on deck and man them around-the-clock."

A tap on the door; Juskoviac leaned in. "You wanted to see the prisoners, sir? Chief Mellows is here."

"Yeah, just a second." Dan sat looking at the chart for a moment more, then stood. "Thanks, Dom, I'm real glad to have you aboard. . . . Yeah, XO, let's get to it."

GADDIS, like most modern combatants other than carriers, had no permanent brig arrangements. When you absolutely, positively had to keep someone overnight, the auxiliary machinery spaces were usually pressed into service. The fan rooms Chief Mellows had put the suspects in were aft on the main deck level, at Frame 128. One was to port, sandwiched between the ship's store and the post office; the other was across the midships passageway. The ship's store was closed, Dan noticed. No wonder; the Plexiglas shelves were empty except for shaving powder and cologne. Juskoviac excused himself, saying he'd be right back as Mellows unsnapped the padlock and held the expanded-metal door for Dan to step through.

Pistolesi looked up from a folding chair on the bare gray-painted deck. Dan noticed he looked even more on edge than when they'd had their little counseling session on getting along with the Pakistanis, back in Philly. He was naked from the waist up, and the tattoo Dan had noticed before was revealed, but it had been so badly executed and was so obscured by a black snake of curly hair writhing up from his dungaree trou he could not tell what it was.

"Stand the fuck up, Pistolesi," said Mellows from the corridor. The fireman waited just long enough, then stood, arms dangling in studied contempt.

"How's it going, Fireman Pistolesi?"

"You made a mistake, Captain. I'm not the guy you want for this one."

Dan tried to discount the Jersey accent and the overtones of *The Godfather* it brought to mind. He leaned against the sheet-steel housing that covered the fan itself. Its muffled roar underlay all their words. "I'd like to believe that, Pistolero. Unfortunately, when we ask ourselves who we got aboard with a bad liberty record and a history of violence, your name pops out of Chief Mellows's computer."

"Yeah, it's pretty airtight. I slammed some brews on the beach. I don't let slanty-eyed asshole cops push me around. Obviously that means I whacked that cocksucker Vorenkamp and the hooker in Singapore."

"And most likely several other women, too." Dan watched the scarred face and concrete eyes as he described the girl in Fayal, what the two detectives said had been done to her. He compared that to the injuries to the corpse that rode beneath them, wrapped in a body bag and chilled to below zero. He wasn't sure what he was looking for; a sparkle of interest, a gleam of regret, a relish for the gory details . . . but he didn't get any of those out of the man before him.

Pistolesi listened, then shrugged. "Just the guy you want to carve your turkey on Thanksgiving. We got a serious head case aboard, all right. But it ain't me, Skipper."

"Just saying that doesn't cut it, Pistolesi. I only see two ways you get out of this fan room. First, confess now. We'll move you to a compartment with air-conditioning, treat you good, till we can turn you over to the pros. Second, if it wasn't you, prove it to me, and you walk out of here."

"Somehow it strikes me as funny there ain't no mast or charges or anything involved in this."

"No, there aren't," Dan told him. "I'd guess we're about two thousand miles from the nearest JAG officer. I know I'm going to get reamed at some point for taking you and Machias into preventive custody. Or maybe not; a commanding officer at sea still has some latitude. But if neither of those two things happens—you confess or you can prove it wasn't you—we'll turn everything over to the Naval Investigative Service when we get to Subic. You can explain it to them."

"Oh, we going to Pubic? I didn't hear that. Hey, I know a bitch in Olongapo, she'll tell you I don't need no knife to make an impression."

"I don't have orders yet, but I've asked for a brief port visit en route to the Phase Three op area," Dan told him. "I also asked for an agent to fly in to Brunei, but I never got an answer to that one. So I'm planning for Subic."

"Well, I'll tell you what *I* hope," Pistolesi told him, flashing small, widely spaced teeth outlined with yellow tartar. "I hope it's Shi-hime. I really hope it is. 'Cause I know it ain't me. And if it ain't him, the sicko who did the faggot is still strolling around giggling under his breath, looking for another chicken tender to carve on. You know what? I like where I am. Keep that door locked on me, Skipper. Keep her locked tight. I may just be the safest son of a bitch aboard this fucking death ship."

JOHNILE "Shi-hime" Machias was extremely tall. The electrician's mate's long, close-cropped head carried heavy lips, a pencil-thin mustache, and large opaque protruding eyes over which strangely corrugated lids half-masted. The first thing he said when Dan opened the cage was, "Is you the man with the cigarettes?"

"Get him some cigarettes, Chief," Dan told Mellows.

"Ship's store's fresh out of 'em, Cap'n."

This was the first he'd heard of it. He didn't smoke, which had made him something of an exception in the Navy when he'd joined, but he knew how much smokers needed the weed. Another negative morale factor. "Well, find a couple someplace."

"It don't need to be cigarette tobacco, Chief!" the prisoner called, stepping to the relocked grating and shaking it violently. Dan saw the slim shoulders held astonishing power. "See-gars. Pipe tobacco. Copie. Whatever you got." He turned back to Lenson. "What you doing down here, Cap'n?"

"I got two guys in custody, Johnile. If I can get a confession out of one of them, I can let the other go."

Machias smiled slowly, and two gold incisors flashed out. "I better see a lawyer."

Dan put his hands into his pockets, very slowly. It occurred to him that they were now alone in the locked-down compartment. He didn't hear anyone from the passageway. From what Mellows had just told him, Shi-hime Machias had actually been behind razor wire in the naval station brig when a pressing need for engineering-qualified bodies had bought him a "get out of jail free" ticket. "A lawyer," he repeated.

"I got a right to an attorney. I don't like being locked up. I got to tell you that. I get to make a phone call, too."

"We don't have phone communications, Petty Officer Machias, and we don't have Miranda warnings and bail and a lot of other things you might rate shoreside. You and Pistolesi are staying locked down till one of two things happens." Dan outlined the same choices as he had for the other sailor. The heavy lids did not quiver. Machias seemed half-asleep.

When Dan was finished, there was a short silence. Then Machias said again, "I better see a lawyer."

"Are you telling me you're guilty?"

In reply he got the communicativeness of a stone wall. Dan regarded him for a moment more, then turned as a chain rattled.

Mellows was back. The chief was letting him out when, with great swiftness, surprising them both, Machias made a break for the door. Dan flung up his arm and knocked him back, nothing more than reflex action, and slipped through and slammed the grate closed with his shoulder against a violent battering till the chief got the padlock snapped shut. Machias snarled through the expanded metal, an edge close to panic in his voice, "You got to let me out. Shackle me, whatever; just get me out of here. I can't take being locked up, man."

"Give him his tobacco," Dan told Mellows. The master-at-arms, holding his body back from the door, poked three White Owls through into the cell. Machias snatched the cigars and turned his back to them. His hands were clapped to his face, and for a moment Dan felt pity. Then he hardened his heart. If Shi-hime was the killer, mercy was a misplaced emotion.

Juskoviac came back down the passageway, rejoining them. "All done, sir?" he said crisply. Dan nodded, thinking that as usual, the exec had managed to be absent when anything actually had to be done.

"It's got to be him," Mellows said, a few steps down the passageway. "He's been twitchy as a bedbug since we put him in there." He stopped and leaned against the Supply

Department bulletin board, took his hat off, and wiped his streaming face. Dan saw perspiration beaded on his shaven scalp.

Juskoviac: "You OK, Chief?"

"Son of a bitch startled me. He's fast."

Dan said, "Why do you say it's got to be him?"

"I mean it's got to be. You know what he was in for, when they sent him to us? Attempted rape."

"And they let him out?"

"The woman dropped it or something. But Shi-hime likes knives. If anybody aboard this ship could cut a guy up like they cut up that kid, it's him."

"I'm not so sure." Dan waited for the chief to recover, glancing back down the corridor to where the gratings faced each other. Two choices, and he didn't like either one. The Italian-American was more vocal in his denials. Dan had heard no false notes, seen nothing that would indicate anything more serious than a certain contempt for authority. The black sailor had clammed. But if Dan carried Machias's history, he'd not say a word without an attorney present, either. Not when the penalty for a mistake was a murder charge.

On the other hand, he was no psychology expert. Living as close to other men as you did aboard ship, trying to lead them, you got a certain basic grounding in human nature. But if they were really facing a psychopath, his guesses and his intuitions were probably worth absolutely zip.

"Nothing on the prints, huh? The ones you dusted for down in the dome?"

"No, sir. Whoever done it was real careful. Maybe had gloves on."

Fucking great, he was thinking when a J-phone squealed on the bulkhead. Mellows snatched it, listened, said, "Yeah, he's here. For you, Skipper," and handed it over.

"Captain."

"Sir, this is Chief Compline. We finally worked that MARS hookup we were talking about; you want to come to Radio."

"MARS hookup . . . oh. Yeah. Be right up." He glanced over and saw that Mellows looked a little better. "OK, let's go," he told them both. "Greg, I want that search I told you about. You're in charge. Zone by zone, locker by locker. Start at the pointy end and finish in the wake."

He left them staring silently at each other.

IN Radio Central, he pulled out a chair in front of a mike as Compline explained what he'd set up. The Military Affiliate Radio System, or MARS, was a military/civilian arrangement where amateur radio operators provided auxiliary comms shoreside during emergencies or equipment failures. Originally a backup for official radio links, it was mostly used these days for personal messages, but the backup function was still operational. Just now they were in luck. The sunspot cycle was right for long-range communications. Compline had a ham from Maryland on single side band on the high end of 13 megahertz and had explained *Gaddis*'s situation. The stateside operator was willing to patch him through to any East Coast phone number, but he had to bear in mind that it was two o'clock in the morning.

Dan thought fast and gave the operator a number.

She picked up on the first ring. "Hello?"

He closed his eyes. She didn't sound as if she'd been asleep. Distant as her voice seemed, ionosphere-crackly, distorted by thirteen thousand miles or more, it swept him with loneliness like a foundering hulk swept by a heavy sea. He couldn't think for a moment, hearing it. The illusion of her presence was so strong, the image or fantasy that he could reach through the microphone somehow and touch her warmth, her tangled hair. For a moment he actually saw her lying in bed in the second-floor Georgetown flat he knew so well. She was sitting up, holding a book. A faint tapping came from outside. The elm tree on the corner, branches whispering beyond her bedroom window . . .

"Hello?" Impatient now, about to hang up.

"Uh . . . Blair? This is Dan, calling on a radio patch. Can you hear me? Over."

"Dan. Dan? Is that you? This is a really lousy connection. Where in heaven's name are you? I got your card from Singapore."

"Uh, you have to say, 'Over,' because we can't both talk at once. I don't know how long we can maintain this patch, but I have a couple of things, if you can grab a pen. Over."

He gave her phone numbers, and brief messages to pass to the appropriate staffies at CINCLANTFLT and at DESRON Twelve and one guy he knew who was still at JCS J-3, Current Ops. She took them down without comment but when he didn't have any more said, "It sounds like you're having some problems. Are you all right out there? Speak as loud as you can; there's a lot of static on this line."

"That's the MARS patch. We'll make it, but we need to phone home with the Navy. We're out here hunting pirates, but I'm beginning to feel like one myself."

"Are you all right? Personally?"

He thought about unloading it on her, the murder, the restive crew, everything, but didn't see the point. "I'll live. I know why some of my COs were so damn short-tempered now, though. How are things on the Hill?"

"Pretty tense at the moment. We're looking at authorizing resolutions for military action in the Gulf. You're probably better off where you are. The China Sea, you said?"

"Uh-huh."

"Should be quiet there."

He told her it wasn't really, that the locals had concerns, what Dr. S. Mei Guo had said about ships disappearing near Hong Kong. Told her about Suriadiredja's suspicions, though without using his name. "They're convinced the Chinese are slowly moving south. First the Paracels, then the Spratleys," he finished. "And they don't think the U.S. will be there for them. We went aboard a PRC survey ship in Brunei. The captain drew a line in the sand north of fifteen degrees. Said that was Chinese coastal waters. Which it isn't."

"I agree, but the policy is not to provoke them. They've got legitimate interests in the region. Remember, the Indonesians killed about a half-million ethnic Chinese in '65. Not to mention their thoroughly barbaric record in East Timor."

"What about this military buildup? All this new equipment the Chinese are buying, these new ships and aircraft, the missiles they're building?"

"There's a good case that's driven by internal dynamics. Jiang Zemin, the new Party head, is probably just buying the support of the military leaders. Over."

Dan glanced at Compline, then grabbed the desk in frustration. "And the spying they did on the Tomahawk seeker? Wait; I know. That's a 'legitimate interest,' driven by 'internal dynamics,' right?"

"Dan, stop it! Which is better, a trading partner or an outright enemy? Which do we have more leverage over? Most people up here think constructive engagement's the best policy in the long run. Treat them like responsible partners on the international scene. Accustom them to the give-and-take between equals. Help them grow economically. Given time, given interaction, their system's going to change the same way the Soviet Union did. Over."

"I seem to recall we had to fight a couple of times while we were waiting for *them* to turn into good guys."

Her voice again, cool and patronizing. The tone he hated. "Let's not argue, Dan. Not at this distance, OK? It's good to hear from you. I'll pass your messages along first thing in the morning. When do you think you'll be back in the country?"

JUSKOVIAC, Mellows, and the assistant masters-at-arms searched the ship for six hours, stem to stern, but found nothing. The crew cooperated, but in an ominous silence. They watched as the chief and his petty officers went through the pitifully small storage compartments under their bunks and the equally minuscule lockers in each berthing area. They found nothing, which meant either that his crew was made up of Eagle Scouts or that they'd anticipated the search. Dan sat glowering on the bridge after

Juskoviac had reported as much. All he'd done was further
estrange the men.

Which most likely explained why the sounding and security watch smelled smoke not too long afterward. When
he went in search of its source he found a smoky blaze in
the wardroom storeroom, an obscure space in an untended
part of the ship, far aft and belowdecks. He put it out with
an extinguisher before reporting it to Main Control. Jim
Armey reported it to Dan, along with his guess: Someone
had thrown hydraulic fluid, fuel, or cleaning fluid through
the gratings, onto the officers' stacked-up luggage and
boxes, and tossed a match in after it.

AS they ran toward their assigned area through that evening
and night and then the next morning, the sea changed. It
shallowed and turned from murky green to a deep transparent emerald. They passed widely scattered islets, and
though Dan kept them far offshore the men concentrated
around the Big Eyes on the 01 level. Palm trees and white
sand beaches glared in the occasional sunlight. The wind
dropped to a breeze. The sky cleared, not entirely, but they
saw blue more often than they had since Singapore. In the
early afternoon the lookouts reported breakers ahead. Chick
Doolan, who had the conn, slammed on the brakes and
called Dan to the bridge. By the time he got there, the
"breakers" had resolved themselves into thousands of bot-
tle-nosed dolphins, furrowing the swirling sea.

They reported on station in patrol area Zamboanga on
the task force coordination frequency at 1400 on the seven-
teenth of November. After he sent the message, Dan lingered uncertainly on the bridge. What was it Barry Niles
had told him once. . . . something about if you ever achieve
command, you'd better keep your doubts to yourself. Be the
picture of confidence. It seemed distant and faraway, in the
face of what was happening aboard *Gaddis*, the seemingly
metastasizing evil within her hull. Irrelevant, in the face of
the pristine and shining sea and sky that surrounded her,

under way at a fuel-conserving five knots in the midst of a
paradise.

THE call came in on Channel 16, 156.8 megahertz, the distress frequency yachtsmen kept dialed in as the default on
their sets. The radioman jotted it and called the bridge. Dan
heard the tail end of his read-back as he woke from an only
partially voluntary nap. " ' . . . boarded by armed men from
small boat.' That was all."

Doolan pressed the worn-smooth transmit lever. "Any
posit?"

"No, sir. That was it. Clear and five by, though, so I'd
guess it's within thirty miles. VHF, you lose it over the
curve of the earth past that."

"Sir?" The weapons officer turned his head toward Dan.

"Say again the whole transmission."

" 'Motor Vessel *Queen Shallop* being boarded by armed
men from small boat.' End of transmission."

"Come to flank and head toward the Strait." Dan was
awake now. "Make sure Combat knows what's going on. If
they transmit again, maybe the ESM team can get a line of
bearing. Get Dom up here right away. And pass this to the
coast guard; make sure they got it, too." Part of the message
setting up their patrol area had specified that two Philippine
coast guard patrol boats would be available close inshore,
ready to move into shallow waters to intercept once *Gaddis*
or *Monginsidi*, which patrolled the next area north, could
relay track information on a suspect craft.

Doolan yelled out the new course to the helmsman. The
engine order telegraph pinged as Dan jumped down from
his chair. The combination of the lean of the deck as *Gaddis*
came to a new course of 135 degrees true and a brush with
his arm knocked a cold cup of coffee from its perch on the
steel U-beam that formed the window ledge. He stepped
over it, not stopping, and went to the chart table, where
Chick joined him after passing on the orders to his junior
OOD, Chief Tosito, and to CIC.

Colosimo arrived, stuffing his shirttails in. Together they discussed the most likely position the distress call had come from, putting together the estimated range, the channel conformation, and what the reserve officer knew about the pirates' preferred method of attack. They came up with an area of sea south of a shotgun blast of islets the chart called the Pilas Islands. By now *Gaddis* was at her maximum speed, almost thirty knots, rolling slightly to the quartering northerly swell, the deck shuddering and the blowers whining and whooshing. Dan backed off from the process, zooming back to get perspective, and keyed CIC again. "Combat, bridge. Did you pass information on *Queen Shallop* intercept to Philippine authorities?"

"Sir, we called on the assigned freq but have no response yet. Will keep calling."

Dan double-tapped the lever in acknowledgment and crossed to the repeater. Found himself confronted by a taped-on paper sign: RADAR FUCKED. "Is this the repeater or the radar?" he yelled angrily.

Heads whipped around, and the boatswain said hastily, "Sir, that's just the repeater; we called the ETs half an hour ago."

"Get Chief Warrant up here ASAP. We need this repeater." He wheeled, straight-armed the door to the ladder, and clattered out one level down in CIC.

The ops specialist had his head down over the big repeater next to the plotting table. He made a careful mark with his grease pencil as Dan came up. "Yeah, we got it," the petty officer observed. "You were gonna ask me if we had a contact bearing about 130, forty thousand yards, right, sir?"

"I like being anticipated. Give me a course and speed to intercept to make my day."

"Another three minutes. There's some intermittents out there, but this is the only one that paints on every sweep." The OS eyed his watch, then etched another mark. Dan saw it was tracking directly in toward the center of the screen. "Dead in the water," the petty officer said, walking his fingers across the glass. "Come left a hair and we'll intercept in . . . forty minutes."

No point getting worked up, Dan cautioned himself. They had no certainty the contact was actually the vessel that had put out the distress call. But still he felt the acceleration of events, the excitement that came so seldom, but that when it did made up for so much boredom, so much routine, stupidity, and repetition. The ladder slanted beneath his half-Wellingtons as he ran up it again. *Gaddis* was flinging herself headlong across the choppy sea, charging to the rescue. Forty minutes, less now, and they'd be in range of the five-inch in about . . . No, goddamnit, they didn't have any five-inch ammunition . . . but the twenties could reach out and touch someone at a good thousand yards. He yelled at Doolan as he emerged onto the bridge, "PCG answer up yet?"

"No, sir, no response on their circuit."

"Have they answered up before? We did a radio check, right?"

"Compline says they had contact when we checked into the net around 1400."

"Sir?" The duty signalman at the wing door. He looked scared. "Captain? Can you come and look at this?"

Dan frowned but stepped out onto the wing. The signalman pointed over the side.

He leaned over the splinter shield, to gaze directly down on what his shocked and disbelieving eye recognized instantly as a tropical coral head. The sea was so clear that in the smooth trough of *Gaddis*'s bow wave, distorting what lay below like curved crown glass, he saw a blue parrot fish frozen against the convoluted background of a brain coral. He stared downward for what seemed like an eternity as *Gaddis* roared on, then spun and screamed through the open wing door, "Depth!"

"Five fathoms under the keel, sir!" Tosito yelled back. Dan felt himself almost literally torn apart between wanting to yell all astern full and wanting to keep on, hoping to reach the now not-so-distant contact while perhaps their quarry for so many days was still aboard or at least nearby. . . . Colosimo, face suddenly bleached, turning from the chart with mouth an open O . . .

"Five fathoms . . . *three* fathoms . . . *shoaling fast!*"

"Back full! All back full, back *emergency!*" He ran back out and stared hypnotized downward again. No question, the seafloor was rising to meet them, already visibly closer. The coral mushrooms reached for *Gaddis*'s thin-plated keel, her even thinner bow dome, bulging and tender as a swollen scrotum, made not even out of steel but of stiffened rubber . . . the stern hammered as the screw reversed. The helmsman spun the wheel left as the stern pulled to port. Still her momentum carried her forward, seemingly without braking effect. He yelled in, "Collision alarm!"

"Stand by for collision. All hands brace for shock," stated the 1MC in Doolan's laconic tones. The collision alarm began an electronic *dit-dit-dit, dit-dit-dit* that set his teeth on edge as he waited for the deceptively gentle shudder that meant a ship was being disemboweled. Please God, he didn't want it to end this way. How had he forgotten, carried flank speed heading inshore? The reef wasn't charted, of course. The printed soundings showed twenty fathoms. But Colosimo had warned him how undependable charts were here. He had no excuse for this little lapse in judgment.

Gaddis began to slow, slewing still farther as the single big prop walked her stern left. Beneath his tranced sight the multicolored reef moved past, brilliant scarlet fire coral, bulbous dark coral heads, deep green canyons or fissures dropping to a glowing white bottom. With a physical tightening throughout his body, throat to anus, he stared across the flat sea to a purple-brown turmoil not a hundred meters to starboard. The gentle swells broke without foam, with a flat, swirling turmoil. He'd done enough scuba diving to know what that meant. The sea there was about four feet deep.

Were they backing down? He nearly screamed into the pilothouse again but saw the EOT handle still racked to back full, the lee helmsman holding them down as if that would help. The speed came off so fucking slowly. . . Another patch of uneasy sea whirled ahead. He watched helplessly as it drew closer. Closer.

Ping. Ping. The EOT handles coming up to "engines stop."

He breathed out, very slowly, feeling the top of his brain trying to push its way out of his head and go floating off like a helium balloon.

Gaddis drifted motionless, hovering in a fluid so transparent he could see each detail of the bottom, see sea fans and large whelks, if that was what they were. So shallow he could make out the trails they'd dug through the sand . . . but she was still floating free; somehow he'd avoided impaling her. His fingers finally got a message through to a brain that had blocked it out till now: *we hurt.* He looked down and saw them clamped like spring clips to the splinter shield. He let go and chafed his palms together self-consciously, feeling eyes pinned to him from within the dark cave of the pilothouse. Seeing something in them for the first time. There had been hostility before and resentment. Now there was something else, something new: doubt and uncertainty and something not far from fear.

He swallowed hard, his relief at being still afloat, immense as it was, erased by the realization that his crew was looking at him the same way the Pakistanis had regarded Hussain Khashar.

THE starboard RHIB purred on ahead, so slowly it hardly drew a ripple across the undulating, gleaming, somehow greasy-looking sea off which sunlight sparkled in an airless calm. Guided by a lookout atop *Gaddis*'s mack with binoculars and PRC-10, the inflatable had first made a wide circle, searching out the route back to deep water. Nudging the bow around with infinite caution, Dan had followed it gradually out of the watery maze of the reef. Far ahead of them the port RHIB, manned by a fire team of gunner's mates with M-16s and an M-60 and officered by Dom Colosimo, was a wasting speck on the heat-wavering seahorizon. Be-

yond that, elevated by refraction, shimmered the violet
rounded ovals of distant islands. The outliers of the Pilas
group, if his increasingly chancy navigation was correct.
The encounter with the reef had delayed their response to
the distress message, but the inflatable would put a small
force on scene. He hoped it would be enough.

"Forward lookout reports sailboat ahead," said Chief
Tosito, poking his head out like an intimidated turtle. Dan
nodded and reached for his binocs.

They made up on it slowly, plodding along behind the
starboard RHIB. Maybe too cautiously; the chart showed
the depths here as sixty fathoms. But he didn't want to repeat that last little thrill. He still couldn't believe she hadn't
bent her prop tips or collapsed the sonar dome. The reports
came in on the PRC-10 from the fire team, running out
ahead at full throttle. The boat was hove to. No sign of anyone on deck. They were approaching. Using the bullhorn.
No response. Moving in on the port quarter. Hailing again.
At last, boarding.

Then silence, for too long. Dan studied the craft ahead,
now clearly visible at four thousand yards. The inflatable
was standing off, motionless in the calming sea. The as-
sisted vessel was a white-hulled, yawl-rigged motor-sailor
of considerable size and breathtakingly graceful lines. Her
poles were bare. He couldn't make out the ensign that hung
down in the lifeless air. He inched the fields of his binoculars left to right, searching the shimmering sea to either
side. The only other signs of human presence were the rain-
bow-striped sails of the Filipino outriggers Colosimo called
vintas. Dan remembered the intermittent contacts the operations specialist had mentioned. The vintas were wooden
and rode low in the water. That would make them almost invisible to radar, whereas the yacht, with metal masts and
what he could make out now as a radar reflector at her main
crosstree, would show up more distinctly.

At last the VHF crackled. It was Colosimo. "Captain?"

"*Gaddis* actual speaking."

"You'd better come aboard here and take a look."

* * *

HE told Doolan to heave to five hundred yards off and climbed down a hastily rigged jacob's ladder into the inflatable. The outboard purred him through the glassclear water. Jewel-like drops of it hung in the air, then plummeted into the hand-polished surface of the fluid boundary between sea and air.

She wasn't the *Queen Shallop* but the *Queen Salotte.* Her stern listed her home port as Christchurch. Close up she was even more beautiful, a white sea bird with sweeping lines and raked masts. Hundreds of thousands of dollars' worth of boat. Fresh blue canvas aft of her main cabin. The sails had been dropped, hastily by the looks of them; they lay tumbled on the booms like kicked-off panties. She had no way on, but an auxiliary generator murmured across the water and a piloting radar rotated atop her mainmast. She looked unharmed till the Johnson dropped a note and he began to judge where he might be able to reach up to pull himself aboard. Then he saw the holes in the shining fiberglass.

A few minutes later he stood in the motor-sailor's pilothouse, looking at a smear of fresh blood on the carpeted deck. The wide windows had two perforations in them, the small, barely cracked penetrations of a high-velocity rifle bullet. He yelled down to the boat, "Head out to the northeast. Look for people or bodies in the water." The coxswain raised his hand in acknowledgment.

"Everything that can be stripped off is gone," Colosimo said, looking up at Dan from below. A cocked-and-locked automatic was thrust under his web belt. "Not a cassette tape left. Binocular stowages empty. Somebody went through the women's quarters. Hard to tell what's missing, but there are clothes all over. There's a safe open in the master cabin. No damage. Whoever opened it knew the combination."

"The master or the owner." Dan followed Colosimo below, down a companionway. An air-conditioning unit was still running, and it was like descending into a colder zone of abandonment and fear. A spacious lounge area shone with hand-fitted teak. Dangling cables showed where some sort of entertainment electronics, a large-screen TV or sound system, had been ripped out. The rotten-fruit smell of alcohol led him to smashed glass below a hastily looted bar. He looked into small but expensively appointed cabins behind louvered doors. The drawers had been pulled out and their contents emptied onto the bunks. A shoe caught his eye, lying in a corner. A woman's espadrille, or maybe a girl's—it was small enough—no longer new but not worn out, either. It was impossible to tell what was missing, and it was unimportant next to the main thing on his mind. "Where do you think they are? The crew? Passengers?"

Colosimo was silent. Dan rubbed his face, wishing this were something as harmless as a nightmare. He kept seeing the shoe. "Shot? Overboard?"

The reservist said, in a low voice, "If they're lucky."

"If they're—" He stopped, not wanting to pursue it any further. Instead he swallowed and said, "We finally raised the PCG. They'll have a boat here in an hour."

"That's good," said Colosimo. He didn't say anything else, just stood brooding, looking around the cabin. Finally he turned and climbed back into the open air again.

Dan kept the RHIBs out searching. They reported back no sign of the crew, alive or dead. No sign of the pirates, either. Only scores of small bancas to the north, any of whom could be those of the people who had killed everybody aboard the *Queen Salotte*. There was no way to tell short of searching them all, which was out of the question. When one coxswain tried, he caught one outrigger, but the others scattered, bursting apart in a swift-running swarm like sardines at the approach of a tuna. They were astonishingly fast, skimming away across the breaking water of shoal patches as their colorful sails dipped and swayed.

Dan stood on the open deck, looking down at where a bullet had scarred its way across the pristine white. He slowly clenched his fists.

17

THE SOUTH CHINA SEA

THEY never actually saw the aircraft. It was a radar detection, a high, crossing contact at 30,000 feet. The news arrived in Dan's cabin via a call from CIC. "The ESM guys say it's radiating long-range surveillance. It's pretty definitely a dedicated overflight, probably out of southern China."

"You're saying it's maritime surveillance? Targeted on us?"

"Overflying the TF, right, sir. They're keeping tabs on us."

"Have you reported it to Clear Bell?"

"Clear Bell" was Suriadiredja's radio voice call. The petty officer said it had gone out over the task force coordination net as soon as he picked it up.

So they were being tracked by the Chinese. Dan reflected, hanging up, that it was hardly worth their while.

The TNTF had lost *Sea Lion* as it crossed the 15° North line. There hadn't been even a lame explanation this time, simply laconic words on the bridge-to-bridge stating she was returning to Singapore. Now only three ships remained, steaming steadily north through slate-blue, wind-harried swells kicked up by the renewed monsoon wind.

The task force had emerged from operations in the Sulu Sea with empty hands. It was perfectly obvious to Dan, in hindsight at least, that its corvettes and frigates were too large and deep-draft for the task. Even the patrol craft had drawn too much water to follow the bancas and vintas across reefs and coral heads. Whenever they tried to close, the small craft skimmed away, vanishing like mosquitoes ahead of a charging sloth. The two Philippine Coast Guard craft had been almost useless, plagued by radio and engine breakdowns.

No one had found a trace of the crew and passengers of *Queen Salotte.*

That was disturbing, their 0 for 0 record so far. But what Dan found just as disturbing was the continued silence from PACFLEET and, indeed, everyone else to whom he had sent a stream of steadily more urgent messages as they'd steamed north through the Mindoro Strait and along the coast of Luzon. The single response Compline had logged was from COMNAVBASE Subic, putting off his request to enter port for overhaul, resupply, and to off-load suspects in the Vorenkamp murder case. Not denying permission, exactly, simply stating that his request had been forwarded. He'd stared at the message—on the reverse side of an older one; the radiomen were down to using both sides of the paper now—with numb disbelief. It was as if he were an outcast, as if he and the ship beneath his feet and the crew that ran her no longer belonged to the U.S. Navy at all.

That evening a flashing light message came over the darkling sea from *Nala:*

> IN VIEW OF REDUCED PARTICIPATION OPERATION OCEANIC PROSPECT TERMINATED X USS GADDIS RELEASED TO PROCEED AS DIRECTED BY NATIONAL AUTHORITIES X OUR FORAY HAS DEMONSTRATED POSSIBILITY OF INTERNATIONAL COOPERATION AND HAS SUCCESSFULLY REDUCED SCALE AND NUMBER OF PIRATICAL INCIDENTS IN AREAS WHERE SUCH HAVE RECENTLY OCCURRED X MANY THANKS TO OFFICERS AND MEN USS GADDIS SIGNED WALUYO SUPRYO SURIADIREDJA ADMIRAL NAVY OF REPUBLIC OF INDONESIA

Shortly thereafter *Nala* and *Monginsidi* turned westward together. They drew off to the west, then swung again, together, headed south. Dave Zabounian called down from the bridge for a new course. Dan had none to give him. The task force had dissolved. The operation was over. They had no orders and nowhere to go.

That evening *Gaddis* lay alone on a sullen sea. She rolled slowly, barely with way on. One boiler lit off, just enough turns on the screw to maintain steerageway. Dan sat on the bridge, watching the terminator sweep toward them. He tented his fingers and listened to the murmur of the quartermaster to the boatswain, the sigh of the monsoon wind as it streamed past the open wing door. To his left the sun sank steadily, drawing a scarlet veil down after it across the darkling sky.

He had to think. Had to find some sense in this.

This was not the way the U. S. Navy operated.

Even steaming on independent duty, a ship was under the operational command of one of the fleet commanders. When it was commissioned, it reported to him for assignment. It operated under his orders, according to his operating schedule. He assigned it to a task force, when it deployed.

Of course, *Gaddis* had not been formally recommissioned. It had been turned over to the Pakistanis, then turned back to him; but he had to admit, it had never actually been reflagged. In a legal sense, it could be argued that she had not been a U.S. Navy ship since leaving Philadelphia.

But he'd dealt with that. He'd reported in to PACFLEET the day he'd gotten under way from Karachi, both by radio and by a cable he had handed to the attaché before getting under way. He'd reviewed Article 606 of Naval Regulations and Naval Warfare Pub Seven, Reporting Requirements, and made his required reports in the clear. He'd given copies of his movement report, combat readiness report, and logistics requirements reports to Captain Sasko as well, to make sure they went out. And never gotten a reply. Dan had assumed that was because he was turned over to a foreign opcon and because he still didn't have covered communication capabilities. As well as the fact that much of the Seventh Fleet had deployed west to support Desert Shield. Hey, he could understand being left on someone's desk for a few days. But still it was disturbing, that he'd never received an acknowledgment.

The next and just as unsettling question was what his own status was. He'd been head of the MTT but, aside from a verbal order from Sasko, had nothing to confirm that he was in command. That hadn't bothered him overmuch. Not at first.

The question was, What did they expect him to do now, with a ship steadily declining in readiness and a crew that ranged from disgruntled to barely this side of mutinous? With a body in chill stores and two murder suspects locked down?

Outside the blackness arrived, the night laying itself over them heavy and dense and yet somehow comforting as a lead X-ray apron. He stared out into it and groped in the darkness, but his outstretched fingers found nothing but a tenuous fog.

THE next morning he was shaving when someone tapped on his door. He half-turned from the mirror, lathered with a Santa Claus beard. "What is it?"

"It's me, Captain."

It was Juskoviac. "What you got, Greg?" Dan asked, turning back to the mirror and lifting his chin to get underneath.

He saw then, in the mirror, that several enlisted men stood behind the exec. He laid down the razor slowly and dried his hands on the towel.

"The crew's presenting a petition, sir."

"A petition," Dan repeated. He looked at them in the mirror, then picked up his razor again. "I'm shaving right now. Give me a few minutes; then meet me on the bridge."

Later, in the fresh khakis Usmani had laid out, Dan stood on the port wing as the cool breeze ruffled his hair. The sky was overcast again, and they'd come far enough north it was time to think about a jacket. *Gaddis* barely stirred through slate gray four-foot seas. Dan had called Mellows up from the chiefs' quarters. The burly master-at-arms stood a few feet aft, arms crossed. Dan watched the men emerge from the signal shack and come forward. One took his hat off; the others didn't. Dan noticed the exec wasn't with them now.

"What's this about a petition?" he said, ignoring the sheet of paper one held out. "I don't want to see that. I want to hear what you've got to say."

"Sir, we want to know what the fuck's going on," said a man Lenson recognized as a machinist's mate third, family in Texas. "We're not getting paid and we're not doing anything out here. We want to know the ship's schedule, find out when we're going home."

"All right. What else?"

Sullen stares directed at their boots. Clearing of throats. Dan said, raising his voice, "You're up here. Let's get it out on the table."

"We ain't had any liberty since we left the Med," said another sailor. "You got the guys cut C.V. locked up in the fan room, Captain. It's either Pistol or Shi-hime. So just to let you know what some people is saying, they say the next time we see land, we're goin' ashore."

Dan said coldly, again, "What else?"

Silence and more glances. "That's about it, Captain," one said. "Just we don't understand what we're doing out here. There ain't even any smokes."

He considered just telling them to go below, cutting them off without an explanation, but that did not seem fair. He'd always found leveling with the American enlisted man paid better than trying to snow or bully him or buy him off. So he pushed down his anger and said, "First off: Whoever gave you the idea you could come up here with a petition is wrong. We don't have a right of petition in the U.S. military. But I will tell you, the early wrap-up on Oceanic Prospect caught everybody flat-footed. I sent a message requesting that we go into port in Subic. We can get resupplied there, get some of our casreps fixed, and jack up the pork chops on our pay problems. They came back that we have no orders from Seventh Fleet to do that, that they have a lot going on with Desert Shield and all, and for us to stand by and we'll be given a date to go in."

They didn't respond, at least not verbally. Somebody shifted in back. The others stared at Dan expectantly.

"Now, this 'petition.' That's not how you present a grievance in the Navy. In fact, it's close to what military law calls 'conspiracy.' I know some things have seemed not so shit hot lately. But this is still a U.S. Navy warship. We still have the UCMJ and you still have a chain of command. Any complaints or suggestions, take them up with your division chiefs or division officers. If what you hear from them doesn't satisfy you, then I'll see any man who has a beef, one-on-one."

A murmur. "What was that?" said Dan sharply.

"You said we got a chain of command. But you don't got any orders, and Mr. Juskoviac does."

Mellows dropped his lounging attitude and moved forward threateningly. "You shut your fucking mouth, Carr."

Dan said, "Wait a minute, Marsh. What do you mean, 'Mr. Juskoviac does'?"

"That's what he said. He said he at least got orders saying he's the XO. You don't have anything says you're in charge."

"That's enough. You people are on the edge of some serious trouble—"

"The chief's right," Dan told them. "You can all go below now." The ones in back started to drift. "No—wait a minute."

He straightened, keeping the anger reined, but letting it show. "For your information, I do have orders. They are verbal, but they are just as effective as paper orders, until those paper orders arrive. So don't allow yourselves or your shipmates any illusions I am not in full command of this ship. Another thing. The next man who circulates a petition will be charged under Article Eighty-one and Article Ninety-four. If you don't know what those articles mean, you'll find the Manual for Courts-Martial in the ship's office. They are the articles in the Uniform Code of Military Justice for conspiracy, mutiny, and sedition.

"Any other questions?"

He held them fixed, but not one returned his look. They stood completely silent. He said, hearing the edge in his voice and also something that, to his surprise, sounded close to contempt: "Dismissed."

"YOU wanted to see me?"

Dan observed himself as if from a distance. He had to get a grip; this anger took him by surprise sometimes. It was the lack of sleep and the continual stress.

He said to Greg Juskoviac, "Yeah, let's take a little stroll."

A fresh wind out of Asia swept the fantail. Dan waited till they were aft of the quad forty tub. The lookout glanced around, then stood quickly from a folding chair set with its front legs on the gunwale strake. Dan took three quick strides to him, jerked the light metal chair up off the deck, held it over the lifeline, then pitched it out and down. It splashed into the whirling foam *Gaddis* dragged behind her. Still visible beneath the water, it glinted for a moment through the bubble-streaked sea, then faded away into the deep green. The lookout gaped, then jerked his binoculars up and turned away hastily, taking refuge behind the black barrels.

"You OK?" Juskoviac said, his voice a blend of alarm and concern.

"No, I'm not OK! What the hell are you telling people? I just had a bunch of white-hats tell me you told them you had orders and I didn't."

Juskoviac licked his lips. "I didn't say that exactly."

"What exactly *did* you say, Greg? I'd very much like to know, because right now I'm thinking of relieving you of your duties."

"They came to me for advice. A lot of these guys, they were jerked in here en route someplace else. They're gap fillers. They want to know when they're going to get back to their commands."

"Don't stop now. Keep explaining."

"So one of them said why were you CO anyway, we

were the same rank. . . . I said something about the MTT and you being senior. Then they asked about my orders, whether I had orders to the ship. I said sure, of course I do. I didn't say anything about command orders. They aren't command orders."

"They sure as shit aren't."

Juskoviac seemed about to say something else. Dan waited, sure he knew what it was. That his own weren't command orders, either; that at best he was head of the training team on a Pakistani frigate named PNS *Tughril*. If he said it, Dan was ready to rip Juskoviac's head off and throw it overboard after the chair. But finally the exec said just, "Yessir."

"OK, so these boys consult with you about their grievances. Great; that's XO territory. But the next thing I know they're in my stateroom, presenting a goddamn petition, for God's sake. And where the hell are you? Leading them! Do you have the faintest, slightest idea that is not your role? Do you have any conception of that?"

Juskoviac said in a sulky tone, "Well, I've been trying to take care of this Vorenkamp thing. You wanted me to write up the investigation."

Dan closed his eyes. It was hopeless explaining or remonstrating. The man did not have it in him. How had he made it to lieutenant commander? The average competent petty officer third had more leadership ability.

"Listen carefully now, Greg, OK? Words of one syllable. I am not happy with your work. Either in this matter or anything else I have asked you to do since I took over this ship. I've tried to give you the benefit of the doubt. I've tried everything I know to motivate you, to explain how to accomplish your duties, and it hasn't worked. I am now terminating my efforts. I considered, on the way down here from the bridge, relieving you and putting Jim Armey in as XO. But I need him in the engine room, and I can't afford to let you fuck things up down there. I'd swap you and Chick, but the same goes for the guns. In fact, I can't think of any-place in the ship for you except maybe the scullery, and that would bring too much discredit on the rest of the ward-room. So I'm going to leave you, officially, with the title of XO. But you are out of the loop from now on command-wise, and the day we touch port you are off this ship."

Dan expected Juskoviac to lash out, at the very least ver-bally, even to punch him. That was why he'd come back to the fantail, where they could have it out without an audi-ence. It would have been a relief, a release. But all the exec did was get a hurt, sad look. "If you weren't happy, you could have told me," he said.

Dan felt himself start to lose it. He stared around wildly and caught the aft lookout glancing at them out of the cor-ner of his eyes and murmuring into the phones. He brought his hands down with an effort. "That's all I have to say. Anybody else comes to you with their problems, send him to Chief Mellows. He's the guy I have to depend on around here. Unfortunately. Do we understand each other?"

Juskoviac said, "And you still want me to do the investi-gation report, right?"

Dan gave up. He started forward. He glanced back, to see the slim figure standing silhouetted against the sky, against the wake; he couldn't see Juskoviac's face, but he could see his hands, held close against his thighs.

Then Dan heard running steps behind him. He whirled, bringing his fists up, but Juskoviac stopped a few feet away. The exec was panting, and Dan saw with stunned fascina-tion how he'd transformed, in that brief period of time, into Juskoviac, Flip Side. For the first time, he wondered if there might be something more going on with the man than being an incompetent no-load; if his Jekyll and Hyde act might have a depth no one had suspected.

"You're not getting away with this," the exec said in a low, tensile voice like a steel strand drawn tight and plucked. His hand shot out to grip the lifeline as *Gaddis* rolled. "You're not going to get away with screwing me again, and all these guys."

"I never meant to screw you, Greg. I don't have anything against you personally—"

"Oh, shut up!" Juskoviac screamed it out, and despite himself Dan took a step back. Glancing up, he saw faces appear above them, peering down over the bent and twisted frames of the helo deck life nets. "I've listened to your gung-ho, Blue and Gold *bullshit* since you pulled your stiletto out of Dick Ottero. 'For the good of the ship.' 'To get us out of the yard early, so we can go to Desert Shield.' It's a load of fucking crap, you don't give a shit about anything but your fucking promotion, and it doesn't fool me or the men anymore. That's the reason they're presenting petitions. That's why they're setting fires. And it's only going to get worse. When they decide they've had enough, I'll be on their side. You've overstepped your authority. No; you don't *have* any authority. You think you're some kind of self-anointed king."

Dan fought for control, aware of those listening above, but also, with one corner of his mind, realizing the situation was moving toward court-martial territory. If it did, witnesses to a scene like this would be invaluable. "Are you threatening me, Greg?"

"Oh, I don't need to threaten you, Dan," Juskoviac said, and the queer knowing little smile he said it with was more unnerving than his words. "*I* don't need to do a damn thing. You're blowing this one all by your lonesome. All *I* have to do is stand by to pick up the pieces after it goes off."

"I won't allow you to take her over, if that's what you're thinking," Dan told him, but even in his own ears his voice sounded blustering, defensive, and weak. He knew he was right. But something in Juskoviac's malevolent certainty had penetrated his confidence like a crossbow bolt through a faulty breastplate.

A murmur and then a scatter of laughter came from above him. He did not look up. He stood rooted as the exec, still with that secret smile, came toward him, brushed by, close enough to touch, then undogged an exterior door and disappeared inside the skin of the ship.

18

THE next afternoon a minuscule darkness took shape on the horizon, a speck in the immensity of sea and sky. Dan broke out the package of charts Suriadiredja's staff had turned over at the briefing in Singapore.

Dahakit was an isolated dot of land far to the west of Luzon. The chart informed him it had been surveyed by Comdr. N. P. H. Harkins, R.N., HMS *Blazon*, in 1894, with additions and corrections from a Japanese survey in 1937. The longitude of all points depended on Tokyo Meteorological Observatory being in Longitude 139° 44' 41" East. It was an atoll formation, with four comma-shaped islands spaced around a central lagoon. The largest was about half a mile long. Dan eyed the chart for a long time, weighing his options. Noting the group of men standing on the bow, looking toward the atoll as it slowly rose from the sea.

Jim Armey, at his elbow, wiping his hands on a rag. The engineer's overalls were filthy and wet. Dark circles rimmed eyes that looked like accesses to hell. He said in an undertone, "Thinking of dropping the hook, Skipper? Swim call, at least?"

"There's no reason to stop here."

"Lot of heat stress down below. Since the air-conditioning went down. We haven't been seeing you in the engine spaces like we used to."

"I've got a lot on my plate up here."

"Sure you do, but you ought to know something else, too. You tie a safety down long enough, something explodes. The word is things are going to start breaking down in earnest if we don't stop at that island."

Dan gritted his teeth. "Not you, too, Jim."

Armey said quietly, "Hey, I'm on your side. Greg came

around to talk to me about you. I told him to pound sand. But if somebody stuffs a rag into an oil line, we're gonna have permanent damage." He shaded his eyes at the island. "Inhabited?"

"Couple of hundred people, according to the sailing directions."

"It's real wearing, steaming shorthanded like we are."

"You want to lay over a couple of days, Jim? Is that what you're saying, in your subtle way?"

"I wouldn't say no," Armey said, looking ahead with a strange, distant expression. "Just to get some shut-eye would be nice. But even if we anchor, I guess we'll have to keep a steaming watch."

Dan weighed it, looking at the chart again. He'd been thinking about anchoring off, using the atoll for a shelter and putting the hook down to the south. But the bottom went almost straight down. They'd have to drop close to some wicked-looking reefs.

Or they could go inside. The eastern entrance was charted at eight fathoms. The lagoon within beckoned with twelve to twenty, adequate depths and good holding ground. That seemed deep for a coral atoll, but he checked three times to make sure it was fathoms, not yards or feet or meters, and fathoms was what the chart said.

He slowly realized everybody in the pilothouse was stealing glances at him. The men on the forecastle were staring up at the bridge. He didn't like the appearance of being forced to acquiesce. But they were right—they'd gone without even a step ashore for a long time. And sometimes giving a crew what they wanted was the best way to reassert control. With the hook down they could save fuel, too. There wasn't much point in steaming around aimlessly, waiting for things to clarify themselves.

"Sea and anchor detail, Mr. Doolan," he said, and suddenly everyone in the pilothouse became very busy.

They approached from the eastward, very slowly, preceded in by the inflatable in case the old charts had missed a pinnacle or did not show a Second World War wreck. The northerly swell boiled cream on long ribbons of reef as they inched toward the eastern gap. Dan searched it with his binoculars as they neared. The hydrography showed the unmistakable slope of a volcanic upthrust, but at the surface it was a classic atoll formation. Level and low, a crew cut of white coral sand and coconut palms, so flat a typhoon must strip it bare.

A clatter from aft. The boatswains, checking out the engine on the other RHIB. The crew gathered along the lifelines, staring shoreward as *Gaddis* moved gradually into shallow turquoise and indigo, between ivory patches of reef. Gulls soared in their wake, crying despairing warnings. Ahead the channel looked emerald deep. The fathometer was tracking with the old survey so far, showing a good six fathoms, twelve meters, beneath the frigate's tentative keel. The entrance gradually narrowed, and Chick slowed to one-third, barely creeping ahead. The bow wave chuckled. The surf boomed and thundered. Shoals seethed to starboard. Squinting into the flat, dull light, Dan shaded his eyes to search for patches closer in. He was not immune to the ever-shifting colors, the play of hue and sound, but his mind was with the ship. If she bent a prop here or gashed her hull plating against a coral head, they might never get out again.

Then she was inside, the churning reef fell astern, and he breathed again. The depth fell away to dark green, then to a hazy, light-filled, translucent blue. The ripple of energy from bow and quarter furrowed the lagoon. White fingernails of surf clawed out toward a close horizon above which the sky bleached pale as if scrubbed with lye. A couple of miles distant he made out boats, moored not far from the flat, dark mass of the principal island.

Doolan gave the word to drop on cross-bearings from cuts on two of the islands. He put the engines astern until Dan was satisfied the anchor was set. They had room to swing. Four thousand yards to the nearest shoal water. He called the engine room and told Armey he could pull fires, but to keep an aux diesel running. The inflatable in the water circled back, the coxswain looking up for instructions. Dan leaned out from the wing and motioned him in.

"SHALLOWING fast, sir."

"We can't draw a lot more than those canoes," Dan told them, pointing to the outriggers drawn up on the beach ahead. "Keep going."

He'd told Chick he had the CDO; he was going ashore to check things out. Making Chick the command duty officer avoided the awkward question of Juskoviac's status. The crew staying behind had watched with a curious mixture of envy and hope as they cast off. Now *Gaddis* was a separate world astern, hunting slowly back and forth to the hook. He gave her one last, long look, then faced forward again.

The island drew slowly closer as they purred on. Wooden-hulled fishing smacks with astern wheelhouses rode off a collapsing pier. The canoes were drawn up under the flickering shadows of the palms. He didn't see any human figures, though as they neared he made out structures beneath the trees that covered the rest of the island. The whole scene lay in an ominous silence, save for the endless sigh of the trade wind under a close gray sky. The water was so clear that looking down, he saw sharks nosing along the bottom.

The coxswain beached them near the pier. Dan stood and looked carefully around. The lagoon was sheltered, but the thunder of the surf still underlay everything, a foundation of sound so steady it was almost silence. The RHIB shrugged in the shallows. He saw nothing moving onshore. Only the coconut palms swayed slowly, and the obscurity beneath them could hide anything. He smelled smoke and something strange he could not identify, that he'd never smelled before. He knelt on the pitching thwart, then levered himself down into water warm as blood and began wading toward shore.

Fifty yards out he made out the first figures, brown against pink-white sand, waiting in the shadows. Twenty yards out a patch suddenly detached itself and moved into the sunlight. It was an old man in a short-sleeved khaki shirt so faded it was closer to white than its original tan. Dan gave him a salute as he splashed up onto the beach, and the old man returned it, snapping to attention and whipping his hand up to his forehead.

"Good morning, sir. I am Philip Kalapadon, Sergeant, Philippine Scouts, Retired."

Dan introduced himself, shaking the fragile hand, uncomfortably conscious of the brown faces that thronged close, gazing up into his. Kalapadon did not release it. Instead he turned and began walking inland, past the shoal of drawn-up outriggers. Dan looked back at the men in the boat, motioned them to stay with it. Then he followed. Kalapadon pushed through the crowd like a canoe through white water. He said something and laughter rippled. Dan nodded, forcing a smile. They came to a coral wall. "What's this?" he said.

"Pig wall."

"What?"

But Kalapadon was climbing over, damn near vaulting it, still holding Dan's hand to steady himself. "Circles the island. We live inland."

They crossed a belt of coconut palms and emerged onto a path. Suddenly the air was cooler, damp-smelling, like a limestone cave. Dan wiped his forehead gratefully. The path was smooth. Not sand but worn white rock. It was not quite wide enough to be called a road. The palms arched over it in a tunnel of whispering shadows.

"The village is that way," Kalapadon said. "You see? Gives shelter from the typhoons."

The path curved and two young girls appeared, hand in hand. They stopped, staring astonished at Dan, then bowed to Kalapadon, greeting him respectfully. He spoke a few words, and they dropped their eyes suddenly, crossing their arms over small adolescent breasts. Then ran, giggling, bare heels and pale soles flying up like the bobbing flags of fleeing deer.

The village was a scatter of open huts built on coconut

logs and roofed with palm thatch or rusty sheet iron. Round-bellied iron pots squatted beneath them on blackened rocks. Fires smoked here and there. A black-and-white sow rooted at the high-tide mark. Four sucklings practiced around her, thrusting their snouts into the sand. A roofless outhouse perched over the water, colored strips of cloth fluttering in the steady wind.

The store was tacked together of weathered plywood and galvanized iron. A woman eyed the stranger as she fetched orange drinks from a kerosene-fueled refrigerator. Dan was relieved to see several cartons of cigarettes, both American brands and Japanese, and some cans of tobacco and rolling papers on the shelves. That would ease the tensions aboard *Gaddis* considerably.

They sat outside, on empty oil drums, as other grayhaired men joined them, squatting one by one on the sand. Naked children and closed-faced women watched from a safe distance.

When some sort of invisible quorum had been reached, Kalapadan cleared his throat politely. He began, "You are the captain of the American destroyer?"

"That's right."

"We did not expect a visit from a U.S. Navy ship."

"I was passing by and decided to stop. Let the men stretch their legs."

"After the war, we saw many Americans. We were glad. Life was hard under the Japanese. An American LCI brought me back to the island from the prison camp. But it has been a long time since then. What brings you to us now?"

"We're on an anti-pirate patrol."

"Ah, pirates." The old man spoke rapidly to the others; a murmur passed around the circle. He was silent for a few seconds, as if deliberating on saying more. Finally he added, "You're hunting them, eh?"

"For a while, anyway," Dan said.

"Good," said Kalapadon. He looked out at the lagoon and sipped the soda slowly. "We're fishermen here. One Fil-

ipino government boat came here years ago. A small landing boat, with soldiers. That was in the Marcos time. We
have not seen them back since."

Dan leaned back against warm iron. Suddenly the can in
his hand began to shake. He'd been under way so long,
pressed with uncertainty and occasional terror. Now the
palms cast dancing shadows on the powdery coral. Flies
buzzed in the cool wind. For a moment fantasy gripped his
mind. Give Juskoviac what he wanted. Let *Gaddis* go off
over the horizon. Stay here; find a native girl; live in a hut
for the rest of his life.

Beside him Kalapadon sat relaxed, body draped over the
drum. He was smiling, watching three naked children playing what looked very much like hopscotch.

Dan cleared his throat. "My men would like very much
to come ashore."

"I think they would be welcome."

"Do we need permission from the—" He'd been about to
say "chief," but that sounded so patronizing he groped for
another word. "The local government. The mayor."

"We don't have a mayor. If we have leaders, it would be
the men you see around you here."

Dan lifted his soft drink to them, and they nodded back
solemnly. "I'd like to bring my crew ashore, half of them at
a time—that would be about fifty men. It would be best if
we had something arranged for them to do. Say if we set up
on a beach, swimming, volleyball, maybe roast a pig—"

"That can be arranged."

They discussed prices. The old men turned out to be
canny bargainers. At last they settled on a hundred dollars
for the feast. Pork, rice, fruit, and fermented coconut juice.
They allowed as how there might even be a band, or at least
that was what Dan understood. They came to an agreement
and shook hands. He made himself get up not too long afterward, or he might have stayed forever, and Kalapadon
led him back to the boat.

The crew was sitting under the trees, with a carpet of
kids and young girls giggling and staring around them. The

men looked pleased but disoriented, the way Dan felt. The ship was a distant gray nightmare beyond them. "OK, let's head back," he told them.

"We going to pull liberty here, Captain? These are real friendly people."

"All arranged. Port and starboard liberty, and a beach party tonight."

They jumped to their feet, and he joined them, shouldering the inflatable from where it had been drawn up on the beach out until it floated free.

THE *Gaddis* men had been swimming and sunning themselves most of the afternoon, not going out far because the islanders warned them about the sharks. Now they gathered self-consciously as their hosts sang what seemed to be a hymn.

They sat together cross-legged on woven mats on the sand. Bowls of rice and taro, fried pork and fish and baskets of hot-hearted doughnuts went from hand to hand. Dan and the elders sat separate, a few yards up the beach. He ate a little rice, then tried the deep-fried tuna. It was crisp and fresh and very salty. He cleared his mouth with a swig of coconut tea. Beyond the shore *Gaddis*'s lights rode steady and reassuring in the descending night. The air shivered to the rumble of surf. And not much later, a guitar began to sing, and girls' voices embarked on a plaintive melody.

They ate for hours, and as the night deepened brought out the *tuba*. Kalapadon explained it was coconut wine, the 10:00 A.M. vintage. Dan passed on it but accepted a hand-rolled cigar from a friendly old woman. He gave it a token puff and passed it on. The elder took it with a nod and settled down to smoke it between swigs of fermented coconut sap.

"Now, about these pirates," Kalapadon said in a low voice. "We know something about them. It may be you know it already, though."

Dan dropped his eyes from the singers. The bancas in the lagoon looked like they had putt-putted many miles.

Fishermen exchanged news. It would be strange indeed if no one on this island knew anything about the incidents to the north. Whether they would say anything or not, of course, he had not been sure of. Now the elder leaned close and murmured beneath the singing, "You know they are Chinese."

"I'd heard that."

"There is a battleship with them. Our boats have seen it. We are too small to bother with. We have nothing valuable. They do not disturb us. We turn and run when we see it."

"A 'battleship'?" Dan couldn't help grinning.

"A navy ship. A big ship."

"I'm looking for pirates. Not a warship."

"This ship works with the pirates. It makes the large ships stop, and then the pirates board them."

Dan stared at the old man. "Where does this happen?"

"West of the Pratas, south of Hong Kong, east of Hainan Dao."

"A big piece of sea."

"Look for the battleship. Viatai here, his son saw it." One of the gray heads nodded vigorously, reaching for a chunk of sizzling-hot pork. "He said it had large guns and many portholes. That is all we can tell you about it. Please, do not let anyone know you found out from us here. Manila is far away, and the Chinese are very close."

Dan thanked them gravely, not putting much stock in the rumor. Someone had glimpsed a Chinese destroyer, and it had become a "battleship." But the news might be worth forwarding up the chain. If they ever reestablished contact or found someone willing to acknowledge the wayward and orphaned *Gaddis*. Which he was beginning to doubt might ever happen. He kept thinking of the Flying Dutchman. Maybe these islanders would tell legends of the Flying American, the ship that steamed off into the wide, flat emptiness and never was seen again.

A group of boys began singing, and the elders joined in, something in Tagalog whose tune sounded familiar but which he could not quite place. Not much later, Dan made his excuses and hoisted himself to his feet, figuring to find a convenient place to relieve his bladder.

The night was fragrant ink. As he stumbled along, he came out suddenly on the path to the village. The worn earth was smooth and cool as fine flour under his bare feet. He smelled moist earth and strange flowers and the sweet breath of rotting coconut. Brush scraped and rustled as the path closed in. Then it widened again and a cloud cleared from a quarter-moon and he could see, a little.

He was standing on the beach alone, looking up at the stars, filled with a slow sweet peace, when he suddenly heard a scream.

It was coming from the village, not the beach. He started walking that way, bare feet slipping in the sand. Then another scream ripped out, and he lurched into a run, hands in front of him to avoid running into the trees that came out of the shadows, turning solid right in front of him.

A woman was wailing by one of the huts. Islanders surrounded her, faces ashen. Flashlights flickered, but kerosene lanterns were more numerous.

"What's going on?" Dan asked.

"You. Captain. He cut my daughter with knife."

"What are you talking about? Who?"

"The sailor. My daughter twelve years old . . . he cut her with knife. She bleeding."

When Dan stepped into the mat-screened interior he caught his breath. Two old women stared up at him with blank ancient faces. One lifted a blood-soaked cloth for a moment. In the buttery light of a kerosene lamp he slowly made sense of what he saw.

The girl had been a chubby-faced, dark-haired island Lolita. Now her right eye was gone, cut from the socket with a crisscross of razor slashes angled in from the circumference. The rest was blood and loathsomeness.

"U.S. sailor," the mother said, spitting the words at Dan. He felt the hostile looks of the islanders, the steady accretion of adult men at the edges of the group. Each carried an unsheathed machete.

"Who was with her?" he asked the old women. No response. He asked the mother, "Does anyone know who it was?"

"We don't know name. Just a sailor."

Marsh Mellows, pushing his way into the hut. He was in khaki cutoffs. His bare chest shone in the kerosene glow. Dan caught the smell of coconut beer as Mellows stared down, then quickly looked away.

"Get down to the beach, Chief," Dan told him. "Take charge and get everybody into the boats. Check every man as he gets in. He's got to have some blood on him. She might have fought back, scratched his face. Ask every man who he was with, what he saw, what he heard."

"Aye, sir." The master-at-arms glanced at the girl once more and left. Dan stood, conscious now of the murmurs and jostling around him. He understood how they felt. This girl was his own daughter's age. He'd brought the killer to them, unleashed whatever beast or horror *Gaddis* carried with her on this innocent island.

Engelhart pushed his way in, dislodging another surf rumble among the islanders. The warrant officer looked at the women. "We found the knife," he said.

"Where? Whose was it?"

"On the path. No telling whose it was, no markings." Engelhart squatted by the girl. The women followed his every movement with flat, wide gazes. "We could take her out to the ship, get Neilsen to clean her up . . . oh. God. Her *eye*—"

"See if you can argue her mother into it," Dan told him. "I'm going down to the beach."

A bony figure in a wraparound joined Dan as he went through the trees down toward the sound of men's voices. It was Kalapadon. Dan said, "Sergeant, I can't tell you how sorry and angry I am about this. I knew we had a killer aboard. I had two suspects locked up, or I wouldn't have let the men come ashore."

"It is very unfortunate." The old man was close to tears. "That girl did not have a good name in the village. She would creep into men's huts at night. But we did not look for this from you."

The liberty party was gathered near where the inflatable was drawn up. The engine was running, and the lights glowed bright. Dan came up to them, and when they saw it was him they parted, letting him through to where, in the center of the group, Chief Mellows stood inspecting a line of men one by one as they waited to step into the RHIB. He looked around as Dan came up to him, and his broad face was expressionless as coral stone. "Here's the knife," he said, thrusting it at Dan so suddenly he winced. It was a hunting blade, a heavy pointed thing that glowed silvery pale under the lanterns. "It was pushed into the sand. There was blood on the hilt."

He stared down at it, unwilling to touch it. The spittle had gone dry in his mouth. He had to think. Already he saw flames guttering in the woods back of the beach, heard shouts and threatening voices. The motor of the other inflatable droned in the darkness, and men splashed out toward it through the shallows. He heard the crackle of a voice on the PRC-10, urgent, peremptory. He dismissed all these things from his mind and said to Mellows, "Any luck, any ideas?" in a voice that sounded thick and slow.

The chief master-at-arms held out a thick forearm, blocking the next man's access to the boat. "OK, that's a load. Cast off, then back here just as soon as you can," he told the coxswain. To Dan he said, "No, just the knife. But I guess it wasn't Shi-hime, like I thought."

"I guess not. Nor Pistol, either."

"This is one sick puppy. Carving on her eye like that—"

"Just like Vorenkamp," Dan said. "Just like the girls in Fayal and Singapore. I'm just glad someone interrupted him at it, this time. I wouldn't blame these people if they killed us all, you know? If those torches start coming down here, I want all you men in those canoes learning to paddle.

They were so glad to see us. . . . How can he keep doing this?"

In a voice so low Dan could barely hear it over the yelling from the village, which was drawing nearer with each passing minute, Mellows murmured, "Oh, he's having too much fun. He loves it. Why should he stop?"

Torches flared and dipped, approaching from the direction of the huts. Dan saw it was the island men, maybe twenty of them, bare-chested, heavily muscled, carrying what looked like rolled palm-frond torches or else kerosene lanterns. And long machetes. The sailors turned to face them, drawing together into a denser mass.

Engelhart, a few feet away in the flickering dark. "Captain? Where are you? Captain?"

"I'm here, Chief Warrant."

"Sir, we got some pissed-off natives on our six. We got them outnumbered, but them choppers look sharp. Suggest we get the hell out of Dodge."

"I agree. Where's the girl? I thought we were taking her out to the ship."

"The old women won't let us take her, sir. And I don't blame 'em."

Just at that moment, the islanders surrounded them in a semicircle, not shouting now, just edging their way forward with the machetes held downward. Some of the sailors snatched up driftwood and rocks.

Dan slogged through the sand and held up his hand between the two groups. The islanders looked at him. "Listen to me," he said. "I am the captain. If you want to kill anyone, kill me first. Where is Kalapadon? Where are the old men? I will speak to them. I am the captain, and I promise you justice."

THEY didn't want to let him go. Only after an hour's angry discussion, punctuated by threats and shouting from the younger men, did Dan succeed in persuading the elders that he would report the crime, that he personally guaranteed that when the perpetrator was found justice would be done, and that he would inform them of it, and of the sentence, when it happened. He also promised sizable cash indemnity to the girl and her family, payable as soon as he could arrange it with the Navy.

Gaddis got under way at first light, bringing the hook up at the first faint silvering of the eastern sky. The withdrawing darkness revealed canoes ringing the ship. The islanders watched them leave without gesture, without motion. The pilothouse, too, was silent, except for the low-voiced updates as they passed through the eastern entrance, between reefs seething like scalded milk. As the atoll sank astern, Dan sat slumped, chin tucked into his chest. Contemplating his failure, his complacency, his fault and guilt.

Around midmorning, after huddling for several hours in the signal shack, the signalmen broke a new flag at the port yardarm. Dan ordered it hauled down the moment he saw it. The signalmen protested that it was a joke. They lowered it sullenly.

It was a black piece of cloth, hastily stitched with a white staring skull and crossed bones.

IV

THE FAR SIDE OF THE LINE

19

19° 14' N, 117° 32' E:

THE SOUTH CHINA SEA

THE dawn broke with him still in his leather CO's chair, staring out at the sea as it created itself from darkness. For all he could tell from the rolling crests, the same polished gray-green as olive leaves, it could have been a billion years ago, before whole biological kingdoms had risen. Only instead it was today, this unavoidable day he had to meet and somehow master. *Gaddis*, dangerously low on fuel, without orders, manned by a sullen and restive crew, saber-sawed again and again into ten-foot seas driven out of the Luzon Strait by the interminable monsoon wind. The surface current here was carrying them north. He had moved with it, urged by a shadowy sense his business lay somewhere in that direction.

"Skipper? Sir, you awake?"

He flinched and sat up, returning to the prickle of unshaven beard, the dry mouth, the anxiety that accompanied him now wherever he went, every eye averted from his. Thank God he no longer drank. Or he'd be down in his cabin, turning into Dick Ottero bottle by bottle. "What you got?" he asked Compline.

"Sir, I don't like the weather picture. Here's the latest."

"I thought we couldn't copy Fleet Weather."

"We can't; I'm eavesdropping on the commercial reports out of Hong Kong. They're only three hundred miles north of us, and I'm getting it pretty clear. This Hercule they're talking about—"

"Make sense, Chief. What 'Hercule'?"

"The typhoon," Compline said, gaining Dan's attention immediately. "It's out around 130 and headed west. They're getting real focused on it, in the Philippines."

Dan told him to bring him every report he could get on it and to have Robidoux put up a typhoon chart for the bridge watch. He sat and worried a bit more after the chief went below.

Even at minimal consumption, they'd suck the last of the Brunei oil out of the bottom tanks in a couple more days. The last evaporator had crapped out, meaning all the fresh-water would soon be gone, with *Gaddis*'s increasingly leaky steam system wasting it. The men were down to a gallon a day, barely enough to shave and wash under their arms. Slowly failing boilers, no water, no air-conditioning, no comms . . . pretty soon this crew would be hoisting pirate flags for real. He didn't know what he was doing or where he was going. Maybe it would have been better if the islanders had done a Captain Cook on him back at Dahakit, grabbed him and chopped him in the surf. No, that was self-pity. He didn't have anything he recognized as a death wish. And without him, the ship would be chaos. Juskoviac would never be able to hold things together. The way he had so far, under some pretty trying circumstances.

Or was he kidding himself?

Sitting alone, he knew that was the most pernicious and inassuagable doubt, that unbeknownst to him he'd lost it, gone too far, he was over the line, and now no one dared tell him he was into Mistah Kurtz territory. That was the curse of command. But in his case there was a hidden flaw, like a bubble in cast metal. He'd always had problems with authority figures. Oh, he knew why. His father, the drunken, failed, strap-wielding cop. Commanders like Ike Sundstrom, Tom Leighty, Ben Shaker. Not always wrong, not always evil, but Dan had suspected and been wary of them all, even the good ones.

He smiled faint and bitter, watching the sea roll past. So

that now he himself was in command, what more natural than that he should doubt himself?

"Bridge, Combat," said the 21MC. Colosimo, who had the watch, glanced up from the radar repeater. Dan said, "I got it, Dom," and hit the lever with his foot. "Captain."

"Sir, distress call coming in from a merchant ship. Being shadowed by unidentified craft. It's open mike; they're still transmitting."

"They give a posit?"

"Coming in now, sir. They're up north of us."

"Let me know as soon as you have it plotted."

"Aye, sir. Permission to respond, sir? Let them know we've copied their distress call?"

"Absolutely."

"Combat aye."

The 21MC went off. Dan leaned back, briefly debating kicking her up to flank, then dismissed it. Why bother? If it was pirates, they either would strike or would not. If they did, it would be over in minutes. A swift attack, a quick departure, melting back into the chaff of fishing craft and small merchants that thronged these shallow seas. Why burn the last of his fuel to no good purpose?

He sank back into his seat, returning to the unpleasant contemplation of a very narrow range of possible actions. The time was coming when he'd have to go into port willy-nilly; otherwise he'd end up drifting around out here with empty tanks. He sure as shit didn't want to have to go through a typhoon in that condition. That was how Halsey and Task Force Thirty-eight had lost three destroyers east of here in 1944. Every seaman knew that story. No, the thing to do was head southeast, back toward Subic. Permission granted or not. Anchor off if there was no space at the pier, but just go in. Go in; give up; give over; throw in his cards; dump *Gaddis* and her hodgepodge crew and the murderous evil lodged at her heart into someone else's lap.

Why put it off any longer?

A weight eased off his shoulders. It was so easy, giving

up. Only the nagging sense he'd failed made it less a resignation than a surrender.

"Captain, Combat."

"Go ahead," he snapped. Why were they still calling him that? He wasn't in command. He never had been. It was time just to accept it.

"Sir, more information on the *Marker Eagle*. The ship shadowing them is a gunboat of some sort. It signaled them to heave to. Two more craft approached. One's attempting to lay alongside. The master has increased speed and is trying to keep them from boarding—"

Dan set his coffee aside, not sure he'd heard that right. "Say again—say again the name of the ship."

"They identify as the *Marker Eagle*, a ro-ro out of Hong Kong."

A restaurant in Little India and a white-bearded fellow who started conversations with strangers. A workaday ship, not new, not yet old; a cabin filled with paintings and good talk and friendliness to a stranger.

He shook himself back to the *Gaddis*'s bridge, to find Colosimo looking at him expectantly. He depressed the key again. "You said you had a posit. Distance to intercept?"

"Ninety-two nautical miles straight-line, sir. I don't know what his turn-away course is, though."

A trifle over three hours, at *Gaddis*'s best speed, Which she could not reach now, with steam leaks and worn pumps, yet still not all that far. Without Dan's understanding why, his heart surged suddenly upward, as if struggling toward the surface from an immense depth. The bare possibility of action transformed the world, the way love changed the look and feel of everything accustomed and everyday. He cleared his throat and said to Colosimo, filtering any hint of excitement from his voice, "Commander, let's come to three-zero-zero and go to flank."

"Flank speed? You sure?"

"Right, I know, we're short on fuel."

"Real short. We sprint too far, we won't make it back to Subic. By the time we get there, it'll all be over, anyway."

Dan ignored the assumption that was their ultimate destination. "Well, without knowing the ship's name, I'd say you'd be right. But I've been aboard the *Marker Eagle*, in Singapore. She was boarded and robbed before, in the Strait of Malacca, and the captain built in some precautions based on that experience. Depends on who's attacking him, but he might be able to hold out long enough we could do him some good."

While they were talking, Compline had been busy at the chart table, but he now turned away from it and approached them and stood silent, waiting for their exchange to end. Dan said, "Yeah, Chief?"

"Sir, uh, just to interject, going north right now isn't going to improve our position in respect to this typhoon."

The radioman had a point, and Dan crossed the bridge and checked the chart Robidoux had taped up. They only had two date-time/lat/long positions on Hercule, but it was obviously headed in their general direction. It would pass over Luzon first, though; that mountainous island was a barrier in its path. The movement roses in the *Sailing Directions* suggested a tropical cyclone coming over Luzon would curve northward. Compline said the forecasts he was monitoring had mentioned this as a likely track, but not as the only possible one; it could head straight west or even hook left, though this was statistically rare. Dan tried to weigh all the factors in his mind, trying to make the right decision. He'd watched the process, watched his previous COs as they thought their way through a go–no go call. Sometimes they'd been right, sometimes not. "We're getting status reports on this out of Hong Kong, right?"

"Yessir—so far," Compline said.

"And we've got a little time to watch him come, see what he does. I don't think another ninety miles north is going to put us in an irretrievable position. Let's bring her around, Dom."

Colosimo looked doubtful but started snapping orders. *Gaddis* swung obediently to the new course. Dan hit the bitch box again to tell Combat to pass to the *Marker Eagle* to hold out and try to shape her course southward if possible. Then he went back to stand by the helm console. The helmsman showed no sign he knew Dan was there, eyes riveted on the gyro, his whole being intent on keeping the ship on course within a tenth of a degree. Slowly, he became aware of a murmured conversation behind them, in the little chart room abaft the pilothouse.

". . . Let me out, but you know the son of a bitch did it still prowling around. Who the fuck knows? And what he doin' about it? He's headed north again. We're not going to Subic. Just steamin' off into fuck knows where."

A mutter in reply, something about the officers. Then, just incrementally louder enough that Dan could make out the words: "Maybe he right. Somebody got to do something about it."

He slammed back the sliding curtain to reveal two startled faces. One was Quartermaster Second Robidoux's. The other was that of Johnile Machias, the third-class Dan had mistakenly confined. Machias stared at him with a brazen, lazy gaze, as if he'd said nothing worthy of note. The QM swallowed, smoothing the charts spread before him. "Yessir? Need something, Skipper?"

"South China coast."

"Out on the table, sir, underneath the one we got out now."

"What are you doing up here, Machias?"

"Just hanging out with my buds, Cap'n. There a problem with that?"

"You're not on watch, you have no business here. Boatswain, show this man below."

"You gonna chain me down in the fan room again, sir?"

Dan turned back, enraged by the heavy-lidded face, the sleepy, contemptuous voice. For a moment he struggled with what to say, while three men watched and waited: the QM, Machias, and the boatswain. "Get below, Machias," Dan said at last.

Instead the enlisted men glanced at one another. They

still didn't move. What the hell was going on? Taken by a sudden disquietude, he glanced back over his shoulder; but the bridge looked normal; no one else was paying any attention. Colosimo and Compline, standing watch as JOOD, were over on the starboard side. He wheeled back as Machias said, "You ain't never apologized for locking me up down there, my man. That was not easy on me."

"If it was a hardship for you, I apologize. I did it for everyone's safety."

"I told you, I can't take that kind of thing. I said—"

Dan said again, "*Below*, Machias," and somehow that broke the spell.

The boatswain grabbed the seaman's arm. Machias said, disgusted, "You ain't gon' get away with this shit much longer," and drifted toward the ladder down, looking back, as if daring Dan to take up the threat. But he ignored the bait, and a moment later the joiner door banged.

"I don't want him on the bridge again. Or anybody else who's not on the watch team," he told Topmark, then raised his voice. "Commander Colosimo? I'm going for a tour of the ship. Keep her headed to intercept the merchant. Pass the word, what's going on, to get your boarding team and the boat crews spun up, but don't call them away yet. I'll call you back for an update in a few minutes."

"Aye aye, sir," said the reservist, eyes masked by binoculars as he stared at the sea ahead.

HE went below and walked the length of the ship, all the way forward on the second deck, then turned at the windlass room and went all the way aft. Pondering, as he slid through office spaces and passageways and test labs. Thinking, as he breasted the too-hot air of the empty mess decks. A solitary sailor in cutoffs, bare shoulders shining with sweat, pushed a listless swab over glistening streaks that dried as dirty as before. The scullery trash had been pushed into corners and forgotten; the stench was choking in the cloying heat. A half-finished repair had left cables dangling from the locked-open door of the package conveyor. He pushed through a watertight door, its ungreased hinges groaning and cracking, and down a narrow hooked passageway that ended at a door that was unlocked and shouldn't be. He pushed it open and looked around at a looted litter of masks and rubber ponchos, the deck covered with the black rubber duck feet of Footwear, Chemical Protective. A cleared space and a blanket.

Wherever he looked he saw the signs of neglect, filth, lack of care. Sure, they were undermanned. But wasn't that what Dick Ottero had said?

A functioning exec would have helped, too. Damn Juskoviac anyway. After their confrontation beneath the helo nets he'd vanished, like the Invisible Man when he unwrapped his bandages. Juskoviac's visibility, his impact on the ship and on Dan's consciousness, minimal before, had ended. He didn't come on the bridge anymore or show up in CIC. Dan wondered fleetingly if he'd done the right thing, securing power to the XO. Maybe any XO was better than no XO . . . no, not in this case. He didn't care what the man was doing, as long as Greg Juskoviac was out of his face.

He dropped down a deck to Main Control, found Jim Armey there, and discussed fuel state and possible ballasting against heavy seas. Then emerged from the hole and headed up, until with sweat dampening his shirt he emerged onto the open main deck on the starboard side aft.

Driven by a cool wind, the green sea surged by, leaping and running like a herd of deer, and he followed it aft to watch the washing-machine surge of it as the square stern dragged itself over the rolling surface. The foam seethed and sucked, and looking down into it he remembered how years before on another ship a man had turned his back on him and stepped out and off the stern, seemingly standing on the air, before dropping away into the vortex. For a moment that endless maelstrom called to him, too, and he leaned forward, gripping the lifeline so hard his fingers hurt. And that, too, brought a memory, of his younger self trying to abandon the doomed and sinking *Reynolds Ryan*, staring down into a fire-lit sea while his fingers cramped on an icy lifeline.

So many memories. So many years at sea. Was this all it had come to? Duty and sacrifice and struggle; was this what he had earned?

What in God's name was happening to him?

Gaddis was bulling through the ocean now at flank speed, and the wind blustered across her deck so strong he had to take shelter under the lee. Leaning again on the lines, he looked down as the combers surged endlessly by, their backs the cool gray-green one saw sometimes in human eyes, but a darker color in their curved hearts.

Standing there, he contemplated the conundrum. And once again, could come to only one conclusion.

It didn't seem logical. He might not be quite sane, even to entertain it. But if it was not the explanation for why he and *Gaddis* were where they were, well then, he had no other theory. The U.S. Navy didn't just misplace combatants, even obsolescent frigates. It didn't detail crews the way it had detailed these misfits and undesirables to him. And it didn't cut off communications or refuse port entry to its own ships.

All right then, he told himself. Reason it out. One step at a time.

Fact: He'd been extended to go with the training team, when usually the XO or the chief engineer was the officer in charge.

Hypothesis: Someone wanted him in command of, or at least aboard, *Gaddis* after her departure from Karachi.

Fact: The USN didn't let a ship's commissioning status drift, even if it was a question of a lapsed or abrogated transfer. It either was a Navy ship or it wasn't. But *Gaddis* had been left in that limbo, despite repeated notification.

Hypothesis: Someone wanted a doubt to exist as to whether *Gaddis* was actually a U.S. warship.

Fact: The Navy didn't refuse port entry when a ship needed resupply and fuel and ammo, "beans and bullets and black oil," in sea parlance.

Hypothesis: They wanted him right where he was, in the northern end of the South China Sea, west of the Luzon Strait.

Boot propped on a chock, staring down into the passing foam as the frigate charged northwest, he gradually realized that facts and deductions, hypotheses and speculation, all added up to a conclusion only if he assumed that everything—his unlikely assignment as *Gaddis*'s CO, her delayed turnover to Pakistani control, everything that had happened since then—had been set up by some single, as yet unrevealed operator, with the tacit or active concurrence and cooperation in varying degrees of COMDESRON Twelve, COMNAVSURFLANT, NAVOTTSA, CINCLANTFLT, PACFLT, and possibly COMIDEASTFOR.

He shook his head slowly, rubbing his mouth as he stared at the rolling horizon. No, no, impossible. Just reciting the list of commands and commanders who would have had to acquiesce made it *prima facie* the paranoid construct of a disordered brain. He'd always pitied those who saw conspiracies at the root of world events. It had seemed a sign of minds too isolated, too simplistic, too enraged at their own powerlessness to deal with the innumerable permutations a messy reality offered up for marvel every day. But then, grimly, he took hold of his doubts and set their faces forward again. Continue the analysis, he ordered himself. Follow to its logically absurd end, and clear your mind of it forever.

What possible rationale would justify such collusion?

He tensed. As soon as he asked the question, the answer was self-evident.

The only reason to have a ship that was not a U.S. ship, under a commander who could be disowned as a U.S. Navy commander, with a crew that was disposable . . . would be to make it possible for that ship and that commander and that crew to take on an enemy that was, for whatever reason, undesirable to confront directly. To make a statement or send a message, while protecting other U.S. interests by making his action plausibly deniable.

With a chill, he realized how neatly it fitted into his own career history. He had decorations, yes, and dedicated service. He had supporters, friends, even a patron or two. But he also had letters of reprimand in his jacket, adverse fitness reports, and a reputation in the Fleet for acting independently, speaking his mind, for being close at times to the proverbial loose cannon. Daniel V. Lenson could easily be labeled a rogue. And how smoothly and gradually it had all been done! On paper *Gaddis* was Pakistani. He had nothing, not a document, not so much as a message, to prove he was entitled to sail her. Everything had been verbal, passed by messengers who could deny any such instructions had been given.

It wasn't the way the Navy he knew did business. But he had to admit, if he wanted to reason in this dark vein, it *did* make a shadowy and frightening sense.

But if that was so, if it was even conceivable that was what was happening . . . then where did his duty lie?

Could the Navy abandon him and still expect him to do his duty?

Or did they expect him to see it was all a front, a cover story or beard or stratagem or whatever you wanted to call it, expect him to penetrate it, recognize it for what it was, and yet persevere?

He rubbed his hand over his jaw again, an unconscious caress to reassure himself, feeling the damp that rose off the restless sea, and his hand came away wet with mingled sweat and salt water. He was replaying in his mind every conversation he could recall back in the States, trying to snag some snippet of meaning he could point to as signifying, We're sending you in under false colors, but we expect you to do your job anyway. Or something like, We'll disown you if you're caught, but that is the code and you will have to stay true to it.

But then he saw that anything like that was impossible. If he went into this knowing what he and his ragtag crew would be expected to do and was captured, it would blow the lid off the whole effort. Moreover, it would expose the

United States as too weak or too divided to take an open stand against the power that loomed over the western Pacific.

For if such a conspiracy existed, it could be aimed at none other than China. The only power on earth that could seemingly not be confronted directly, either by the United States itself or via a client state or ally. The only power that had expansionist interests in the China Sea . . . and the only one that was underwriting piracy as a tool of hegemony.

He clung to the lifeline as the sense of doomed inevitability chilled his bones. Because they'd picked the right man. He had good reason to hate the Chinese. He'd lost Kerry to them, on a deserted towpath years before in Washington, and had to watch as the guilty danced away from punishment. Yeah, he had unsettled business with the People's Republic of China.

And also because, God help him, he'd always tried his best to do his duty, as far as he understood it. It wasn't so much loyalty to his superiors, nor even to his orders. It was an obligation to honor and to the United States, and even beyond that. Hard to discern as it sometimes was, he had always tried to do what he thought was right.

Could duty exist without orders? Of course it could.

Could a mission exist without orders? He had to admit it seemed unlikely.

But he couldn't think of any other explanation that would lead to a ship without a flag, a captain who was no captain, a stateless and abandoned crew.

He stared into the passing sea till he felt squeezed and wrung and his brain would no longer track down the mazes and switchbacks that opened before it. Then shook himself free and went inside the black-bulkheaded quarterdeck compartment and spun the crank on the phone.

Colosimo answered. No further transmissions from the *Marker Eagle*. They were not yet on radar. Lieutenant Doolan was mustering and arming the boarding party. Dan hung up and went back out onto the weather deck.

The gray sky hurtled past above, driven on an endless conveyor belt of high-altitude winds. Covering the heaven that presumably lay above it with an impenetrable mask.

HE stopped in Combat and listened to the ops specialist call the *Marker Eagle*. Radio confirmed that the transmission was going out, but only the hiss of empty ether replied. He crossed to the electronic warfare station and watched the petty officer as he stared at the screen.

The SLQ-32 electronic surveillance display console looked like an oversize desktop computer. A green bull's-eye pattern glowed on the monitor. Since there was no realistic way to measure how far away the emitters the electronic warfare gear eavesdropped on were, at least for a single ship, the display didn't show range, the way a radar screen did. Instead it placed own-ship and friendly emitters in the center, hostile missile radars on the appropriate bearing in the middle ring, and hostile nonmissile sources such as aircraft or ships along the outer perimeter. "What have you got?" Dan asked the operator, who flinched at the interruption.

He said he had two Skin Head I-band radars, a Soviet-style surface search radar used on light patrol craft, occasional VHF voice transmissions, and a commercial radar he assumed was the ro-ro's, all coming in from 000 to 007 degrees relative. "There's something else I get an occasional mutter of. Haven't been able to pin it down yet, though. Weak and intermittent."

Dan asked him, "Those Skin Heads could be Chinese, right?"

The petty officer said it was consistent with light Chinese units; his guess was Shanghai-class gunboats. Dan nodded, thinking it through. It wasn't too late to change his mind, turn back. That could be justified. He let himself be tempted, just to make sure he was making the right decision. Then he turned and ran lightly up the ladder.

When he got to the bridge Chick Doolan was taking over

as OOD. He and Colosimo saluted, and Dan acknowledged the turnover. Doolan said, "We have a radar contact now where our guy's supposed to be. I altered course to intercept."

"Just one contact?"

"One fat one, yeah. How big's this ship you were on?"

"Maybe fifteen thousand tons. High freeboard. That'd give you a big return, beam aspect."

"Not this big. I'm thinking multiple returns, too close to paint separate."

Dan said grimly it could very well be that whoever Wedlake had reported as boarding him could still be alongside and that from the ESM picture he anticipated light patrol or fast attack craft.

"That brings up another point," Chick said. "That we're going into this with just about empty magazines. We never caught up to *Malvar* for forty-mil, so the heaviest we got is twenty. You *have* thought of that, right, sir?"

Dan wasn't sure he liked the weapons officer's lighthearted tone. "I thought about it, Chick. But what's our alternative? Stand aside?"

"Oh, I fully concur, Skipper. Just wanted to bring it to your attention." Doolan grinned.

Dan told him he wanted the machine guns and twenties manned and loaded and the boarding party protected with helmets and flak jackets. Chick said they were mustering on the boat deck. Colosimo would be in charge. Lenson nodded. The guy might be a reservist, but he had good judgment, he spun up incredibly fast, and he seemed to know all there was to know about the piracy situation out here. He went out to the wing and had a short shouted conversation with the fire team leaders on the boarding party.

When he came in, he snapped, "Let's go to GQ." Doolan nodded to the boatswain, who stepped to the alarm panel. The electronic tones pealed out over the ship, with Topmark's harsh announcement afterward. When he made to rebracket the mike, Dan reached out. He cradled it for a moment, mustering his words, then pressed the button.

"This is the captain speaking.

"For almost two weeks now we've been out searching for pirates. First with the TNTF, then on our own. We had two close shaves, but they got away.

"It looks like we might have another chance today."

He told the crew briefly about *Marker Eagle*'s distress transmission and explained he'd been aboard the ship in question, that it had been attacked before, and that the master had since taken precautions. "We're seeing a larger-than-usual radar paint here on the bridge. Mr. Doolan thinks it's possible the boarders are still alongside. I suspect they are rogue Chinese Navy gunboats, operating on their own hook to halt and loot merchant shipping.

"If they are, my intention is to give them a chance to depart the scene peacefully. If they do not, we will warn them off with the fifty-cals. We should outgun any light patrol craft and we're a much more stable platform to shoot from. I will hold the boarding party inside the skin of the ship until I'm sure it's safe to lower the RHIBs. I don't want them bobbing around when there's lead in the air." He let up on the button and gave it a moment, making sure there was nothing else he wanted to tell them, then realized there was.

"I know some of you feel abandoned by the Navy. To some extent, we seem to be out here on our own. But I want to reassure you that it is only a temporary comm problem. They'll be in touch soon. Till then, we will stay at sea and carry out our previously assigned tasking.

"We are now proceeding to render aid to a ship and crew who have called for our help. That is an essential part of any warship's mission.

"I am very proud of how well you are doing, considering equipment failures and shortages of parts. I am proud of you and of USS *Oliver C. Gaddis*.

"That is all. Perform all last-minute ordnance checks. Ensure ready service ammunition is available at each weapons station."

He had no more than hung the mike up when a loud crack sounded on the starboard side. Heads whipped around, and the starboard lookout ducked. The phone talker yelled, "Accidental discharge, starboard twenty-mil!"

"Casualties?"

"No casualties, round unloaded outboard."

Dan told the talker to have the mount captain report to the bridge, applied his face to the radar hood, and racked the bearing knob around and laid the range pip against the contact ahead. Twenty thousand yards. Ten nautical miles. She ought to be in visual range. It did look as if there were more than one contact there, but the separation, if any, was beyond the ability of the radar to resolve or the scope to display.

The 21MC. "Bridge, Signal bridge. Surface ship bearing 350 relative."

"I hold it," Chief Tosito yelled in from the port wing. "A big white merchant."

"Anybody else?"

"Don't see anybody else, sir."

Dan whipped his binocs up, searching, then had it. It was the ro-ro, all right. She looked smaller out here at sea than she had alongside the pier with her ramp down.

The 21MC, Armey's voice: "Bridge, Main Control: Lube oil pressure alarm. Remote bearing header pressure, down to eleven psi and dropping. Cutting on both service pumps, we need to close the throttle and stop the shaft—"

"Negative, goddamnit, Jim, we're on our way into a situation—"

"Captain, you wanted to see me about that stray round—"

He snapped responses from the center of the bridge, acknowledging Main Control and Combat, sending the twenty-mil gunner back to his post on the double, sparing a quick look around to make sure everyone was in helmet and flash gear. To his surprise, he found he was wearing a helmet and that his made-up Mae West was snapped around his waist. He didn't recall putting them on.

Topmark: "Condition Zebra set throughout the ship, sir."

"Very well," he and Doolan said, both together at the same moment. All hatches and scuttles were closed and dogged. *Gaddis* was now divided into a series of watertight compartments.

Doolan, beside him. The weapons officer had one earphone clamped to one ear, the other dangling free. He said, "General Quarters set throughout the ship."

"Very well. That was fast."

"Minute and a half. New record. I'm going to let Dave take the deck. I might hold Chief Tosito here, too, unless you think we need him in Sonar."

Dave Zabounian, saluting: "Sir, I have the watch as General Quarters JOOD."

"Very well. . . . That sounds good, Mr. Doolan. This is when you notice a serious shortage of junior officers." Dan lifted his glasses again, checking the already noticeably nearer shape ahead. *Gaddis* was covering nearly a thousand yards with every passing minute. So far, he saw no evidence anyone had detected them. Sheer good luck that the ro-ro had ended up on their side, masking their approach from whatever was alongside. Her high superstructure even cast a radar shadow behind it, screening the hell-for-leather approach of the cavalry.

Zabounian, from the radar: "Contact ahead separating."

"Say again."

"Two smaller contacts separating from the centroid pip."

The gunboats whose search radars ESM had detected, no doubt. They had to be on the other side; that was why Dan hadn't seen them. But they'd reacted too slowly. They would be in *Gaddis*'s line of fire as soon as she cleared the bow of the ro-ro. At the speed he was traveling, there was no way they were going to escape being in range.

Beside him Doolan was saying into the sound-powered mike, "Your target, two small surface craft, bearing zero-zero-five relative, masked by white merchant vessel, range thirteen thousand yards."

"Remind them batteries tight, Chick. I don't want any more loose rounds out there."

"I'd sure as hell like to have the forties and the five-inch operational, sir."

"I would, too, but twenty-millimeters should be suffi-cient," Dan said. "These contacts are small; they're proba-bly trawler-size. A couple of twin thirty-sevens, without director control. A burst across the bow, point the forward mount at them, and they'll realize resistance is futile."

"I hope so," said Doolan, but he didn't sound intimi-dated. He looked happy, eager for a fight, and Dan studied him for a second, unsure whether to leave him in that state or bring him down to earth. Any eagerness he himself might have had once for combat had disappeared the first time he'd seen the butchery an exploding shell made of human bodies.

But it was obvious that the prospect of action kicked the mustached lieutenant into turbo mode. And suddenly a sus-picion glowed to life. Was it combat that excited Doolan or danger itself? And if danger turned him on, what was more dangerous, unpredictable, fatal, and thrilling than murder?

"Captain. Captain! Signal Bridge wants to know what flag to hoist. You want the battle ensign or—"

Dan jerked his mind back and almost said, "The battle ensign, of course," then stopped. Did he want to hoist the oversize Stars and Stripes it was traditional to fly into battle?

Wasn't that the whole point?

"Hoist no flag," he said at last.

"Sir? You want the battle flag?"

"No. No! I said no flag at all. I want bare halliards, un-derstand? Get the U.S. ensign down."

They gaped as if he'd gone crazy, and maybe he had. But he screwed the binoculars back into his eye sockets and after a moment Doolan yelled, "You heard him! Bare poles. ASAP, you son of a bitch!"

"Don't curse at the men, Lieutenant."

"Sorry, sir. Got excited."

"I need you to stay cool, Chick. Let's buckle down and stay focused."

But then everything went to hell and his battle plan with it. The 21MC said, "Bridge, Combat: ESM reports X-band fire control radar activated bearing three-zero-five."

Dan hesitated, mouth open to speak and brain racing to supply content. But none came.

Patrol craft didn't carry X-band radar.

A white flare rose slowly from the deck of the ro-ro. Wedlake was signaling, apparently. Dan frowned at it, gripping his binoculars half-raised. It didn't peak, then gradually fall, though, like a signal flare ought to. It kept climbing, straight up, leaving a thick white cone of smoke below it. A second and then a third flare appeared, rising lazily toward the gray clouds.

"Chaff!" he screamed, understanding all at once. Simultaneously Doolan jumped across the bridge, grabbed the pivoting key that fired the RBOC, and yanked it over. A warning bell cut on.

Above the freighter, the cones of white-hot flame and swiftly shredding smoke began to tip downward.

They weren't flares, and they hadn't been climbing vertically.

They were missiles of some kind, and they were headed straight for the onrushing *Gaddis*. They arched down over the drifting freighter and swung left, then right, hunting to and fro before steadying the weapons themselves visible now as dark hearts to the cones of flame, coming fast and straight down their throat.

Six sharp thuds came from aft, and Dan heard screams along with them. He clenched the barrels of the glasses, staring up at the incoming weapons, knowing that the chaff canisters took at least ten seconds to travel far enough from the ship to detonate into a milling midge-cloud of radar-reflective foil. The version *Gaddis* carried had an infrared decoy, too, but it took even longer for the heat source to ignite. It was designed to divert and confuse an incoming Styx or Silkworm. But for whatever was coming at them, smaller and faster and at a deadly short range, it did not look to him as if it would be effective soon enough.

The paralysis snapped and he loped across the pilothouse, shoved the boatswain aside as Topmark stared petrified out the window, and yelled into the 1MC, "Missile incoming, starboard bow!" He dropped the mike, wheeled, and searched a suddenly empty mind for another action to take. The first incoming round hovered, moving almost imperceptibly against the hurtling clouds, then plunged with the terrible grace of a diving hawk.

". . . the deck!" somebody yelled, as in the last ending seconds a clatter of .50-cal fire burst out on the upper deck, a despairing skyward burst, a last futile gesture of defiance as the smoke trail plunged down at near-supersonic velocity.

The blast snapped the deck away under their faces, and an instant later a rain of fragments clattered across the overhead. A second whip-cracked behind it, fast and deafening as stringed firecrackers going off a yard from one's ear. Bulletlike shards whipped through the open port wing door and whined about the interior of the pilothouse. As if by some magic, Chief Tosito's shirt suddenly turned bloody. Dan crouched, taking partial cover behind the heavy aluminum casing of the repeater, though his back and side were still exposed. He waited for the third explosion, but it didn't come. *Gaddis* plunged on, shaking off smoke and the remains of fire scattered about her boat deck.

Up again, and amid the strange soundless ringing aftersilence Dan stepped to one of the cracked windows, peering ahead. To his enormous relief, there didn't seem to be any more missiles on the way. After a moment he raised his binoculars, which he discovered were still around his neck.

Something had changed about the *Marker Eagle*. She seemed to have elongated at one end, as if telescoping outward at her stern. For a moment, confused, his eye told him she was swinging her stern ramp outward. Then he blinked and understood.

What he was seeing wasn't an extension of the merchant. It was the raked gray stem of a warship, emerging from behind the ro-ro. As he watched, the forecastle came into view and then the unmistakable silhouettes of turreted guns and directors, rising swiftly to a strange stepped pyramid of superstructure.

"Holy shit," Zabounian muttered beside him. "That's no fucking gunboat. What the hell *is* it?"

Suddenly other voices, other sounds penetrated the anechoic bubble around him, and he caught the dying whine from all around him as the power went down. The 21MC made a choked noise and went silent. The phone talkers and the QM were bent over Tosito. Blood was still jetting out of his shoulder. Some large, very sharp sushi blade had sliced him so deep Dan could see the raw pulsation of his lung. The Guatemalan gave him a steady despairing look. Dan almost knelt, then remembered: he had a ship to save, and a hundred men, and turned front again and tried to make sense out of what he was seeing.

The warship that had fired on them was still moving out from behind the merchant, a white bone growing at her strangely curved stem. Now he could see nearly her whole length. She was broken-decked, with very little sheer. Like a British *Leander* or Type Twelve, but he'd steamed with them in the Med and Caribbean; she wasn't either of those. The single huge raked-aft funnel looked almost Japanese. It was followed by a long, low, almost featureless midships area, with two more turrets superposed aft and a straight transom stern.

"Son of a bitch, she's big," Zabounian breathed.

Dan stared, his mind churning through observation and reasoning to conclusions about ten times faster than it usually operated. He had no idea who this ship was, but her armament and size made one thing perfectly plain. The other, fleeing contacts might be gunboats. This was something more like a light cruiser, at least twice *Gaddis*'s displacement, and unless he did something very quickly those guns, already training slowly around his way, were going to sink him. But without ammunition for the forties and five-inch, and without power to run the mounts even if he had it, he was helpless. The gun crews could fire the fifties and twenties without power, but they'd just dent the plating on something like this. The other ship could stand off and shell them to pieces, or put more of the missiles into them.

Only great good luck that first salvo had detonated high, a mission kill in their mack and upperworks but still not a mortal wound. Not yet. Not if he could persuade—

He wheeled and grabbed up the black canister that sat just within the wing door, yanked off the tape that held its top on, and shouldered his way outside. He tore the tab off and upended the canister over the side. It lightened abruptly as the weight within dropped away. He yelled to the boatswain. "Pass the word to the lookouts, all the smoke floats! Over the side! *Now!*"

When he wheeled back to raise his glasses again, the other ship was fully unmasked, clear of the *Marker Eagle* and moving ahead with swiftly gathering speed through the choppy sea. He narrowed his eyes and squinted as over the three miles of water he suddenly saw clearly detail, shape, armament and superstructure arrangement, radars, and antenna.

"Large guns, and many portholes," the fishermen on Dahakit Atoll had said. Dan had chuckled indulgently. Now here it was, the high freeboard of the forward hull dotted with dozens of the tiny circles.

Gaddis coasted forward, more and more slowly as the way came off her. The phone talkers and lookouts heaved the last of the smoke floats over the side. From midships, the one Dan had dropped burst into a brief flame, then began venting huge clouds of milling smoke the color of library paste. They were designed to be seen from miles away at sea or from the air, and now up around and behind the helpless frigate a great towering pillar built toward the hurtling sky.

Below him the boat crew, understanding suddenly, spun the lids off the red metal cans that held gasoline for the inboard-outboards. When the gas hit the water it spread, a silvery-blue sheen on the uneasy sea, before its edge reached one of the burning smoke floats and a sudden sheet of white-yellow flame roared up the side of the helplessly rolling frigate.

He didn't really think it would work. But it was the only chance they had.

Ahead, the gray silhouette shortened, curving gently as she gathered speed toward her wallowing and helpless opponent. Dan screwed the glasses into his eyes, blinking sweat away, searching through the thickening smoke for some sign of its nationality. Now that it was closer, he saw how old it looked, like newsreels of ships from the thirties and forties. The portholes—no modern destroyer type had *portholes*, not in the *hull*—were each bearded with a russet streak of rust. She looked like the pictures of prewar cans he recalled from the history texts at Annapolis, the old—what were they called? He couldn't remember. He lifted his glasses to search the mast again.

She flew no ensign.

Just as he flew none.

The bridge was dead silent around him. *Gaddis* surged back and forth as she slewed around beam on to the prevailing sea. He became aware that he hadn't breathed for a long time and forced himself to draw a lungful. He was choking on mortal fear and helpless rage. Watching, through the field of the binoculars, for the first flash from the muzzles of those short, grim-looking barrels that aimed now directly across two thousand yards of heaving sea at the wallowing frigate.

Then her hull began to shorten.

He watched in astonishment, fighting to keep his knees from folding. It did not seem possible. But as bow and stern drew closer together, then collapsed to a stern quarter position angle, he couldn't deny it, couldn't understand it, but had to accept it nonetheless.

His unexpected antagonist was turning away, showing him the white toss and burble at her stern. He held his breath and refocused the glasses, fighting the tremor in his hands, the shaky blur it made of vision, hoping to make out something on her counter, some clue to who or what she was, but whatever had been there once, it had been painted out.

Just as *Gaddis*'s hull number had vanished, in Singapore.
"They're running away," somebody said. "Hauling ass."
"Son of a bitch."

Dan said nothing, sucking in breath after breath. Smoky
air had never tasted sweeter. He'd expected to be swimming
by now or fighting fires and flooding from armor-piercing
projectiles. *Gaddis*'s own hull plating was only half an inch
thick, barely enough to stop a rifle bullet.

The warship shrank steadily, moving off to the southwest. Dan got a bearing and best-guessed her course. Then
he cranked the sound-powered phone and asked Armey
when they were going to have the emergency generator
started and how soon they could get way on again.

Doolan slammed a big blue book down in front of him.
Jane's, an old edition. Doolan flipped it open to an outline
drawing. Dan stared, grinding his mouth with his knuckles.

"That what we just saw?"

"Sure looks like it. Without this top hamper here and
those things aft of the stack—are those cranes?"

"Floatplane catapults." The weapons officer lifted his
hand, revealing the text. "Get this: Built for the Imperial
Japanese Navy. Katori-class cruisers. Commissioned 1940
through '41. Most of them lost in WW Two. One used as a
test ship at Bikini. China got the last one afloat as repara-
tions after the war. The Nationalists left it in Shanghai in
'49. This says it was laid up, going to be broken up."

Neilsen, behind them: "We could use some help with
this stretcher, sir."

They grabbed the head end of the litter, helping to ease
Tosito down the ladder on his way to sick bay, then came
back to the chart table and stared down at the book. Dan was
trying to wrap his mind around the concept of an ex-Japanese
cruiser, a ghost from the Second World War, roaming the sea
as a Chinese commerce raider. He couldn't imagine a more
intimidating one. "Obviously somebody decided not to scrap
it. What kind of guns were those? Does it say?"

"Four six-inch fifty-cal and scads of AA. Range not
given, but it's got to be more than our five-inch."

Suddenly all the radio remotes began to hiss, the radarscope cooling fans came on, pilot lights winked to life. Dan pushed buttons. "Main Control, Bridge: We have power back up here. When are we going to be able to move?"

Sansone said they were relighting one-alfa now and should have enough steam for steerageway in fifteen to twenty minutes. Dan considered, staring around the horizon. It was empty now, except for the hurtling clouds, the ever-lasting march of swells, and the white bulk of the *Marker Eagle*. He said to Doolan, "OK, call away the boarding party. Let's see just how bad things are over there."

THE boarding party radioed back that everyone aboard the merchant was dead. They had found the master on the bridge, shot through the head. The other crew members were either dead or missing, presumably lost overboard. Hundreds of spent 7.62×39 cartridge casings on the deck told the rest of the story. There had apparently been a hasty effort to scuttle, perhaps triggered by *Gaddis*'s sudden appearance on the horizon. The hull forward had been blown in either by a shell exploding close aboard or by some form of demolition charge. Dom Colosimo reported water coming in steadily, too much, in his judgment, to stanch with the men and gear they had available. He'd gotten enough watertight doors dogged to slow the flooding, but that was all they could do, postpone her final plunge for a few hours.

Dan stood on the bridge after he acknowledged, scratching his chin and thinking. Remembering the bluff captain who'd been so sure he could handle anything. His sparrow-like, vivacious American wife. Both dead. . . . And wondering how he was going to find, let alone attack, a ship that outgunned him four to one, that could range over a vast area of ocean, that operated in conjunction with fast patrol craft, that carried missiles he was helpless to retaliate against or counter.

A few minutes later, Dom called back to announce that

their first report had been in error. There was one survivor. A woman who identified herself as Roberta Wedlake had barricaded herself in a laundry room behind the captain's cabin with a revolver. She wanted to stay with the *Marker Eagle* and her husband. Dan said that was impossible. The ro-ro was going down. She'd have to gather what personal gear she needed and come back to *Gaddis* in the RHIB. Then he added, "Dom, I'm going to test your resourcefulness. Can you and Pistol locate any hose over there? Fire hose or maybe something down in the engine spaces? As large-diameter as you can handle. Something that looks like it'll float."

An hour later, with the white ship's bow riding noticeably lower in the water, the reservist reported back that Pistolesi had things jury-rigged about as well as they could expect. Dan moved in then and put *Gaddis* as close alongside upwind as he dared. Both ships had been drifting downwind all this time, propelled by the steady monsoon. The huge sail area of the merchant drove her faster than the relatively low frigate. The deck gang fired over a shot line, followed by a nine-thread. They hauled back a heavy manila line with one of the merchant's fire hoses slung beneath it. The snipes toiled cursing down on the main deck, spattered by surprisingly cold breaking seas, but at last reported they had a makeshift connection at the fuel riser. Dan told Colosimo to start the pumps when he was ready.

The two ships rode downwind coupled as if for a battlefield transfusion for an hour and a half, till *Gaddis*'s tanks were overflowing-full with diesel from the doomed merchant's bunkers. It wasn't Distillate Fuel, Marine, but Armey assured Dan they could adjust the sprayer plates and burners to accommodate it. After which Dan cast his end of the rig loose for the sinking ro-ro to take down with her, circled around to the lee side, and ordered the inflatables back aboard.

The RHIBs plowed slowly back, buffeted by seas driven higher by a rising wind. They were loaded deep with the food, grease, consumables, and spare parts he'd ordered them to ransack the sinking ship for. It wasn't looting, exactly. *Gaddis* needed fuel and stores, and there was no point letting them go to the bottom. Behind them *Marker Eagle* was listing to starboard, down so far by the head now that her foredeck was awash in the breaking rollers.

When the boats were yet a couple of hundred yards off he could make out the woman's face. It was pale as a patch of spume, cupped by short dark hair. She was gazing up at the frigate as *Gaddis* loomed closer, then towered over her as the boat slowed, heaving violently, the coxswain snatching a sea painter tossed down from the main deck. Dan waved at her from the bridge but couldn't tell if she saw him, if she recalled him, if she recognized him; could not tell whether she was seeing, at that moment, anything at all.

20

THE next morning he stood in sick bay as the ship heaved and strained around them, feeling the delicate bones within Bobbie Wedlake's motionless hand. She lay huddled beneath a sheet on the upper bunk, the reliefs of her spindly arms and legs reminding him of a fallen bird. Her face was colorless as wax. The manic energy he'd seen in Singapore was gone. The corpsman had given her some kind of tranquilizer, but she was awake enough to talk. She'd told Dan what she knew, what she'd seen and heard during the boarding. He'd told her Eric had died a hero; she could be proud of him. She squeezed her eyes shut and murmured, barely moving her lips, "If he hadn't fought back, they'd have let us go."

"You better not stay too much longer, Captain," said Neilsen.

"I don't think they would have, Bobbie. Not these guys."

"I told him, 'You're not in the bloody Royal Navy anymore.' I heard them shooting down below. He told me to go to the hidey-hole, bar the door, and stay away from it, and that's what I did. He said he'd come back down and get me, when they left, not to open up for anybody till then." She rolled her head on the pillow, then abruptly sat up. Clutched her temples, pulling the skin around her eyes back till he could see her skull beneath the flesh. "Oh, God. I feel so dizzy."

The corpsman rushed over, putting his arm around her shoulder and giving Dan a warning glare. "You're gonna be fine," Nielsen said. "All you need is rest. Do you want another shot?"

"No, I don't want any more fucking shots. And you get away from me." She pushed him away and swung her legs

over and slid down. Dan took her arm and she swayed there
for a few seconds, fighting the ship's motion, then sagged
and collapsed back against the frame of the bunk. "Maybe
I'll try that again later," she whispered.

Neilsen came back, silently disapproving, and together
they lifted her back into the bunk. "You come up to the
bridge whenever you feel up to it," Dan told her. "Mean-
time, I'm going to be doing some thinking."

Her eyelids fluttered closed, and a moment later her
breathing smoothed out.

Lenson bent to check on Tosito, in the lower bunk. The
sonarman chief was snoring stertorously, a plasma drip
taped to his outboard arm. Dan crooked a finger at Neilsen.
He asked for a prognosis in the passageway. Neilsen said
the chief was stable; it seemed to be a clean wound; he was
full of antibiotics and plasma. They just had to wait.

"OK, you seem to be coping. I just want to make sure
you keep all accesses to sick bay locked at all times. If you
need a piss break or want to go to chow, call Marsh Mellows and get one of his masters-at-arms down here to relieve you. Don't leave her alone, and don't let her leave."

"She's restricted to sick bay? Didn't you just invite her
to the bridge?"

"I changed my mind," Dan told him. "I forgot we've still
got somebody aboard who likes to kill people. Understand?
Keep her here as long as you can. And don't leave her alone
for a second without a guard."

THEY met in his sea cabin, Dan, Jim Armey, Chick
Doolan, and Dom Colosimo. Dan hadn't invited Juskoviac.
Zabounian was on the bridge, holding her bow on into the
increasingly heavy seas, and Englehart was still getting the
missile damage repaired and the radars back up. The first
thing Lenson told them, after getting them down around
the table that the heavy pitching had wiped clear, dumping
everything off onto the deck, was, "This is a council of
war."

"We're not at war, sir," Armey said. He leaned back, his

long, slim frame radiating fatigue and tension even as it relaxed slowly into the cushions of the settee.

"Yes, we are. Ask Chief Tosito. But first, how we doing with that diesel fuel?"

The chief engineer cleared his throat. "Well, what we got from the merchant tests real close to the JP-5 we use in the generators. So I changed out the burner barrels to a smaller orifice, to tune for the right air/fuel mixture. Then I checked for leaks on the burner front. The flash point for JP-5 and DFM is the same at 140 degrees, but the diesel's a lot less viscous. You'll burn white due to the air/fuel mix—"

"Burn white. More white smoke?"

"Correct."

"Are we going to make as many RPMs?"

"I guess the short answer, we ain't gonna make thirty-one knots anymore no matter what we burn. We're using baling wire and Band-Aids down there, sir. And diesel burns hotter than regular fuel. More dangerous, less margin for error." Armey hesitated. "What's this typhoon doing?"

"Robidoux says it's parked over Luzon for the moment. He's watching it."

"Did you look in on Tostito? I've been on the bridge," Doolan said, tapping a pencil, his face withdrawn, watchful.

"Neilsen's got him stabilized. Says the wound's clean."

"That's good. OK. Why did you say we're at war?"

Dan leaned back and laid out an abbreviated version of Bobbie Wedlake's story.

She'd been on the bridge when the two gunboats appeared. Eric had been unconcerned at first. Then, as their shadowers drew nearer on converging courses, suddenly became agitated. He'd called all hands on deck and ordered them to man fire hoses. At that time he had sent the first distress message, the one *Gaddis* had intercepted ninety miles to the south.

The craft, which Bobbie described as large gray speedboats with guns, had closed rapidly from two directions, closing a pincers on their solitary prey. At a range of about half a mile, one had signaled them with what she called an

Aldis lamp. Instead of replying or heaving to, Wedlake had
increased speed and sent another distress message.

At that point, with the crew mustered and under cover,
he'd opened the lockers and distributed the shotguns.

"I told him not to fight," she'd told Dan, looking straight
up at the overhead from tearless eyes. "That they'd rob us
but let us go. But he said if everybody thought that way, it
would just keep happening. If once in a while a master
upped the price, the bastards wouldn't consider them all
easy pickings."

Dan had sat awkwardly silent, not sure what to say. It
was one of those situations where there was right on both
sides. It had just happened to fall out that this time the captain had gambled and lost.

The end had been signaled by a sudden burst of automatic gunfire from both boats. One had fired into the superstructure, aft of the bridge, obviously trying for the radio
room. The other had let loose two spaced rounds into
Marker Eagle's engine spaces. At that point the engineers
had stopped the diesels, despite Wedlake's keeping the
throttle forward from the bridge. As she lost way, the at-
tackers had swung in and boarded over the stern. The stern
ramp itself was swung up, like the drawbridge of a garrisoned castle, but a platform the men smoked and fished
from off watch had been undefended. Dan nodded, remembering the Sikh watching TV there, armed with a baseball
bat. The boarders had shot the lock off the door and
swarmed forward through the cavernous vehicle storage
area.

Several crewmen had made a stand there, firing back
amid the containers and vehicles, but had been shot down.

At that point, Bobbie told him, Eric had ordered her to
the hiding place. He'd prepared three spaces for an extended siege: the crew's workout room, the purser's office,
and the master's cabin. She'd begged him to come with her,
but he'd refused. Said his place was on the bridge. He'd
given her a quick, apologetic peck on the cheek, then turned
away and begun shouting at his men, as if to avoid speaking

to her again. So at last she'd obeyed. Gone below, bolted the door, and dropped the steel locking bar into the brackets he'd had welded to the bulkhead after they'd been boarded in the Strait. Then crawled into the little laundry space and waited.

"So you never actually saw who boarded you?" Dan had asked her.

She said yes, she had. She'd been curious, so just before going to earth she'd undogged a porthole and stuck her head out. To find herself looking at the backs of four men standing just aft of the bridge area.

They wore green fatigue uniforms and olive balaclavas and carried AK-47s. They were quiet and orderly. Someone, maybe an officer, was shouting up at them from the craft close alongside. Roberta: "I heard what he said. It was, 'Ba ta ca ganjing.'"

Dan had asked her, "Do you know what that means?"

"Clean it up, make it all clean—something like that. When he stopped, one of the men with the gun yelled back down. He said yes, he would do that."

Dan had asked her if she spoke much Chinese. She said only a little; she'd been studying Pinyin on tape in order to be able to bargain in the shops.

He told his officers all this as they sat in his cabin. When he finished, they sat without speaking. At last Armey murmured, "They don't sound like pirates to me."

"They're pirates, all right. But I know what you mean. The discipline, the uniforms, the weapons. They're not Malaccan bandits or ragtag sea beggars like the guys we were chasing in the Sulu Sea."

"PLA navy?" said Doolan.

"I'd say yes and no," Dan said. "They're obviously Chinese, according to what Bobbie overheard. And they're obviously freelancers in some sense. But you're right—they've got uniforms, discipline, arms. They're operating out of a base, with regular logistic support."

"Probably Zhanjaing," said Colosimo.

"Which is where?"

"The Leizhon peninsula. North of Hainan Island."

Dan asked the reservist, "OK, what else do you know about this? Obviously more than we do."

"Actually not much more. But I read the IMO circulars in my reserve job and *Commercial Crime International*, and I get to see the transportation intelligence out of US-TRANSCOM and the Office of Naval Intelligence Merchant Desk. Like Dr. Guo said in Singapore, they're freebooting elements of the Chinese military. It's like a car-stealing ring. The real junkers just vanish. The more modern ships turn up in Zhanjaing and get ransomed back to their owners, minus cargo. That's probably what they had planned for this one, only we rode over the hill." Colosimo shook his head. "They've obviously got official sanction at some level. In a sense, they're not so much pirates as something else—something like privateers."

"My understanding of privateers was that they were licensed and it was wartime."

"Maybe a better analogy is the Elizabethans. Hawkins and Drake and Henry Morgan. The Spanish called them pirates. The English called them raiders or adventurers. Spain and England were not officially at war, but Drake still kept his plunder. The queen got a healthy cut for her failure to prosecute."

"That's probably exactly what's happening here."

"Well, not only that," said Colosimo. "Ask yourself: Why would the Chinese permit pirates to operate from their waters?"

"Because someone up the line is getting paid off?"

"Certainly that's happening, but how do *they* justify it to their superiors? I think somebody's playing a deeper game. Pirates operate in the China Sea—other nations aren't up to suppressing them—so China must step in and impose order throughout the region. It's another excuse for hegemony, as they call it."

Doolan said, "But wasn't that what Suriadiredja and the

task force were aiming to do in Phase Three? Come up here and take these guys on?"

"Only everybody wimped out on him."

Colosimo: "Sure. Nobody's willing to step up to the dirty dishes. The smaller nations are afraid to antagonize the Chinese."

Dan remembered the investigation into Kerry's murder, and his voice took on a less detached tone. "It works in the U.S., too. So they just keep going. Ship after ship. Island after island. Now they're moving south toward the Spratleys, and all the seabed and oil between here and Borneo."

"You don't seriously think *we're* going to stop them," Armey said.

"No. I don't. But it would be nice to catch them bending over and kick 'em in the ass." Dan took a breath. "Here's what I'm concluding about all this. I don't think ending up here, the way we are, is as random as it looks. They're operating without a flag, so the Chinese can disavow them if anybody complains. I think we've been set up as the same kind of unidentifiable throw-down piece. Like a gun with the serial number ground off, you can't tell who it belongs to, where it came from."

To his relief, they didn't seem to think he was nuts, or at least didn't say so. Armey and Doolan nodded thoughtfully. Colosimo said, "I haven't been aboard here very long. But I was active side surface line, and I have to admit, this is way out of the ballpark, what I'm used to."

"If someone was to be positioned to go against these freelancers—"

"Then they'd have to be outside the system," Dan said softly. "Deniable. Without orders. Like they used to say on *Mission: Impossible*: 'If you are captured, the government will disavow any knowledge of your actions.' "

"It's pretty off the wall, all right," said Doolan after a long moment.

Dan looked from face to face. "Well. I can't be sure. But if it was. If that's why we're here and what they expect us to do and if I decided to roll those dice . . . are we up to it?"

"I wouldn't mind shooting back," Doolan said. "If we had something to shoot."

But Jim Armey didn't respond. He looked worried. "Yeah?" Dan prompted him.

"I don't think it's that way at all, Skipper. Even if you're right, even if that was our—mission?—they'd have let one of us know. They'd have let *you* know."

Dan said, "OK, you think I'm wrong?"

"Not exactly, but maybe too eager? Considering we're in the neighborhood of a major storm, we aren't in the best shape materiel-wise. We could take a lot of damage, maybe lose some guys out here." He stopped.

"Damn it, Jim, if you can persuade me I'm going nutzoid on this, I'll be the happiest guy on this ship. I'm not trying to push a rock uphill on this one; I'm trying to avoid a boulder coming at me downhill."

The chief engineer hesitated, then added, "Skipper, you're the man in charge here. You point this sonofabitch, I'll make it go there. But if they wanted us on some kind of secret mission, this isn't the way they'd go about it. In my opinion. And they'd have armed and fueled us and given us better manning than these wharf rats and bottom scrapings we've got."

"You don't think the CO's right and they gave us expendable people?" Doolan asked Armey.

"No, I don't. If I got a fire in the main spaces, I don't send Fireman Fuckup to put it out. I send the first team. So I don't know. . . . Plus, now we got a typhoon sitting on Luzon, trying to decide whether to come after us. How much longer are we going to stay out here? I hope it's not so long we find ourselves in the dangerous semicircle with the propulsion plant in the condition it's in."

The chief engineer looked around almost desperately. "Look; like I said, I'm with you. All I'm saying is we got to make a decision. We just don't have a lot of time to dick around out here."

Dan waited, but Armey added nothing more, nor did any of the others comment. "All right," he said, getting up. They rose, too. "Let's leave it at that for now. We'll keep an eye on the storm track and reevaluate our options as we go. Make sure your departments are rigged for heavy weather."

"Was that a decision, Skipper?" Doolan asked in a low voice, jamming his hands in his pockets and not moving as the others filed out. "Look; I need to know. Jim needs to know. And the guys are asking us, every hour on the hour."

"I plan to stay out here till either we find these assholes or Hercule forces us south. So let's start thinking about how we're going to catch up with them and what we can do if we do."

He'd intended it as dismissal, but the weapons officer didn't take it that way. Doolan put his hand on Dan's shoulder, stopping him. The door closed behind Armey, and they were alone. "One last word?"

"I'm all ears, Chick."

"This is with all due respect. We don't have the ammunition to go looking for trouble. We find that cruiser again, he won't turn away the next time. He'll blow us out of the water with those six-inchers."

"I hear you," said Dan. "But we can't go into Subic now. Even if they gave us clearance, we couldn't go in with the typhoon parked over the island. We have sea room here. We have fuel. So for now, here's where we're going to stay."

Doolan held Dan's gaze for a second or two, as if trying to read what he found there, then dropped his eyes. "Aye, aye, sir. Am I dismissed?"

"You're dismissed, Chick."

USMANI brought in Dan's lunch. He ate it wordlessly, mind a thousand miles away. He was wondering, again, what he was supposed to do. No, not what he was supposed to do, what he ought to do. Because he didn't *have* to do anything, in the sense of having orders. The only orders were the absence of orders, and what he had to infer from that void.

He'd groped his way through this before and come to no conclusion. He'd puzzled over it sitting on the bridge at night. His brain had returned to it time after time; it had obsessed him even in sleep. Now he believed he glimpsed an outline beneath the veil.

The key was putting himself in the place of whatever intelligence had conceived this bizarre and dubious mission.

Whoever had put him here would anticipate he'd raise this question, even if only internally. They'd expect him to look forward to his eventual return and the questions that would be asked. And they'd expect him to understand that they had anticipated his doubts.

He stared at the bulkhead till the little stateroom started closing in on him. He tossed down his napkin and left. Stopped at the bridge, where Dave Zabounian was holding the fort against the assault of squalls and fifteen-foot seas.

Compline's storm chart showed the typhoon stationary six hundred kilometers to the east, bringing devastation, no doubt, to thousands on the heavily populated northern island. It might stay there, lose energy, and gradually exhaust itself in rain. It might start west again. Or spin north or even south, wobbling and meandering like the immense gyroscope it was. No one could tell.

If it went due west, it would put *Gaddis* in the position of a #1 pin in the path of a twenty-pound ball. But in the Northern Hemisphere, cyclones tended to spin to the right of their direction of movement like a cue ball with english on it. If this one did that, rolled west and then hooked, they'd find themselves in the dangerous semicircle, where the storm's forward speed added to its wind velocity.

If he'd listened to the quartermaster, Dan would have headed south long before. As it was, he'd tied himself to this square of ocean, and his options were growing steadily less attractive. Move too far west and he'd fetch up in Vietnamese waters. He was bounded on the north by Hainan and the coast of China. The Paracels lay to the south, but even if they hadn't been Chinese, the scatter of reefs and low islands offered no shelter or lee—rather, a mortal threat. And steaming east would take him straight into the murderous onrush of the typhoon.

Yeah, you've set things up real well, Dan told himself. He didn't like the looks of these seas. Not only were they building, but he was also seeing the long rolling swells he remembered from hurricanes in the Caribbean. He did not like the weird greenish tinge to the gray light. He stood with his hands in his pockets for a while, peering up into a charcoal sky from which fluttered pale ribbons of rain. The monsoon cover masked any cirrus development, but he could see how the wind aloft had increased; the close clouds raced overhead, curved like the paws of panthers.

He let himself out the starboard wing door and drifted aft, pushed by cold gusts. He checked himself on the midships flat, and blinked over the side at the rushing sea as his internal dialogue resumed.

If they expected him to doubt, the answer had to be that they expected him to assume he'd be rewarded for his covert action and for silence afterward.

If he was right and *Gaddis* swam now beyond the ken of national governments by design.

A burst of singing came from aft, carried against the wind, and he turned his head, half-listening. He was still thinking. Thinking that in that case, they'd miscalculated.

He did not need the assurance of reward.

Now that he'd seen the kind of things these bastards did, he wanted to sweep them from the seas.

It would mean personal danger and not only the kind you ran in combat. If he was wrong, if *Gaddis*'s situation was an artifact of coincidence and official neglect, the price would be steep for any casualties he took opening unauthorized action. The UCMJ still imposed the death sentence for murder and other capital crimes. He was no lawyer, but pillaging and looting, endangering the safety of the command, uttering fraudulent checks, and improper hazarding of a vessel also came to mind. Capture was not inconceivable, either. He might find himself turned over to an international or, worse yet, a Chinese court.

He shook his head impatiently. From above came the

whine of the wind and a clatter and buzz of tools as hull techs and ETs, lashed tight against the constant pitching, ripped shredded metal off the mack. One of the missiles had hit it dead center, blowing a big hole in the aluminum skin. Other techs were working on the radar, repairing the waveguides.

Whether or not he was right, a secondary consideration supervened. Doolan and Armey had both pointed it out. How could he bring these freebooters and murderers to bay when the enemy both outgunned and outnumbered him? Why would anyone send a frigate on such a mission, anyway? Wouldn't it be cleaner and simpler, if a message had to be sent, to send a sub in to put a torpedo into the pirate leader?

He still suspected the bottom line was deniability. If *Gaddis* was caught or sunk, she and Dan Lenson could be disowned. A commissioned, first-line submarine could not.

The singing came again, louder, and he stared aft. Something about it made him listen more closely. Then he frowned.

He walked aft, circled the helo hangar, and came out on the flight deck.

The first thing he smelled was charcoal, then roasting meat. The torched-in-half fifty-five-gallon drums the Supply Department kept for ship's picnics had been set up inside the empty hangar, shielded from the wind and rain and spray. And despite the pitching, the rain, the howl of the wind outside, the party was going full blast.

Everybody had a cigarette in his mouth, even sailors Dan had never seen smoking before. A boom box detonated with rhythmic thuds. The men did not look at him as he walked by. They were eating T-bone steaks off paper plates. One of the supply petty officers stood behind the grill, teeth gleaming, chef's cap perched on the back of his head, spearing and rearranging white-veined chunks of meat with a long, wicked-looking stainless-steel serving fork. Dan said, "Smells good."

"This one here got your name on it, Cap'n."

"Where'd these steaks come from, Machowski? I thought we were out of chill stores."

"These here come off the merchie, Cap'n. Pistolesi and them brought 'em. How you like yours, rare?"

"I'll pass." Dan told his disquiet, So what? If we didn't eat them, the fish would. They were lawful salvage.

He stood for a moment, watching. The men wore a casual mix of uniforms: dungarees and coveralls, blue jackets or foul-weather jackets, shoes and steel-toed boots. They swayed as the deck rolled beneath them. A thin film of salt water surged across the nonskid at the hangar door, pooled in the scuppers, then vanished over the side. Their uniforms were filthy, unwashed, but that wasn't their fault. Because of the shortage of freshwater, the ship's laundry had been shut down since they left Brunei. Ditto for their dirty, too-long hair. Some were unshaven. He noticed they still wouldn't meet his eyes. They stared at their plates or talked animatedly to each other, avoiding his glance. What the hell was going on? He didn't mind their enjoying themselves. He wished he could cut loose himself. But there was something off about their casual chatter, the way they spooned canned beans rapidly into their faces. As if hiding something.

He wheeled suddenly and grabbed the man who was trying to edge past, making him clutch at his plate. It was Greg Juskoviac. Dan pulled him close and lifted the cup from his hand. The sweet solvent odor told him all he needed to know.

The defrocked exec snapped his mouth closed, looking frightened and then, a moment later, angry.

Dan tossed the liquor out onto the flight deck, put the cup back in Juskoviac's hand, and shoved him away. He looked around, then noticed the one area on deck everyone had drifted away from as he'd entered. Everyone except Machias. The sleepy-looking petty officer was sitting cross-legged on a red-painted rescue-and-assistance gear box next to the barbecue grill. A cigarette dangled from his lips.

Dan strode across the slanting deck and motioned him up. Machias glanced up, blinking, then hoisted his long body till he towered. Dan reached behind him and jerked the cover up.

Rank on rank of flower-decorated bottles.

Pistolesi came out of the crowd. "The captain's cabin?" Dan asked him. The fireman scowled, arms folded. Dan braced his boot on the locker and eyed the distance to the deck edge.

"You don't want to do that, my man," Machias said in a low, somnolent voice.

When he turned his head, Dan saw all the men in the hangar were getting to their feet. The music played on, but the singing had stopped. The smoke from the cooking steaks writhed in eye-stinging clouds just beneath the floodlights.

"Say again, Shi-hime?"

Machias's eyes were nearly closed. He looked down with a faint smile bending the thin mustache. He did not answer.

Pistolesi plucked a fifth out of the box. He spun the cap off and held it out. "Jap whiskey, sir. That's your bottle. The rest of these is ours."

"Navy ships are dry, Pistol."

Machias murmured, barely moving his lips, "News flash, Boss Man. You ain't on no fucking Navy ship no more."

The eyes around him had turned opaque. They were all standing now. Dan looked at Pistolesi. "Don't push this one, sir," the fireman said in a low voice. "Roll with it. Take a drink."

"An' how about the split-tail?" said another man, staggering across the deck as it pitched violently. "Little dried up, but not bad-looking. See'f she wants to come out an' have a drink with us—"

Instead of taking the proffered bottle, Dan turned his head and yelled, "Juskoviac!"

The XO flinched. His narrow, balding pate searched

around. Then he put his plate down on the deck and trotted over reluctantly.

At the same moment, Machias reached behind his back.

His hand came out holding a hunting-style blade, still pointed downward as it had slicked out of the sheath or maybe just from riding tucked into the small of his back. It seemed to Dan to move very slowly. By then he was moving, too, circling slowly to his right, toward where the steaks smoked on hot metal. The men around them shuffled their boots, falling back to form a cleared space in the center of the hangar.

"You fucked everything up since you come aboard," Machias said. "You know that? Fucked up with the Pakis. Fucked up with fucking Vorenkamp. Fucked us up all the way out to ass end a noplace."

"Your point?" Dan said.

"My *point.* Man want to know, do I got a *point.* I got one, all right. You ain't gon' like it when you get it, either."

The knife turned slowly in the long, dark hand, tip wheeling upward.

Dan flicked the serving fork up, three feet of sturdy U.S. government-issue stainless-steel servingware ending in two icepick-sharp tines aimed right at Machias's windpipe.

For a moment neither of them moved.

"Take his knife, somebody. Before I turn Shi-hime here into shish kebab."

"Shit, Johnile—"

The electrician had lost his sleepy expression. He stared down with undisguised hatred.

When the knife was in custody Dan tossed the fork back to the gaping barbecue chef, then bent. He hauled four bottles out and handed them to Pistolesi, so that he had five now, with the one he'd offered, and his arms were full. Dan turned to face the men. It took an effort of will to put his back to the motionless Machias, like a matador turning away from an unreliable bull.

"Shi-hime tells me we aren't on a Navy ship anymore," he yelled into the monsoon wind and the crackle of charcoal. "There's something to that. But we're still on a ship I command."

Silence.

"What Pistol's got in his arms right now's enough to light everybody up. I don't have any problem with a party. If I still drank, I'd have a shot with you. But this is it for today. We could run into a major confrontation at any time. XO, take the rest of this down to Supply and lock it up. Decide on a fair ration and issue it daily."

Juskoviac opened his mouth, seemed to think it over, then closed it again. From the men, silence still. Dan eyed Machias once more. The sleepy look was back, the arms crossed, the cigarette dangling. Dan turned from him again and said to the supply petty officer, "OK, I'll take that steak now."

HE stopped again outside sick bay on the way back to the bridge. Wanting to go in, but not sure he should. Wanting to ask Neilsen for something for his own nerves, goddamn it. His knees were shaking. He couldn't believe the rebelliousness he'd seen in the hangar. He couldn't believe he'd had to face down a man with a knife. The crew was coming apart at the seams. He had no exec, hardly any midgrade petty officer structure to stiffen discipline. In sailing ship days, a captain at sea had a squad of marines with bayonets to keep order when the chips were down. All he had to lean on was Mellows and his masters-at-arms.

And now he had to plan around Bobbie Wedlake's presence. He was glad she was alive, but having her aboard complicated things. Not just because of the killer, though God knew that was dangerous enough. But he had a slew of bad actors aboard now, lads like Machias. If anyone got out of hand, it could be ugly. Some men lost all control when they drank.

You should know, he told himself. For an unsettling moment, the old craving had coaxed him to take a mouthful. It had reminded him of the relief from tension and worry alcohol had always brought. But he knew he couldn't stop with one. If he'd so much as tipped that bottle Pistolesi had offered, he'd end up stinking oblivious, useless to the ship and to himself.

Still, he'd barely been able to walk away.

Rung by rung, he and *Gaddis* were descending the ladder.

He had to decide what they were going to do. He couldn't put it off any longer. A prudent mariner would dodge south, get out of the vicinity of the storm, then come back when it was past. A responsible commander would take *Gaddis* into Subic permission or no, decline whatever game the gods were playing with her. Not stay out here, looking down the barrel of a typhoon, with a ship that was falling apart and a crew three millimeters from mutiny.

He decided to give it one more day.

But when he got back up to the bridge he found Compline standing at the storm chart, pouchy face ashen. Robidoux was crouched forward, etching in a position. "What's up, Roy? What you got, Louis?" Dan said, already feeling the knife edge of dread.

The QM said, "The tracking reports got sent twice."

"Give me the bad news, guys. It doesn't improve with age."

The radioman chief said that one of the position reports had been retransmitted without being updated. Hercule had not been hovering stationary over Luzon, as they had thought. "It must have a real strong subtropical high pushing it along. It's been roaring west at twenty-two knots for eight hours, while we thought it was in park."

Dan bent to the chart as the bow dropped away into a trough, leaving his head floating and his gut dragging along somewhere behind. The sky to the east was turning a dead, woolly dark that made his mouth go dry in sheer physical fear. It was black as a coal face, laced with hot platinum wires of lightning. The red *X* Robidoux had just lifted his grease pencil off showed the typhoon 150 nautical miles west of Cape Bolinao and starting to hook north.

He'd lingered too long, trying to make up his mind. They

were pinned against the China coast, trapped, and they were going to have to do exactly what he'd feared most: go through the right-hand dangerous semicircle.

The bow slammed down, foam and green water spurting up through the bullnose, and the shock of salt sea against steel shook the pilothouse with a deep strumming boom like a dropped piano. He raised his eyes to see every member of the bridge team staring at him, some with terror in their eyes. And through his own fear, for he had seen tropical cyclones and knew what they could do, he had to smile reassuringly and pump confidence into his voice. He had to. Nobody else.

He was in command.

21

HE was nodding out in his seat, buckled tight, when in the heaving, plunging darkness someone shook him. "Sir, Dave Zabounian here. The SPS-10's out again."

Dan grunted an acknowledgment, blinking as his mind reeled from uneasy dream back to the real world, or what passed for it: this lightning-grayed rain-streaked obscurity that surrounded them, the stagger and shock as *Gaddis* blocked and wove and counterpunched the screaming wind and mountainous seas of an oncoming typhoon.

For the last day and night they'd steamed north, then northeast, fighting to keep the wind on the starboard bow when the seas let them. Usually they didn't. In all that time the swells had grown, harried and maddened hour after hour by a roaring blast varied only by battering gusts that had hauled steadily around as the storm hurtled toward them. His apprehension rose as the bottom fell out of the barometer. Hercule was obviously a fast-moving storm. They shouldn't have to fight it for long. But the winds were passing sixty knots now, gusting to eighty, and they would be higher, much higher, as the wall of the eye neared.

Despite the fouled-up transmission, he couldn't help feeling he was at fault. He'd had plenty of time to get clear. He'd stayed north of fifteen degrees and north of the Xishas, despite advice from his officers. He remembered a story he'd read once about a captain too stupid or too stubborn to evade a typhoon when he could and who'd barely survived. But it was too late for second thoughts or beating himself up. He'd made his decision, and now everyone aboard was going to be royally screwed for it.

No, he thought, half-listening in the flickering darkness as the supply officer's voice brought Chick Doolan up-to-date on wind and sea and the engineering plant lineup. It wasn't really the ship he was worried about. He'd seen some horrific storms before. The hurricane in the Santarén Channel, bailing his butt off for two days and nights in a leaky skiff with a Cuban kid and a pregnant woman. Or the weeks-long Arctic hell north of Iceland in winter, the endless hammering before *Reynolds Ryan* had finally turned south. Unless something went very, very wrong, *Gaddis* could take heavy weather. It was her crew that really worried him.

Zabounian interrupted his musings. "Captain, Mr. Doolan has the deck and the conn."

"Sir, I have the deck and the conn. I'm going to break Chief Mellows here in as JOOD, since Chief Tosito's hard down."

Dan told them, "Very well," and added a couple of encouraging words to Zabounian. Dave said, "Yessir, well, it's my first big storm as OOD."

"You're doing a super job, Dave. You and Roy go below and try to get your heads down. We're going to be in this awhile."

The jaygee hesitated, gauging the motion of the deck, then let go Dan's chair and slid the length of the pilothouse, ending up at the ladder. Then he was gone, and Doolan said, "Jim seems to be doing OK with that diesel fuel."

"Yeah, I wouldn't have wanted to go into this with empty tanks. Dave tell you about the radar?"

"I don't like having the ten and the forty both down."

"Engelhart's doing the best he can, given the weather and parts situations. I told him I didn't want anybody aloft on the mack with this much wind. We still have the Raytheon. Not as much range, but it'll let you know if there's somebody else really dumb out here. Make sure Mellows knows how to keep it tuned and we ought to be OK."

"Well, I got it. You ought to pack it in; you look like hell. Sir."

Dan said reluctantly, "Maybe for a little while. The wind and seas may stay about like this. They may increase. Depends on how far away the storm center passes." He passed a few more cautions. Doolan listened patiently, smiling a little, as if humoring Dan, who found this infuriating. When he was done his department head nodded slowly, looking out at a huge sea that swept in, like a slowly approaching tennis court set on end, and the bow climbed to meet it and suddenly knifed it apart, bursting upward in an explosion of glowing foam.

Doolan murmured, "You know that time in Fayal you saw me with that girl?"

Dan said, surprised, it was so out of left field, "Uh . . . the dark-haired girl? The one from, uh, Portugal?"

"Yeah. Lavina. Well, I wanted to say something about that."

"You don't owe me any explanations, Chick."

"I know, but I'm gonna make one anyway, all right? It's about Jill."

Dan remembered *Tughril*'s commissioning party, a twisted, child-tiny woman in a wheelchair. He said uncomfortably, "You don't need to tell me this, Chick."

"I don't need to tell you? Then you understand?"

"I don't know if I 'understand,' but I don't need to. Your sex life is your own damn private business as far as I'm concerned."

"Well, you know, you respect somebody, you want to get things straight. I don't know why I care what you think, but I do. All I want to say is, Jill knows. All right? She knows and it's all right with her."

Dan cleared his throat. The husky lieutenant seemed to want some kind of forgiveness or at least comprehension. The skipper as father confessor. But instead of absolution or sympathy or whatever Doolan was asking for, all Dan's suspicions about him suddenly reenergized. If Doolan was the one they dreaded, lying about the state of his marriage was a negligible offense in comparison with his other acts.

Dan said in a low voice, "I hear you, Chick. Anything else you want to get off your chest?"

"No, that's it. Just wanted to let you know I wasn't

sneaking around behind her back. I love my wife. I'm not proud of this. But it's all out in the open."

"I hear you," Dan said again after a moment. So that was it, then; Doolan wasn't going to confess anything else.

They stood together without speaking for a long time, while the storm boomed and rushed against the echoing steel box they were surrounded by, protected by, and caged by, halfway round the world from home.

HE woke suddenly at the axis of black night, suddenly and fully, as if some obscure never-sleeping nexus in his brain had all at once concluded from its patient monitoring that he was in mortal danger. He sat up, body tense, staring into the dark.

He'd hit his rack at 0400, figuring on two or three hours before dawn broke. Lashed himself in with his bunk strap and a rolled-up blanket to wedge himself in. So this creaking, seesawing, darkness surrounding him must be his cabin; this sensation of leaping and bounding along through the air was *Gaddis*, pitching and surging to an even heavier sea. Closer to the eye, then, but he didn't think they'd have to go through it. The way the wind had veered before midnight told him the center would pass to the south. Unless, of course, it hooked again. . . . His ear tuned to a chain-rattle from somewhere far away, conducted through the metal to his ear. Then he realized what was so strange about the dark. Aboard ship, no silence was ever completely silent, and no darkness ever completely black. Light filtered through perforations in joiner bulkheads, shone from power-on lights, trickled scarlet as blood from the meshed ventilation gratings that opened on the passageway.

But around him now was the utter black of a cave, and as he swung stocking feet down to cold tile, heart picking up speed, he realized what else was missing: the thousand mechanical sounds that formed the backdrop and warp against which the sounds of the ship in motion existed; a susurrating obbligato as much or as little present to his consciousness as the chirp of crickets and hiccup of frogs were of a summer night. His groping fingertips found his trousers, hung from the speaking tube by his ear, and he got them on and slipped on his Klax and opened the door.

Darkness, except for the yellow glow at the end of the corridor. An emergency lantern, the relay-operated type that only came on when ship's power failed.

He leaned back in and pulled his khaki jacket over his T-shirt, then headed for the bridge as the buzzer sounded behind him. His flashlight sent a red oval dancing ahead. He double-timed up the ladder, grabbing for a handhold as the ship began a roll. In any ship, losing electrical power was a major problem. But in the fast frigates, it could turn very rapidly into a disaster.

The pilothouse was relatively bright with the crossed beams of four emergency lanterns. Chief Compline clung to the gyro. Dan looked for the OOD. The helmsman was standing back from the console, staring at it in consternation. Dan timed himself, lurched forward. He grabbed the hand line a moment before he crashed into Dom Colosimo.

"Just buzzed your cabin, sir. Guess you were on your way up." The reservist's face gleamed with sweat despite the cold, and Dan knew why.

Knox-class frigates ran on power generated by three steam-powered turbogenerators, 750 kilowatts each, any one of which could handle the normal electrical load. Their sixty-cycle, 450-volt three-phase output was stepped down to 115 volts for hotel services and lighting and stepped up by a motor-generator set to 400 hertz to run the radios, radars, and the other electronic equipment. But that wasn't all you needed power for on this ship.

"What's up?" Dan said quietly.

Colosimo told him their first indication of trouble had been a current reversal in one of the switchboards. At that point they had #2 and #3 ship's service turbogenerators on the line. Apparently the automatic bus transfer had failed, dropping the load.

"Emergency power?" Dan said, pulling the sound-powered handset out of its clip.

"Hasn't come on line for some reason. We've lost steering and—"

At the same moment a light flickered back in the nav shack. Then the radios hissed on, the helm console hummed. The fathometer beeped, and neon numbers flickered too fast to read as it re-initialized. The helmsman whipped the wheel right and left, then cried, "I have control back!"

Colosimo pressed the switch on the reenergized 21MC and began an exchange with Main Control. Dan hoisted himself into his chair, but two sentences into the exchange every pilot light on the bridge suddenly brightened, going intensely hot as if jammed with lightning, then went off again. This time the darkness lasted for about a second and a half before power returned. Dan started to sweat. Surges and outages were not good for equipment. He pulled out the handset in front of the CO's chair, clicked the dial to the forward switchboard, gave the crank a spin.

"Machias, main switchboard."

"Captain, Shi-hime. The hell's going on down there?"

"We were standing by to shift over to number three generator. It didn't take and now voltage is jumping around all over the place. I slammed in the main bus transfer to give you juice up there on the steering. You got it back?"

"We had a couple intermittents, but it's on right now. If we lose rudder control in these seas it's gonna be nasty. How about the other emergency loads? Fire control, radar, mounts?"

Machias said they'd try to keep those, and Dan said no, cut them off. "The only vital loads we got tonight are steering and blower fans. If those fans go, the boilers will snuff out. You know that. Then we'll really be screwed."

The electrician's mate hesitated. "You want me to cut 'em off, you got it. But shouldn't Mr. Armey be passin' these orders?"

"Right, yeah, I'll call Main Control. Give me a second, then request permission to secure the nonvital loads."

Machias rogered that and hung up. Dan threw a look

around the bridge, then through the windshield. The faint red light from the pilothouse penetrated the Plexiglas just far enough to show him windshield wipers flailing away underwater. Beyond that was just heaving black. He bent and whipped the crank again, this time clicking to Main Control.

"Skipper?"

"Here, Jim. Main switchboard call in, about securing power to the mounts, and so forth?"

"I think that's Johnile on the bitch box—yeah."

"What's going on down there? We're getting surges; then it cuts off."

"Best I can figure, we skipped the warmup procedure when we were putting number three SSTG on the line. Overload, overspeed, speed variation, voltage all over the place."

To the accompaniment of cries of alarm, the steering console and lights and radios and the light on the gyro binnacle went out again. "Ca-rap," Armey said. "We're losing it down here."

"We're black dark up here, too, Jim. How about the diesel generators? We've got to have power or we'll broach."

"Lemme get on this; call you right back." The handset on the other end rattled down.

Dan glanced to where Colosimo and Compline stood centerline, staring ahead. Then the power came back on, inside and out. At the same moment, the roar of rain slacked off. A white seethe from outside snatched at his eye, and he glanced out through the window, then leaned closer, appalled at what the flickering radiance of the reilluminated forward running light had suddenly pulled from the surrounding night.

The sea surface was covered with long patches of beaten foam. They glowed incandescent silver in the pale rolling light. In the black hours the seas had grown from twelve-to-fifteen-footers, heavy but no real threat to the ship, into deep-troughed monsters that had to be forty feet high. As he watched, one crashed down over the gun mount, burying it till only the mount captain's bubble on top swam above the boiling froth, and berserked aft as if for him personally and tore itself apart around the ASROC launcher. He could see it shaking on its steel pedestal. Then the spray flew up solid and smacked the windows, covering them, and for a few seconds it was as if *Gaddis* were already vanquished and buried, plunging on her last voyage bottomward.

His hands tightened on the radar repeater, fighting both terror and a sudden and unexpected hate. The fear because without power a sea like this could destroy them. Like most destroyer types, the Knoxes had more "sail area," more wind-catching superstructure, forward than aft. Without power her head would fall off, the pressure of wind and sea driving her bow around till she was beam on to the oncoming breakers. The sea would have them, and it had no mercy. It would capsize a ship and bludgeon it down without thought and without regret. Would batter and submerge whatever survivors fought free, till at last they slipped below, to eternal peace beneath the raging storm.

The hate was new. He'd never felt that for the sea before. The thought bewildered him for a moment before he pushed it aside.

His head jerked around as he heard someone say, "Abandon," or maybe only thought he did. Remembering the Pakistani crew. He waited through several wild rolls and plunges till she floated almost level for a moment, then slid down and headed across the deck toward the typhoon chart. The surface beneath his feet began tilting again as he neared, and he ran the last few steps up a steep slope. He grabbed the table and hung on as *Gaddis* howled over the top of a sea and rolled like a horse trying to shake off its rider before trampling him to death.

Compline panted, "Sir, I was coming over to brief you, after I saw where it plotted—"

"That's OK, Chief. What's it doing?" He aimed the red spot of his flashlight as the chart table light flickered again, off, then on.

Colosimo: "Looks like it's tracking west again now."

The ship crashed down so hard every plate and beam flexed. The wipers stopped dead before starting again. Dan's knees sagged under the abrupt increase in his weight. He heard retching from the far end of the pilothouse: the phone talker, doubled over an inverted battle helmet.

"We're only getting updates every eight hours. It could be looping and wobbling all over the chart." He swallowed; in the heaving darkness, the violent, visually unreferenced motion, even the best sailors got queasy. "I guess I screwed up, getting us into this."

"Forget it, sir. If we went south, it'd 've come after us there, too."

Compline read the rest of the message out. Hong Kong predicted hundred-knot winds near the eye, with gusts to a hundred and fifty. He grabbed for the safety line, a steel cable tensioned athwartships above their heads, as *Gaddis* heeled farther over.

Robidoux lurched out of the chart room. For a second Dan wondered if the quartermaster was drunk as he zigzagged over the deck, but it was just ship's motion. He joined them at the chart table. "Sir, I'd recommend we come about and put the seas on our quarter."

"That would reduce this slamming," Colosimo said.

"I'll keep that recommendation in mind, gentlemen. But if we do that in the dangerous semicircle, it's going to blow us right into the eye."

Without warning the console went dead again. The white seas outside the window vanished. *Gaddis* rolled long and hard, steel groaning and wailing in utter blackness broken only by the yellow beams of the emergency lanterns. When she went over the wind seemed to lessen. When she straightened it shrieked around the pilothouse. Dan bent a leg around the radar repeater and picked up the sound-powered handset again, but couldn't get Armey back. Well, if anyone could get power back, his CHENG could. If only they had more electricians. . . .

In the howl of the wind and the creaking and clanging as

the hull twisted and rose and slammed down, the drum of spray and rain on the windows, he never heard the engines stop. There was just too much sea noise, too much wind. This high and this far forward you couldn't hear the screw turning even in utter calm. The only indication was a yell from the helmsman. Dan put his flashlight spot on the gyrocompass repeater, saw it clicking over to the right as the ship's head swung, slowly at first, then faster as the wind seized it. He bent to peer out but saw nothing, tuned his senses instead to the wind direction.

No question, they were falling off rapidly.

As she gave way, a huge sea bore down on her. *Gaddis* poised herself at the top of a leap, then began toppling and didn't stop till they were all hanging from gear and handholds, feet dangling and kicking. She came back a few degrees; then Dan felt her stagger anew as another thousand tons of typhoon-driven water slammed into the side.

Was there anything more he could do? Not up here. He let go of the rail and skidded toward the ladder down, fetching up against the scuttlebutt. Then clung, uncertain what to do as another huge wave smashed into the darkened ship broadside. Clanging echoed up from belowdecks, and the stuttering groan of heavy gear getting ready to shear its bolts. The steel rails holding pubs in their shelves in the nav shack gave way, avalanching hundreds of pounds of paper out onto the deck. He wanted to go below, help Armey get the engines lit off again. But he didn't like the way Compline and Colosimo clung silently to handholds.

At last Dan clawed back toward his chair, hauling himself like a rock climber over the helm console. In the flickering flashlights and battle lanterns the enlisted looked like a gathering of the damned. They clung chalk-faced to the wheel and lee helm, staring at him as if their fates were in his hands alone. He held their eyes for a moment, trying his very best to look confident. Maybe it worked; one or two gave back a weak quirk of the lips that might have been intended as a smile.

"Sir, anything I ought to be doing?" Dom yelled over the

deafening clamor of the sea hammering at the windows. The port door groaned and flexed, and suddenly thin streams of water jetted straight out around its oval outline.

Dan jerked his eyes away from it, suppressing a desire to ask the reservist if he really wouldn't rather be back comparing growth funds in Cincinnati. "What's Main Control say?"

"No word yet."

"We should have had the emergency diesel generators cut in as soon as we had serious fluctuations from the SSTGs."

Compline: "I'll call Aux Two, find out why the diesel generator set hasn't kicked in."

"No, let them fucking work; don't keep calling them."

The phone talker, in a hoarse voice: "Sir, as soon as they lost draft they had to cut the burners. They can purge and try to relight, but without electrical power it's going to be real rough."

The pilothouse rolled back and forward, cracking the whip as the hull beneath twisted, and one of the men clinging to the helm console lost his grip. Robidoux fell twenty feet, kicking and grabbing for grip on the smooth tile, and succeeded only in cracking his head against the ladder stanchion. He slid limply into the corner of the bulkhead. Compline caught the body on the second pass and hauled him under the chart table, lashing him in place with a gas mask strap under the arms.

Colosimo cracked out orders. He was holding up, Dan thought; he didn't sound frightened or overwhelmed. Once again, Dan was torn between going down to Aux Two and getting the gen set started and staying here and trying to hold the center together. But the question answered itself. He was the only CO *Gaddis* had. Armey and Sansone could handle the generators better than he could.

His job was to save the ship.

A tremendous wall of water crashed suddenly into the side, far more violently than any before it. The windows flexed inward and the warping door pissed water in power-ful streams and he had a flicker glimpse of one of the grat-ings flashing past—waterborne, airborne, he didn't know. The worst of it was how little he could see. Just hear the chaotic howl of shouts, the shrieking wind, the agonized groan and scream of the ship as she staggered back upright, a Niagara torrent roaring off her canted forecastle. The rumble and crash of something carrying away on the flag bridge or off the damaged mack.

She couldn't take much more. The question was, What could he do?

"Sir." Colosimo's strained voice. "I don't think she'll take too much of this."

"Just what I was thinking, Dom. Jim's got to get those generators going."

"How far will she roll before she goes over?"

His flashlight found the clinometer on the bulkhead. It stood at forty degrees just then, but that last roll had been much more violent. If she went far enough to gulp water down her uptakes, the boilers would flood out. Beyond that, and she'd never come up again.

He forced his mind to close down, to think it through coldly as a classroom problem in seamanship and damage control.

Faced with heavy weather, topside icing, and a light ship in an Arctic storm, Jimmy Packer, his CO on his first ship, had flooded deep tanks and chain lockers and blown off the air search antenna with a demo charge to reduce weight high in the ship. Thank God they weren't carrying ice now, but Dan had no confidence in the ability of this crew to carry out controlled flooding. If it wasn't done perfectly, the combination of off-center weight and free surface would make *Gaddis* even less stable. He didn't want to go that route.

The textbook answer to lost power in a storm was to stream a sea anchor and run downwind, but he didn't think the reduced, half-trained crew he had could do that, either.

Wrestle heavy timbers into position on a wave-washed, rolling deck, he'd lose guys over the side. Pity it wasn't shallower; they could anchor and ride it out. But his last look at the chart had showed over fourteen hundred fathoms. No way to anchor, no way to put drag on the bow.

An image teased for a moment but shrank back when he reached for it. He groped for a second, then let it go and went on.

Some authorities advised putting your stern to the seas in a terminal situation. As Robidoux had recommended. But damn it, not only would that head him into the storm center; he couldn't do that without power, either. It might have worked when they first lost steerageway. Slamming the rudder to leeward, using her momentum to carry her through the trough. But now they were trapped.

Without electrical power and engine power, they were helpless. He cursed the designers who'd made this a single-screw class. In most destroyer types you had two separate engine rooms, two separate plants. The Knoxes not only had just one, but it also depended on electrical power to keep the boilers lit off. When you lost power, you were up a tree for real.

The squeal of the sound-powered phone, like a squirrel being crushed. He beat Colosimo to it. "Lenson."

"Armey here. We're taking water down here."

More good news. "Water? From where?"

"Main deck, I think. I'm not sure exactly where yet, but the guys think the aluminum-to-steel interface on the main deck's starting to separate. You know, where Khashar rammed us into that liner, in Fayal? The sea leans on the deckhouse while the hull's trying to roll up. That's a hell of a stress, and that's a weak seam anyway with the dissimilar-metal riveting. I sent the hull techs up to check it out, but I don't know what they can do in the middle of this."

This was serious. Loose water, rolling back and forth without swash plates, was terrifically dangerous in heavy seas. It dropped stability even worse than simple flooding, and if it reached the switchboards they could forget about ever getting power back. Dan felt ice touch his spine. "What about the bus transfer?"

"I can't get it to take. We're gonna have to do a thorough troubleshoot on that panel. Right now I'm rigging casualty power cables up from the de-gen set."

"Are the diesels running?"

"Tried to start 'em twice. We got enough compressed air for one more try."

Dan felt sweat break under his arms despite the cold. "If you run those air banks down and the diesels don't start—"

"Right, then we're really fucked. Believe me, I know. What's the situation up there?"

"Beam to and rolling like hell. I can hear gear coming off topside."

"Yeah, we're getting flung around down here. I cracked my fucking arm against the panel and damn near broke it. Can't you do a sea anchor or something?"

"I'd have to put guys out on deck." Dan swallowed, looking out at the black howling waste outside. "Without lights, too. We'll lose some of 'em."

"We'll lose everybody if this bitch goes over."

He sucked air, scared suddenly to the depths of his guts. But the engineer was right. Some, rather than all.

"OK, you convinced me. I'll get Chick and Topmark to pull a party together. Give me a call when you're ready to use that last slug of air." He slammed the phone down and swung on Colosimo. Dan was opening his mouth when black jaws closed suddenly over the pilothouse and the deck jerked out from under his feet, leaving him floating, one hand locked desperately to the windshield wiper motor box.

The ship shuddered all over, whipsawing from one end to the other. He could actually feel the hull flexing as the immense sea Rolfed it from stem to stern. Water covered the windows, black as oil, sucking in the few random photons shed by the dimming battle lanterns. He had no idea how deep they were buried. When she staggered back up, the roar of water sluicing off the flying bridge, just above their heads, was so loud his voice was lost under it. He tried again. "Dom. Dom!" Colosimo turned a startlingly pale face. Dan yelled, "We need to get some men out there, rig a sea anchor. Get the word to Doolan and Topmark."

"They'll never make it."

"Some of them, probably not. But we've got to do it. No time to rig one out of dunnage and awnings. I figured, one of the RHIBs, on a long line, drag it sideways, that'll keep our bow to the wind—"

"How are they going to get it over the side, rolling like this?"

The ship leaned desperately and men clung to each other. Robidoux moaned suddenly from under the chart table, coming to. Aside from his groans, several minutes went by with no one speaking. More seas battered into them, though none as bad as that last big one. She was down, and the sea was taking its chance, kicking and smothering her at the same time. If another monster came in, they could go over. The total blackness, without even masthead and range lights to show what was bearing down on them, made it ten times as terrifying. If only he could fucking *see*—

Wheep-wheep-wheep, then the rattling bang as Compline grabbed the handset. A moment later it clacked as he slammed it back into the holder.

"What is it, Chief?"

"Mr. Armey," said Compline. "He used the last of the air. The generators didn't start."

Dan stared at him. Exclamations, curses, and quickly choked-back cries came from elsewhere about the darkened bridge. They were finished, then. There was no way to start the boilers without power. Nor did they have bilge pumps without electricity. They'd roll till they took enough water, then capsize.

The J-phone *wheeped* again, interrupting his thoughts before he had a chance to follow them through. He cursed as Compline held it out to him again. "Jim? That you?"

It wasn't Armey. It was Neilsen, calling from sick bay. His voice was unsteady. He said, "Captain, we need you down here."

"Christ, Neilsen, I've kind of got my hands full; you're gonna have to wait."

"You better get down here, sir. It's Mrs. Wedlake. We had a visitor."

Oh, no, he said to himself, feeling hopelessness and horror. He closed his eyes for a fraction of a second, then jerked them open. "I'll be right down," he said, thrust the phone into the chief's hands, and turned to the ladder.

"What is it, sir?" Colosimo, blocking his path. "Where are you going?"

"Dom, you're gonna have to hold the status quo here for a couple of minutes. You can reach me in sick bay if it really goes to shit. Chick should be up any second. Tell him what's going on and what he needs to do, on the sea anchor, and he's got to do it most rikki-tik now."

"We need you up here, Skipper."

"I know that, goddamnit." He blinked and tightened his jaw against an uninvited image: the girl on Dahakit Atoll, the shallow network of knife cuts around the bloodied socket . . . Bobbie Wedlake's elvish face . . . "Get the hell out of my way."

"Sir, you can't leave the bridge."

"I've got to, Dom. Just do one thing for me, OK? Just keep her afloat till I get back."

THE midships passageway was empty, leading aft through Officers' Country. It was dark except for the saffron gleams of the emergency lighting. The deck took another tremendous lean as he worked his way aft along it, creaking and screaming, and for the first time he heard metal popping, breaking, like a human spine twisted sideways and then slowly being buckled by some enormous weight. He staggered into the bulkhead opposite Juskoviac's door, then dropped to his hands and knees and crept along, more on the bulkhead than on the deck, sucking the slanting, jolting air in dry sobs. He didn't want to see this. Didn't want to.

Sick bay was open and a tropical sun shone out of it into the careening, pitching passageway. He blinked into the glare. Neilsen had turned on the battery-powered operating lamp, installed for emergency surgery.

The first thing he saw was Bobbie Wedlake, sitting bolt upright in a chair lashed to the sink. Her dark eyes stared out of a face white as sea foam. She held a snub-nosed revolver on her lap, thin fingers wrapped like white wires around the grip. Neilsen stood on the far side of the compartment, clinging to the bunk frame where Chief Tosito lay, still out, apparently. Dan took it all in with one sweep of his sight, and his knees went weak. Then relief turned to rage. If she wasn't hurt, why had they called him? *Gaddis* could go over any moment and never come up again.

"OK, goddamnit, what is it?"

"I had to go out for a minute," Neilsen said defensively. "And you said call the masters-at-arms . . . so I did. Then I left. Should have waited for 'em, but I couldn't. Only for a second. But while I was out somebody tried to break in."

"He *did* break in," Wedlake said. Her voice was soft and low but very focused.

Dan took another took at the gun. "Uh, could you take your finger off the trigger now, Mrs. Wedlake? Thanks. Did you see him? Could you identify him?"

"He used a key. It was dark. All I saw was somebody very large."

"Black? White?"

"I think white. I think. No, I'm not sure about that."

"Did he say anything?"

"No, but I saw something gleam."

"Then what?"

"Then I cocked the gun. He heard it. And I said, "Stop. Get out of here, or I'll kill you." I would have, too. I can hit what I aim at. He stood there for a second or two. Then he left."

Lenson swung on the corpsman. "You didn't lock her in. I gave you a direct order—"

"He did," said Wedlake. She lifted the gun, hands still locked on it, to push back a strand of black hair. In the blinding light, close as he was to her, he saw gray roots beneath. "I heard it click as he went out. I told you, the man who came in had a key."

"Who else has a key to this compartment?" Dan asked Neilsen. The corpsman said as far as he knew, nobody. The controlled substances safe was in sick bay. Access was as tightly controlled as to Crypto and the magazines. Dan hesitated, chewing that one over.

Or had there really been an intruder at all? He glanced at Wedlake again, bolt-erect in the chair, taut upright but swaying forward as the ship took another gigantic squealing roll and the sea thundered over them, shaking their metal shell as if the storm knew they were in here, as if determined to crack it apart and devour them all. What kind of drugs had Neilsen given her?

As if on cue, a slow voice piped from the lower bunk, "She's right, Captain. I saw him, too."

"Chief Tosito. You back with us?"

"I was awake. Don' feel so good, but I could see. Just like she said."

"Who was it?"

"Couldn't be many guys. He was real big."

"Tall, you mean? Or hefty?"

"Real big."

The voice trailed away, and Dan reached out and squeezed Tosito's leg reassuringly. "Thanks, Chief. You get some sleep now, OK? Get better." Then he switched back to Mrs. Wedlake. "Did he touch anything while he was in here?"

"No . . . but he backed out and he tripped on the, on the sill, as he went out. I ran to the door and locked it again, then jammed the chair against it. But I heard him fall down outside. There was a lot of noise."

Dan glanced at the J-phone, remembering he had to get back topside, had to figure out some way to save the ship. They'd missed this psycho yet again, but they had another hint. There were only so many "big men" in the crew. He and Mellows would narrow the interrogations accordingly. Eventually one would crack. He nodded curtly to them both and to Tosito, who had closed his eyes again and lay back exhausted. "All right. Keep it locked after I leave. We'll get it sorted out in the morning. If we're still here."

"I want another lock on this door," she said. "I'm telling you, he came right in."

The corpsman offered to rig a padlock and chain, and Dan said to make it so. The need to get back to the bridge became overwhelming then. He jerked the door open and stepped out into the passageway.

Just then the ship went over again, this time farther than before, till he was lying on his back looking terrified up at the opposite bulkhead. The hull boomed deafeningly, jerking under him. The impact of thousands of cubic meters of water was skidding her bodily sideways through the sea. He tried to regain his feet but went down again as the ship fell away beneath him, then rose again with dizzying speed. He waited, pinned helplessly, for her to go over, for them all to start drowning, those who weren't battered to death first by shifting machinery.

Something cold submerged the backs of his legs.

The deck came back to the upright a few degrees, then a bit more. She was losing stability with each roll, but she was still fighting. He flicked on his light. A stream was pouring down the passageway, funneled into the corner made by deck and bulkhead. The parting main deck seams . . . then the cold poured over the tops of his half-Wellingtons.

As he glanced down he saw something glint in the water. He bent, felt around, picked it up. Shook the salt sea off and held it under his light.

It was gray plastic. The shattered-off back of a Polaroid camera. He turned it over and read the inscription. Faded black Magic Marker read: PROPERTY OF USS GADDIS.

He nodded once, there in the heaving dark. Understanding at last. Because just that simply, just seeing that, so much that had gone on so puzzlingly and for so long became suddenly and perfectly clear.

HE climbed back to the bridge to find everyone clinging to handholds in the flickery dark. He stuffed the whole issue with Bobbie and the intruder then, jammed it under a rock in his head till they were out of this. *If* they made it out of this. If not, this night would see justice done to innocent and guilty alike. Your will, he thought, not mine. I'll do my best, but if that's what you want, I'm ready.

Brief as the prayer was, it steadied him.

Lieutenant Commander Colosimo was waiting at the top for him. "Chick getting his team together?" were the first words out of Dan's mouth.

"He hasn't shown up. I called again but—"

"Here I am, goddamnit!" Doolan, on the ladder just below Dan. "Jesus. What the hell's going on? Where's the power?"

"Fires are out, and the de-gens won't start. Where the hell you been? We've got to get a sea anchor out."

"I fell down the goddamn ladder," Chick said, and this time Dan saw the blood black on his face, on his mustache. "Slipped and did a Superman all the way to the bottom. You ran right past me as I was lyin' there."

"We're stuck in the trough. Jim tried to start the diesel gens. Till there wasn't any more compressed air."

"Oh, shit." Doolan rubbed his head, staring at the ominous black outside the window. Dan couldn't believe it was still dark; it felt like they'd been fighting this for days. "Oh, *shit.*"

Dan stared out, too, suddenly going still as it rushed back into his mind at last, what he'd almost grasped a few minutes before. How he could put drag on the bow. He spun and yelled at them both, "OK, here it is. Forget the RHIB. Chick, get your team ready to drop anchor."

"What? We're way off soundings. What are you thinking of—" Then Colosimo stopped. Dan saw Doolan's eyes snap open, too. They nodded, not looking at him. Then the weapons officer picked up the phone.

A few hours later he sat exhausted on the wardroom sofa, staring with the blank regard of utter exhaustion at the lashed-down chairs and the bare table. The hull still

strained and creaked around him. He could still make out
the whish of breakers going past, the crash and roar and
shudder as a big greenie smashed itself apart over the main
deck. But the eye had passed, *Gaddis* drove now through
still-heavy but less mountainous afterseas, and, most vital
of all, she had way on again. The low, nearly imperceptible
hum of the turbines, the beat of the screw, were a steady re-
assurance. The overhead fluorescents burned flickerless, intense. He was soaked and filthy. His khakis were sodden,
his back and arms were bruised, and terror was still fresh in
his mind. He knew he wasn't the only one. Every man
aboard had probably gone over his accounts due this dark
night.

In the first black light of dawn Doolan and Topmark had
led a party of volunteers out on the forecastle, a damn brave
act, and run forward with safety lines and clung as the cold
gray sea hammered over them, then dashed forward again,
like marines, some covering as others rushed, and at last
managed to reach the ground tackle at the extremity of the
bow. A slash of knives, a couple of judiciously applied
steel-toes, and the pelican hooks had flicked free and the
chain slipped, clanked, then thundered out. The boatswain
rode the brake, half-submerged at frequent intervals on the
control station, till all twelve shots, fifteen fathoms a shot, a
total of 1,080 feet of steel with each link weighing twenty-
two pounds, were out and the big bow anchor was swinging
far down there in the darkness. And the drag of all that
metal through the depths had brought her back, brought the
bullnose slowly around into the teeth of wind and sea, the
water foaming white as it broke and seethed and swept her
all the way to the pilothouse, but at least she wasn't rolling
beam on now.

And after two and a half hours like that, with everyone
sweating bullets and wondering when a weak link or
cracked shackle would give way, Armey had suddenly reported he had one-bravo boiler lit off again. Somehow Sansone had managed it without electricity, kindled it with a

tank of welding oxygen, a smoky, dangerous, half-assed fire but one that gradually brewed enough steam to restart a turbo generator, then the fans, then the bilge pumps, and finally the shaft began to spin and she'd forged ahead to breast the oncoming seas once again as they brought the anchor back aboard.

Yeah, everyone had been scared. Some had met it boldly. Others had acted only when it was thrust on them. But for once, goddamn it, the crew had worked together.

Weary as he was, a glow of satisfaction warmed him as he sprawled exhausted in the deserted wardroom, eyes empty as a lightless sky.

There might be hope for *Gaddis* yet. It wouldn't make a lot of difference in the great scheme of things, but it made him feel better. As if he'd done something worth doing. More than that, he wished her well. He knew it was pure sentiment. "She" was just a piece of steel, iron and carbon bound by chemical attraction yet separated by the mutual repulsion, the jealous guarding of selfhood every atom of matter maintained against every other. But that was the way he felt.

Another thing occurred to him then, and any elation at survival dropped instantly away. He rubbed his face, hard, as if hand-sanding a block of walnut. The matter he'd shoved under a rock while he waited to see if they'd still be afloat come dawn. He had to make a decision. In a sense it was made for him, but he wanted to make sure it was the right one. If it was wrong, the consequences, both for himself and for others, were too terrible to contemplate.

And right or wrong, his own life would never be the same.

A gray piece of plastic marked USS GADDIS.

A big man, with access to the most restricted spaces of the ship.

Dan sat there for a few minutes more, too battered and wrung out to push himself erect; trying to concentrate, trying to think. Instead he found himself bobbing back for a

moment above the slick black surface of a tormented hallu-
cination, neck kinked painfully by the arm of the sofa. He
heaved himself up and wended his way down the darkened,
swaying corridor, fingers splayed to the slanting bulkheads,
back to his cabin to snatch an hour's sleep.

22

THE chief's quarters, and the tension level was high. Chief Compline and Chief Warrant Engelhart, Al Sansone, and both the assistant masters-at-arms stood witnessing as Dan checked the name on the locker. The chiefs had bigger lockers than the junior enlisted, but they still weren't over-generous. Padlocks tapped as *Gaddis* rolled.

Dan rubbed his mouth, trying to push away his desperation for sleep. He'd only managed a few minutes of shut-eye, for the simple reason that he couldn't just turn off the terror and energy the typhoon had unleashed. He was glimpsing weird animals at the corner of vision that when he focused weren't there. Plus, he couldn't stop wondering what they were going to find this morning. It was only the second time in his career he'd had to witness a non-consensual search. They were only legal with probable cause, or in an emergency, both of which justifications he figured applied to a murderer aboard ship. He felt torn, both eager for a final answer and dreading what that answer would demand in its train.

"Where's Commander J.?" he grunted.

One of the masters-at-arms said, "Uh, he said you decided you didn't need him to be the exec, sir, so he ain't gonna be part of whatever you're putting over here. Is what he said."

"You're the one who keeps custody of the evidence camera, right? Has it shown up yet?"

"No, sir, haven't seen it since the chief checked it out to do the sonar trunk, you know, the kid they found sliced and diced down there."

"Does he check it out often? When he does, does he keep it long?"

"He keeps it right much of the time," said the petty officer. He kept his tone bland and uncommitted.

Marsh Mellows was topside, on bridge watch with Chick Doolan. It was his locker they were looking at here in the CPO quarters. Dan finally nodded to the guy with the "Magic Key," the big bolt cutters every ship kept for when someone forgot his combination. "OK, open it up. Chief Warrant, why don't you go through the stuff, and Chief Compline can take the inventory." The other MAA handed the radioman the clipboard and a cocked ballpoint.

When the hasp separated the locker door swung open with a tinny pop. Dan bent to peer inside but didn't see anything interesting. He deliberately stayed several feet from it, well out of arm's reach. Engelhart reached up a folding chair, snapped it open with a motion like cracking a whip, and perched on it back to front. He started from the bottom. Shoes came out first, then a black-lacquered shore patrol nightstick. Then a gray metal box that looked like Navy issue. It had a smaller padlock on it and Engelhart started to set it aside with the shoes, but Dan said, "Open it."

Inside was a rubber-banded roll of cash, fives and twenties, an old faded box of Trojans, some letters, and a pink partial denture in a Ziploc bag. A handful of coins from every port in the world. On the bottom, magazines with trussed-up women on the pulp covers. Two Beta videotapes, volumes 2 and 4 of something called *Faces of Death*.

Beneath them, a worn maroon leatherette photo holder. Engelhart opened it and said, "Christ." The album trembled in his hands for a moment, and then he touched one of the celluloid pockets with the nail of his thumb and flipped it over to the next, then held it up so that they all could see.

There were four photos of women and one that had been taken in the sonar dome.

Dan took a deep shaky breath and held it. He looked around at the others, at their varying reactions: some ashen, others flushed, hands to their mouths or faces.

"Now we know why we never had any leads or any fingerprints," he said softly. "Why our investigations never went anywhere. Why we were locking up people who didn't have anything to do with it.

"Chief Compline, report to the bridge. Tell Lieutenant Doolan you are relieving Chief Mellows, that I want to see him ASAP about master-at-arms business in the supply passageway. Once Marsh leaves, tell Mr. Doolan to send his two most trustworthy gunner's mates, armed, down to the port fan room as soon as possible."

"I hope you thought this through, Cap'n," said Engelhart. The warrant flipped the folder closed and dropped it back into the box. He wiped his hands on his trou. "Marsh has got a lot of admirers. Among the new guys, mostly, but a lot of the *Gaddis* original flavors, too. I been in for thirty-two years, and I've never seen a ship this close to blowing, not even in Vietnam."

"I've been thinking about that since about 0400, Ben." Dan beckoned to him and to the two masters-at-arms. They left the chiefs' quarters and headed for the supply corridor.

What he was considering was illegal, of course. He had no power to try capital crimes. But he also had no idea how much longer they would be at sea. Only ruthless and instant action would stave off the total disintegration of the crew.

He would adhere as closely as he could to the forms. But if USS *Gaddis* sailed now beyond the law, she could never sail so far as to be beyond justice.

THE special court-martial met at 1400 in the wardroom. As the convening authority, Dan could not sit on it, nor did he attempt to direct or influence the proceedings in any way. Doolan was the president. The members were Compline, Zabounian, and Colosimo. Chief Warrant Officer Engelhart acted as counsel for the defense. Chief Sansone served as the recording secretary. The charge was murder. Dan had expected a protest from some of the members, as to the court's legality, but none came. They seemed to have no compunction about rendering judgment in the case at hand without benefit of attorneys, JAG officers, trial counsel, or

any other expert advisers. The proceedings took an hour
and a half.

DAN read the record of the trial in his cabin, with Doolan,
Sansone, and Mellows before him. The chief was handcuffed, his ankles shackled. Dan asked Mellows if he had
any complaints about the way he had been treated. He
shook his bald head wordlessly.

"Chief Mellows, I convened a special court aboard *Gaddis* because I do not feel we can hold this matter for a shoreside court. If my judgment is wrong I will have to meet any
consequences.

"That court has found you guilty of murder. The sentence under Article 118 of the Uniform Code, aggravated
by Clause One, which is premeditation, is death. Do you
have any statement to make?"

Dan had expected Mellows to protest what was in effect
a drumhead court, to ask for a stay or postponement until
the proceedings could be reviewed. But Mellows said nothing about this. Instead he shook his shoulders and said,
"Where's Mr. Juskoviac?"

"The exec is not part of these proceedings."

"He should be. He'd have spoken up for me. I'd like to
get these handcuffs off."

"Can't. You're big enough to take any two of us." Dan
paused. "Why did you do it, Marsh?"

Mellows didn't seem inclined to talk. He glanced toward
Dan's porthole. "Who cares? Why should I say anything?"

"Because I have to approve the sentence. Do you admit
killing the women whose photos we found in your locker
and Seaman Vorenkamp, attacking the girl on Dahakit
Atoll, and trying to attack Mrs. Wedlake last night?"

"You found the pictures, sir. You don't need me to admit
anything."

Dan looked away, so he didn't have to meet Mellows's
eyes. The truly disturbing thing was that this was exactly
the same Marsh Mellows Dan had known from the day he
stepped aboard USS *Gaddis*. He had the same bluff cheer-

fulness, the same hearty self-confidence he'd had at mast on the bridge, briefing Dan on the state of the crew's morale, or at any of the other hundreds of times he and the senior enlisted adviser had seen each other in the past three months. Dan coughed into his fist and looked up again to the condescending gaze that met his without flinch or evasion.

"All right, we'll take that as a confession. And you won't discuss your reasons."

"Would it help any?"

"I can't tell you that till I hear it. But we're shipmates. Don't we owe each other the truth?"

The J-phone chose that moment to go off. Dan turned away and answered it, listened to the OOD's report of a crossing contact, and said, "Very well. Let me know if it comes within five thousand yards," then hung up and turned back to the matter at hand. "Well, Chief?"

"Why did I do it. Well, at first, because I had a mission."

"A mission."

"Yeah. To protect the young sailors from the suckoff queens that hang around you when you go into New York. That was the first one, Times Square."

"Go on." Dan flicked his eyes to see that Compline had perched himself on the side settee and was jotting notes. "You said 'at first.' "

"Right. Then in Philly, one came up and grabbed my cock. You know how they do."

" 'They' being prostitutes."

"Yessir."

"Who were these women? Did you know their names?"

"Never asked. They were just whores."

"Why specifically prostitutes?"

"Well, it wasn't, later. Like when Vorenkamp came on to me. And the little bitch on the island. But I don't think anyone's going to miss any of them."

The cabin was quiet except for the steady rush of the sea. Dan held Mellows's gaze for a moment, then had to look back at the documents. His fingers were trembling. He said, "Chief, I believe each of us is completely and totally re-

sponsible for what he does. There can be predisposing circumstances. I can see cutting slack for that at times. But
we're not machines, or robots. Unless we're totally insane,
we are making the decisions. And I don't think a man who
can carry out his duties as competently as you have can be
called crazy. You knew what you did was murder and that it
was wrong."

"I don't have any regrets, sir, if that's what you're trying
to get at." Mellows held Dan's gaze.

Dan swallowed something in his throat and tried to
harden his voice. "Very well. I will proceed to sentencing.

"The Manual for Courts-Martial of the United States
normally limits the power of a commanding officer at sea.
He cannot award capital punishment, even if the crime is
proven and the prescribed punishment is death. However,
this ship is no longer operating within the limits of the Uniform Code of Military Justice or of the laws of the United
States. It is obvious from repeated failures to respond to requests for orders, guidance, and logistical support that we
are no longer acknowledged as a U.S.-flag warship.

"But even pirates, by definition outside the law, historically had law among themselves. If we are outside a formal
system of justice, a more ancient code prevails: the code of
judgment by one's peers, the right of self-defense, both of
the individual and of the group, and the duty of those in
command to maintain order and punish wrongdoing regard-
less of the presence or absence of higher authority.

"Though I have no written orders as CO of this ship, I
am the senior officer present and acknowledged as the de
facto commanding officer by the crew, facing a situation of
the most serious and overwhelming necessity. A hundred
years ago, when Navy ships sailed independently, the Articles of War gave commanders the power of life and death
over their crews. That same circumstance applies now
aboard *Gaddis*. I therefore approve this sentence, and in
view of the ship's danger, both external and from within, I
see no reason to postpone its execution.

"Chief Mellows, I hereby approve the findings of the

court and, in accordance with the customs and traditions of the sea, order you to be hanged by the neck until dead at sunrise tomorrow." He signed two papers on the clipboard, flipped it closed, and handed it to Sansone. "God have mercy on your soul. Dismissed; return him to the brig."

"A-bout face." Mellows paled at last, started to protest, but was jerked around and hustled out none too gently by his escorts.

"Mr. Doolan, stand by for a moment," Dan said as the weapons officer made as if to follow. "One last thing. I want you to issue side arms to all officers, chiefs, and first-class petty officers. Hold a familiarization firing on the fantail this evening. Put the word out it's to prepare to repel boarders."

He caught the looks Sansone and Doolan gave each other, the way the boilerman puckered his lips to in a noiseless whistle.

"You really want to turn the ship into an armed camp, sir?"

"It *is* an armed camp, Chick. Since Pistolesi brought that booze aboard and started them thinking about loot. I damn near got my throat cut before the storm. And then there's Mrs. Wedlake. I can think of a whole lot of bad things that can happen with guys who think they're out of reach of the law. I want double guards on Mellows tonight, in case someone takes it into his head to break him out. *Not* the masters-at-arms; I don't want them guarding their boss. I want us all to keep a real close watch on Bobbie, too."

"He's probably right there, Mr. Doolan," Sansone said. "I hear the guys talking. We've got some mad dogs aboard right now I wouldn't put a damn thing past them, from rape to taking the ship over."

Chick nodded. "All right, I'll issue pistols and two mags of hardball each, as we report to the fantail. No point mentioning it before then."

"Now we're thinking along the same lines. I hope nobody has to use them."

A moment later he was gone. Sansone stared at his

notes. Then the boilerman glanced at him. "Sir, you serious about this? About Mellows? I don't say 'Chief' because he ain't one anymore in my book. But you really going to hang him?"

"Never been more serious in my life."

"They'll hang *you,* sir. By the balls. Once we get back to civilization."

"What is civilization, Al? Isn't justice part of it?"

"It used to be."

"Then we'll see it done at least once in our lives." Dan got up and reached for his cap.

But Sansone wasn't finished. "Sure, and a lot of people will think it's great. But are you gonna like the bill when you get it?"

The boilerman waited for a second and then, when Dan didn't answer, made that soundless whistle again, and left without saying another word.

THE sign he had been waiting for so long came that night, well into the midwatch, when the sea was sealed dark and no stars shone through the murky sheet that had lingered all that day. It arrived in the form of an insistent buzz that jerked him out of a sleep so deep he came to already holding the phone to his ear. "Yeah," he coughed.

"Skipper? That you?"

"Who the hell else sleeps in my cabin, Chief Warrant?"

"We're getting flashing light from a contact to the south. Mr. Zabounian said to get that info down to you."

Dan was on the bridge in his trou and Klax twenty seconds later. The supply officer took his arm as he stood blind and led him to the port wing. He stared out to where the light winked rapidly in the windy dark. Complete and utter sightlessness, black on black, with only the single distant pinprick of illumination occulting far off. He went in and checked the contact on the radar, then let the chief warrant brief him. It had come in from the southwest and had a closest point of approach of about seven thousand yards, which it would not reach for a while yet.

The flashing light winked out suddenly, returning the world to formlessness and the void. A few minutes later the signalman clattered in and handed something to Engelhart. He handed it on to Dan.

It read: COME ALONGSIDE ME ON COURSE 030 SPEED 10 PREPARE TO RECEIVE HIGHLINE AND FUEL TRANSFER.

"No identifier," the signalman added.

"Request they identify themselves."

"I did, sir. No reply."

"Skunk Alfa altering course to port," the CIC phone talker said.

"They're coming to zero-three-zero, like they said," Zabounian said, coming in from the wing. "What do you want to do, sir? Do you want me to shoot for an approach?"

"Uh, yeah, I guess start getting into position," Dan said. His mind raced as he tried to put this together. All the messages he'd sent requesting fuel and ammunition. Was this his answer? But then why hadn't there been an advance message, outlining the rendezvous point? Could it be a trap? He shook off ratiocination. "Get Mr. Doolan up here ASAP. Bo's'n Topmark, too. Set the starlight scope up. If he won't tell us, maybe we can see who the hell it is."

Over the next half hour, twenties and fifties manned just in case, they made up on the unidentified ship. The signalmen said they couldn't locate the starlight scope, had not seen it since Karachi. Most likely one of the Pakistanis had taken it ashore; that kind of item brought top dollar in the bazaar. Dan turned away with compressed lips and kept trying with his night glasses. But he couldn't really tell what he was looking at. It didn't seem to be an oiler or ammo ship. She was radiating a commercial radar. Sonar reported the steady thump of one screw driven by low-speed diesels. It was smaller than a U.S. replenishment ship, though still larger than *Gaddis*, and there was something off about the bridge and sterncastle arrangement. At one point he was sure he was looking at a three-island superstructure, but then booms or stick masts came into view and he lost his mental picture. She was running darkened except for a

wake light, a faint white light high on her stern. It glim-
mered dimly off the cresting swells.

He didn't like this. It didn't seem like a trap, but it wasn't
going to be simple, either. Nighttime underway replenish-
ments, "unreps," were standard in the USN repertoire. But
he'd never practiced one on *Gaddis*, nor had his makeshift
deck crew. Fortunately, the wire highline was the simplest
method of transfer and required the least complex rigging.
It was simply a trolley block rolling on a man-tensioned
span wire, with the load hauled, braked, and managed with
heavy manila lines. It could be screwed up, but it was about
as conceptually transparent at least as any deck evolution
ever got.

Over the next few minutes they closed slowly from
astern, slightly offset to port. The wake light drew gradually
closer. Following NATO practice, the transferring ship
should have been considerably better lighted, with contour
lights to give him a fix on how close he was getting to the
other hull. That was vital; a mistake on the helm or even a
rogue sea could slam the two ships together with catas-
trophic results. Dan thought for a moment of putting a
searchlight on the other, see exactly what he was dealing
with. Some inchoate reluctance made him decide not to, at
least not just then.

Topmark reported by phone from the starboard transfer
station that he could see light boxes for fuel transfer forward and ammo aft. Dan put his glasses to his eyes and
made them out, too, an inverted T signal forward and a
shape like an E aft. He noticed other lights, too, much
fainter, a swarm of indistinct red fireflies moving about
along the steadily nearing shadow's port side.

"Keep going in, Skipper?" Zabounian, behind him.

"Continue your approach, Dave. Have the chief warrant
keep a close eye on the helmsman. Drop your turn count
when the bridge passes her stern."

Gaddis bored in steadily, the rush of wind and the crash
of seas growing louder as they were reflected from the nearing hull of the other ship. The shadow grew to a dimly visi-

ble tracery of masts and booms and topping lifts complicating the black sky.

Then they were alongside, racing along together, and the roar of the bows-on wind in the narrowed venturi between the hulls, the surging frenzied leap of trapped seas, the plunging and rolling and the lack of visual clues were like riding a liquid-damped roller coaster through complete darkness. He braced himself on the wing, looking across at the ruddy pinpoints he could see now were men moving about with dimmed flashlights. Zabounian added a couple RPMs back on the screw and *Gaddis* clamped into the notch, and a faint pop came from across the water and the lighted head of a line projectile drew a luminous arch in the sky.

THEY ran side by side for nearly an hour. Armey reported from Main Control that they didn't have the tankage for much more fuel, unless they dumped the diesel they'd topped off with from the *Marker Eagle*, so Dan cut that transfer off after taking aboard 3,600 gallons. The incoming loads touched down back aft. After two loads had come over, Doolan rang the bridge. He told Dan it was ammunition, five-inch and forty-millimeter. The weapons officer had examined it by flashlight and had something interesting to report.

"Don't play with me, Chick. I'm trying to run an unrep up here without lights or comms or even knowing whose dick I'm holding. Spit it out and get off the line."

"You're getting to be one of those cranky COs, Dan."

"God damn it—"

"All right, all right. This stuff is USN-issue, but it's old. The five-inch is dated 1970 and 1971. The forty-mil's even older, 1960s. Some of it—get this—it's got RVN markings."

"Vietnamese? South Vietnamese?"

"Yeah, it looks to me like stuff we shipped the Vietnamese Navy back during the war."

"Is that going to be any good? That's twenty-plus years old."

"The propellant and primers should be fine. The fuzes could give us trouble. I don't think safety-wise, but we might have some duds."

"Well, I'm not doing the gift horse routine. How much are we getting?"

"Don't know. It's still coming over."

"Sort it by date, if you can. Then strike it below."

"Aye aye aye."

"Two ayes are enough, Chick. You sound like you're getting short on sleep."

"So do you. One more thing. There's something here addressed to 'CO, *Oliver C. Gaddis*.' Want me to open it?"

Dan took a deep breath and closed his eyes in thanks. "No. Run it up here right away. And for Christ's sake, give it to somebody who's not going to let it blow over the side."

USMANI brought hot coffee and he gulped it down, not waiting for it to cool, great slugs of it searing his throat. It didn't help much; he was still slipping off into dream even as he stood watching the replenishment.

The contents of the manila envelope did more to keep him awake.

As soon as they broke away and he was satisfied they were clear, the unidentified replenishment ship or freighter moving off still darkened, till she fell off *Gaddis*'s radar screen and the edge of the world, he went into the chart room, threw Robidoux out, snapped the accordion door closed, and switched on the white light. Pulled up a stool, and slit the envelope with a pair of dividers.

The paper within was light and flimsy. Fax paper. The typed words were blurred, as if they'd been photocopied before they'd been faxed. There was no salutation or header and, of course, no signature, either.

The memo or message or order—whatever it was—both reproached him for not conducting a more expeditious search and apologized for the belated realization that *Gaddis* had been forced to leave most of her ammo in Karachi. It directed him to proceed to an area that, when he tickled a chart, lay 200 miles east of Hainan Island and 180 north of the Xisha Quindao or Paracels. An open and undistinguished stretch of ocean about 250 miles due south of Hong Kong. He drew a triangle on the chart, then erased it after reading the last lines: *"Keep these instructions secret from officers and crew. Destroy this note. Final targeting information will be provided en route. Inflict maximum possible damage to outlaw forces. Retire at best speed to the south."*

He erased the tiny triangle so thoroughly that not on the closest inspection could he find a sign of it. He memorized the position, read the message three more times, till he could recite it from memory, then flicked on the shredder.

A dark form awaited him outside the chartroom divider. His flashlight illuminated one of the assistant masters-at-arms. "What is it?" he said.

"Chief Mellows, sir, he wants to talk to you."

"Why? What for?" But the man didn't answer. Dan hesitated, then sighed. "All right. I'll be right down."

"CHIEF. You asked to see me?"

Silence, but accompanied with a nod of the smooth, bare scalp, barely visible through the grating. The perforated metal separated them, the one in the half-lighted corridor, the other submerged in the dark. The guard stood back a few feet, weapon casting a gnomonic shadow. Another was perched on a chair at the far end of the passageway.

"I already passed sentence. You had a chance to speak then."

Mellows said hoarsely, "I couldn't think of anything then."

Despite himself, an iota of pity crept past the fatigue. Yes, the man before him was a murderer. Torturer. And mutilator. But now he was facing the common fate, and, by the sound of his voice, not having an easy time of it. Dan motioned the guard farther away, then put his face to the grating. "All right. What have you got to say?"

"This stuff about hanging me—that's a joke, right, sir?"

"I thought about this a long time, Chief. About whether I

should just keep you locked down, turn you over if and when we get back. But there's no question you're the killer. You're going to be an example, Marsh.

"But if you want to talk about . . . what you told me before, you killed them because they were prostitutes, that's not it. God damn it, *why?*"

"They came to me. That's why."

"What are you talking about? They came to you to get gutted like chickens?"

"There is an Angel of Death. There is a Sword of God."

Lenson felt his balls shrivel in horror. The voice was that of a man he knew or had thought he knew, but now he heard something else speaking to him through it. He dismissed the message he'd just received, everything else, from his mind and focused on the man-shaped darkness hunched rocking to and fro.

His own voice sounded thick and slow. "Did Seaman Vorenkamp come to you that way, Marsh?"

"He came on to me, yeah. Just like the whores did. I wouldn't have done it to someone who didn't deserve it."

"You had to know something was wrong, Marsh. If you felt like you had to do this, if you couldn't stop yourself, why didn't you turn yourself in? Try to get help?"

In a voice so low Dan could barely hear it over the humming roar of the blowers, Mellows murmured, "Why bother? It's all going to be dark soon anyway."

"What does that mean?"

"Nothing. It was fun while it lasted, though. Like a game. You really would have turned Pistol and Johnile over to the NIS, wouldn't you?"

Engelhart, up the passageway. "Captain? Where are you?"

"Here, Chief Warrant. What you need?"

"I got some preparations to make, sir. So do you. Dawn's gonna be here, couple hours. Listening to whatever sick shit that son of a bitch in there is ladling out isn't going to change a thing."

"You're not going to hang me, Ben. This is some kind of trick. You're just trying to scare me."

Engelhart: "Oh, yeah? You think I'm fucking with your mind? This is the Old Navy again, asshole. You get off cutting on people? Fine. We're gonna swing you off the fucking yardarm, teach the rest of these motherfuckers a lesson."

"You can't do that. I got rights—"

"Hey, so'd your shipmate Vorenkamp. So'd the girl on Dahakit and all the whores you cut up. I'm out of here, asshole. See you at dawn. Skipper! Let's go! He's not worth wasting rack time on."

Dan moved away from the grille, his momentary weakness braced by the old warrant's blunt comeback. Out of nowhere came what Dr. Guo had said, in Singapore, something about pirates, about all criminals, being rational but not moral, seeking gains to themselves, but shifting the costs to others. This was what lay at the end of that path. A being willing to destroy others not for its survival, nor even for its advantage, but simply for its transient and passing pleasure. He said, "Ben's right. Society's a bargain. You break the rules, you pay. And from what I'm hearing, you can't give me a better reason for killing them than that you enjoyed it."

Silence. Then: "You people are such a bunch of fucking hypocrites."

"Why are we hypocrites, Marsh?"

"Because every man alive would love to do the same thing."

Dan sat silent as the chief went on, describing the things he'd done. Gradually, he began to sweat.

Mellows was right.

Suddenly, in this heaving cage of steel, he recognized the face of his own darkest fantasies. Desires he'd almost forgotten, which he'd never acknowledged in the light of day.

He felt perspiration roll down his back and dragged his sleeve across his mouth, fighting nausea and guilt. He'd

faced evil men before. But he'd never before felt so close to
the evil within himself. Another self, which pushed back
the gravestone he'd always covered it with and whispered
now into his inmost ear, *He's right. You are the same.*

Mellows muttered, "You know what I'm talking about,
don't you? Hear it by the way you're breathing. Smell it by
the way you stink. And you're punishing *me?*"

Dan said through the horror, "I thought about it. When I
was fifteen. Sixteen. Then I realized it was sick and wrong
and pushed it away. Again and again, until it stopped coming back.

"Maybe we had the same fantasies. Maybe everybody
does. But instead of fighting them, you fed them. Went over
and over it in your mind. Read about it. Watched the tapes.
Till finally it seemed like you had to do it. And then you
did. You *did* it, Marsh."

Mellows leaned close to the mesh now, so close Dan
could feel his breath. He pulled back instinctively, as if
something infectious and malevolent might pass between
them on that warm current. "And you didn't have the balls
to," came the whisper.

"It doesn't take 'balls'—"

"No, it does, and you just don't have them. That's the
only difference! I had the courage to say to hell with what
they tell you's right and wrong. Don't push it away, deny it,
pretend it isn't there. It's what we really are! You can make
me some kind of devil, so you won't have to admit the truth.
But there's others starting to think like me. Go ahead, hang
me. You aren't taking away anything I'm not going to lose
anyway. But I won't be the last. You'll see."

"I'm out of here," Dan said to the guard. "Nobody else
sees this son of a bitch. Nobody else talks to him." The gunner's mate nodded grimly. But even when he came up out of
the supply passageway, Dan still heard the chilling whisper
of Mellows's final testament.

23

THEY hadn't seen the sun for weeks, and it was a blinding and awesome thing. He watched it mount passing clouds as he sat on the bridge like a cat bathing in the floods of heat. Still, he felt empty. Cold.

Miles astern now, two bodies were sinking toward the ocean floor. Mellows and his final victim, Vorenkamp.

The execution had gone at dawn, as scheduled. Chief Warrant Engelhart had taken charge in the helo hangar, on the upper catwalk where the sonobuoys were stored. The line was manila, made up to a hoisting point on the overhead.

The ship's lay leader had stepped up with a Bible in his hand, but Mellows had ignored him, staring stolidly ahead as they put the blindfold on. Engelhart had looked to Dan. Who had nodded, and with a simultaneous push of several arms the condemned man had toppled off the platform, plunged fifteen feet, and jerked to an abrupt stop just above the nonskid. The snap and crack had been as loud as a shot in the closed-in, echoing steel space.

Dan massaged his eyeballs as perspiration needled his forehead. He felt unreal, as if this were all dream or nightmare. But it was real.

It would take a long time to forget that sound. If he ever did.

Now every officer, chief, and first-class aboard *Gaddis* carried a loaded side arm and watched his back in the passageways. But Dan had to put all that aside for now. Entirely apart from the question of justice, *Gaddis* could not go into battle with any question as to who was in command. He had established his authority in the starkest way imaginable. And it was perfectly plain where they were headed, just as soon as he got the targeting information last night's message promised.

As the two ships had separated, he'd told Zabounian, who had taken over the watch from the chief warrant, to come to 270. If Colosimo was right and the freebooters were out of the Leizhon peninsula, going west made sense. As long as he was not so close to the Chinese coast that air surveillance could nail him, and of course he had to keep the weather in mind; despite this morning's glimpse of sun, this was still storm season, and the break would not last long. He picked up the CO's clipboard. Compline had gotten a weather chart from somewhere, and Dan contemplated what looked like a string of low-pressure areas moving west, trailing like bubbles in the wake of Hercule, which was up in southern China now.

A stir roved the bridge, the throat-clearing and furtive checking of flies and hitching up of belts men do when they unexpectedly encounter a woman. He looked up to see Bobbie Wedlake's pale, pinched face emerge from the companionway, Neilsen close behind. He stared, then remembered himself and tried to smile. "Good morning."

"Good morning."

He asked her if she'd had breakfast yet but got only a wordless stare. The corpsman shrugged. Dan turned back to Wedlake and offered her his seat. She swung up into the leather chair, then sat motionless and silent, blinking in the radiance. She'd lost weight. Now the fine bones engraved her skin from beneath. He could see each tendon and carpal in her hands.

She said, "I heard another engine last night, lying with my head against the frame of my bed."

"We were refueling and rearming."

"Out here? From another ship?"

"That's right." He cleared his throat and told her the other piece of news he figured she might be interested in. "The man who broke in on you, night before last? We found out who it was. I executed him this morning and buried him at sea, along with a young man he murdered two weeks ago."

"Executed? Right here aboard?"

"I felt I had to."

To his relief, she didn't probe that wound further, simply said, "Where are we bound now?"

"I'm heading west, looking for the people who attacked you. *Marker Eagle* wasn't the first ship they've looted and taken over."

"So you're really going after them. And if you find them?"

"I'll bring them to battle and, I hope, win."

"You didn't do so well last time."

"You're absolutely right, but they took me by surprise. I expected patrol craft. I didn't expect what seems to be a cruiser."

"I saw it close up. It's larger than your ship here. Though yours looks newer. And you think you can beat them?"

"Well, we have to try. The tough part may be getting in close enough."

"Any woman can tell you how to do that," she said, and a faint sarcasm edged her voice.

"She can? I mean, you can?"

"Sure. Just make yourself look like something he wants. Now. Tell me: What can I do to help? Eric broke me in on the bridge. The radar and how to do the chart work. I'm a pretty competent second mate."

"I'm sure you are, but Navy procedures are different. I've got my watch teams pretty well shaken down."

"I want something to do. I *need* something to do."

He thought of the crowd at the flight-deck picnic, the remarks Sansone had overheard. "Well, I could put you on as an assistant JOOD. But I'll level with you, Bobbie. It would be best if you stayed out of sight as much as possible. Usmani will bring you your meals. Don't roam around the ship. I think you know why. The man we hung is not the only possible danger aboard."

"Then you don't want me in sick bay. People are always knocking at the door, wanting the corpsman."

Dan considered. "I'd give you my cabin, but I have to be close to the bridge. . . . You still have your revolver, right?"

"I still have it."

"Well, what the hell, I spend most of my time up here anyway. Bo's'n! Show Mrs. Wedlake to my cabin, and tell Usmani to put my shaving kit in the officers' washroom."

She thanked him with the quiet dignity of a medieval lady. Watched the sea for a few minutes longer, a distant look in gray eyes, then climbed down from the chair and went below.

"THIS is a drill. Now General Quarters, General Quarters." The 1MC's bark caromed off bulkheads. *Gaddis*, rolling hard as she plodded westward, echoed with running feet. Dan let Doolan run the exercises, which he did slowly, stopping for instruction and explanation, getting the phone talkers and designation personnel, the gun crews and ammunition handlers, back into practice.

Dan went aft and stood a few feet from the quad forty, observing as the loaders, arms nearly covered by heavy protective gloves, pushed four-round clips of the foot-long shells down into the loader guides atop each gun. The pointer and trainer were hunched over their handwheels, helmets shading their faces as they peered through the ring sights. The mount captain jerked back the hand operating lever, closing the breech with a metallic clank. The loaders stood ready with the next clips. All signs of hesitation or apathy had disappeared. The men were intent on learning as quickly as possible and moving as fast as they could.

Yeah, the prospect of a fight pulled together the most unpromising crew. But *Gaddis*'s skimpy compliment and the heavy manpower requirements of the old twenties and forties meant that when he went to GQ he'd have just enough hands to steam her, conn her, and fight her. If they took hits, he'd have to choose between continuing to fight and letting her sink under them. Not an appealing prospect in this corner of the world. He had little expectation any friendlies would turn up to rescue them if they ended up treading water.

The answer, of course, was that if he engaged, he'd damn well better make sure he won in round one. He couldn't let it turn into a slugging match.

When the shoot was over he convened another war council, this time in the wardroom, since Wedlake was in his cabin.

Chick and the leading gunner's mate reported that they were seeing about 30 percent duds with the five-inch proximity-fuzed ammunition, most likely due to simple age. That didn't mean they wouldn't explode; a VT shell carried a point detonating fuze too. But it would make it more difficult to neutralize the gunboats. The weapons officer recommended that they dedicate the five-inch to the cruiser and let the forties and twenties deal with the light craft. Dan had to disagree. They might have to engage the Shanghais first, and in that case, he didn't want to hold back his longest-ranged weapon. "How many rounds does that leave us with, by the way?" he asked Doolan. "And how much did we use this morning?"

Chick said they'd received 300 rounds of 5"/54 powder and projectiles, half a normal loadout, and 3,000 rounds of 40mm. They'd fired 29 rounds of five-inch and 307 rounds of 40mm that morning.

"I want to drill again this afternoon. Aimed slow fire at long ranges, director-controlled. Next issue. How's Chief Tosito holding out?"

"Tostito's in pain. Keeps eating pills. But he's parked down there in the sonar room, keeping the scan going. The ping jockey on watch got a signature off the Katori. If it's around, he'll find it." Doolan hesitated. "But there's a lot of sea out here. How are we gonna localize this guy?"

Dan had considered this, how he was going to get them to the position the sealed orders had given without telling the crew about the orders themselves. "Well, we think we know where they're out of. Question is, Do we go in and get them or wait for them to come out?"

"Zhanjaing's the headquarters of the Southern Fleet," Armey said. "If you decide you're going in there, leave me behind in a life raft, OK?"

"Just kidding, Jim. We've got to catch them out of their hole. So I asked Commander Colosimo to check out their target set and see if that narrows things down for us any, gives us some idea where to look. Dom?"

The reservist unfolded a chart. "Basically I just plotted reported attacks from IMO and industry records over the last four years. We didn't wake up to the problem till then."

Examining the results, Dan saw immediately that the second largest group of small circles lay north of the Paracels, grouped around the position he'd memorized. When you looked at the shipping routes, the reason was evident to the most casual observer: that was where the Singapore–Shanghai, Hong Kong–Jakarta, and Japan–Singapore routes crossed. Predators followed prey. He placed his finger there. "Looks perfectly obvious to me where we're headed."

"And if this next depression stays on course, it'll come right over us."

"Well, we've come through a typhoon; we can take another storm." Armey shifted in his seat, and Dan prompted him, "Go on, Jim. Don't leave us in suspense."

"Our last refrigeration unit is out. We have two operating firepumps left. We got the strake patched, but I don't think we're in shape to take on another storm—or a battle, for that matter."

"Sorry, Jim, we haven't come this far to turn back for anything short of a major materiel casualty." When Armey had no comeback, Dan tapped the chart again. "So that's it. And not that far away. We can be there in two days."

They didn't look convinced, but not even Armey had an audible objection. Dan refolded the chart and handed it to Colosimo. They were gathering their legs under them, getting ready to leave, when he added, "One last thing. Watch your backs. I had a very disturbing encounter with one of our less career-oriented petty officers just before the storm. And I've been getting threats on the sound-powered circuits."

Engelhart grunted, "You mean when you and Machias faced off in the hangar? I heard about it. Ever since then I've had people nagging me about their whiskey ration."

"I told Juskoviac to administer the booze."

Doolan said, "You think it's smart, putting Greg in charge of that?"

"I don't think he wants my job anymore," Dan told him. "If he ever really did. What I don't want to do is make him some kind of martyr. You got a better idea, you can implement it when you're CO, OK?"

"Sure, Skipper." Doolan pushed air away with both hands. "Take it easy. Just asking. And about Machias, I'd have locked him up, if I were you. After he pulled the knife on you."

"I can't lock everybody up, Chick. Nor can I spare the people to guard them. We'll need every hand we've got if we run into the Katori again."

"But will they fight?" said Engelhart dourly. "And can we keep the lid on 'em till then?"

"I think they'll fight," said Dan. "Anyway, stay alert. And wear those side arms."

"You never picked yours up," Chick pointed out. "We had it back on the fantail, waiting for you."

"I don't think that would send the right message, to have me wearing one. All right, gentlemen. I believe that will be all."

THAT afternoon he was sitting on the wing, half-asleep, when Doolan came up and laid the dense weight of a holstered pistol in his lap.

When the weps officer left, he sat rubbing his eyes, listening to the firing commands going out for the afternoon drills. Wondering if he *could* get Juskoviac to take over as CO. He no longer wanted this mission or assignment or whatever it was. He didn't have any objection to taking on the Chinese. But he didn't like the idea of having a crew he couldn't depend on, a failing ship, anonymous logistics, and, instead of orders, operating contingent on the guessed-at intent of concealed, unnameable higher-ups.

Along with that, he was grappling with a tactical problem.

Coldly and dispassionately as he could, he had analyzed the coming battle. Had sketched several tactical approaches on a maneuvering board, and even done some Lanchester and probability of kill calculations.

Both sides had radar, but he felt he could assume *Gaddis* had better sensors—better ESM and sonar—and more skillful operators.

In terms of speed, the gunboats gave the other side the edge, though if he caught the cruiser alone, he thought he could most likely match her. Some Second World War warships had been built for astonishing speeds, but he doubted if boilers that old could be pressed to their design limits.

As far as armament went, they were roughly equal. The old cruiser had bigger guns and more of them, but *Gaddis*'s automatic five-inch could fire faster and probably had more accurate radar control. With one glaring exception. The cruiser had missiles. He wasn't sure what they were and he didn't think they had over-the-horizon targeting capability, but even without it there was a significant range band where his opponent could hit *Gaddis* and he could not strike back.

How could he transit that zone and come to grips with them?

Any woman can tell you that, Bobbie Wedlake had said. You make yourself look like something he wants.

He sat with the pistol on his lap as men shouted on the boat deck and a clanking came from the feeding mechanism of the guns. The forties cracked again, and the sulphur reek of propellant filled his nose as the smoke of the guns shrouded the ship, plunging west.

24

HE stopped the fourth merchant vessel they passed the next day but changed his mind after they hove to and let them go, not giving any justification or rationale, simply blinking a curt international-code: "Continue on your original course." The reason he gave the bridge team being that another contact was bearing down on them and he didn't want any more witnesses to this than he had to have. They accepted it, but the truth was he'd simply lost his nerve at the last minute.

This skull-and-crossbones stuff was a high-stress occupation. And he had to get some sleep. He couldn't keep driving himself, on the bridge day and night.

The next ship he stopped was a small engines-aft merchant whose decks were piled high with containers. She hove to obediently at the flashing-light message, and he got Pistolesi and his boys in the water and on their way before he could change his mind again. Then paced the bridge, biting his lips and telling himself he had to do this, that it was inherent in the mission.

They were over there a long time, while *Gaddis* stood by, monitoring the distress channels and maintaining steerageway into the seas. At last he saw activity. One of the smaller containers, the international standard twenty-foot boxes, began inching toward the stern. With the binoculars, he made out a yellow forklift pushing it. The container paused at the deck edge, teetered, then toppled into the sea. Several more followed it over the side.

"Tell him two more and that's enough. And hurry it up. I want him back aboard," Dan told Doolan. The weapons officer raised the PRC-10 and relayed the order.

By the time the merchant was a departing dot on the

gun-gray sea, the containers were aboard. The deck gang got them aboard with some difficulty. Being a warship, *Gaddis* had very little in the way of hoisting gear, but since the containers were empty, they eventually succeeded. Six of the 8×8×20 boxes rested now on the forecastle; the rest stood about on the fantail, where they were being cut in two to the accompaniment of the whine of pneumatic saws and dazzling firefalls of sparks.

Now Dan sat in the wardroom with Compline, Zabounian, and Pistolesi standing before him, his chin propped on locked knuckles as he contemplated a rich selection of pocketables spread out on the tablecloth.

He'd told the masters-at-arms—overseen now by Chief Compline, whom he'd asked to take over Mellows's former duty as chief master-at-arms—to be waiting on the boat deck to search Pistolesi and his returning boat crew. Along with the things they'd been sent over to secure—paint, pump motors, wire, house flags, and lighting gear—they'd come back with a sizable hoard of South Korean, Japanese, and U.S. currency, a dozen watches, pornographic videotapes with titles in Chinese, and a fat Ziploc stuffed with a brownish shredded material of vegetable origin.

Finally he raised his eyes to the man who stood unhumbled at the head of the table. "You couldn't keep your hands to yourself, Fireman Pistolesi. Could you."

"Sir, the guys put it to me on the way over. We ain't been paid in a month. Even if we was, there's nothing in the ship's store but belt buckles and Aqua Velva. So we decided to take it out in trade. The master over there, he had no problem with that. Soon as we boarded, he took us down to the safe. I never even had to ask. Which was good, because I don't think he and I would have made a lot of sense to each other. Anyway, we did like you said, kept the cold-weather masks on the whole time."

"He gave you these watches, too? And the grass?"

"I told you, these were very hospitable guys, Skipper. We didn't do no inventory. He just cleared out the safe, shoved everything in Marky's bag. He just wanted us to leave, was the feeling I got. I never saw the grass till now. If that's what it is." He raised his eyes to the overhead. The wardroom was silent except for the slow creaking of the bulkheads and the whine of power saws from aft.

"Mr. Zabounian."

"Sir." The supply officer came to attention.

"The cash, the watches, and the tapes go in your safe. If and when we make port again, you will mail them direct to the master of that ship Pistolesi just robbed. No return address. Just mail it without one."

"Aye aye, sir."

"The marijuana or hash or whatever this is goes over the side. Roy, I want witnesses to the destruction. I also want one of those search-and-seizure forms completed and filed."

"Sir, you ain't going to charge me with—"

"The question of what I am going to charge you with, Pistolesi, is suspended until the completion of this operation," Dan told him. "It may be that none of us are coming back. In that case, it doesn't matter. It may also be that we survive, steam into Subic, and I've forgotten about this incident and the forms got lost. Considering your positive contributions. But damn it, we're all walking a narrow line out here. We get over the edge too far and we're never going to make it back."

"Sir, this is blackmail. That ain't the way you should deal with me."

Dan regarded him for a moment more, then shrugged. "Maybe you're right. You don't want to play that game? OK, we won't."

"That's good, Skipper. I figured you'd—"

"Chief Compline: Take this man back to the fantail. Mr. Zabounian: My compliments to Mr. Doolan, and ask him to muster a five-man firing party. M-16s, each loaded with one round, total four rounds of ball ammo and one blank. For disobeying orders in the face of the enemy, Fireman Joseph E. Pistolesi is hereby condemned to—"

"Jesus God, sir!"

"Are you listening to me now, Pistol? You're over there shaking these poor bastards down, and meanwhile I have to sweat every closing contact. You know why? Because if any of them's a warship—it doesn't matter whose, Japanese or Korean, Dutch, French, Russian, whatever—if it's a warship, he's duty-bound to come to their assistance on the high seas. Then what? Either we take them under fire, other navymen doing their duty, or else the mission's down the tubes and we're all up for trial. And not in a U.S. court, either."

"Look, I didn't know that, sir. Forget I said anything. You make out any form you want. We're playing by your rules now. Jesus God!"

Sweat was trickling down the fireman's cheeks now, and his beard stubble showed dark. But maybe they were both playing, Dan thought. Certainly he was trying desperately to imitate someone who knew what he was doing. He was abruptly sick of the game. He snapped, "Get this shit out of my sight. And frog-march this son of a bitch out of here."

HE prowled restlessly about all that afternoon, inspecting the preparations, making suggestions, putting his shoulder to it when his weight was needed. The pillaged containers, each sliced in half, were being manhandled and come-alonged into position along *Gaddis*'s deck edges, facing outboard. That is, their open interiors faced inboard; their ends, decorated with the logos of shipping lines and trucking lines, faced out.

He'd puzzled over the frigate's hull. They couldn't leave it gray and have any hope of being taken for other than what they were. But it wasn't possible in seas that continued this heavy to even think of putting men overside to paint. Then Topmark had proposed a white band along the deck edge. If the light was right, the boatswain said, it might look like the color scheme on some of the merchants they had passed.

Dan had gotten the germ of the idea from Bobbie Wedlake's sardonic remark, added it to a *ruse de guerre* Capt. Thomas Leighty had come up with off the coast of Cuba, hunting USS *City of Corpus Christi* during a barrier exercise, and mixed in an antisubmarine tactic the British had tried in the First World War, something called a Q ship. Bobbie had done the actual design. Sketching the outline of a 1052 on a drawing pad, she'd first truncated the damaged mack, slicing metal off its telltale shape to make it more closely resemble a merchant ship's stack. Stacked forward and aft, the containers would imitate deck cargo. The guns, barrels depressed as far as they would go, would be covered with tarps. Put together, it all might create the illusion that *Gaddis* was a rather small breakbulk steamer with an opportunity deck load of containers.

Until the observer was close enough, of course. At a certain range all illusion would evaporate, revealing a destroyer-type warship, rake-bowed and low to the water, clumsily painted and furbeloyed into the image of a seatramp. He could only hope the masquerade got him inside gun range. Well, the weather was cooperating. The advance fringes of the next storm were pushing downpours and squalls ahead of it. The frigate rolled steadily through them, rain clattering down now and then as the crew jockeyed the last containers into position and griped them down against the corkscrewing bucks and slams of a ten-foot sea on the quarter.

He was on the helo deck inspecting the tiedowns, satisfying himself they were solid yet could be quickly released, when *Gaddis* leaned into a series of prolonged rolls. He glanced uneasily at the seas behind them, then at a steadily blackening sky. Not again, he thought. If the seas grew much heavier, he'd have to abort the whole operation. Beyond a certain sea state the gunboats couldn't board, and if they couldn't board, they'd probably retire to port.

"Captain? Have a word with you?"

It was Juskoviac, to Dan's surprise. The XO had not addressed him for days, even when they brushed by each other in the passageways. Dan led the way toward the aft edge of the flight deck. The clanging and cursing were a little less loud there, and no one could overhear them.

"Yeah, Greg. What you got?"

"I want you to know there's significant doubt about the way you're running this ship."

"Doubt in your mind or someone else's?"

"I mean in everybody's mind. I understand you authorized arming the officers."

"I did, along with the chiefs and first-class. In case of attempted boarding. Where's your side arm, XO?"

"In my safe, in my stateroom. It's not an antiboarding measure. Nobody bought that. I don't think this is the way to maintain a good relationship with the crew." Juskoviac hesitated, then added, "Nor is, uh, *hanging* people. No matter what they may have done. Or threatening to shoot them, like you did with Pistolesi."

Dan almost smiled. If his purpose in dealing summarily with Mellows had been to inspire fear, he'd succeeded with the exec. "This is not a normal underway period, Greg. In several significant ways." He waited, but the exec didn't respond. "So, what did you decide on the liquor issue?"

"Half a pint, at noon."

"Seems like we ought to pipe 'up spirits,' eh?"

But Juskoviac didn't smile. His sullen, stubborn expression was grating, but Dan tried to maintain his patience. Doolan was right; he was turning into the kind of cranky, touchy CO he'd always disliked himself. By now he'd figured out what he was doing with Juskoviac, more instinctively than by plan. He was using the XO as a lightning rod, providing a ready channel for incipient unrest, figuring that if it truly became imminent the exec would remember a shred of loyalty or, failing that, of fear.

"Any more petitions circulating, Greg?"

"It won't be limited to petitions this time," Juskoviac said. He looked over his shoulder at the guys finishing the griping down. A squall was emerging astern, taking on solidity and mass as it overtook them from the overlooming darkness to the east. Dan considered altering course, then decided not to. He had clear orders at last; he'd head directly to the indicated point.

But with that decision fresh worry gnawed. Sure, he'd gotten orders. But from whom? Was it possible that they weren't Navy orders? His mind skittered back and forth like a squirrel in traffic. Were they caught in the toils of a plot so subtle he still had not grasped it? They were almost on station. Shouldn't he have gotten the promised targeting message by now? "Final targeting information will be provided en route"—but how? *Gaddis* carried Link Fourteen, a nonautomated interface with the Naval Tactical Data System, but the frequency was dead; no one was transmitting. Compline had no access to Fleet Broadcast. Dan had Radio and CIC monitoring all the uncovered channels he could think of, but he didn't see how it could come in that way without running the risk it could be intercepted, overheard by Chinese listening posts, and recorded. Saying "so long" to the deniability of the whole operation.

He came back to *Gaddis*'s helo deck to feel the first cold exhalation of the oncoming squall. Juskoviac was regarding him strangely. He cast back to whatever they'd been talking about. Oh . . . petitions, and the XO had said it wouldn't be limited to that. Dan cleared his throat. "No? Then what will it be?"

"This time the word in the p-ways is they're just going to kill you."

"OK, Greg. So on the one hand, I'm overreacting by issuing side arms. And on the other, you tell me the lowlifes have a contract out on me."

"It isn't just me. Jim Armey thinks we ought to turn back, too."

"Jim's shared his doubts with me, Greg, more than once. He's up-front with it. Then he salutes and goes down below and keeps things running. You ever noticed that? What he says'll get done, well, damn! It gets done. Not because he sits in his office playing with his snake. Because he goes down there and works it and bird-dogs it till it's done."

"You've got them believing you, Lenson. I don't know how. My own sense—"

"Yeah? What sense is that, Greg?"

Sentence by sentence, they'd passed from wariness to enmity. The equivocal construction of Dan's last remark nudged it past recovery. He felt it happening, but he was too tired to care, too fatigued to dissemble anymore with the man he'd carried on his back since the day they met. He did not clarify or recall his statement.

Juskoviac flushed, gripping the lifeline as the deck slanted beneath their boots. Suddenly words tumbled from his mouth. "You know, I saw from the second you came aboard to stab Dick Ottero in the back that you were an arrogant, devious son of a bitch. I could live with that. You run into them now and then in this organization. But you're so far over the line now that—I know you hate the Chinese. They hurt your fiancée or something—"

"They killed her, Greg. Hired some D.C. gang bangers to rape her and kill her."

"OK, they killed her. That's rough. But you're so obsessed you've become what you think you're fighting. You're becoming a pirate yourself, and dragging the rest of us down with you. You think you're Captain Kidd. But you're not. You're not Captain Queeg, either."

Dan said dryly, figuring this was the time to let the man spit all the poison he'd stored up, "Then who am I, Greg?"

"You're Captain Ahab."

"And you're Starbuck? I don't think so, Greg. The men respected him."

Dan knew the second it was out of his mouth he shouldn't have said it. Up to now the exec had been ineffective, undependable, a pain in the ass, but he was at least nominally still responsible to the command. After he got his whining over with, he'd have turned back into his inadequate, harmless self. But now Juskoviac's eyes blazed in a way Dan had not seen before. His face went the mottled red and white of someone who's been out walking in deep winter and come in suddenly to a suffocatingly hot room.

"You son of a bitch," he said in a low, tormented voice. "Just remember: What goes around comes around. There's gonna be a reckoning for this someday. When it happens, I intend to testify to the truth."

He turned on his heel. Dan reached out, half-intending to call him back, then gave up and just called after him, "Wear your side arm, Greg."

The men looked toward Dan as the first drops of rain arrived, plopping first on the fantail, then around them on the black nonskid, clapping heavily down one by one, then more and more swiftly until he had to jog toward the hangar. He took shelter there with the sweating crewmen in long-unlaundered dungarees and T-shirts, in a sudden silence. Shoulders pressed into his; he felt someone shift and move behind him.

Suddenly his mouth grew dry. It was all he could do not to turn around, to stare out at the dancing silver mist as if the idea of a blade suddenly thrust into his back was not all that filled his mind.

BUT the squall passed without incident. As it eased off, he worked his way through the crowd and forward and then up to CIC to check on the radio and sonar searches. Thence to Radio, and thence to the bridge. Where he stayed perched in his chair, alternately trying to nap and pacing the deck for the rest of the afternoon.

By dusk preparations were close to complete. The power cabling for the new lights was still being connected, but the rigging of the lights themselves, the alterations to ship's structure, and placing of the containers were finished. *Gaddis* heaved steadily now through a darkening gloom penetrated only by occasional bursts of heavy, almost drowning rain, so sudden and concentrated it was as if she'd sailed under a waterfall. He went down to Radio again to get another message off to Subic, then came back up to the bridge. Chick had prepared an emissions bill and had assigned his JOOD to check it off. Dan called for a status on the dark bridge and was startled when a woman's voice answered.

"That you, Bobbie?"

"You said I could sign on as a mate. I can't sit down there any longer looking at that revolver."

Dan remembered being there. He'd confronted that choice himself, on a divan in front of a telephone, a six-pack, and a pistol, after Kerry died. After he'd realized that all evils do not have remedies, that not all malevolence is punished, that all stories do not tie up neatly at the ends. That some losses can never be avenged or remedied, only outlived.

Could it be possible that Juskoviac was right, that he was over the line? That he was—what had the exec's word been—obsessed?

He became conscious she was still staring at him, invisible in the dark, but he could still feel her eyes, and he cleared his throat, pushing doubt and self-questioning back into the shadowy place where it lived always. "Well . . . OK. How are we looking?"

"I don't understand all of these things. People call up and tell me they're done, or I call them and ask, and then I check them off. Turn count set and masking, what's that?"

"That's holding our speed to one consistent with a merchant . . . and there's some other dirty tricks there, so we sound more like one. In case somebody's tracking us with passive sonar."

"IFF off and tagged?"

"Identification Friend or Foe; that's an electronic responder that tells another U.S. ship we're a U.S. ship."

"Don't we want that left on?"

"No. Believe me on that one."

"Fire control radars, tagged out and breakers removed—"

"So we don't give ourselves away as a warship."

"Deceptive lighting measures."

"That's the lights and gear we were setting up on the flying bridge and up on the mack. A merchant shows a lot more lights under way than we do. Actually, if we could manage to come up on these guys at night, we can probably get within spitting distance before they figure out we're not what they think."

"What are the chances of that?"

He told her he didn't have any way of calculating it; all they could do was try and hope for the best. He thanked her for helping out, then moved on through the darkened pilot-house, among the silent anticipating shapes of helmsman and lee helm, boatswain and quartermaster.

And once again fear squirmed in his belly. It would be child's play for someone to take him out up here. A knife in the side, then escape in the dark and confusion. A side arm wouldn't do a damn bit of good. He'd need a suit of armor. His mouth parched again, and he went to the urn. The coffee was bitter and overcooked, it tasted like licking the inside of a cap gun, but he drained the dregs anyway. If somebody wanted him out of the way, there wasn't much he could do about it. He was pretty sure he could count on the bridge team, anyway.

Yeah, and when this was all over, he was going to have to find some way to reward the guys who'd stuck with him. Like Doolan and Topmark and Zabounian, Chief Compline and Sansone and Usmani. Had to find some way to get Usmani into the country. Didn't service in the armed forces help you in applying for citizenship? He ought to get Compline to swear the son of a bitch in. After Bobbie gave him a few pointers on how not to treat women in America. And Chief Tosito, sitting down there in Sonar with the torment from his stitched-up chest plain from the very stoniness of his features. Should be flat on his back in sick bay. Instead he was patiently searching out ahead for any screw beat, any machinery tonal, anything that might indicate the presence of their quarry. They deserved praise and more than praise. Maybe when this was over—if they all came through whatever lay over the horizon—their hard work would be rewarded.

And that made him wonder again, not with any hope of resolving what he had puzzled at now for too long, what *they* had in mind for him. What web those inaccessible deities—he thought of them that way now, like the gods who had pushed Odysseus around the sea like a living toy—were spinning as his fate and destiny.

He'd taken *Gaddis* on with the naïve assumption that what he saw was what he would get, that it was what it had been presented as, a chance at a temporary command. Since then the assignment had morphed into the strangest of his career. He'd pursued it halfway round the planet and endured Khashar and Juskoviac and Machias. Had passed a sentence that left him with a cold hole where his soul had been, a judgment that would always make him doubt the meaning of justice and retribution. He'd proceeded on faith, faith that these unseen immortals would make everything right, that they knew all, foresaw all, and would end all in some way that would transform the wayward course of his long voyage into a logical mission. And only once through that entire time had their presence been made manifest, incarnated in a shadow out of the dark, a ship he'd never fully seen, peopled by red-lit shadows, who had gifted him with the power of destruction, but flawed, aged, and thoroughly and completely deniable. Twenty-year-old ammunition. A ship manned by outcasts, with an outcast for her captain, named after the great outcast of mankind . . . no, that had been USS *Caine*. Shit, he couldn't blame Armey or Juskoviac if they didn't buy his take on this. He'd been skating on the edge of disbelief himself when the replenishment message came blinking through the dark.

"Bridge, Sonar." The 21MC. One of the wraiths pressed the key to acknowledge. "Captain up there?"

"Sittin' here listening. Inform us."

"He might want to come down here. We got somebody trying to call us."

TOSITO was stretched out at full length in the dim red light of the alcove that opened off CIC, his chair reclined like a dentist's. Headphones vised his skull. A third-class sat with him, glancing up as Dan rattled the curtain aside. Narrow and equipment-walled, the sonar space smelled of ozone and floor wax and rubber and old burnt coffee from the hot plate bolted to the bulkhead. The sonar stacks were shut down for all but passive listening. Tape reels rotated smoothly behind a transparent shield. Dan placed his hand carefully on the unbandaged shoulder, and Tosito looked up. "Somebody trying to call us on Gertrude, Captain," he said.

"Gertrude" was the AN/WQC-2A, a seldom-used underwater telephone. Dan had seen it employed occasionally to communicate with submerged submarines during exercises, but subs were wary about talking to anyone at the best of times. Sound refracted through water layers and turbulences at different rates, varying with frequency, and someone speaking over Gertrude sounded as if he were underwater at the bottom of a deep well. Their distorted, echoing words came accompanied by eerie gurgling, clicks, whistles, and distant tolling bells. "There he is again," said the chief. He motioned to the sonarman, winced, and sank back.

"You better take it easy, Chief."

"I'm OK, sir. Turn it up on the speaker."

They sat hunched in the red light as a bubbling, clicking groan was penetrated by what might be a human voice speaking far away. The words were indistinguishable. "Is that English?" Dan said.

"It's degraded now, but it was coming through a couple of minutes ago. When I called you. They said very clearly, 'U.S. ship *Oliver Gaddis*.' "

"That's an odd form of address," Dan said, looking at the green cloth-bound comm log the petty officer put in his hands.

"I can play it back. We started taping as soon as I heard it."

"Did it sound like an American accent?"

"No, sir, it didn't."

"Did you answer?"

"Not yet. Wanted to get your permission before we put sound in the water."

"In case it was the Chinese," the petty officer said.

Dan nodded, commending them silently on recognizing the possibility of a snare. Then they sat quiet again, listening to the distant whirring and clicking. Tosito whispered that those were shrimp. These shallow seas were full of fish and biologicals, and a lot of them made noise.

Suddenly the petty officer half-turned on his chair, staring at the pattern of light marching upward across the screen in front of him. Dan saw no discernible change, but the man was edging dials around, expanding one section of the screen. Tosito struggled to sit up, staring at it, too.

"What is it?" Dan asked.

"Reduction gears. See that tonal?"

"No."

"This isn't Chinese."

"No?"

"No. They sound like a fleet of dump trucks on a rocky road. This is real quiet, but—"

Dan waited while they pulled pubs down. Finally Tosito said, "I'm not sure exactly what it is. It's not ours."

"What could it be?"

"The possibilities are French, British, and Russki."

"If it was Russian, what class would it be?"

"It's getting hard to pin them down, sir. They've gotten a lot quieter in the last ten years."

The WQC speaker, which had clicked and groaned intermittently as they tried to identify the tonal, now said very weakly but fairly distinctly, "U.S. ship *Oliver Gaddis*. Over." The voice was male and tenor. The third-class reached a mike down and cupped it, glancing at Dan.

"Respond," he said at last. "But keep it brief."

"This is USS *Oliver Gaddis*. Go ahead. Over," the petty officer said. Some seconds passed while they listened to the shrimp.

"Your target bears . . . ," the voice said; then clicking and gurgling drowned it out. ". . . kilometers, over," it ended.

"You are coming through garbled. Say again, over."

After five repetitions through steadily increasing noise, they pieced together a complete transmission consisting of: "Your target bears 110 from you, range fifty-five kilometers." The voice had an accent, but not a readily classifiable one.

Dan said, "Can he hear us better than we hear him? Or is it about the same?"

"Hard to tell, sir. Sound can take different channels going back."

"Read it back. See if he rogers." Dan got up and almost clapped Tosito on the shoulder before he remembered. "Take care of yourself, now. I want you to be in good shape to go up for senior chief." Then he pushed through the curtain and hammered his half-Wellingtons up the ladder.

They hadn't seen the stars for days, but here in the northern end of the China Sea they had good electronic navigation, Loran-A sky wave coverage from Japanese chains, Loran-C ground wave from the Philippines, and the more modern and dependable Omega coverage from pair E-H. He laid off a dead reckoning line from their last fix and marked his estimated position as of ten minutes before, when the submarine transmission had begun, then ran another line out from that along 110 degrees true, found the kilometer scale on the chart, and put a half-circle fifty-five kilometers out. It occurred to him that it might be a good time to get Combat manned up and start trying to correlate that position with a contact.

"Who's got the conn?" he yelled into the darkness.

"I do, sir."

"Oh, Bobbie, sorry I yelled. . . . How about bringing her around to 115 and slowing to five knots." He didn't want to come crashing in at high speed before he was ready. "OOD!"

"Here, sir."

"Pass the word to CIC to man up. Pass to the department heads that we have an estimated target position."

After he had delivered all the orders he could think of,

set the others running to prepare, he stood for a moment in the center of the bridge. Then said to Wedlake, "I'll be out on the wing."

Leaning against the splinter shield, the wind in his face, he looked down into the darkness that plunged and roared ahead. It was time to put it all to the test, throw all he had on the table and roll the dice. A cliché, sure. But at that moment it captured the idea of the reckless gamble.

Standing there, bracing his body against the pitch and then the long, hard heave *Gaddis* had taken on with the added weight on her upper decks, he let the fear that had accompanied him for so long, across so many miles, out at last. Like a large cat, it hesitated at the opened door of its cage, then sidled out. As it came forward step by stealthy step, sweat broke on his arms and back, turned his skin icy, accelerated his breathing to a pant. He let it approach until its cold breath bathed his face like the precursor of a squall.

He admitted he was leading them into a trap, against a superior force, closer to enemy reinforcements than to any friendly support and assistance. He agreed that men would die tomorrow, that he himself might die. Death was cruel anywhere, but the sea had honed its techniques. A man could die in battle, fall perforated by shell splinters or with the life blown out of him by blast; die fast, screaming entombed by flame, or with hellish slowness, trapped in a flooding compartment or adrift without hope of rescue.

Gripping the saltgreasy steel, he heard again a sound he had not heard for years: the hopeless screams of dying men, howling in the North Atlantic blackness as a broken ship drifted burning and another, grim and gigantic and inescapable as death itself, completed its long turn and came back purposefully to smash and grind those survivors down forever and ever into the depths of the bitter sea amen.

Standing alone in the dark, he let the fear grow until it mastered him, till he could no longer breathe and his heart pattered in helpless terror. Until it crested and toppled and then like a dread tide gradually receded, dragging reluctance and hope and many other things behind. Leaving only a purged emptiness.

He was here to do a job. The rest was in other hands than his, and as he resigned it, his heart grew quiet at last.

When he looked at his watch it was 0200. He owed it to his men to catch a few hours' sleep, to gird up the resolution and judgment he would need when they came into the presence of the enemy.

Soaked with sweat and spray and rain, he turned from the dark sea and went below.

25

THE hateful buzzing went on and on as he groped for the source. The speaking tube, that curious survival of nine-teenth-century technology down to the fag end of the twentieth. A hollowness of brass, its shiny cover unpolished these latter days of *Gaddis*'s long decline, like the unshaven faces of her crew and the rusty flaking paint around her scuppers. He finally got it located about the time he remembered where and when he was and what the racked creaking fabric around him, complaining as it leaned to the rush of the sea, was racing toward. "Captain," he grunted.

"Officer of the deck, sir. ESM reports a Skin Head radar bearing 010 true."

His brain leaped toward alertness. "Any correlation with the radar picture?"

"Raytheon's not worth shit this morning, sir. Wind's picking up again. Too much sea return."

He muttered something and clamped the tube closed. Blinked into the darkness as his body rushed from wanting to burrow back into the warm bunk to a sudden acceleration of the pulse, a deep-sucked breath, a nervous thrill along his limbs. He clicked the light on and reached for his trou.

He had to cease climbing and cling to the ladder as the metal world around him leaned far over in a prolonged roll to port.

Five-fifteen. Should be dawn, but the sky was as opaque as if it had been 0015. A cold, misty drizzle, dull silver like sprayed mercury, speckled the pilothouse windows between whining sweeps of the wipers, which were set on slow. He studied the typhoon chart, now engraved with new symbology showing the oncoming low-pressure areas, and sucked air through his teeth as he glanced at the barometer.

It didn't take a cyclone to build up mountainous seas; in fact, in some ways the rapid passage and changing winds of a fast cyclone like Hercule militated against them. All it took was a strong, steady wind from the same quarter, operating over a few hundred miles' fetch. Just like what was shaping up out here now.

Engelhart joined him at the chart table, eyebrows gloomy as the weather, and Bobbie Wedlake stood by as the chief warrant laconically outlined the surface picture. Two tankers had passed during the night, both headed north at a speed that must have pushed their engines to the limit. Trying to make Macao or Guangzhou before it was too late, clawing their way around the oncoming weather. The ESM "racket," or contact, had faded a few minutes before.

"Faded or stopped?" Dan asked him.

"Stopped all at once. Turned off, my guess."

"What have we got out there on radar?"

The little Raytheon, Engelhart told him, was handicapped by the building seas; they covered the screen with a speckle of informationless light. Dan chewed at the inside of his mouth, seeing everything headed down the tubes. The Shanghais would have to run for port soon, if they hadn't already left. The Katori would go with them, and he'd be left out here to battle the storm. He didn't think the crew would be with him after another like the last. He'd called again and again on their tenacity and perseverance, and he knew it was at an end.

Bobbie was thinking, too. Finally she lifted her head, and in the ashen morning radiance he saw the marks of time around her eyes, the fine hachure around her lips.

She said, "You've got to call them to you."

"Call them to me. How?"

"Send an SOS. Like the *Titanic*. Say you're in trouble, sinking. Or no, not sinking, just say you need help. Let them come to you."

Engelhart frowned. "You don't send a distress call when you're not in distress."

"I'm past worrying about that, Ben," Dan told him.

"Come on; help us out on this. OK, Bobbie, you mean make us look like an easy target, a crippled duck. So what are we going to say? That we're broken down?"

"No. Then we couldn't maneuver. We want to continue to close on this course, right?"

"Yeah, we got to get in as close as we can."

"A fire? Flooding? Medical emergency?"

"I like flooding," said Colosimo, who had joined them out of the gloom. "That could explain our lack of freeboard. A destroyer type sits lower in the water than a merchant. It might get us a couple hundred yards closer before they tumble to what we are."

"Make us up a message, Dom. Put it out on International Maritime Distress. Give a position about ten nautical miles ahead of our actual running EP, though."

"You don't want to give our actual position?"

"No, I want to hold back any surprise I can."

They left him at the chart table. Dan stood irresolute again, staring out into the very gradually lightening dawn. Squalls surrounded them, turning the fine drizzle to heavy rain as they passed or as *Gaddis* passed beneath them. He shivered, remembering the Santarén Channel, a twelve-foot skiff with hull boards so rotten he could see between them. He'd never found out what had happened to the woman he'd shared it with and the boy. At least, fleeing Cuba, they hadn't had to worry about pirates. The kind of bloodsuckers who hovered now a few miles ahead.

BUT the message brought no response. Dan ordered it sent again at 0900, but again no one answered. The sea seemed empty. *Gaddis* churned on, swept by violent squallbursts and heavy rain. They were spaced closer together now, Dan noticed.

At 1020, Chief Tosito called up to report screw noises to the north. Confused and intermittent, he said, most likely because of the storm-driven mixing of the surface layer. Zabounian had the deck now. Dan listened as he quizzed the chief over the bitch box. No, he couldn't say what type

of ships they were. No, he could not give an estimated
range. "How about a zone, then?" the supply officer
pressed. Tosito, sounding distant and listless, said they
could be as close as ten miles and as far away as forty.

As soon as he went off, Doolan called asking for the
skipper. Dan tapped the lever with his foot from his reclined
position in the chair. "Lenson here."

"Sir, Chick, down in CIC. I've been trying to put these
indications together on the dead reckoning tracer. Could
use some overarching intelligence."

"Be right down." He swung to the scuffed tile and told
Zabounian where he was headed, told him to keep the lookouts sharp and to notify him instantly of anything out of the
ordinary.

CIC was dim and hot, with fans and blowers racketing
away to take the place of the broken-down air-conditioning.
He worried briefly about the effect of ambient temperature
on the electronics, then dismissed it. One way or the other,
it would not be his problem. The OSes and fire control technicians were stripped to the waist and gleaming with sweat.
Doolan had peeled his T-shirt off, too, and with the mat of
hair on his broad chest he looked more than ever like the
young Hemingway. Dan joined him at the belt-height table
of the dead-reckoning tracer. Topped with glass, the DRT
contained electric motors and gearing that drove a spot of
light across the paper taped atop it. The projected spot rep-
resented *Gaddis*. When relative bearings and ranges to intercepts and radar contacts were plotted relative to that
moving point, a true geographic plot gradually emerged.

"Like I said, I've been trying to put these together."
Chick swept a hand across the flat white surface that repre-
sented the open sea this iron morning. "Trying to correlate
everything, sonar, ESM, what we know about the way they
operate."

"So you see 'em out here," Dan said, leaning over what
seemed to be where these various and fuzzy indicators
pointed. "Say fifteen miles."

"Can't pinpoint, but yeah, I'm getting a vague cut out

here to the west. Maybe thirty, forty thousand yards, if they're holding the same course over the last hour or two."

"Should we come left?"

"If they're tracking us, it'll look suspicious."

"We still look like a merchie to them, turn count, radar characteristics."

"Correct. At least, as far as we know."

He was staring at the paper, trying to make a decision, when the 21MC above his head said, "Combat, Bridge: Skipper, problem on the mess decks."

He reached above his head without looking. "Captain here. What kind of problem?"

"Sounds like a riot, sir," Zabounian's voice said. Behind him, Dan could hear the whining slap of the windshield wipers and then the hollow roar of rain.

THEY were sitting on the deck, because all the plastic chairs were stacked and lashed along the bulkheads, secured for heavy seas. That was the first thing he noticed: the men sitting down. The second was the haze of cigarette smoke, and then, the smell of the whiskey. Dan saw that Compline was being held by two men just inside the scullery.

"Sorry, sir," said the chief. Then he doubled forward as one of his captors grunted, "I told you to shut up," and punched him in the stomach.

Dan raised his voice. "Who's the leader?"

"We don't have one," said a voice behind him.

When he turned, four men grabbed his arms and hands. He did not bother struggling as they took his automatic from the holster. There were at least thirty men down here, half on their feet around him and Compline, the others sitting, passing bottles around.

He said, hearing his voice hoarse and angry, "OK, you've made your point. We won't resist. What do you want?"

It was Pistolesi, to Dan's regret, who stepped forward. The fireman looked ill at ease but determined. "Cap'n, sorry to tell you this. But we ain't manning up for GQ any-more, and we ain't going another mile north. Pick up that squealer, call the bridge, and tell 'em to shag ass for Subic."

"You don't walk off the field in the middle of the play, guys. That's what this is, last quarter, last down."

"Too bad, we're out. The boys voted for a strike."

"There's another name for that in the Navy, Pistolesi. One none of you are gonna want on your record."

"We're not stupid, Skipper. We been talking this over for a long time."

"OK, I'll say it. Mutiny. Your ticket to Fort Leavenworth. You considered that?"

"You got to be on a USN ship to commit mutiny, Mr. Lenson. This hasn't been one for a long time. Anyway, you can call it whatever you want. We ain't doing shit till we're headed for Olongapo."

Dan felt his heart sink. They couldn't take on an armed enemy with a third of the crew out of ranks. The mission was finished and so was he. All he could do now was mini-mize the damage. He took a deep breath, trying to keep his voice steady. "OK. I hear you. But there's still a lot of bad weather between us and the Philippines."

"Then let's boogie south. We don't care; just get us out of Chinese waters." Pistolesi glanced at the men behind him. "Hey, just so's you know, some of these assholes wanted to shoot all the officers and throw them overboard. I told them that wouldn't be cool, good as it sounded."

"Thanks for that, Pistol."

"Shut it, OK? Only reason why not, we ever get home, we don't want murder on the record. But there's still some wouldn't mind taking you back to the fantail."

A seaman jerked the handset out of its retaining clips and held it out. Pistolesi snapped the dial to 01, Bridge, and said, "Go on. Tell 'em."

"If I don't?"

He heard a click not far from his ear and turned his head to find himself looking into the black cavernous bore of the handgun.

Wedlake answered. "Bridge."

Dan fought to keep his voice level. The rage and disappointment were like an obstruction in his trachea, making it hard even to breathe. "This is the . . . this is the captain. Give me Mr. Doolan, if he's up there. Otherwise the OOD."

"Just a minute." A click, then Zabounian's voice said, "OOD."

"Lenson here." The muzzle of the pistol moved nearer, pressed itself in a cold circle against the side of his head.

"Yessir. Everything cool down there?"

"Not really. I need you to come left. Carefully, because we're top-heavy. Time your swing through the trough to minimize roll. Steady on one-eight-zero true and click her up knot by knot to what she'll take without too much motion."

"Sir, I don't advise that. I was about to pass the word for you. CIC advises ESM racket resumed, very loud, very close—"

Dan said angrily, knowing this was the wreck of everything and all he had hoped for, "Don't advise me; just do it. Come left to one-eight-zero. Increase your speed to fifteen knots if the seas permit, once you're on that course."

A confused burst of sound from the bridge, the babble of several voices at once. He ignored it, slammed the handset back into its bracket. "There, I told him," he said to the men around him. "He'll come around as soon as he sees a trough between the swells."

For answer his hands were yanked around behind him and hard metal bit his wrists. A rasping click, and he realized when he tried to pull them around again that he couldn't. He was handcuffed, secured to a stanchion beside the long-empty soft ice-cream machine.

Then somebody coughed, and he looked up to a familiar pair of malevolent, swollen, heavy-lidded eyes.

"Sorry to see you fucked up like this, Cap'n."

"I'm sure you are, Johnile."

"You could be fucked up a lot worse."

Pistolesi was nowhere in sight; he must have left right

after Dan made the call. The other mutineers watched, some avid, others looking doubtful, but no one offering to interfere. Machias brought the knife up and put the point under his chin, against the soft flesh of his throat. He whispered, "You know I said I didn't like being locked up. Didn't make no never mind to you."

"I told you I made a mistake. I apologized."

"That ain't enough. You lorded it over us too long, you sorry motherfucker. You need to bleed."

They were standing like that, face-to-face, when the crack and flash deafened them all. For a moment Dan couldn't move, as around him men dived for the dirty terrazzo. Then he squatted as a second, louder explosion slammed the metal around them, as if a bulldozer had been dropped onto the main deck from about eighty feet up. Fluorescent tubes quivered and burst, spraying a mist of glass and poisonous powder into the closed air of the mess decks.

Only in the ear-ringing aftersound did he hear, dimly, the electronic *bong* of the general alarm. Men scrambled up, some cradling the bottles like infants, others flinging them to smash on the deck. They scattered while he yelled into the pandemonium for somebody to unlock the handcuffs.

Then he was alone. The deck began to slant, not in a roll, but in a shuddering application of power that meant the screws were biting in with full force, 100 percent pitch, either full ahead or full astern. It seemed to be a crashback, all back emergency. He fought against the unyielding steel, twisting his hands until the pain lanced sharp and he sagged back, gasping.

"Open fire," he yelled desperately, as if the bridge team could hear him through three levels of solid steel and a third of the length of the ship. "*Open fire*! Don't let them *board*!"

Instead a crashing boom, hollow and grinding, shook the ship. It seemed to come from forward, not a detonation but something slower and more prolonged. He had no idea what it was. He wrenched his wrists again, savagely, helplessly, against the metal, then gave up and hung, trying to quiet his thudding runaway heart as minutes crept past slowly as worms.

A husky-chested HT came running from aft, pounded past him, then braked and spun and gaped at him. Dan yelled, "We're being attacked! That was shellfire, hitting aft. Get me off here! Get Pistolesi; he's got the key."

Instead the man wheeled and dashed in the opposite direction. Dan cursed him and all his tribe and surged against his restraints as the grinding came again from forward, the ship responding with a shudder through her length.

"Stand by to receive boarders, starboard side," announced the 1MC in a voice he didn't recognize. Yes, he did. It was Topmark's, but raised an octave. A thunder of boots and a clatter as of dragged chain came from just overhead. Then silence as he wrenched again, feeling his skin abrading off.

The HT came back, lugging the Magic Key at port arms. "Lean back, sir; lemme see some slack," he said. Dan sagged against the stanchion and thrust his arms out stiffly behind him. A moment later a clicking snap announced he was free, or at least that the steel chain that restrained him had parted.

He was heading forward when small-arms fire broke out on the deck above.

BY the time he got topside the shooting seemed to be nearly over. He gripped the rail in the blowing mist, peering into the unremitting wind on the midships flat. Taking in the hundred feet of light gray paint and wicked-looking automatic guns that lay a few yards off to starboard, rolling till it showed black boot topping and barnacles. A line slacked between them as the smaller craft swung in to smash violently into *Gaddis*'s side, then ripped dripping up out of the green and suddenly drew bar-tight between them, slicing through the passing seas that crested and surged as the two hulls swung apart again. The rumble of engines penetrated his consciousness, along with the strangely muffled crack of shots.

He lowered his eyes to the crumpled bodies, huddled as if they'd died of cold in the corner of the boat deck. Weapons lay around them. Blood pooled in the scuppers, eddying with the roll. Another clatter of fire, and he looked up again, unable to piece sense for a moment out of what was happening.

A door slammed open suddenly on the low pilothouse opposite. It swung closed as the Shanghai-class gunboat surged upward, climbing a green-black mountain, then flopped open again, tolling a mournful note like a bell buoy. A moment later a body hurtled out. The Asian clung to the handrail, staring across at Dan. He looked surprised. Then his hands slowly loosened their grip, and he toppled down a ladder to the main deck. Dan could make out forms moving inside the pilothouse. Then one came out on the little wing platform and saw him watching.

It was Usmani, holding an M-16. He pumped it over his head like a fedayee, grinning, and then went running down the ladder. He vanished into a canvas shelter between the bridge and a smaller deckhouse that supported what looked like an antiaircraft mounting.

Pistolesi and four other *Gaddis* crewmen emerged from behind the superstructure and raced forward. They discovered a hatch in the deck, jerked it open, fired down. Casings spun, raining into the sea. The fireman pulled an object from his pocket, fiddled with it, and dropped it through the hatch. Black smoke gushed out, whipped away by the rising wind.

Dan jerked himself out of his astonishment and sprinted for the bridge.

Doolan and Colosimo whipped helmeted heads around as he burst in. Wedlake, who'd reached for the small of her back, paused. He said rapidly, "They had me restrained below. I heard explosions. What happened?"

Chick explained tersely that the Shanghai had come out of the mist and drizzle without warning. It had popped up on the radar, vanished, then appeared again inside two thousand yards. Inside of a minute later, coming in at high speed from upsea, it had begun firing. The first burst had ripped up the water ahead of the stem, obviously a signal to heave to. The bridge team, trying desperately to locate Dan, had maintained course and speed. The second burst had been the one he heard. Three shells from an automatic gun had penetrated the starboard side about Frame 130, one exploding in the chiefs' head and shower, the others in the mooring and towing gear locker on the main deck. That was when Zabounian had pulled the GQ alarm.

At that point, Juskoviac had ordered them to heave to. "I didn't want to, but I had no choice," Colosimo said tightly. "He said he was next in command and ordered me to go to 'all stop.' I didn't know where you were. So I obeyed him. Then they came alongside."

"Where is he? You say he left the bridge?"

"Right, when he saw they intended to board. I don't know where he is now."

Dan thought rapidly, staring into the radar screen. They were on 300 now, making about seven knots, maintaining steerageway against huge green seas from the starboard bow. The Shanghai had come in, not from the west, where Doolan had guessed the enemy group lay, but from the north. Downwind and downsea, which meant she could use her superior speed to close rapidly from a quarter already obscured by rain.

But if Chick's DRT plot was right, the Katori and perhaps the other gunboat were still out there.

"Bobbie," he said slowly, "how did you say these people attacked the *Marker Eagle*?"

"Just like this. One came in from starboard, made us heave to, and boarded. The other came in from the opposite side. The big ship stayed about a mile away."

Dan told Chick to get the lookouts on a close visual search to port. He jogged uphill to the wing as *Gaddis* rolled, cupping his face against a renewed volley of rain. To the east the sky was black as asphalt, and the wind was rising minute by minute. The seas were building, too, bulling in from the northeast. So high and with so much water in the air that the piloting radar could not pick up a solid contact only a couple thousand yards away.

But if that was true for them—

He ducked back inside and said tersely, "Did this guy alongside us ever get any message off? Call Radio. Check with CIC. See if they intercepted anything." The reservist turned away to obey, and Dan asked Bobbie, "When this gunboat closed, when they were making up, tell me exactly what happened."

"Like Dom said, they came alongside. We put down the jacob's ladder. It took a while because it's so rough. They were looking back over their shoulders and shouting to the men on the boat. Then when all of them were on board, I guess it was seven or eight of them, all of a sudden one yelled something. That was when the shooting started."

Topmark said, "Pistolesi and them were waiting behind the RHIBs. The boys got the drop on them, just blew 'em all away. I don't think they even got to shoot back."

Colosimo: "Sir, checking the times in the ESM logs against the deck log: A couple of transmissions while they must have been approaching us. No transmissions intercepted once contact began."

"And then we boarded them back and took out the crew they left behind."

They nodded, and he contemplated the near-incredible fact that the gunboat had closed, fired on, and at last even boarded them without detecting their masquerade. Hard to credit, but then he wasn't seeing a low-lying and unfamiliar ship between bursts of squall, from the deck of a pitching vessel much smaller and lower than his own. The containers, the gun covers, the nose job on the mack had done their work.

Now it was time to throw off the disguise, and reveal the predator within.

Dan looked back at the Shanghai, to see the dungaree-clad *Gaddis* seamen knotted on the bow, waving across to their compadres on the boat deck. They were carrying AK-47s slung over their shoulders, carrying pistols, some toting three or four weapons.

"Boarding party requests permission to come back aboard," said the phone talker.

"Give me the bullhorn," Dan snapped. He twisted the switch on and went out on the wing. Pointed it at the tossing craft, the faces that lifted as he said, "On the gunboat. Can you hear me?"

They nodded. "I want all of you back aboard, but first I want you to get all the flammables and loose ammo you can find belowdecks and stack it under that canvas. All the fuel and gas and pyro you can find. And get rid of those souvenirs! You're not going to make it back across carrying all that weight." A couple of them glanced across the foaming gap, the looming side of the ship; black rifle shapes flew over the side and disappeared into the ever-ravenous maw of the sea.

The phone talker: "CIC reports intermittent contact bearing 252, eleven thousand yards."

"That's them," said Doolan urgently. "It's in gun range. We can get a fast solution—"

"We're not trained up for long-range fire, Chick." It was attractive, but an extreme range gun duel was not going to win him this battle. Long before they had the other ship's range, missiles would come burning through the mist, homing on them.

He had to get in killing-close. Close enough to shove a snub-nose into the other ship's belly and pull the trigger.

He thought for a moment more, then put fenders over to starboard, lessening the battering *Gaddis*'s hull was taking from the gunboat, and bent a longer line on the sea painter, so if he ordered her paid out and trailed astern it could be done instantly. He adjusted course by gradual increments to port, putting the prevailing sea on the quarter, till they were running west by southwest. Then snapped more orders, the boatswain and phone talker relaying them.

The containers on the starboard side stayed; those to port

were released and shoved over the side. They splashed and fell aft, some sinking immediately, others rolling low on the surface. The gunners and loaders swarmed over the mounts to port, ripping off the tentlike gun covers.

"Range and bearing to the intermittent," he said, not taking his eyes from the binoculars or the binoculars from the mist.

"Skunk Delta: two-five-zero, seven thousand yards."

Three and a half miles. Every yard closer increased the effectiveness of his guns, but what was all-important now was the angle at which they met. He kept his glasses on a darker patch of sky off the starboard bow. If the contact they were calling Skunk Delta was the second Shanghai, he could take it out without risking much damage from return fire. Five or six thousand yards, in this weather, would be extreme range for what had looked, on the craft he still towed along wallowing off his starboard side, like a Soviet-style optical-sighted thirty-seven-millimeter. But if Delta turned out to be the cruiser, he'd have to make an instant decision.

"All containers free, port side."

"Guns manned, port side."

"Very well. Pass to all stations, weapons tight," Dan said, just to make sure they knew not to fire until he gave the word. "Range and bearing, Skunk Delta."

"Skunk Delta: two-five-five true, four thousand five hundred yards."

The obscured sky, the occasional blasts of rain made the pilothouse dim. The gray drizzly light made it seem like they were underwater. He glanced at Bobbie, who had read the range and bearing off the repeater. She was there still, only the back of her thin neck visible as she nestled her face into the black rubber light hood. The butt of her revolver stuck up out of her jeans; the gray steel battle helmet looked enormous on her. He could not decide if she looked vulnerable or intimidating. Maybe both. Past her Robidoux stood at the chart table, staring at the Fathometer. The chromed V of a pair of dividers glittered in a silver cone as he twirled them rapidly round and round. Colosimo was staring forward, fingers pale on the barrels of his binocs. As he caught Dan's eyes, he gave back a tight grin. Doolan stood to his right, gaze distant, listening to the gun control circuit whose headphones were wrapped around his skull.

A nudge; Dan looked down; the boatswain was holding out a flak jacket. "Mr. Doolan said to send them up here," he said. Dan told him good, make sure everyone had them on, everyone on the guns, too. As he struggled into it, the steel plates weighed him down, but its heavy, warming embrace felt good. He took the battle helmet with less enthusiasm.

"I'm going out on the wing. Keep those ranges and bearings coming, Bobbie. Watch for any other pop-ups; they could come from any quarter. Chick, make sure the fire control radars stay off till I tell you to illuminate. Our only chance of pulling this off—"

"I know; I know," Doolan snapped. Dan regarded him for a second, then let it pass. Chick didn't seem nearly as happy about going into battle the second time around.

On the wing the fine driven mist-drizzle wetted him through at once. Wedlake yelled through the open door, "Delta, two-six-zero, three thousand . . . seven hundred yards!" It sounded odd to be getting reports in a woman's voice. The CIC phone talker seconded that with a course and speed of 030 at ten knots.

He stared into the blowing rain, into the darkness in the midst of day. They *had* to see something soon. If Delta was the Katori class cruiser, it was tracking slowly across his bow, her course keeping her into the sea for comfort while closing the merchant contact she'd sent her gunboat in to board and search. Right now, she had to be waiting for a radio report. He wished he had a native Chinese speaker aboard. But even if he did he wouldn't know prowords, call signs, proper terminology.

"Skunk Delta, 260, three thousand yards."

He had barely time to register that the bearing was unchanged—that most likely meant the other ship had turned toward him, was no longer on 060 but something closer to the reciprocal of his own course—when a gray form condensed suddenly out of the squall. It was low to the sea, so close he flinched back as it jumped toward him out of rain-fog and darkness to fill nearly the whole field of his binoculars. She was coming at *Gaddis* bow on, so close he could see the distinct leaps and splashings of the white foam boundary where her stem wedged the sea apart. Her guns were leveled, pointing so directly at him that he could see the black emptinesses within the tubes.

Three thousand yards, a mile and a half. She was close, by one reckoning. But he wanted her closer still. For a moment his mind searched frantically. Then he turned his head and yelled, "To the signal bridge: Hoist the black ensign!"

"Hoist what, sir?"

"That flag the signalmen made up. The skull and bones. Break it at the masthead! Dip it; hoist it; do it three times. Do it!"

A moment later came shouts from aft, the snap and flutter of cloth going up the halliard. He studied the oncoming bridge but saw no flicker of response. Well, response didn't matter. All he had to do was confuse whoever stood in the other pilothouse, trying to interpret the apparition looming out of the mist ahead, trying to read a nationality from a wind-whipped flag; trying to make sense of a confusing outline of containers and superstructure, the gunboat riding close alongside, obviously either boarding or about to board. All he had to do was keep that one man off balance, keep him undecided long enough to get *Gaddis*'s hungry gun muzzles a few hundred yards closer.

"Skunk Delta, two thousand three hundred yards, closing!"

"Very well," he said, keeping his tone bored. "Weapons officer: All guns, load."

He heard the command recede down the line mouth to mouthpiece, mouth to mouth. Heard the hollow clanking and thumping down on the forecastle as the first seventy-pound five-inch shell came up the hoist and went into the transfer tray, was swung to the proper angle parallel to the barrel axis, transferred, backed up by its propellant charge, and rammed home into the breech. Heard the familiar clang as the fifties charged, one abaft each wing, two on the flying bridge over his head.

"Chick, pass the following to all mounts. The target is a cruiser on our starboard bow. All fire will be visual sights and local control; Fifties will concentrate on the bridge; twenties, on the forward guns; forty-mil and five-inch, superstructure for the first few rounds, then lower sights and fire into the hull centroid. The main battery will fire armor-piercing projectiles until exhausted, then shift to VT. There will be no further targeting commands during the engagement. Each mount captain will keep his gun in action as long as he has ammunition and the target is on a safe firing bearing."

"Aye, sir. Permission to man up the starboard side mounts."

"Negative; hold the starboard gun crews inside the skin of the ship. They've got glasses on us, too. Chick: Backstop me on this; what's the arming distance for five-inch armor-piercing?"

"About five hundred yards, I think."

Wedlake, her voice going higher: "Range is now two thousand yards even, closing very fast!"

Colosimo, mouth distorted as he stared ahead: "How fucking close are you *going?*"

Dan lowered his binoculars, seeing now with unaided sight how shockingly near the other ship really was. He could see pale ovals in the round bridge windows that had to be faces. Mist, rain, and deception could only shroud him for so long. Any second now, they would see *Gaddis* for what she was.

"Weapons officer: Train port batteries out to three-zero-zero relative. Stand by for batteries released. OOD: Increase speed to flank."

The shouted orders filled the bridge. The EOT pinged. *Gaddis* could not exactly surge ahead—no steam-powered ship did—but inside of two or three minutes, when he'd need all the speed he could muster, she'd be accelerating in earnest.

For a few minutes he'd been afraid. The dread was still down there, crawling around in the basement, but it was giving way now to something cooler and less human, of which he was always faintly ashamed afterward; to the remote ironic detachment that always came over him in battle. Aloud he said, "You want to know, how close, Dom?"

"How *fucking* close, I said, sir!"

"Well, let's see. I would call it *R* plus one-half *T*. Take half of our tactical diameter, *T*, at this speed, which is the distance we'll travel as we come right ninety degrees. *R*, arming distance on the five-inch, before the shell's ready to explode, is five hundred yards. That means I commence my turn . . ."

He ducked back out on the wing, and picked out one of the seas that came steadily in on their quarter. Waited till it had almost reached them, till it would in fifteen seconds more begin to lift *Gaddis*'s stern, and turned his head and yelled, "Right about . . . *now. Right full rudder*, steady course three-five-zero! Mr. Doolan! Port side batteries, local control, fire for effect, your target: cruiser, three-three-zero relative, continue firing until target is obscured or destroyed—*batteries released!* Starboard side, clear the containers over the side, clear the gun covers; starboard batteries, *man and load!*"

Gaddis staggered sideways. Taken by the mounting of an overtaking sea as her rudder began to bite, body-blocked suddenly sideways by thousands of tons of cresting water, her bow whipped hard right and she snap-rolled nearly to her scuppers. Dan grabbed the safety line as the deck dropped away beneath his boots like the trap of a gallows. He dangled for a moment like a kid on the monkey bars, then clawed his way up to a more secure handhold as the rapidly swinging bow, like some deadly indicator, pointed for an instant at the onrushing cruiser, then swept on, past it, unmasking the port side abruptly to the oncoming enemy.

The swell swept past with the roaring of a thousand birds starting from their roosts, and as the deck rolled back upright the sights of all the port-side guns, lifting from their aim down into the sea, rose to bear directly on the oncoming ship.

The 40mm and 20mm and fifties opened fire simultaneously, a crash and firestorm of noise and fury. Crossing the pilothouse at a run, Lenson emerged onto the port wing to a blasting confusion of gun-flashes, dirty brown nitrate-stinking propellant smoke, and a spewing rain of hot cartridge cases from directly above. He clung to the splinter shield, deafened and half-blinded, peering out over the surging sea. Tracers in red, yellow, and orange flew lazily upward, hung in the air, hardly seeming to move, then plunged precipitously, puckering the sea like heavy raindrops around the still-approaching cruiser. It seemed to him that none of them were hitting. He opened his mouth to yell, then slammed his teeth closed; any shout was futile in the ongoing clamor; realizing, too, that hits would barely show, that the fifties and perhaps the twenties might glance off, but that the larger calibers would penetrate, wreaking most of their damage within, out of his sight.

With a bellowing blast and a huge sphere of orange flash, the five-inch let go. The long tapered barrel recoiled slightly. The gas ejector whiffed black smoke out the muzzle. The empty propellant case clanged out on the deck as the barrel rose a trifle, tracking the target through *Gaddis*'s roll. Then it fired again, shaking the whole forepart of the ship. The smoke was whipped away instantly by the storm wind, obscuring the oncoming silhouette, yet not enough, he hoped, to deflect his gunners' aim.

For it was up to them now, the fire controlmen and gunners and loading crews. He'd done all he could. He'd taken them in close, caught the enemy by surprise, and crossed his T in a maneuver that probably owed more to luck, bad weather, and complacency on the part of his opponent than to skill on his. But at this angle, nearly all *Gaddis*'s guns could bear, as against only the forward mounts of the enemy. A hit would travel the length of the cruiser, punching through transverse bulkheads and equipment, scattering a widening cone of secondary projectiles until at last it detonated, deep in the ship. It was the aim and rate of fire now that would determine the outcome of the battle. He didn't know how much damage he could expect from the fifties and twenties. Probably not much, though they would mow down personnel. But the fast-firing forties, with their two-pound shells, could wreck a ship in minutes, and the seventy-pound hardened-steel five-inch projectiles would punch through a ship like buckshot through a beer can before their slow-acting fuze ignited the bursting charge.

A flash from the Katori's forward mount, and a howl overhead. She was firing back at last. His men didn't have much longer to get rounds out without taking damage themselves. He estimated the angle on the other ship, then thrust his head inside.

Doolan was standing just within the shelter of the pilothouse, cheeks white as chalk. Dan yelled another rudder order past him, and the helmsman stared, face pale, too, then spun the wheel as Topmark shoved his shoulder and snarled.

Now *Gaddis* swung left, more slowly this time, because he had forgotten to synchronize the turn with the seas. It was more difficult, too, for a ship to fight her way out of the trough, once she'd fallen into it, than to continue through. The steadily building seas, driven by a wind that was now driving straight trails of spume downwind, came with increasing rage out of the nearing blackness that was the front bumper of the storm front. Once it was on them, all thought of battle or even holding a given course would become moot. He could not have long before that time, and as *Gaddis* gathered herself and began a sluggish swing, he ran to the starboard side and saw the last of the sawn-off containers topple over the side, saw the crews jerking the tarps off and climbing into firing positions.

Back to the port side, pushing his way past Doolan. The weapons officer was braced in the wing door, watching the

fiery rainbows. Only seconds had passed since the first
round went out, but it seemed to Dan like ages. The five-
inch paused, then resumed its steady *ka-WHAM . . . ka-
WHAM* at three or four seconds' interval. The forties
cracked their distinctive rapid *pom pom, pom pom*. He found
his glasses at his eyes as *Gaddis* steadied on two-four-zero.

As the Katori's starboard side came into view he yelled
to Doolan, "Shift fire aft! Concentrate on the engine room."
One of *Gaddis*'s rounds plowed into the water and burst
short of its target, throwing up an immense plume of white
against the darkening sky. He started to snap an order, then
restrained himself. The mount captain could see through his
sights as well as or better than Dan could from the bridge. A
short round was better than a long one; it could ricochet
into the hull or even punch through the underwater plating.

"We're going to pass close aboard," he yelled into
Doolan's ear. "Stand by to cease fire on the five-inch."

The weapons officer came out of his trance. "No, sir, no!
Recommend we keep firing with all calibers."

"We're inside arming range. The rounds will go right
through her."

"Doesn't matter; they'll still open her up."

Gaddis's hard-reefed port turn was taking her inside the
other ship, sliding down side to side, and he could see now
how dreadfully close it was going to be. The Katori seemed
to be slowing, the white bone at her teeth lessening as she
absorbed round after round, even though she did not yet
show damage. For a dreadful moment he wondered if this
ancient cruiser was armored, if the reason she showed so
little hurt was that she was shrugging off all he was throwing at her. Then as *Gaddis* plunged to a stern-mounting sea,
he caught just before the spray hit a momentary glimpse of
the other's length, saw the twisted metal, the gaping rips in
the gray plating. Saw black smoke pouring from midships,
and men strung along a hose drop it and run in terror as a
hurricane of fire floated down to trip a fiery dance among
them, blasting some bodily over the side, tearing others
apart, wiping yet others out in flame and smoke that ob-

scured all vision of their ends. He ground his teeth at the visceral horror of watching human beings die. But the cold, calculating being who was in command noted only the sudden lowering of long twin barrels amidships, the flashes and the glowing wires that seemed suddenly drawn out of hot copper in their direction.

Simultaneously he became aware of a slight figure beside him, extended arms terminating in blue metal. A pop, a ghost of smoke . . . it was Bobbie Wedlake, hands thrust over the splinter shield, cranking off rounds from her little revolver at the gray monster that plunged and roared back at her. Without thinking, he grabbed her and dragged her down. Her last shot went off nearly in his ear.

The high-explosive cracks of light-caliber shells came from above, exploding in the remains of the mack, showering splinters down on them. Something whacked into his thigh. The impacts walked aft, into the hangar, distinct amid the deeper detonations of *Gaddis*'s guns. As soon as their point of impact shifted, he jumped back to his feet.

The other ship was close, *close*. He saw the helmets of the men operating the twin mount. The aft turret was training around, stubby barrels reaching out to bear. He pointed at the fifty gunner above his head, then to the ship. Yelled in the storm of sound but knew none of his words could possibly penetrate. The man understood, though, nodded, took a renewed grip, and resumed firing, crouched low.

Both ships streaming smoke now, they passed close aboard, hardly rolling as the sea creamed and surged between them; and though their combined speeds had to be over thirty knots, they passed with what seemed to Dan and every man on board incredible slowness. So that the total time they were actually beam to beam and gun to gun could have been no more than half a minute, yet it felt as if every one of those infinitely elongated seconds endured for an appreciable percentage of their lives.

Then they were past, and the five-inch, trained all the way around aft till he was damn near looking down the barrel, let go one last round that nearly blew him off the wing, and deafened and blinded him anew. Then it and the boat deck forties fell silent, though he could hear the stern quad mount still pounding away as the cruiser fell astern.

"Cease fire," he said. Behind him Doolan yelled it, repeating it into his mike. Dan could not believe that he was still alive, that they were all, apparently, still alive. "Damage report, casualty reports ASAP," he snapped to the phone talker.

Zabounian, eager as a puppy: "That was fantastic, the way you crossed her T. Classic surface action, Skipper."

Dan didn't waste time answering. Ears singing strange high songs, he plunged his face into the Raytheon and found it dark. Running his gaze swiftly along the line of windows, the mad chaos of sea and sky without, he took stock of where they were: alone, facing the oncoming storm.

"Skunk Delta coming around left!" said the phone talker, and Dan jerked his attention back to the situation at hand. He was moving downwind and downsea, fast, and opening range second by second. Well, that was OK, as long as—

The missiles. Jesus Christ, he'd forgotten the missiles. He couldn't dance off, duel at long range or even medium range. He had to stay inside, stay in the clinch, and keep hammering until his opponent was on the canvas. Or until he himself went down.

A flash from the mist underlined his decision, as did a column of water that blasted up suddenly just short of the bow. The Katori was shooting again, and getting the range now.

He told Colosimo, "Come left; use hard rudder; use full power; keep it tight. We've got to stay close and keep hammering. We'll do another pass, let the starboard mounts have a chance."

"I don't think we want to do that," said Doolan. "You took them by surprise pulling that hard turn at the last minute, unmasking the guns. It won't work twice."

He could see her now, through the open bridge door.

More flashes sparkled along the deadly low silhouette, lengthening steadily as it hauled around. Not much farther and she'd be broadside, all her guns able to bear. Four major-caliber tubes to his one. He said rapidly, "I don't expect it to work again, Chick."

"They'll be ready this time. We hurt them, but they've got a lot more men over there than we have. They can reman the gun crews—"

"He's still got missiles. HN-5s or Strelas or whatever those were."

"He hasn't used them yet. Maybe we knocked them out."

Dan noticed the helmsman following the argument back and forth, looking confused. He swung on the OOD. "Come *left*, goddamn it! I gave you an order!"

Face grim, Colosimo repeated it to the helmsman.

The roar of the wind rose to a keen as *Gaddis* came into its teeth once more, and she half-surmounted, half-smashed her way through a towering sea the color of melted Coke bottles. Another column of spray and smoke sprang up, loomed over them in the unremitting rain, then collapsed and showered down, shredded by the furious wind.

Dan stared out, clutching the smooth, rounded corners of the dead repeater.

He couldn't open the range.

He couldn't continue the duel at this distance, either. Not only was the storm bearing down; he could not afford to let the other ship's weight of metal, four major-caliber guns against his one, decide the contest.

He was steaming bow on to the other as the cruiser straightened onto a crossing tack, presenting its port side. Flashes now from forward as well: They'd gotten one of those mounts going again. Shells bored in closer. Then a crunch and shudder through the ribs and stringers, a quivering deep *bong* that meant a solid hit. That meant men dead, equipment destroyed, fire, fragments, flooding.

The Chinese weren't going to crumple, as he'd half-hoped. They were going to fight. The longer he dithered out here, the more damage he'd take.

There were no alternatives. No more tricks or strategies or evasions. He thrust dry tongue against drier lips, and said over his shoulder, "All right, Dom. Take her in one more time."

HE saw immediately that this pass would be different. The Katori was being handled more alertly this time, though she did not seem to have much propulsion power available; she maneuvered sluggishly, but with cunning. Some of his shells must have found the engineering spaces. She kept her beam to him as he came in at flank speed, rolling and pitching through the oncoming sea. She, too, was rolling desperately, and that made aiming difficult on both sides. Still shells whined close over the bridge, or plowed up curtains of spray just short, and all too often and with growing frequency slammed full into *Gaddis*. Dan aimed her grimly a little to starboard of the other. The weather gage, seamen had called it once. It didn't give him any tactical advantage now, but instinctively he wanted to be upwind. He looked down from the wing at the gunners on the boat deck. The loaders stood or leaned with relaxed alertness, staring at the oncoming ship. Their long-sleeved dungarees were dark with rain and sea spray. They looked in some way timeless, their attitudes the same as those one saw in paintings of men before battle or before death. Surely they must be seeing their fate ahead, emerging from the mist as—

"Missiles!"

This time the chaff mortars barked nearly simultaneously with the lifting of the white plumes from the ship now barely visible through a passing gray veil of squall. The rising cones of flame dazzled against the growing lightlessness of the sky. He gripped the splinter shield, fighting a sudden need to run. The clatter of one of the twenty-millimeters aft recalled him, and he whipped around.

A huge fireball was lifting to the clouds. He stared in horror, then realized it was the gunboat, cast loose with her midships cargoed with flammables and pyrotechnics, and fired into till it ignited. The writhing balloon of flame

changed almost at once into a black sphere, pushed rapidly
downwind, succeeded by a column of orange-white fire that
sent up smaller fireballs from the deck of the Shanghai, visible now, drifting and rolling in *Gaddis*'s crushed-down
wake.

He whipped his head back to see the missiles already in
their plunge. A distant crack echoed back from the wind-
whipped emptiness to port; that would be one of the chaff
projectiles exploding. . . . He didn't know what kind of
homers these things had, radar or infrared, bias seekers or
what . . . three, maybe more behind them. . . . He yelled angrily into the pilothouse, "All ahead emergency! Slam those
handles forward again; we need more speed!"

The missiles came down almost vertically, and he dived
for the cover of the pilothouse as explosions, so close together he couldn't count them, came from astern and
around him. He hugged the dirty shoe-scuffed tile, then felt
it slide out from beneath him. The ship lifted till it seemed
about to take flight, then plunged madly downward, burying
her bullnose beneath a swelling bulge of grass-green sea
that shattered into a percolating welter of white-glowing
foam. "Damage report!" he yelled, his voice grating in his
chest. He pushed himself up with an enormous effort of will
onto hands and knees, though all he wanted to do was
grovel on his belly.

"Fire, fire, fire in Torpedo Room Number One," the 1MC
announced. Dan wrenched his mind away from the desire to
cower and forced himself to his feet. Thank God there were
no torpedoes back there, just flammable stores and a couple
of dummy shapes for loading practice. The other reports
came in no damage; he had no idea where the other rounds
had gone, didn't need to know, didn't have time to think
about that—

The forward five-inch took him by surprise when it fired,
just as *Gaddis* hesitated at the crest of an immense sea. The
smoke and flame whipped aft past the pilothouse, and he
saw for a moment through it the other ship, clear, turning
left now to parallel them. Imminent again and close. An-

other port to port passage, another headlong charge past each other . . . but with both adversaries crippled, now, with *Gaddis* battling a fire aft and the Chinese warship smoking heavily, too, and with a long-period roll that mean to Dan she was taking on water. "Batteries released, fire as you bear!" he yelled redundantly to Doolan, and took his position on the centerline of the bridge.

When she rose again to the sea, they were nearly alongside. He saw men opposite staring at him. They wore green helmets, and as he watched the forties began to fire and then above him, clattering once again, the twenties and fifties.

Then they were beam to beam, and the tracers burned their way through the gathering dark in both directions. An enemy shell screamed low over the forecastle, so close he seemed to catch a confused glimpse of it, although he knew that was impossible, maybe just the trail it made through the smoke and mist. The five-inch belched out globes of yellow fire, then black fumes, catapulting out empty casings to roll down the crazily slanting deck. A heavy, deck-shaking slam just below the bridge, and all the lights and remotes went out and the helmsman stepped back, holding his hands up in token he had lost control, at the same moment a white flash occulted all vision and smashed him backward against the chart table.

HE lay for an immeasurable soaring time watching sheets of white fire shatter and rearrange themselves. He couldn't see past the white fire, or only in glimpses, as if between the cars of a passing train made of incandescent steel. He kept trying to get up again and at last did, or at least imagined that he had; he wasn't quite sure. In one of the fiery between-glimpses he seemed to see a body, nearly headless, wires dangling from ripped-apart flesh. In the next flash frame it spun, groping out a blind hand, then pitched over suddenly and collapsed, pumping jets of bright red across the black rubber matting behind *Gaddis*'s lee helm. The matting had tiny parallel ribs running along its surface. He saw this very vividly and distinctly, while registering only a blurred impression of everything else, of an unending clamor of exploding shells, firing guns, screaming mouths.

Then for the second time that day the cold detachment took him and he turned his back on the corpse, staring through the white lightning that came slightly less often now, maybe he wasn't going to be blind, directly across the heaving foamstreaked waste of black sea at a dark mass studded with flashes and the black puffs of bursting high-explosive as the twenties and forties stitched downward into the hull, just as he had ordered. He clung staring, unable to so much as blink as the terrifying spectacle went on and on, neither *Gaddis* nor the other seeming to move, time occurring now not on a human scale but in the millisecond-by-millisecond recounting of detonating primers and wheeling masses of violently accelerated metal.

A brutal jolt battered at the windows, cracking all those to port and shattering several. Flames and smoke streamed in, heavy white smoke, he didn't know where from, but it was strangling. He gagged, too stunned still to even think of his gas mask. His hand when he explored his temple came away coated with blood. Without thought, he ripped his helmet off and threw it through one of the gaping window sockets through which rain and spray streamed in, borne by a shrieking wind. As his vision cleared still more, he saw other bodies scattered on the deck. The JA phone talker was crouched behind the metal bulk of the helm console. Dan blinked again and saw no one behind it; the helmsman and lee helmsman, Topmark, too, lay grotesquely twisted on the bloody tile. Dan stepped across them, tore off a set of phones, and put their blood-slick wetness over his own ringing ears. "After steering, Bridge." His voice, Christ, he couldn't hear his own voice.

"After steering, aye."

"Lost helm control on the bridge. Give me left ten degrees rudder."

"Taking control aft. Testing rudder. I have control. Left ten degrees rudder, no course given."

Bobbie Wedlake at his side, he had no idea from where,

had not thought of her or really of anyone else, either, only of *Gaddis* and how to fight and preserve her. Bobbie was shouting something about broken fuel lines, a major fire in the boiler spaces. But he already knew that. He couldn't say how, only that he and the shattered bleeding fabric that surrounded and bore them were one now, one and the same, he and she. He felt every blow to her reeling hull like a hook to his own ribs. He fought every stagger and reel as she battled the storm with his own muscles, grunting and jerking as if he could force her back upright against the seas that swept her forecastle and starboard lifelines as she came around to the manually controlled rudder, bracing her beam to the seas as downwind of her the Chinese cruiser came around, too, both wounded warships grappled now in a tail-chasing spiral downwind, each fighting to keep its guns bearing without exposing its own length to the steel and fire of the other. Boatswain Topmark struggling to his feet, blinking at the unmanned helm; another crewman, stepping off the ladder from below, looking down in horror at the slaughter-house pool around his boots. The radios suddenly hissed, numbers flickered on the fathometer, the binnacle light glowed back on in the dusky gloom. Emergency power.

He wrenched his attention back to the maelstrom outside, where the wind was shearing the tops off the waves and laying lashes of spray across the heaving glossy backs of the swells. The sky was the same black as the sea, sinister, lightless, light-absorbing, so that the ship across from him seemed to glow with some pallid internal radiance. Her stern tipped down to an oncoming sea, and the snowy foam shot upward as it struck and covered what looked like minelaying rails and swept on to crest and break around the after mount like surf over a half-submerged rock. He stared at the aft turret, waiting for the next gun-flash with his hands crimped so tightly on the mouthpiece of the phone his fingers dug deep into the rubber. *Gaddis* was losing way. She was losing steam, losing power, losing the ability to maneuver. Once he lost mobility, this battle was over.

The other ship would take position on her stern and sledge-hammer him to pieces.

Then he noticed something strange.

The Katori wasn't firing anymore. No more bursts of light flickered from the dark pyramid. No more dangling wires of tracer probed from her upper decks. She was rolling slowly, sluggishly, wallowing as the swells passed over and under her.

Gaddis's five-inch fired again, and the forties resumed slamming away. Dan stared, seeing the rounds' red-hot flight end as they plunged point-blank into the dark mass that he saw now was streaming smoke from end to end. He hadn't made it out before because it was blowing down-wind, away from him, and the smoke was the same color as the storm and the sea and the mist.

Then, before his fixed and disbelieving eyes, the long, slim, smoldering ruin tilted with enormous deliberation over to port.

Zabounian, stepping out onto the bridge from his GQ station in Combat, gaped at the carnage. Dan grabbed him. "Stop!" he yelled. "Stop it! Cease fire!"

"No, we can't do that—"

"*Cease fire*, I said!"

The other ship hesitated for a long time on the edge of going over, and the sea foamed and seethed up over its stern with an obscene and impatient craving. Staring, he could imagine the panic onboard: the struggle for ladders and escape trunks, men trampled and fighting and falling. The most rigid discipline could give way at such moments. The last moments, for all too many, of their lives. He knew. He'd been there, on a dying ship, and not the faintest spark of glee or triumph or even relief penetrated the blank horror he felt now, watching it happen to other men.

She was nearly beam on to the storm seas now, and if she struggled to rise the repeated blows of the swells kept driving her down. Dan watched, seeing not just her but *Gaddis* as she'd struggled helplessly in the typhoon. Each time she lifted, a little less of her fantail was visible; the sea crept up her strakes till at last steam burst at her crosstrees, and faintly through the wailing wind came a despairing, nearly human shriek.

Then she capsized. The sheer strake came up and beneath it the long black length of her, bilge keels thrust up like stubby fins. The screws, still ticking over, beat in slow futility at the turbulent sprayfilled air. *Gaddis* was still coming around, moving on her momentum, and he saw holes in the cruiser's bottom where the armor-piercing projectiles had gone clear through, plunging downward. A visible stream of spray and smoke blew from each, a dying breath exhaled from the now rapidly compressing atmosphere within the sinking hull. The sea surged, and for a moment nothing showed above the roiling foam. Then, like a surfacing whale, still blowing from multiple rents, it resurfaced, yet now only a few feet projected above the triumphant sea.

As they watched, each clinging to some handhold in total silence, the bow began to rise. It came up with terrible slowness, then paused, hanging in the gray air. The rest of the doomed ship had disappeared beneath a greasy black-gray froth, dotted with spumy geysers of smoke and spray and oil and air. Raked and sharp, anchor chains thundering free as it pointed straight up, it aimed itself into the stormy sky for what seemed a last, long, straining effort, the final, dying struggle of a living creature.

Then, with an indescribable combination of grace and horror, it slipped slowly beneath the maelstrom that surged and boiled still where it had disappeared.

Lenson stared, unable to move or think. Faintly he heard someone shouting orders; saw *Gaddis*'s own prow dip as if in salute, no, simply a plunge to an overtaking sea, and then swing hard right. Then the deck beneath him went over so savagely he was pinned against the coaming by his own weight. The jagged white shapes laced his vision again, and he became conscious of an immense pain in his head.

Bobbie Wedlake's voice in his ear, her hand on his arm.

"Come inside the pilothouse. I'm getting Neilsen up here to look at you."

"Forget that. Have him take care of the wounded."

"News flash: That includes you. There's blood all over your face. Your leg, too."

"Find out what's happening down below. Call Jim; fight the fire. If we don't get power back, we're not going to come through this storm—"

She didn't answer, just half-led, half-dragged him inside. He collapsed just inside the knee knocker, and she eased him down in a practiced way that made him wonder remotely where she'd learned it. Her wiry frame was stronger than it looked.

Then he went away for a while.

When he came to he was slumped against the bulkhead. He sat motionless, frowning. Someone was exploring his scalp with his fingers. But that wasn't it.

For a moment he'd heard screaming, far away, on the wind.

No, he thought. Not again. Not the eternal dead who had shipped with him on every cruise since *Reynolds Ryan*. He had not heard their cries for years. He shook his head, denying them, and someone said sharply, "Hold still."

But then it came again, louder, and closer, and he realized with a shuddering breath that it was not in his mind.

He struggled upward, pushing the corpsman away. Grabbed the dogging bar for support, then staggered out on the wing.

Clinging to the gyro repeater, he stared down at the passing sea.

Oil slicked the waves, gentling them into ghosts of themselves. Limp, unmoving bodies, life jackets, debris, rose and fell on the anointed sea.

And among them, creatures who waved at the ship that drifted slowly past, who gestured helplessly, some in defiance, others in imploring surrender, yet others who simply regarded him silently, rising and falling with the swells as he looked down. His mind skittered madly, like an operating system hunting here and there on a hard disk for a program it could not find.

Zabounian, beside him, tentatively. "We could put a few of the life rafts over."

"Yeah, I—no. We can't."

"Why not?"

"They've got U.S. markings on them."

A knot of Chinese moved down *Gaddis*'s side, about thirty yards off. An easy toss with a heaving line. Their keening came through even the howl of the wind. Dan swallowed. They reached blackened oil-smeared arms up in supplication. They were the damned in hell, he looking down like the saints in heaven. They were holding up their arms to *him*—

Bobbie said from behind him, "To hell with them."

Dan glanced at her set white lips. "If I don't help, they'll all drown," he said. Barely able to speak, because looking out, he was one with them. He'd known that same shock and hopelessness, not once but twice; in the chill water of the North Atlantic and in the warm shark-prowled Gulf. Now he looked out on it again and grasped from another angle the suffering and waste of battle. He licked his lips and tried once more. "You don't understand. The storm—"

"Too fucking bad," she said coldly. "They killed everybody aboard when they attacked us. How many others do you think they've murdered out here?"

"What do you think, Louis? Can we pick them up?"

"They're pirates, sir," said the quartermaster "Their hands against every man and every man's hand against them. We don't have anyplace to put them anyway."

Dan limped out on the wing again, gripping his thigh as if he could hold back the growing pain. He couldn't seem to make up his mind. He wasn't even sure he had a mind anymore. Everything seemed suffused with light. He must have lost a lot of blood. Finally he said, "All right, get BM1 Topmark up here."

He ordered the boatswain to station a man at each abandon ship station, instructed to stand by to trigger half the
ship's life rafts. *Gaddis* carried inflatable rafts sealed inside
fiberglass capsules that lined the rails. Hydrostatic pistols
released them if the ship went down, but they could be triggered manually as well. "Half of them—every other one.
That'll leave enough for us; we don't have half our rated
crew anyway."

To his surprise, they didn't protest, even looked relieved,
as if redeemed from their own vengefulness. Topmark left,
and Dan told the OOD to use whatever waning engine
power they had left to steer upwind of the drifting survivors.

Still it would not save them all. Some had already
slipped beneath the angry sea. Others would die in overloaded rafts, or of exposure, or of wounds that, tended,
might not have proven fatal.

And that was not all. Something else nagged at him.
Something he'd overlooked. Something important.

He stood silently on the bridge, wondering what it was.
He felt strange, as if he himself had died, maybe with those
who had died long ago, maybe those who were dying out
there now, screaming and pleading against the howl of the
wind.

Topmark came back a few minutes later. "Life pre-
servers and rafts going over, sir."

"Very well."

Zabounian came up and stood beside Dan again. In a
low voice he said, "Sir, we got the Raytheon up again.
We've got another contact coming in."

Dan nodded slowly. That was what he'd been trying to
remember.

Gaddis coasted at last to a halt and began to drift downwind in the oil-slicked sea. Slowly at first, then with gathering speed. Picking up the roll of the swells. He wondered
fuzzily what he should do. Rig a sea anchor? Deploy the
anchor again? He'd better get them started. Yet it seemed so
futile.

"There it is," said Topmark, lowering the binoculars and pointing something out to Zabounian. "To the right of that low cloud. About one-one-zero relative."

They stood watching the shape coalesce from the fog. It was moving fast. They could see that even without radar. As it broke through, they saw what it was.

The second Shanghai. Undamaged, fresh, and angry, the gunboat was roaring in toward them as they wallowed helplessly in the heavy seas.

Then suddenly it seemed to stop, between one wave and the next, and a ripple of spray showed along its side. Not high, not an explosion like a torpedo strike or a mine detonation, just a momentary flash of white, like the instantaneous revelation of skirt by a flamenco dancer.

Dan leaned against the riddled, scarred splinter shield, screwing his face into the binoculars. Blocking from his brain the cries and screams of the wounded, the snap and crackle of fire aft.

A squall edge swept over the gunboat, and when it emerged again from the trailing skirts of rain, something had changed. It was riding lower in the water.

Zabounian muttered, "Isn't that about where we dropped the containers?"

And Dan saw that it was true, the racing gunboat had plowed straight over one of the still-floating container sections at full speed and ripped its bottom out or at least mangled its screw and punched holes in the thin, light planing hull.

Zabounian plucked a handset off the bulkhead and snapped the selector switch to the fire control circuit. He snapped, "Mount fifty-one? Bridge. Your target, gunboat. Bears one-ten relative, five thousand yards. With ten rounds VT—"

"No," Dan said. Then louder, grabbing him by the shoulder and wheeling him around: "No! God damn it, cease fire!"

He hesitated for a long moment, eyes locked on Dan's

face, then said quietly into the mike, "Belay that; I have a check-fire order from the CO. Stand by."

He let up on the transmit button, but before he could speak, Dan said, "What do you see out there?"

"I see our last target. What do you see, sir?" Almost suspiciously, as if he suspected Dan's judgment. God knows, he suspected it himself. But he was pretty sure this was right.

He looked around the bridge, seeing blood splashes, seeing, recognizing, for the first time Chick Doolan's smashed body huddled near the wing door, the bullet holes, the scarred raw metal where fragments had sliced open aluminum. Knowing that all this, all of it, was in vain if no one returned. Total victory was as useless to the penumbral cause in which they soldiered as total defeat. *Gaddis* had come halfway round the world to convey a message. If that message was not delivered, they might as well never have come, never have made the long voyage, never have endured the ordeal and made the sacrifice.

He said slowly, "I see a messenger."

"You mean we let them go?"

"We let them go. Otherwise, who'll tell the story?" He pushed himself off the bulkhead, timed his crossing to the lean of the ship, and limped across to the bitch box. "Main Control, Bridge. Jim, how's it going down there? Any headway on the fire?"

A heavy, exhausted voice came up in reply, one Dan knew but could not quite yet identify. "Bridge, Main Control: Status report. Main space fire extinguished. Reflash watch set in the fireroom. Five more minutes, we'll give you one-bravo boiler operational at reduced steam capacity. Max estimated speed at that time ten knots."

"Who's speaking? Is Commander Armey still in the fireroom?"

The dragging voice coughed and coughed and said, "Mr. Armey's in pretty bad shape, sir. He was on the boiler flat when one of those shells came through."

Dan let up on the lever for a moment as his throat closed, then took a fresh grip on it and on himself and asked, "Who else is down? How's our casualty list look?"

"Not good, sir. We've got a lot of wounded and four or five dead."

"Who am I talking to? Who's in charge down there?"

"This is Sansone, sir."

"Have you got enough men to steam, Al?"

"We'll cook you some fuckin' steam, sir. Don't worry about that."

"Roger, Chief. We've got a lot of casualties up here, too. We're going to head south as soon as you can get the screw turning again. Try to get out of the way of this storm. At least, try to duck the worst of it."

"Aye, sir. I'll advise when we can answer bells."

Sansone signed off. Dan clicked off and looked around the bridge, at the smoke-blackened, shocked faces. The boatswain stared back, eyes red-rimmed and weary. "Good job, sir," he said.

"You, too, Petty Officer Topmark."

One of the signalmen, at the wing door. "Sir, permission to hoist the U.S. colors."

"Do it, and—no, wait. Bring that black rag up here."

He brought it up a few moments later. Dan held the black cloth for a few seconds, feeling their eyes on him. Then he hobbled out onto the wing. The deck was littered with .50-caliber and twenty-millimeter cartridge cases. He knotted a handful of the blackened brass into the flag, so that there was no chance it would float. Then he leaned over the splinter shield and dropped it straight down into the sea. It splashed; bobbed for a second or two, already swept aft by the motion of the ship, then vanished as the bow wave broke over it white and clean.

He still felt dizzy, but a little strength had returned. He gave Zabounian his instructions, then gathered himself, and, limping slowly and deliberately, headed down to check out his ship.

THE AFTERIMAGE

ROYAL THAI NAVAL BASE COMPLEX, SATTAHIP, CHUK SAMET, THAILAND

IT felt like *déjà vu* all over again. The ranks of Asians in uniform, swinging in to take their places on the pier. The band, better than he'd expected; they'd warmed up with some Eastern-flavored marches he'd never heard before. The reviewing stand, replete with dignitaries and saffron-robed monks. And behind them, the flag- and flower-festooned length of a freshly painted Knox-class frigate, gleaming in the sun that now and then broke through the clouds over the soft green hills and danced flashing off the waters of the bay.

The Thai national anthem came to an end, and Dan broke his salute crisply. He waited until the others glanced around for their seats, then let himself down. A government official stepped to the podium. Lenson crossed his legs, careful not to show the soles of his shoes, and feigned attention to the steady stream of language he did not understand. His own turn would come soon. He had been carefully instructed in what he was to say, and more specifically on the many things he was not to mention. Still, it was a momentous occasion, and he felt thankful to be here.

After *Gaddis*'s action against the Chinese cruiser and her subsequent battering in two more days of heavy weather, he'd taken her south till he got the message directing him to his next port of call. The orders had pointed him west, to transit to the Gulf of Thailand with no intermediate landfalls. He had the fuel to make it, but barely; the frigate's tanks had been nearly dry when she arrived off Phra Island. A Thai patrol craft had escorted her at night into Sattahip, where she'd immediately been dry-docked for hull inspection, sonar dome and shaft X rays, repairs, and blasting and painting.

By then, of course, those wounded whom Neilsen couldn't save had died, and those who were going to recover were on the way. The final count had been eight dead among the ninety-plus who'd taken *Gaddis* into battle, counting among them Chick Doolan, Johnile Machias, Roy Compline, and Ben Engelhart.

Dan was still angry about the casualties. Intensely angry. But apparently those numbers had been acceptable to whoever had planned their equivocal and obscure mission.

It was perfectly obvious they'd all been expendable.

He suddenly became aware that the official had switched to English.

". . . that the government of the United States has seen fit to transfer this notable addition to the Royal Thai Navy, for the purpose of extending our reach offshore and to police the continuing unrest in the Vietnam-Kampuchea area of the Indochinese subcontinent. It is with much gratitude on the part of the Thai people, government, and Crown that we accept the gift in the spirit in which it is offered.

"I will now introduce Daniel Lenson, commanding officer of USS *Marcus Goodrich*."

Yes, he thought as he stood, they'd even disguised her name.

An interview with Jack Byrne had set him straight on his own responsibilities in the matter. *Gaddis* had never been north of the fifteen-degree line. What had happened in the South China Sea had never happened. Both Mellows and Vorenkamp, along with those lost in battle, had died in an action with a heavily armed Filipino extremist group off Mindanao. But Dan had presented a couple of non-negotiable demands of his own. Those surviving crew members who had not participated in the abortive revolt would get a step up in grade and their choice of assignment. The dead got posthumous Bronze Stars for their actions off "Mindanao" and the living wounded Purple Hearts.

Bobbie Wedlake had agreed to confidentiality; she had what she wanted, which she'd explained simply enough as "revenge." Dan had driven her up to Bangkok, to catch her flight home.

The only other loose end was Juskoviac, who had survived the battle locked in his stateroom. Byrne had "persuaded" the exec to trade his silence for dismissal of any charges relating to inciting to mutiny, and a shore billet at a training command where he could navigate a desk with perfect safety to all concerned till a not-very-far-off mandatory retirement. Any objections the Thai government might have had to being accessories to such smoke and mirrors had been quelled by the gift of a much-needed frigate.

Byrne had seemed taken aback when Dan presented his after-action report but had accepted it, promising to forward it and the recommendations it contained to the appropriate authorities. He handed over in exchange an envelope containing Dan's own orders, as Tomahawk targeting officer with the staff of the Commander, U.S. Naval Forces, Central Command, in Mina Salman, Bahrain.

An envelope that remained in Dan's briefcase now. They were interesting orders, he had to admit. He'd operated in the Gulf before, as exec of *Van Zandt* during the strike that had destroyed half the Iranian fleet. This assignment might be even more dangerous, if the offensive against Iraq, built up and planned over the last five months in Operation Desert Shield, was finally unleashed. Byrne had intimated that war was imminent and had recommended Dan get himself in top physical shape; despite his being assigned to a staff billet, it was possible he might see action ashore.

But they weren't command at sea orders, and he doubted they could measure up to where he'd gone and what he'd done with the officers and men of USS *Oliver C. Gaddis*.

Since then workmen had swarmed over the ship, repairing damage, restoring her to her pre-Pakistani configuration. She was still not fully ready for sea, but there seemed to be considerable impetus to get him and his crew out of the country fast. He'd only had a couple of meetings with his relief, barely enough to brief him on the maneuvering characteristics of his new ship.

And now it was time to lay down the office he'd never really had. His first command, in a way, and he was pretty certain there'd never be another. Officially, he'd never really been her captain. But he knew better, and he felt sure the ship did, too. He could feel her behind him, a conscious presence in the flickering sunlight. As if she were listening, waiting to hear how he would salute her and how he would remember her.

He took the podium, looking down at the men standing at parade rest to his left. At Jim Armey, Chief Tosito, and the other wounded sitting in the front row. They were too shaky yet to stand in ranks, but he'd wanted them at the ceremony. At Usmani, grinning up in his brand-new blues. He was a U.S. Navy sailor now, and proud as hell.

"I will make my remarks short," Dan said. "Not because I want to, but because I've been asked to." Slight frowns, uneasy shifts behind him on the dais; yeah, they knew.

"So I will be brief. To the outgoing crew: You overcame a lot of obstacles, but you acquitted yourselves nobly. I'm proud to have served with you, and maybe we'll run into each other again, down the road.

"To Captain Chandvirach and his men: Treat *Bangpakong* well, and she'll come through for you. She's a solid ship, a dependable ship. I wish you fair winds and following seas."

There, that ought to be short enough. He turned to his relief, a tall man for a Thai, stiff and resplendent in whites and gold braid. He, too, would know the burden of command and the inestimable reward.

What was command? He knew now he had only glimpsed the edge of it . . . but he *had* glimpsed the edge.

If professionalism was responsibility for yourself, and placing duty before self, then command at sea was that, squared. It meant being responsible for others, and for placing their welfare over your own.

And yet more. He knew now that to lead contained a

hard contradiction. It was to love those others to a degree surpassing self . . . and yet to be ready, if necessity so ordered, to place the mission before your career, your life, your men's lives, and the very existence of your ship.

For that was why the people of the United States sent fleets out to the seas and straits of the planet: to have a sharp tool ready, against the hour of mortal need.

Command was not a reward. It was not a perk. It was not just another step in a career at sea. It was not a lark, though there were times when it held as deep a pleasure as he'd ever felt. For the first time, he'd found a task that demanded everything he had in him, every ounce of professional skill, every gram of courage, every grain of insight and patience, integrity and character, self-control and wisdom. He did not know if he would ever be called to it again. But he was glad to have been there, if only for a little while.

"I relieve you, sir," said Chandvirach, lifting his hand briefly to his cap. Dan returned the salute, then reached out to shake the other man's hand.

He said, "I stand relieved."

BEIJING

THE swarthy, barrel-chested officer in blues sat watching the bare snow-dusted streets pass by. Pleasant as it was in summer, Beijing was a murderous post in January, with the Siberian winds keeping the temperatures somewhere between zero and minus thirty Centigrade. When the embassy Citation turned off Baishiqiao at North Circular Road, Jack Byrne flipped the collar up on his bridge coat. Stood for a moment on the pavement after he got out, looking around. It was a habit he'd picked up from years in the USSR and Eastern Europe. Take your time. Be aware of your environment. Always have an escape route.

When he felt secure, he followed the signs and the straggling crowd toward the exhibition hall.

Tonight's event had not been scheduled in the reddish-gold blaze of the Forbidden City. The Youyi Binguan lay in the direction of the Summer Palace, but the "Friendship

Guest House" had none of the suffocating late Qing ostentation of that resort of the final Manchu empress. It was not
a "house," either. The acres of hotel blocks, apartment
blocks, auditoriums, and meeting halls, mostly of reinforced concrete, had been built in the 1950s to house Russian advisers and their families.

But at least, he reflected, it had not been "purified" with
hammers during the Great Proletarian Cultural Revolution.

The main exhibit hall was thronged with smiling Westerners and expressionless Chinese in uniforms and blue
business suits. Banners proclaimed corporate allegiances
above tables and booths: IDS, IBM, Wang, Hughes, Westinghouse, Lotus, Microsoft, Intel, Apple, GE, Lockheed,
Oracle, Acme, Ventura, Compaq, Systems Bull, Osborne. A
banner more enormous than all the rest together, hung from
one side of the hall to the other, announced in English and
French, *Welcome to the Annual Beijing Computer-Electronics Exhibition.*

Jack Byrne slowly took off his dark glasses, polished
them, and slipped them inside his service dress blue blouse.
He accepted a brochure from a Japanese woman wearing a
Toshiba button, checked the schedule of events, and headed
across the exhibition floor—Leading Edge, Hewlett-
Packard, Adobe, MicroPro, XyQuest—and down a short
hallway.

The reception room was considerably more luxurious,
and warm enough that he could leave his coat at the check
table. Buffet tables held a selection of California delicacies,
and older men clustered around them and around a small
bar. On second glance, he saw they were staring at a television behind it. The set was connected to an astonishingly
small satellite dish, not much bigger than the serving plate
he held in his hand. A placard behind it; some vendor had
had the bright idea of setting up in here. As he approached,
he saw it was tuned to CNN. Wolf Blitzer was holding
forth, interspersed with images of a darkened city naked
under the night sky. Streams of tracers clawed skyward, the

gunners groping desperately for an enemy that eluded their grasp with ease.

He recognized it. Baghdad, reprised images from the opening of the Desert Storm air war, the night before.

He was holding a plastic-stemmed glass of *sudashui* when he saw the cherub-faced man in gray civilian suit smoking a cigarette near the buffet. He glanced around, then drifted toward him.

"Admiral Mi. Nice to see you, sir."

The Chinese blinked. "Captain Byrne."

"Your aide's not with you?"

"I don't take him everywhere," Mi said. His eyes slid past Byrne, toward the buffet table. The attaché turned gracefully, suggesting with his body that they proceed in that direction, but the admiral did not stir.

Instead Mi nodded toward the screen. "Have you been watching CNN?"

"The bombing of Baghdad. Very impressive."

"Saddam depends too much on Soviet-style weaponry. No one will make that mistake again. The technological supremacy of the West is quite clear now."

Mi's face had hardened as he spoke, watching the images of a heavily armed but helpless city. Suddenly he swung away, toward the bar. Byrne glanced round again and followed him. But halfway there the senior officer swung his bulk sideways and stopped. He and a bald husky European in a blazer exchanged several sentences in German. Byrne waited patiently, smiling, till Mi was free again, then said, "I understand the South Sea Fleet was recently engaged off Hainan."

Mi's eyes flickered, but only for a microsecond. He said evenly, "Only certain elements of that fleet, deployed on a peaceful mission. They were treacherously attacked, without warning, and the survivors abandoned with great cruelty and loss of life."

"Tragic. Any idea who was responsible?"

"Pirates."

"Pirates! How terrible. I have heard they are a serious problem in certain quarters of the China Sea."

"They have been for many centuries," said Mi. The Chinese attendant had a drink waiting when he reached the bar. The admiral devoured it in one bite.

"What is the Chinese Navy's view of that incident?"

"Of the incident off Hainan?"

Byrne nodded. Mi turned his eyes away, then back. "We must suppress these bandits of the sea," he said at last. "All of them. They threaten us all."

Byrne looked slowly around at the chattering salespeople, at the banners touting faster RAM chips and Ethernet connectivity. "You know, it's all too easy to believe commercial interests are all that matters to the West," he said. "But that's not the whole story."

"You first came to China as pirates," said Mi.

"We came in many roles, as I understand it," said Byrne. "As pirates and adventurers, certainly, but also as traders, as missionaries, as those genuinely extending the hand of friendship. I can imagine it must have been difficult for the rulers of those days to distinguish among them. To sort out those who merely wanted to profit, with no thought beyond that, from those who had more fundamental interests and would defend them. All the more so since their governments, too, did not always convey a consistent attitude."

Mi nodded thoughtfully, lighting another cigarette. He said nothing more, simply staring at the screen, so after a moment Byrne excused himself and got a drink, now that the business of the evening was over, now that he'd made the point he wanted to make.

For just a moment, holding a pale golden wine, he allowed himself to wonder if it had been worth it. He knew not only what Mi knew—National Security Agency intercepts of certain transmissions after the sinking of the cruiser had made interesting reading—but he knew also what those higher officers to whom he himself reported thought. He knew their doubts as to whether the mission might succeed and their caution in dissociating themselves from any hint of official sponsorship.

He nodded slowly, realizing Mi had said the right things. Very cautiously, he allowed himself to hope that the message had been received. But he also knew what all diplomats learned sooner or later: that no message ever meant to the hearer exactly what the sender intended. What the oligarchs of the New China made of this one remained to be seen. But it had been transmitted. Until matters developed further, his responsibility, and that of the U.S. Navy, could be considered at an end.

Only time would tell if the game had been worth the candle, or if history and politics and the ineradicable streak of something not quite sane in the human heart meant a titanic struggle still lay ahead. He himself did not believe in inevitable conflicts. He hoped what they'd done had pushed the possibility of this one a little further away.

Drinking off the rather-too-sweet wine, he grimaced and set the glass down. And a moment later, lost himself in the crowd.

Turn the page for a sneak preview of
David Poyer's next exciting book

BLACK STORM

Coming soon in hardcover from
St. Martin's Press

1

0100 18 FEBRUARY 1991: THE SAUDI DESERT

No one spoke after the helicopter lifted off. There wouldn't have been any point, even if they'd wanted to; the engine noise was deafening. The deck shuddered, tilting as the pilot pulled into a hard bank. Beyond the windshield, beyond the open doors where crewmen sat hunched over the pintle mounts for the M60s, impenetrable night hurtled by as they gathered speed.

The winter of the war was cold and rainy, the worst in thirty years. The desert stars had been sealed off for days by an overcast that opened now and again to loose spatters of sooty, oil-smelling, dust-gritty rain over the half million men who waited, scattered far and wide across the western desert, for the word to go.

The helo steadied, dropping till it hurtled onward barely a hundred feet above the desert.

Seven dark figures lay tumbled together in the crew compartment, where they'd hauled themselves in during the thirty seconds the Navy Combat Search and Rescue HH-60 had touched down at the pickup point. The compartment was too low to stand up. There weren't any seats, just bare aluminum-walled space lit by faint green lights to port and starboard. Their camouflage uniforms had no rank insignia and no unit patches. They lay on top of their gear and rucks and weapons and each other, mingled like a composite organism that had only just begun to gain consciousness of itself.

The pilot tilted his head back, peering beneath his night vision goggles when a brilliant line of evenly spaced blue-white lights lifted over the horizon. The pipeline road stretched parallel to the border twenty-five miles north. It was lit all night long. Both lanes were filled with double columns of tanker trucks and tank transporters heading

slowly west. The lights passed beneath them, and fell quickly
aft. As darkness retook the world he looked through the goggles again. And suddenly the scene shifted from inchoate and
unrevealing darkness to a strange green-on-black world of
barren sand-ridges and blasted wadis, a dry undulating sea of
sand and sand and sand, and close above it the haloed green
flare, pulled from the deep infrared by the circuitry of the
heavy goggles, of the hot exhaust of another larger aircraft.

The black helicopter ahead was an Air Force Pave Hawk
bird. It had better avionics and weapons, including a sophisticated terrain-avoidance radar, but the Navy helo had
better navigation. The pilot tracked it through the NVGs,
rising when it rose, dropping when it dropped. When he had
the rhythm he said softly into the intercom, "Team leader,
you on the line yet? Slap a cranial on him, Minky."

"Six team leader on the line," said a voice. "This the
pilot?"

"Welcome aboard, I'm your taxi driver tonight. Crawl
up here and tell my copilot where you want to go."

A faint green light clicked on, focused on an air chart.
Across the lower quarter a dotted stripe zagged from left to
right, gradually angling down. North of it was a series of
carefully hand-drawn threat circles. They grew denser and
more closely spaced toward the top of the chart, and many
of them overlapped.

A gloved finger reached out and pressed a point west of
a blue-tinted scatter of lakes and marshland. It was covered
by two of the circles, which marked the location and effective radius of Iraqi antiair missile batteries.

After a moment the copilot said, "I was afraid that's
where you wanted to go."

"What is this, sir? You were at the briefing, weren't you?"

"I'm just pulling your chain. Just making sure we're on
the same sheet of music."

"Just get us there," said the team leader.

The team leader looked closely at the map, going over the
route and the plan for the hundredth time in his mind.

Turnaround and jumpoff, Point Charlie, Point Delta, objective. In an hour and a half they'd be on the ground a hundred and forty miles inside Iraq. Once landed, they'd link up with an advance party, exchange information, then start the mission. The turnover had to go fast. They'd be inserting close to powerful enemy forces enraged by being bombed for weeks without being able to strike back.

The air war had been underway since the UN deadline expired on 17 January. The Air Force and Navy had been pounding the Iraqis for four weeks now, starting with air defenses, command and communications nodes in downtown Baghdad, and then shifting to the ground forces dug in around Kuwait. Some of the briefers had said they were decimated. Others said the Republican Guard was dug in so deep the bombing barely scratched them. He knew the fog and overcast and rain hadn't helped.

But he'd seen what happened when you underestimated your enemy. As a private, hot off the griddle at Parris Island. Night after night on the perimeter in Beirut, listening to the crackle of gunfire as the Syrians, the Israelis, the Palestinians, the Hezbollah, and practically every other terrorist faction in the Middle East fought it out. Someone with a direct line to God had set the Marines down on the airfield in the middle of it. He'd thought the locals understood they were protecting them. Till he'd been awakened one October night in '83 by an enormous explosion.

The truck bomb had killed two hundred and forty-one marines, four of them his buddies.

You didn't underestimate Arabs. They were courteous. They were proud. They were patient. It was when you thought they were finished, helpless, that they became truly dangerous. Then they didn't care if they lived or died, as long as they could take you with them.

He stared into the absolute darkness ahead of the pilot's outline. If he put on his NVGs, he'd presumably see as well as the pilot. But he wasn't flying. It would be better to conserve batteries for when they were on the ground. For the mission. For a second he felt the fear course through him, pounding, tangible, like something sharp just under his heart. Then he turned away from it. He was trained for this. He had a good team. They had a solid plan. Good equipment. They'd briefed and trained, not as much as he would have liked, but enough. For a moment he felt more confident. Then the unease surged up again, making his mouth dry, his heart pound.

Because he knew no mission ever went as it was planned. And really no one knew what lay ahead in the dark, on the far side of the invisible line in the desert that separated the two massive armies built up over the last six months. Two massive armies, moving inexorably toward war.

The pilot asked the copilot for the next vector. He forgot the man behind him. He was wrapped in the hairy effort of flying thirty feet off the ground.

The Navy helo and the Pave Hawk had taken off from the Allied base at Al Jouf on a false course, then angled north and picked up the team off a deserted stretch of road. So far neither helicopter had come up on the radio. The Pave Hawk blinked its IR position lights each time they went over a check point. They'd preplanned and timed the routes in and out, routing them through or beneath blind zones in the coverage of the SA-8 and Roland sites that were still operational. If they did it right, they could finish the insertion without a single radio transmission.

This would be eminently desirable, considering the French- and Russian-trained technicians who manned the direction-finding posts, electronic intelligence posts, radar sites, and antiaircraft missile batteries between which they'd be flying.

"Cougar, Red Wolf Two."

"Roll to Indigo, Red Wolf Two."

He snapped to the new frequency and picked up. "Red Wolf Two plus one, gate Tarzan, thence to x-ray kilo oscar papa, thence kilo uniform victor delta, charlie charlie mike papa, lima alfa uniform bravo. Read back, over."

The distant AWACS bird, orbiting in great slow circles

thirty thousand feet above the Gulf, rogered his presence
and read back his intended flight path. Now they were safe
from the hunters above the clouds, USAF F-15s, Navy
F-18s, German and Italian and British Tornados.

Unless someone made a mistake.

He was worrying about that, about what they called
"blue on blue," when suddenly the Pave Hawk jinked violently. He hauled around too, just as a dune loomed up out
of the dark ahead and flashed past their rotor tips at a hundred and twenty miles an hour.

Instead of rising the two aircraft dipped even lower, into
a wadi. They were traveling barely twenty feet off the
ground now.

The assistant team leader was huddled close to the van-
ishingly dim green light in the crew compartment, a cover-
less, dog-eared, cola-spotted paperback book held four
inches in front of his eyes. He was leaning against the med
kit, which he carried along with the usual weapon and 782
gear. He wasn't thinking about the mission now, though.
The turbines howled, the fuselage swayed, G forces pressed
him against the bulkhead, but he didn't react. He wasn't
even there. He was in the Caribbean with Dirk Pitt, three
hundred feet beneath the sparkling sea.

"Thirty seconds to the gate," said the copilot, who was simultaneously kneeboarding his map, working the GPS, and
plotting each waypoint on the Tacnav display, a green
screen in the middle of the instrument panel. The pilot
risked a quick glance, then jerked his eyes back to the
ground as it rose again, as if the land itself was reaching up
to grab and stop them. He blinked sweat out of his eyes,
wishing he could see more clearly. Through the goggles the
hurtling desert floor was blur and shadows, boiling with the
random energy of amplified photons. He blinked again and
squeezed his eyes shut, then popped them open and hauled
hard on the collective as, beside him, his copilot sucked in
his breath involuntarily.

If they hit one of those dunes, they'd never have time to realize they were dead.

At the rear of the crew compartment, the naval officer squirmed upright. He'd lain quiet for the first few minutes, trying to get control of his breathing. Feeling the others around him, pressed against him, feeling the hardness of the Hechler and Koch nine-millimeter under his legs.

Now he rolled over and pushed himself upright. An arm's-reach away the port gunner craned down, looking into the blast of wind and noise and darkness, as if darkness itself was solid and came blasting through at them. The air was icy cold.

What the hell am I doing here? he asked himself. He'd served in the Gulf before, but as the exec of a missile frigate. He should be twenty miles offshore, navigating a destroyer through Saddam's minefields toward a naval gun-fire support position. What was he doing with his face smeared with green and black camo paint, carrying a sub-machine gun and grenades and an eighty-pound pack?

He touched the various pieces of equipment lashed and clipped to his load-bearing gear. Night vision goggles. Gas gear. Canteens. Knife, flashlight, magazine pouch, compass, everything ranger-corded so he couldn't lose it in the dark, no matter how clumsy or how sleep-deprived he got. They'd only had a day to train. Just enough time to get thoroughly confused.

If they found what they were looking for, he'd have to destroy it. In the hard flat pack in his thigh pocket, and in his head, he had all he needed to do that.

He felt sick as he remembered what else he carried. Information that, if the Iraqis should ever find it out, would compromise the entire Allied war plan: the details of the massive amphibious assault that would finally liberate Kuwait.

He hoped the men around him were good. Because as far as he could see, he was only going to be a burden to them until they got to the objective. Once they did that, once they got there, he was pretty sure he could do what a very angry four-star general had ordered him to do.

If they could get there alive.

"Penetration checklist rechecked complete," the copilot said over the intercom.

The pilot licked his lips but didn't answer. He squatted the helicopter even lower, shaving the last inches away between the terrain and the hurtling aircraft's belly. Now all light was gone. Neither sky nor desert yielded the faintest luminosity. Even through the goggles, the only illumination was the jittering, fanlike glow of the Pave Hawk's engine-heat two hundred meters ahead.

"Wadi coming up. Tarzan gate, twenty seconds."

The "Tarzan gate" was a low-lying ravine, or wadi, that snaked across the border leading west to east. Border-crossers could use it as a tunnel under the Iraqi ground radars.

But only if you flew low enough. He pushed the cyclic forward even more, fighting his way down closer to the earth. The earth was safety. But it was also mortal danger.

"There's the entrance," said the copilot, and at the same moment the Pave Hawk swerved. The pilot moved the stick slightly and the twenty-one tons of helicopter and crew and passengers, lying silent and motionless behind him, swung onto the new heading and tracked down the looming escarpments, down through the blowing darkness, the clatter-slam of their rotating blades carrying far out over the night-shrouded land.

At the very back of the compartment, the youngest member of the team held tight to the butt of the Glock he'd stuffed into his cargo pocket after the preloading inspection, after the brass turned away. He was sweating all over. He'd moved away from the team to drop his trousers twice as they waited at the pickup site, and now his guts rumbled and he knew he had to go again. It was the lousy raghead water. That and the shitty food, the Pak rice and the lettuce they trucked down from the Bekaa. He shouldn't have ate that lettuce. Everybody knew they shit right on the lettuce to make it grow, that was their fertilizer, goddamn it, goddamn.

Once they hit the ground he'd be out in front. He was the scout. The point. Everybody'd be depending on him. If he fucked up, they'd get blown away. It was desert down there. Not all that different from Montana. Not as rocky, they said. Sand and gravel. He'd have to be real fucking sharp. The Gunny and the Staff would be on his ass. This was the first time he'd ever been in combat. Fucking ragheads. He hoped he got to score. God, come on, let me score.

His hand found the butt of the Glock again, and his finger lightly touched the trigger safety.

"Mark, the border," said the copilot, over the intercom so the gunners and their passengers could hear.

The pilot grunted. He was down to twenty feet now, and totally fixated on not flying into the ground. Flying into that granite cumulus. Voiding that ground-contact warranty. Gluing the shadow to the airplane. You couldn't beat the low altitude flying record; the best you could hope for was a tie. Jokes, his brain feeding back jokes so he didn't actually have to think about how close death was. It had happened to several crews, using the goggles. You didn't have any depth perception at all with them, just light and shade and the blurry speckling seethe of amplified light. An H-60 made a hell of a big hole.

The Pave Hawk swung hard left and tracked up a side wadi, the bluff edges closing in, then rose, rose, as the land climbed; and he pulled the collective and climbed too, following, then suddenly popped up over a rise, and went right over a Bedouin camp about ten feet up. He only realized what it was after they were past, retrieving from memory the conical tents a fraction of a second before they rocketed over them, a sparkle of gun-flashes dotted among them. The Bedouin gypsied back and forth over the border. Some were

Iraqi, others Saudi, most pretty much independent of both sides, as far as the briefers had said. Like all the Arabs were supposed to be, me and my brother against my cousin, me and my cousins against the infidel.

The pilot hoped he never went down out here. He was Jewish.

A brilliant flash jerked his head around. A climbing flame rose majestically out of the dark. He ignored it, knowing it probably didn't have a lock-on. So did the gunners, the machine-guns stayed silent. The border Arabs had Strelas, but they didn't know how to use them. It was hard to get a lock-on in the dark, and they'd fire blindly, without waiting for a fire-acquisition tone. True to form, the glare wavered, then fell aft and at last plunged downward to lose itself again in the chalk-dust and sand-cloud plume the two low-flying helicopters were dragging across the desert floor behind them.

The Air Force chopper was getting too far ahead. He couldn't lose sight of it. They needed two birds in case one went down. Pushing the cyclic forward as he added power, he breathed very slowly in and out, and with tiny, nearly imperceptible movements of the stick threaded the hurtling needle of night.

The communicator rolled himself awkwardly upright, like a beached walrus, humping the weight of his ruck and the radio and batteries and ammo slowly up the back of the aluminum column that enclosed the landing gear shock absorbers, till he could sit upright. Rifle and radio, if you had those you could get through just about anything. Defend yourself with one, save yourself with the other. Call in fire. Call in air support. Call in exfil if things went to shit.

He couldn't get over how cold it was. Nothing like Texas. Seemed like the coldest place he'd ever been.

The vibrating darkness reminded him of Liberia. The float where everything had gone to shit, and they'd gotten called back even when they were steaming home and suddenly it had all gone down, and they'd had to go in as another African country slid down the toilet into rebellion and war.

He squeezed his eyes closed and saw the map of the RV point. And made himself relax and go over it all again, how they were going to make the rendezvous, the passwords, the identifiers.

Somewhere in there, thinking about it, the radio man went to sleep.

The copilot sat tensely in his padded seat, plotting the fixes and trying to keep his hands from shaking. He wanted a cigarette, but he knew he couldn't have one. The ground flashed by too close for him to look at. So he didn't, just kept his eyeballs pressed to the map and then the Tacnav, trying to keep his jitters under control and mainly succeeding.

An hour went by that way, and nothing changed except that they were now a hundred miles inside Iraq. The fuel onboard gauge dropped gradually as they headed northeast, threading between two SA-8 sites and then swinging due east to pass the Roland battery at Mudaysis. The ground maybe getting a bit flatter, less cut by wadis. The relief going away, going flat into what looked like meticulously graded gravel or sand.

What he found really terrifying out here was the emptiness. On and on and nothing living, no vegetation, no trees, not the smallest stunted bush. As if death itself had moved over this empty terrain. Some immense evil in the shadow of which nothing could live. Occasionally a tone in their earphones signaled the edges of a missile envelope, the invisible brushing fingers of a fire-control radar. But each time they heard it the Pave Hawk had already turned away, and they banked to follow and the deadly whine faded.

The sniper was from South Carolina. He'd rolled aboard folded over his rifle, tucking the separate hump of the scope into the angle in his gut, protecting the zero. He'd shot it in every day during the lockdown. Day or night, he could put a bullet through a man's eye socket at two hundred meters. The nine-mils were okay for close quarters, but you could reach out and touch someone with the 5.56.

Like he had at Khafji. When the Iraqi armor had come through, and they were surrounded in the deserted town.

The colonel had climbed out of the tank in his natty greens and black beret like Saddam himself. And from atop a building overlooking a shabby square the sniper had put the crosshairs down on him. He'd taken one more click for the wind, taken a slow breath and half let it out, and then slowly squeezed the trigger and shot him and then shot the three other officers who sat frozen in the staff car, a moment before talking to the man whose skull had suddenly opened like a grisly tulip in front of them, the enlisted boys recovering and diving for cover but the staffies just sitting there with their seat belts still buckled, looking around in alarm as he killed them one after the other, a downhill shot so he held a little high, just above their heads, and when they were crossed off he'd gone back to the tank and shot the colonel again just to make sure till he rolled off his still-seated perch on the frontal armor and fell facedown into a long sky-streaked puddle-rut filled with the rain that had fallen all that day.

He hadn't felt much about it. The man was a soldier. If he didn't want to get his ass shot, he shouldn't have put on the uniform and invaded somebody else's country.

Rifle tucked protectively along his side, he stared out into the passing night.

At 0150, the whole desert ahead suddenly turned to white fire. It outlined the lead helicopter with a rapidly growing halo of brilliant light. The pilot could see its rotors going around.

He hauled into a hard bank, his goggles flaring into a solid blinding brilliance as the light kept increasing. He pushed them up, close to panic, and saw the light pouring down across the desert as the fire climbed toward the sky. For a moment he couldn't tell what it was.

"It's a fucking SCUD," breathed his copilot.

"Tag the waypoint, god damn it, tag it now. Intel officers love that shit."

A wall of tracers rose suddenly and all at once out of the black desert, blazing toward and then over them. They were huge, brilliant, but the pilot could barely see them. Dazzling afterimages chased themselves across his blinded retinas, fear chased itself through his hands. They were ZSU-23s. A four-barreled, twenty-three-millimeter son of a bitch with a dish radar on a tank chassis, and for every one of those huge balls of tracer there were three in between that weren't. If they got him locked up on radar, he was dead. He popped chaff but knew it might not help.

Out of control, the helicopter lurched to starboard, rotor tips clawing toward the sand.

The National Guard major lay with her eyes fixed on the overhead, trying not to throw up. She'd felt sick since they took off. She hated helicopters. She didn't think this was going to work. She'd said so over and over. A squad of grunts, on foot, trying to stop what a mad dictator had had years and billions to prepare? What the CIA said it couldn't find, and the Air Force said it couldn't attack? It was ludicrous. It wasn't the way the Army she knew operated. These people were insane. Totally unconnected to reality.

But they wouldn't listen to her. Oh, she knew why. When four stars gave an order, that was the burning bush. All the regulars had to salaam. But it wasn't just that. Even she had to admit that.

For just a moment she wondered if it could be true. She knew Doctor Rihab Taha. She was smart and she was cold. But could she do something like this? Could any physician? No, it was bullshit. It had to be bullshit.

But with a million innocent lives at stake—men, women, and children—you couldn't take a chance. Not with something like that.

When they asked her, she had to say she'd try.

And horrible though it had been so far, it was getting

worse now. Something was going on outside. A terrifying roar came through the tortured howl of the engine. Light played through the canted windows, throwing flickering shadows across the greasepainted faces around her. She flung her arms out instinctively as the nose pitched up, as gay bright Independence Day sparklers she recognized after a horrified instant as tracers burned past the door gunner. Then the flame was in with them, a jolt and a deafening bang cracked through the metal around her. And God help her, she hadn't meant to, but that was her screaming as they went down.

The team leader reached out and grabbed the two people closest to him. They weren't restrained. If the helo went in they'd all ballistic through the cockpit windshield a fraction of a second after the pilots. But that was what you did, held on to those closest to you. Because that was all there was to do.

The M60 gunner was firing, not bursts like you were trained to, just a steady clatter. The muzzle was outboard the aircraft and it sounded distant, like it was in a far room. Another round came through the fuselage, blinding bright and loud as a stun grenade in a close room. Blinded, deafened, he braced for the impact. So this was the end. They were right, the ones who'd said it was too risky. He'd pulled the team together in haste, and only half-trained it. He'd told the CO he didn't think it would work. If what they wanted him to find even existed. But the boss had said do it, and Semper Fi. Hey diddle diddle, right up the middle.

And now they were heading for the desert floor, and bodies were sliding toward him and then lifting off the deck as the aircraft nosed over and headed down again.

Clamping his teeth together, holding tight to the men he'd hoped to lead, he closed his eyes and waited for the end.

TOMAHAWK
DAVID POYER

Once Lieutenant Dan Lenson had a ship and a family. Now he is on his own, deep within Washington's military industrial complex. His task: shepherd a controversial weapon through the Navy's testing process to deployment. But powerful forces are lined up against the Tomahawk missile—and against Lenson. And for Dan Lenson, separating his enemies from his friends is the beginning of the most dangerous war of all…

"There can be no better writer of modern sea adventure around today."
—Clive Cussler

"This demanding, excellent novel is probably the best so far in a major contemporary seafaring saga."
—*Booklist*

"An imaginative, thought-provoking premise rich in possibilities."
—*USA Today*

DAVID POYER

AUTHOR OF *THE GULF* AND *THE MED*

"There can be no better writer of modern sea adventure around today."

—Clive Cussler

The tight-lipped residents of Hatteras Island aren't talking about the bodies of the three U-boat crewmen that have mysteriously surfaced after more than forty years. But their reappearance has unleashed a tide of powerful forces—Nazis with a ruthless plan to corner the South American drug market, and a shadowy figure with his own dangerous agenda.

Whatever's out there, someone besides salvage diver Tiller Galloway is interested. Someone prepared to bomb his boat and kill any witnesses. And when Tiller finally meets face-to-face with his pursuers, it's in a violent, gut-wrenching firefight that climaxes hundreds of feet below the surface.

"I couldn't turn the pages fast enough!"

—Greg Dinallo, author of *Purpose of Evasion*

HATTERAS BLUE

HBLUE 10/97

THE
PASSAGE
DAVID POYER

The Navy's most sophisticated destroyer, the USS Barrett, carries a top-secret computer that can pilot an unmanned ship and send it into battle. As the weapons officer charged with its first mission, Lieutenant Dan Lenson has a chance to make naval history. But when the system develops a sinister virus and a sailor takes his own life amid ugly allegations, Lenson finds himself caught in a web of betrayal. Now, on the treacherous Windward Passage between the U.S. and Cuba, he'll undergo the ultimate test of honor and faith—one that could cost him his career, his ship, and even his life.

"There can be no better writer of modern sea adventure around today."
—Clive Cussler

"Poyer knows what he is writing about when it comes to anything on, above, or below the water."
—*The New York Times Book Review*

"One of the outstanding bodies of nautical fiction during the last half-century."
—*Booklist*

P 1/01

For four years at Annapolis he prepared for this, pledging his youth, his ambition, and even his life. But when junior officer Dan Lenson finally gets his commission, it's aboard the U.S.S. *Ryan*, an aging World War II destroyer. Now, with a mix of pride and fear, he heads into the world's most dangerous seas.

As the *Ryan* plunges into the dark waters of the Arctic Circle at the height of storm season, Lenson and the crew pursue a mysterious and menacing enemy. But he soon discovers a foe even more dangerous within the *Ryan*, advancing a shocking agenda that drives the ship closer and closer to disaster—testing Lenson's life and loyalty to their very limit.

THE
CIRCLE
DAVID POYER

"POYER KNOWS WHAT HE IS WRITING ABOUT WHEN IT COMES
TO ANYTHING ON, ABOVE, OR BELOW THE WATER."
—*The New York Times Book Review*

AVAILABLE WHEREVER BOOKS ARE SOLD
FROM ST. MARTIN'S PAPERBACKS

CIRCLE 2/97